GREATEST SHORT STORIES FOR CHILDREN

CLASSICS

Published 2024
FINGERPRINT! CLASSICS
An imprint of Prakash Books India Pvt. Ltd

113/A, Darya Ganj,
New Delhi-110 002
Email: info@prakashbooks.com/sales@prakashbooks.com

Fingerprint Publishing
@FingerprintP
@fingerprintpublishingbooks
www.fingerprintpublishing.com

ISBN: 978 93 5856 678 9

Processed & printed in India

"Most of the people who will walk after me will be children, so make the beat keep time with short steps."

—Hans Christian Andersen

The oral tradition of narrating stories to children has been going on since time immemorial. From this, children's literature has evolved into a rich tapestry of enchanting fairy tales, instructive fables, age-old folktales, soothing hymns, and gentle lullabies. Today, this diverse tradition encompasses a wide range of forms, including intricate picture books, concise short fiction, immersive novels, and inventive adaptations and retellings of beloved stories.

Today, this genre boasts of innumerable endearing stories written by gifted storytellers. These stories are a delight for a child's imagination and continue to linger in one's mind even into adulthood. The earliest stories for children are believed to be from *Panchatantra* and *Aesop's Fables*, which were written around 400 AD and 200 AD, respectively. Prior to the eighteenth century, almost all of children's literature was purely instructional or aimed at inculcating piety and good morals. This trend changed with John Locke's treatise *Some Thoughts Concerning Education* (1693), which talked of 'gentler ways of treating children'. One of these ways was through books specifically written to entertain children.

Therefore, from the eighteenth century onwards, children's literature appeared in a distinct form. It came to encapsulate a world, not of simply informing and educating, but one filled with wonder and excitement—a world that the children were excited to be lost in. This world may be familiar, working like a mirror and reflecting the child's real world, or it may be strange and magical, offering a window to transform the child's experience. For adults, children's stories are like blanket—offering comfort and at times, a nostalgic motivation. As adults, we come back to them again and again, finally aware of the depth of these stories, of their hidden meanings and emotions that we were not able to decipher while reading them in our childhood.

This edition includes some stories known all over the world—fairy tales of Cinderella and the Sleeping Beauty, retold for children by renowned French author Charles Perrault, the adventure stories of Aladdin and Sindbad, written for children by Andrew Lang, and stories from *Aesop's Fables* and *Panchatantra*, forming perfect blend of entertainment and life lessons. In addition to this, this edition features excerpts from timeless classics like Oliver Twist and Gulliver's Travels, stories that continue to captivate readers even centuries after their initial publication. Alongside these iconic works, it includes humorous, poignant, and unforgettable short stories penned by literary giants such as Oscar Wilde, Rudyard Kipling, Edith Nesbit, O. Henry, and more, making it a timeless must-have collection for your library.

CONTENTS

CINDERELLA

Charles Perrault

Published in *The Tales of Mother Goose* in 1697
Translated from French by Charles Welsh in 1901

Once upon a time there was a gentleman who married, for his second wife, the proudest and most haughty woman that ever was seen. She had two daughters of her own, who were, indeed, exactly like her in all things. The gentleman had also a young daughter, of rare goodness and sweetness of temper, which she took from her mother, who was the best creature in the world.

The wedding was scarcely over, when the stepmother's bad temper began to show itself. She could not bear the goodness of this young girl, because it made her own daughters appear the more odious. The stepmother gave her the meanest work in the house to do; she had to scour the dishes, tables, etc., and to scrub the floors and clean out the bedrooms. The poor girl had to sleep in the garret, upon a wretched straw bed, while her sisters lay in fine rooms with inlaid floors, upon beds of the very newest fashion, and where they had looking-glasses so large that they might see themselves at their full length. The poor girl bore all patiently, and dared not complain to her father, who would have scolded her if she had done so, for his wife governed him entirely.

When she had done her work, she used to go into the chimney corner, and sit down among the cinders, hence she was called Cinderwench. The younger sister of the two, who was not so rude and uncivil as the elder, called her Cinderella. However, Cinderella, in spite of her mean apparel, was a hundred times more handsome than her sisters, though they were always richly dressed.

It happened that the King's son gave a ball, and invited to it all persons of fashion. Our young misses were also invited, for they cut a very grand figure among the people of the country-side. They were highly delighted with the invitation, and wonderfully busy in choosing the gowns, petticoats, and head-dresses which might best become them. This made Cinderella's lot still harder, for it was she who ironed her sisters' linen and plaited their ruffles. They talked all day long of nothing but how they should be dressed.

"For my part," said the elder, "I will wear my red velvet suit with French trimmings."

"And I," said the younger, "shall wear my usual skirt; but then, to make amends for that I will put on my gold-flowered mantle, and my diamond stomacher, which is far from being the most ordinary one in the world." They sent for the best hairdressers they could get to make up their hair in fashionable style, and bought patches for their cheeks. Cinderella was consulted in all these matters, for she had good taste. She advised them always for the best, and even offered her services to dress their hair, which they were very willing she should do.

As she was doing this, they said to her:—

"Cinderella, would you not be glad to go to the ball?"

"Young ladies," she said, "you only jeer at me; it is not for such as I am to go there."

"You are right," they replied; "people would laugh to see a Cinderwench at a ball."

Any one but Cinderella would have dressed their hair awry, but she was good-natured, and arranged it perfectly well. They were almost two days without eating, so much were they transported with joy. They broke above a dozen laces in trying to lace themselves tight, that they might have a fine, slender shape, and they were continually at their looking-glass.

At last the happy day came; they went to Court, and Cinderella followed them with her eyes as long as she could, and when she had lost sight of them, she fell a-crying.

Her godmother, who saw her all in tears, asked her what was the matter.

"I wish I could—I wish I could—" but she could not finish for sobbing.

Her godmother, who was a fairy, said to her, "You wish you could go to the ball; is it not so?"

"Alas, yes," said Cinderella, sighing.

"Well," said her godmother, "be but a good girl, and I will see that you go." Then she took her into her chamber, and said to her, "Run into the garden, and bring me a pumpkin."

Cinderella went at once to gather the finest she could get, and brought it to her godmother, not being able to imagine how this pumpkin could help her to go to the ball. Her godmother scooped out all the inside of it, leaving nothing but the rind. Then she struck it with her wand, and the pumpkin was instantly turned into a fine gilded coach.

She then went to look into the mouse-trap, where she found six mice, all alive. She ordered Cinderella to lift the trap-door, when, giving each mouse, as it went out, a little tap with her wand, it was that moment turned into a fine horse, and the six mice made a fine set of six horses of a beautiful mouse-coloured, dapple gray.

Being at a loss for a coachman, Cinderella said, "I will go and see if there is not a rat in the rat-trap—we may make a coachman of him."

"You are right," replied her godmother; "go and look."

Cinderella brought the rat-trap to her, and in it there were three huge rats. The fairy chose the one which had the largest beard, and, having touched him with her wand, he was turned into a fat coachman with the finest moustache and whiskers ever seen.

After that, she said to her:—

"Go into the garden, and you will find six lizards behind the watering-pot; bring them to me."

She had no sooner done so than her godmother turned them into six footmen, who skipped up immediately behind the coach, with their liveries all trimmed with gold and silver, and they held on as if they had done nothing else their whole lives.

The fairy then said to Cinderella, "Well, you see here a carriage fit to go to the ball in; are you not pleased with it?"

"Oh, yes!" she cried; "but must I go as I am in these rags?"

Her godmother simply touched her with her wand, and, at the same moment, her clothes were turned into cloth of gold and silver, all decked with jewels. This done, she gave her a pair of the prettiest glass slippers in the whole world. Being thus attired, she got into the carriage, her godmother commanding her, above all things, not to stay till after midnight, and telling her, at the same time, that if she stayed one moment longer, the coach would be a pumpkin again, her horses mice, her coachman a rat, her footmen lizards, and her clothes would become just as they were before.

She promised her godmother she would not fail to leave the ball before midnight. She drove away, scarce able to contain herself for joy.

The King's son, who was told that a great princess, whom nobody knew, was come, ran out to receive her. He gave her his hand as she alighted from the coach, and led her into the hall where the company were assembled. There was at once a profound silence; every one left off dancing, and the violins ceased to play, so attracted was every one by the singular beauties of the unknown newcomer. Nothing was then heard but a confused sound of voices saying:—

"Ha! how beautiful she is! Ha! how beautiful she is!"

The King himself, old as he was, could not keep his eyes off her, and he told the Queen under his breath that it was a long time since he had seen so beautiful and lovely a creature.

All the ladies were busy studying her clothes and head-dress, so that they might have theirs made next day after the same pattern, provided they could meet with such fine materials and able hands to make them.

The King's son conducted her to the seat of honour, and afterwards took her out to dance with him. She danced so very gracefully that they all admired her more and more. A fine collation was served, but the young Prince ate not a morsel, so intently was he occupied with her.

She went and sat down beside her sisters, showing them a thousand civilities, and giving them among other things part of the oranges and citrons with which the Prince had regaled her. This very much surprised them, for they had not been presented to her.

Cinderella heard the clock strike a quarter to twelve. She at once made her adieus to the company and hastened away as fast as she could.

As soon as she got home, she ran to find her godmother, and, after having thanked her, she said she much wished she might go to the ball the next day, because the King's son had asked her to do so. As she was eagerly telling her godmother all that happened at the ball, her two sisters knocked at the door; Cinderella opened it. "How long you have stayed!" said she, yawning, rubbing her eyes, and stretching herself as if she had been just awakened. She had not, however, had any desire to sleep since they went from home.

"If you had been at the ball," said one of her sisters, "you would not have been tired with it. There came thither the finest princess, the most beautiful ever was seen with mortal eyes. She showed us a thousand civilities, and gave us oranges and citrons."

Cinderella did not show any pleasure at this. Indeed, she asked them the name of the princess; but they told her they did not know it, and that the King's son was very much concerned, and would give all the world to know who she was. At this Cinderella, smiling, replied:—

"Was she then so very beautiful? How fortunate you have been! Could I not see her? Ah! dear Miss Charlotte, do lend me your yellow suit of clothes which you wear every day."

"Ay, to be sure!" cried Miss Charlotte; "lend my clothes to such a dirty Cinderwench as thou art! I should be out of my mind to do so."

Cinderella, indeed, expected such an answer and was very glad of the refusal; for she would have been sadly troubled if her sister had lent her what she jestingly asked for. The next day the two sisters went to the ball, and so did Cinderella, but dressed more magnificently than before. The King's son was always by her side, and his pretty speeches to her never ceased. These by no means annoyed the young lady. Indeed, she quite forgot her godmother's orders to her, so that she heard the clock begin to strike twelve when she thought it could not be more than eleven. She then rose up and fled, as nimble as a deer. The Prince followed, but could not overtake her. She left behind one of her glass slippers, which the Prince took up most carefully. She got home, but quite out of breath, without her carriage, and in her old clothes, having nothing left her of all her finery but one of the little slippers, fellow to the one she had dropped. The guards at the palace gate were asked if they had not seen a princess go out, and they replied they had seen nobody go out but a young girl, very meanly dressed, and who had more the air of a poor country girl than of a young lady.

When the two sisters returned from the ball, Cinderella asked them if they had had a pleasant time, and if the fine lady had been there. They told her, yes; but that she hurried away the moment it struck twelve, and with so much haste that she dropped one of her little glass slippers, the prettiest in the world, which the King's son had taken up. They said, further, that he had done nothing but look at her all the time, and that most certainly he was very much in love with the beautiful owner of the glass slipper.

What they said was true; for a few days after the King's son caused it to be proclaimed, by sound of trumpet, that he would marry her whose foot this slipper would fit exactly. They began to try it on the princesses, then on the duchesses, and then on all the ladies of the Court; but in vain.

It was brought to the two sisters, who did all they possibly could to thrust a foot into the slipper, but they could not succeed. Cinderella, who saw this, and knew her slipper, said to them, laughing:—

"Let me see if it will not fit me."

Her sisters burst out a-laughing, and began to banter her. The gentleman who was sent to try the slipper looked earnestly at Cinderella, and, finding her very handsome, said it was but just that she should try, and that he had orders to let every lady try it on.

He obliged Cinderella to sit down, and, putting the slipper to her little foot, he found it went on very easily, and fitted her as if it had been made of wax. The astonishment of her two sisters was great, but it was still greater when Cinderella pulled out of her pocket the other slipper and put it on her foot. Thereupon, in came her godmother, who, having touched Cinderella's clothes with her wand, made them more magnificent than those she had worn before.

THE SLEEPING BEAUTY IN THE WOODS

Charles Perrault

First published in *The Tales of Mother Goose* in 1697
Translated from French by Charles Welsh in 1901

Once upon a time there was a king and a queen, who were very sorry that they had no children,—so sorry that it cannot be told.

At last, however, the Queen had a daughter. There was a very fine christening; and the Princess had for her godmothers all the fairies they could find in the whole kingdom (there were seven of them), so that every one of them might confer a gift upon her, as was the custom of fairies in those days. By this means the Princess had all the perfections imaginable.

After the christening was over, the company returned to the King's palace, where was prepared a great feast for the fairies. There was placed before every one of them a magnificent cover with a case of massive gold, wherein were a spoon, and a knife and fork, all of pure gold set with diamonds and rubies. But as they were all sitting down at table they saw a very old fairy come into the hall. She had not been invited, because for more than fifty years she had not been out of a certain tower, and she was believed to be either dead or enchanted.

The King ordered her a cover, but he could not give her a case of gold as the others had, because seven only had been made for the seven fairies. The old fairy fancied she was slighted, and muttered threats between her teeth. One of the young fairies who sat near heard her, and, judging that she might give the little Princess some unlucky gift, hid herself behind the curtains as soon as they left the table. She hoped that she might speak last and undo as much as she could the evil which the old fairy might do.

In the meanwhile all the fairies began to give their gifts to the Princess. The youngest gave her for her gift that she should be the most beautiful person in the world; the next, that she should have the wit of an angel; the third, that she should be able to do everything she did gracefully; the fourth, that she should dance perfectly; the fifth, that she should sing like a nightingale; and the sixth, that she should play all kinds of musical instruments to the fullest perfection.

The old fairy's turn coming next, her head shaking more with spite than with age, she said that the Princess should pierce her hand with a spindle and die of the wound. This terrible gift made the whole company tremble, and everybody fell a-crying.

At this very instant the young fairy came from behind the curtains and said these words in a loud voice:—

"Assure yourselves, O King and Queen, that your daughter shall not die of this disaster. It is true, I have no power to undo entirely what my elder has done. The Princess shall indeed pierce her hand with a spindle; but, instead of dying, she shall only fall into a deep sleep, which shall last a hundred years, at the end of which a king's son shall come and awake her."

The King, to avoid the misfortune foretold by the old fairy, issued orders forbidding any one, on pain of death, to spin with a distaff and spindle, or to have a spindle in his house. About fifteen or sixteen years after, the King and Queen being absent at one of their country villas, the young Princess was one day running up and down the palace; she went from room to room, and at last she came into a little garret on the top of the tower, where a good old woman, alone, was spinning with her spindle. This good woman had never heard of the King's orders against spindles.

"What are you doing there, my good woman?" said the Princess.

"I am spinning, my pretty child," said the old woman, who did not know who the Princess was.

"Ha!" said the Princess, "this is very pretty; how do you do it? Give it to me. Let me see if I can do it."

She had no sooner taken it into her hand than, either because she was too quick and heedless, or because the decree of the fairy had so ordained, it ran into her hand, and she fell down in a swoon.

The good old woman, not knowing what to do, cried out for help. People came in from every quarter; they threw water upon the face of the Princess, unlaced her, struck her on the palms of her hands, and rubbed her temples with cologne water; but nothing would bring her to herself.

Then the King, who came up at hearing the noise, remembered what the fairies had foretold. He knew very well that this must come to pass, since the fairies had foretold it, and he caused the Princess to be carried into the finest room in his palace, and to be laid upon a bed all embroidered with gold and silver. One would have taken her for a little angel, she was so beautiful; for her swooning had not dimmed the brightness of her complexion: her cheeks were carnation, and her lips coral. It is true her eyes were shut, but she was heard to breathe softly, which satisfied those about her that she was not dead.

The King gave orders that they should let her sleep quietly till the time came for her to awake. The good fairy who had saved her life by condemning her to sleep a hundred years was in the kingdom of Matakin, twelve thousand leagues off, when this accident befell the Princess; but she was instantly informed of it by a little dwarf, who had seven-leagued boots, that is, boots with which he could stride over seven leagues of ground at once. The fairy started off at once, and arrived, about an hour later, in a fiery chariot drawn by dragons.

The King handed her out of the chariot, and she approved everything he had done; but as she had very great foresight, she thought that when the Princess should awake she might not know what to do with herself, if she was all alone in this old palace. This was what she did: she touched with her wand everything in the palace (except the King and Queen),—governesses, maids of honor, ladies of the bedchamber, gentlemen, officers, stewards, cooks, undercooks, kitchen maids, guards with their porters, pages, and footmen; she likewise touched all the horses which were in the stables, the cart horses, the hunters and the saddle horses, the grooms, the great dogs in the outward court, and little Mopsey, too, the Princess's spaniel, which was lying on the bed.

As soon as she touched them they all fell asleep, not to awake again until their mistress did, that they might be ready to wait upon her when she wanted them. The very spits at the fire, as full as they could hold of partridges and pheasants, fell asleep, and the fire itself as well. All this was done in a moment. Fairies are not long in doing their work.

And now the King and Queen, having kissed their dear child without waking her, went out of the palace and sent forth orders that nobody should come near it.

These orders were not necessary; for in a quarter of an hour's time there grew up all round about the park such a vast number of trees, great and small, bushes and brambles, twining one within another, that neither man nor beast could pass through; so that nothing could be seen but the very top of the towers of the palace; and that, too, only from afar off. Every one knew that this also was the work of the fairy in order that while the Princess slept she should have nothing to fear from curious people.

After a hundred years the son of the King then reigning, who was of another family from that of the sleeping Princess, was a-hunting on that side of the country, and he asked what those towers were which he saw in the middle of a great thick wood. Every one answered according as they had heard. Some said that it was an old haunted castle, others that all the witches of the country held their midnight revels there, but the common opinion was that it was an ogre's dwelling, and that he carried to it all the little children he could catch, so as to eat them up at his leisure, without any one being able to follow him, for he alone had the power to make his way through the wood.

The Prince did not know what to believe, and presently a very aged countryman spake to him thus:—

"May it please your royal Highness, more than fifty years since I heard from my father that there was then in this castle the most beautiful princess that was ever seen; that she must sleep there a hundred years, and that she should be waked by a king's son, for whom she was reserved."

The young Prince on hearing this was all on fire. He thought, without weighing the matter, that he could put an end to this rare adventure; and, pushed on by love and the desire of glory, resolved at once to look into it.

As soon as he began to get near to the wood, all the great trees, the bushes, and brambles gave way of themselves to let him pass through. He walked up to the castle which he saw at the end of a large avenue; and you can imagine he was a good deal surprised when he saw none of his people following him, because the trees closed again as soon as he had passed through them. However, he did not cease from continuing his way; a young prince in search of glory is ever valiant.

He came into a spacious outer court, and what he saw was enough to freeze him with horror. A frightful silence reigned over all; the image of death was everywhere, and there was nothing to be seen but what seemed to be the outstretched bodies of dead men and animals. He, however, very well knew, by the ruby faces and pimpled noses of the porters, that they were only asleep; and their goblets, wherein still remained some drops of wine, showed plainly that they had fallen asleep while drinking their wine.

He then crossed a court paved with marble, went up the stairs, and came into the guard chamber, where guards were standing in their ranks, with their muskets upon their shoulders, and snoring with all their might. He went through several rooms full of gentlemen and ladies, some standing and others sitting, but all were asleep. He came into a gilded chamber, where he saw upon a bed, the curtains of which were all open, the most beautiful sight ever beheld—a princess who appeared to be about fifteen or sixteen years of age, and whose bright and resplendent beauty had something divine in it. He approached with trembling and admiration, and fell down upon his knees before her.

Then, as the end of the enchantment was come, the Princess awoke, and looking on him with eyes more tender than could have been expected at first sight, said:—

"Is it you, my Prince? You have waited a long while."

The Prince, charmed with these words, and much more with the manner in which they were spoken, knew not how to show his joy and gratitude; he assured her that he loved her better than he did himself. Their discourse was not very connected, but they were the better pleased, for where there is much love there is little eloquence. He was more at a loss than she, and we need not wonder at it; she had had time to think of what to say to him; for it is evident (though history says nothing of it) that the good fairy, during so long a sleep, had given her very pleasant dreams. In short, they talked together for four hours, and then they said not half they had to say.

In the meanwhile all the palace had woke up with the Princess; every one thought upon his own business, and as they were not in love, they were ready to die of hunger. The lady of honour, being as sharp set as the other folks, grew very impatient, and told the Princess aloud that the meal was served. The Prince helped the Princess to rise. She was entirely and very magnificently dressed; but his royal Highness took care not to tell her that she was dressed like his great-grandmother, and had a high collar. She looked not a bit the less charming and beautiful for all that.

They went into the great mirrored hall, where they supped, and were served by the officers of the Princess's household. The violins and haut boys played old tunes, but they were excellent, though they had not been played for a hundred years; and after supper, without losing any time, the lord almoner married them in the chapel of the castle. They had but very little sleep—the Princess scarcely needed any; and the Prince left her next morning to return into the city, where his father was greatly troubled about him.

The Prince told him that he lost his way in the forest as he was hunting, and that he had slept in the cottage of a charcoal-burner, who gave him cheese and brown bread.

The King, his father, who was a good man, believed him; but his mother could not be persuaded that it was true; and seeing that he went almost every day a-hunting, and that he always had some excuse ready for so doing, though he had been out three or four nights together, she began to suspect that he was married; for he lived thus with the Princess above two whole years, during which they had two children, the elder, a daughter, was named Dawn, and the younger, a son, they called Day, because he was a great deal handsomer than his sister.

The Queen spoke several times to her son, to learn after what manner he was passing his time, and told him that in this he ought in duty to satisfy her. But he never dared to trust her with his secret; he feared her, though he loved her, for she was of the race of the Ogres, and the King married her for her vast riches alone. It was even whispered about the Court that she had Ogreish inclinations, and that, whenever she saw little children passing by, she had all the difficulty in the world to prevent herself from falling upon them. And so the Prince would never tell her one word.

But when the King was dead, which happened about two years afterward, and he saw himself lord and master, he openly declared his marriage: and he went in great state to conduct his Queen to the palace. They made a magnificent entry into the capital city, she riding between her two children.

Soon after, the King made war on Emperor Cantalabutte, his neighbour. He left the government of the kingdom to the Queen, his mother, and earnestly commended his wife and children to her care. He was obliged to carry on the war all the summer, and as soon as he left, the Queen-mother sent her daughter-in-law and her children to a country house among the woods, that she might with the more ease gratify her horrible longing. Some few days afterward she went thither herself, and said to her head cook:—

"I intend to eat little Dawn for my dinner tomorrow."

"O! madam!" cried the head cook.

"I will have it so," replied the Queen (and this she spoke in the tone of an Ogress who had a strong desire to eat fresh meat), "and will eat her with a sharp sauce."

The poor man, knowing very well that he must not play tricks with Ogresses, took his great knife and went up into little Dawn's chamber. She was then nearly four years old, and came up to him, jumping and laughing, to put her arms round his neck, and ask him for some sugar-candy. Upon which he began to weep, the great knife fell out of his hand, and he went into the back yard and killed a little lamb, and dressed it with such good sauce that his mistress assured him she had never eaten anything so good in her life. He had at the same time taken up little Dawn and carried her to his wife, to conceal her in his lodging at the end of the courtyard.

Eight days afterwards the wicked Queen said to the chief cook, "I will sup upon little Day."

He answered not a word, being resolved to cheat her again as he had done before. He went to find little Day, and saw him with a foil in his hand, with which he was fencing with a great monkey: the child was then only three years of age. He took him up in his arms and carried him to his wife, that she might conceal him in her chamber along with his sister, and instead of little Day he served up a young and very tender kid, which the Ogress found to be wonderfully good.

All had gone well up to now; but one evening this wicked Queen said to her chief cook:—

"I will eat the Queen with the same sauce I had with her children."

Now the poor chief cook was in despair and could not imagine how to deceive her again. The young Queen was over twenty years old, not reckoning the hundred years she had been asleep: and how to find something to take her place greatly puzzled him. He then decided, to save his own life, to cut the Queen's throat; and going up into her chamber, with intent to do it at once, he put himself into as great fury as he possibly could, and came into the young Queen's room with his dagger in his hand. He would not, however, deceive her, but told her, with a great deal of respect, the orders he had received from the Queen-mother.

"Do it; do it," she said, stretching out her neck. "Carry out your orders, and then I shall go and see my children, my poor children, whom I loved so much and so tenderly."

For she thought them dead, since they had been taken away without her knowledge.

"No, no, madam," cried the poor chief cook, all in tears; "you shall not die, and you shall see your children again at once. But then you must go home with me to my lodgings, where I have concealed them, and I will deceive the Queen once more, by giving her a young hind in your stead."

Upon this he forthwith conducted her to his room, where, leaving her to embrace her children, and cry along with them, he went and dressed a young hind, which the Queen had for her supper, and devoured with as much appetite as if it had been the young Queen. She was now well satisfied with her cruel deeds, and she invented a story to tell the King on his return, of how the Queen his wife and her two children had been devoured by mad wolves.

One evening, as she was, according to her custom, rambling round about the courts and yards of the palace to see if she could smell any fresh meat, she heard, in a room on the ground floor, little Day crying, for his mamma was going to whip him, because he had been naughty; and she heard, at the same time, little Dawn begging mercy for her brother.

The Ogress knew the voice of the Queen and her children at once, and being furious at having been thus deceived, she gave orders (in a most horrible voice which made everybody tremble) that, next morning by break of day, they should bring into the middle of the great court a large tub filled with toads, vipers, snakes, and all sorts of serpents, in order to have the Queen and her children, the chief cook, his wife and maid, thrown into it, all of whom were to be brought thither with their hands tied behind them.

They were brought out accordingly, and the executioners were just going to throw them into the tub, when the King, who was not so soon expected, entered the court on horseback and asked, with the utmost astonishment, what was the meaning of that horrible spectacle.

No one dared to tell him, when the Ogress, all enraged to see what had happened, threw herself head foremost into the tub, and was instantly devoured by the ugly creatures she had ordered to be thrown into it to kill the others. The King was of course very sorry, for she was his mother; but he soon comforted himself with his beautiful wife and his pretty children.

A VOYAGE TO LILLIPUT (AN EXCERPT)

Jonathan Swift

Published in *Gulliver's Travels* in 1726

The author gives some account of himself and family. His first inducements to travel. He is shipwrecked, and swims for his life, gets safe on shore in the country of Lilliput; is made a prisoner, and carried up the country.

My father had a small estate in Nottinghamshire; I was the third of five sons. He sent me to Emanuel College in Cambridge at fourteen years old, where I resided three years, and applied myself close to my studies; but the charge of maintaining me, although I had a very scanty allowance, being too great for a narrow fortune, I was bound apprentice to Mr. James Bates, an eminent surgeon in London, with whom I continued four years. My father now and then sending me small sums of money, I laid them out in learning navigation, and other parts of the mathematics, useful to those who intend to travel, as I always believed it would be, some time or other, my fortune to do. When I left Mr. Bates, I went down to my father: where, by the assistance of him and my uncle John, and some other relations, I got forty pounds, and a promise of thirty pounds a year to maintain me at Leyden: there I studied physic two years and seven months, knowing it would be useful in long voyages.

Soon after my return from Leyden, I was recommended by my good master, Mr. Bates, to be surgeon to the Swallow, Captain Abraham Pannel, commander; with whom I continued three years and a half, making a voyage or two into the Levant, and some other parts. When I came back I resolved to settle in London; to which Mr. Bates, my master, encouraged me, and by him I was recommended to several patients. I took part of a small house in the Old Jewry; and being advised to alter my condition, I married Mrs. Mary Burton, second daughter to Mr. Edmund Burton, hosier, in Newgate-street, with whom I received four hundred pounds for a portion.

But my good master Bates dying in two years after, and I having few friends, my business began to fail; for my conscience would not suffer me to imitate the bad practice of too many among my brethren. Having therefore consulted with my wife, and some of my acquaintance, I determined to go again to sea. I was surgeon successively in two ships, and made several voyages, for six years, to the East and West Indies, by which I got some addition to my fortune. My hours of leisure I spent in reading the best authors, ancient and modern, being always provided with a good number of books; and when I was ashore, in observing the manners and dispositions of the people, as well as learning their language; wherein I had a great facility, by the strength of my memory.

The last of these voyages not proving very fortunate, I grew weary of the sea, and intended to stay at home with my wife and family. I removed from the Old Jewry to Fetter Lane, and from thence to Wapping, hoping to get business among the sailors; but it would not turn to account. After three years expectation that things would mend, I accepted an advantageous offer from Captain William Prichard, master of the Antelope, who was making a voyage to the South Sea. We set sail from Bristol, May 4, 1699, and our voyage was at first very prosperous.

It would not be proper, for some reasons, to trouble the reader with the particulars of our adventures in those seas; let it suffice to inform him, that in our passage from thence to the East Indies, we were driven by a violent storm to the north-west of Van Diemen's Land. By an observation, we found ourselves in the latitude of 30 degrees 2 minutes south. Twelve of our crew were dead by immoderate labour and ill food; the rest were in a very weak condition. On the 5th of November, which was the beginning of summer in those parts, the weather being very hazy, the seamen spied a rock within half a cable's length of the ship; but the wind was so strong, that we were driven directly upon it, and immediately split. Six of the crew, of whom I was one, having let down the boat into the sea, made a shift to get clear of the ship and the rock. We rowed, by my computation, about three leagues, till we were able to work no longer, being already spent with labour while we were in the ship. We therefore trusted ourselves to the mercy of the waves, and in about half an hour the boat was overset by a sudden flurry from the north. What became of my companions in the boat, as well as of those who escaped on the rock, or were left in the vessel, I cannot tell; but conclude they were all lost. For my own part, I swam as fortune directed me, and was pushed forward by wind and tide. I often let my legs drop, and could feel no bottom; but when I was almost gone, and able to struggle no longer, I found myself within my depth; and by this time the storm was much abated. The declivity was so small, that I walked near a mile before I got to the shore, which I conjectured was about eight o'clock in the evening. I then advanced forward near half a mile, but could not discover any sign of houses or inhabitants; at least I was in so weak a condition, that I did not observe them. I was extremely tired, and with that, and the heat of the weather, and about half a pint of brandy that I drank as I left the ship, I found myself much inclined to sleep. I lay down on the grass, which was very short and soft, where I slept sounder than ever I remembered to have done in my life, and, as I reckoned, about nine hours; for when I awaked, it was just daylight. I attempted to rise, but was not able to stir: for, as I happened to lie on my back, I found my arms and legs were strongly fastened on each side to the ground; and my hair, which was long and thick, tied down in the same manner. I likewise felt several slender ligatures across my body, from my armpits to my thighs. I could only look upwards; the sun began to grow hot, and the light offended my eyes. I heard a confused noise about me; but in the posture I lay, could see nothing except the sky. In a little time I felt something alive moving on my left leg, which advancing gently forward over my breast, came almost up to my chin; when, bending my eyes downwards as much as I could, I perceived it to be a human creature not six inches high, with a bow and arrow in his hands, and a quiver at his back. In the meantime, I felt at least forty more of the same kind (as I conjectured) following the first. I was in the utmost astonishment, and roared so loud, that they all ran back in a fright; and some of them, as I was afterwards told, were hurt with the falls they got by leaping from my sides upon the ground. However, they soon returned, and one of them, who ventured so far as to get a full sight of my face, lifting up his hands and eyes by way of admiration, cried out in a shrill but distinct voice, *Hekinah degul*: the others repeated the same words several times, but then I knew not what they meant. I lay all this while, as the reader may believe, in great uneasiness. At length, struggling to get loose, I had the fortune to break the strings, and wrench out the pegs that fastened my left arm to the ground; for, by lifting it up to my face, I discovered the methods they had taken to bind me, and at the same time with a violent pull, which gave me excessive pain, I a little loosened the strings that tied down my hair on the left side, so that I was just able to turn my head about two inches. But the creatures ran off a second time, before I could seize them; whereupon there was a great shout in a very shrill accent, and after it ceased I heard one of them cry aloud *Tolgo phonac*; when in an instant I felt above a hundred arrows discharged on my left hand, which, pricked me like so many needles; and besides, they shot another flight into the air, as we do bombs in Europe, whereof many, I suppose, fell on my body, (though I felt them not), and some on my face, which I immediately covered with my left hand. When this shower of arrows was over, I fell a groaning with grief and pain; and then striving again to get loose, they discharged another volley larger than the first, and some of them attempted with spears to stick me in the sides; but by good luck I had on a buff jerkin, which they could not pierce. I thought it the most prudent method to lie still, and my design was to continue so till night, when, my left hand being already loose, I could easily free myself: and as for the inhabitants, I had reason to believe I might be a match for the greatest army they could bring against me, if they were all of the same size with him that I saw. But fortune disposed otherwise of me. When the people observed I was quiet, they discharged no more arrows; but, by the noise I heard, I knew their numbers increased; and about four yards from me, over against my right ear, I heard a knocking for above an hour, like that of people at work; when turning my head that way, as well as the pegs and strings would permit me, I saw a stage erected about a foot and a half from the ground, capable of holding four of the inhabitants, with two or three ladders to mount it: from whence one of them, who seemed to be a person of quality, made me a long speech, whereof I understood not one syllable. But I should have mentioned, that before the principal person began his oration, he cried out three times, *Langro dehul san* (these words and the former were afterwards repeated and explained to me); whereupon, immediately, about fifty of the inhabitants came and cut the strings that fastened the left side of my head, which gave me the liberty of turning it to the right, and of observing the person and gesture of him that was to speak. He appeared to be of a middle age, and taller than any of the other three who attended him, whereof one was a page that held up his train, and seemed to be somewhat longer than my middle finger; the other two stood one on each side to support him. He acted every part of an orator, and I could observe many periods of threatenings, and others of promises, pity, and kindness. I answered in a few words, but in the most submissive manner, lifting up my left hand, and both my eyes to the sun, as calling him for a witness; and being almost famished with hunger, having not eaten a morsel for some hours before I left the ship, I found the demands of nature so strong upon me, that I could not forbear showing my impatience (perhaps against the strict rules of decency) by putting my finger frequently to my mouth, to signify that I wanted food. The *hurgo* (for so they call a great lord, as I afterwards learnt) understood me very well. He descended from the stage, and commanded that several ladders should be applied to my sides, on which above a hundred of the inhabitants mounted and walked towards my mouth, laden with baskets full of meat, which had been provided and sent thither by the king's orders, upon the first intelligence he received of me. I observed there was the flesh of several animals, but could not distinguish them by the taste. There were shoulders, legs, and loins, shaped like those of mutton, and very well dressed, but smaller than the wings of a lark. I ate them by two or three at a mouthful, and took three loaves at a time, about the bigness of musket bullets. They supplied me as fast as they could, showing a thousand marks of wonder and astonishment at my bulk and appetite. I then made another sign, that I wanted drink. They found by my eating that a small quantity would not suffice me; and being a most ingenious people, they slung up, with great dexterity, one of their largest hogsheads, then rolled it towards my hand, and beat out the top; I drank it off at a draught, which I might well do, for it did not hold half a pint, and tasted like a small wine of Burgundy, but much more delicious. They brought me a second hogshead, which I drank in the same manner, and made signs for more; but they had none to give me. When I had performed these wonders, they shouted for joy, and danced upon my breast, repeating several times as they did at first, *Hekinah degul.* They made me a sign that I should throw down the two hogsheads, but first warning the people below to stand out of the way, crying aloud, *Borach mevolah*; and when they saw the vessels in the air, there was a universal shout of *Hekinah degul.* I confess I was often tempted, while they were passing backwards and forwards on my body, to seize forty or fifty of the first that came in my reach, and dash them against the ground. But the remembrance of what I had felt, which probably might not be the worst they could do, and the promise of honour I made them—for so I interpreted my submissive behaviour—soon drove out these imaginations. Besides, I now considered myself as bound by the laws of hospitality, to a people who had treated me with so much expense and magnificence.

However, in my thoughts I could not sufficiently wonder at the intrepidity of these diminutive mortals, who durst venture to mount and walk upon my body, while one of my hands was at liberty, without trembling at the very sight of so prodigious a creature as I must appear to them. After some time, when they observed that I made no more demands for meat, there appeared before me a person of high rank from his imperial majesty. His excellency, having mounted on the small of my right leg, advanced forwards up to my face, with about a dozen of his retinue; and producing his credentials under the signet royal, which he applied close to my eyes, spoke about ten minutes without any signs of anger, but with a kind of determinate resolution, often pointing forwards, which, as I afterwards found, was towards the capital city, about half a mile distant; whither it was agreed by his majesty in council that I must be conveyed. I answered in few words, but to no purpose, and made a sign with my hand that was loose, putting it to the other (but over his excellency's head for fear of hurting him or his train) and then to my own head and body, to signify that I desired my liberty. It appeared that he understood me well enough, for he shook his head by way of disapprobation, and held his hand in a posture to show that I must be carried as a prisoner. However, he made other signs to let me understand that I should have meat and drink enough, and very good treatment. Whereupon I once more thought of attempting to break my bonds; but again, when I felt the smart of their arrows upon my face and hands, which were all in blisters, and many of the darts still sticking in them, and observing likewise that the number of my enemies increased, I gave tokens to let them know that they might do with me what they pleased. Upon this, the *hurgo* and his train withdrew, with much civility and cheerful countenances. Soon after I heard a general shout, with frequent repetitions of the words *Peplom selan*; and I felt great numbers of people on my left side relaxing the cords to such a degree, that I was able to turn upon my right, and to ease myself with making water; which I very plentifully did, to the great astonishment of the people; who, conjecturing by my motion what I was going to do, immediately opened to the right and left on that side, to avoid the torrent, which fell with such noise and violence from me. But before this, they had daubed my face and both my hands with a sort of ointment, very pleasant to the smell, which, in a few minutes, removed all the smart of their arrows. These circumstances, added to the refreshment I had received by their victuals and drink, which were very nourishing, disposed me to sleep. I slept about eight hours, as I was afterwards assured; and it was no wonder, for the physicians, by the emperor's order, had mingled a sleepy potion in the hogsheads of wine.

It seems, that upon the first moment I was discovered sleeping on the ground, after my landing, the emperor had early notice of it by an express; and determined in council, that I should be tied in the manner I have related, (which was done in the night while I slept;) that plenty of meat and drink should be sent to me, and a machine prepared to carry me to the capital city.

This resolution perhaps may appear very bold and dangerous, and I am confident would not be imitated by any prince in Europe on the like occasion. However, in my opinion, it was extremely prudent, as well as generous: for, supposing these people had endeavoured to kill me with their spears and arrows, while I was asleep, I should certainly have awaked with the first sense of smart, which might so far have roused my rage and strength, as to have enabled me to break the strings wherewith I was tied; after which, as they were not able to make resistance, so they could expect no mercy.

These people are most excellent mathematicians, and arrived to a great perfection in mechanics, by the countenance and encouragement of the emperor, who is a renowned patron of learning. This prince has several machines fixed on wheels, for the carriage of trees and other great weights. He often builds his largest men of war, whereof some are nine feet long, in the woods where the timber grows, and has them carried on these engines three or four hundred yards to the sea. Five hundred carpenters and engineers were immediately set at work to prepare the greatest engine they had. It was a frame of wood raised three inches from the ground, about seven feet long, and four wide, moving upon twenty-two wheels. The shout I heard was upon the arrival of this engine, which, it seems, set out in four hours after my landing. It was brought parallel to me, as I lay. But the principal difficulty was to raise and place me in this vehicle. Eighty poles, each of one foot high, were erected for this purpose, and very strong cords, of the bigness of packthread, were fastened by hooks to many bandages, which the workmen had girt round my neck, my hands, my body, and my legs. Nine hundred of the strongest men were employed to draw up these cords, by many pulleys fastened on the poles; and thus, in less than three hours, I was raised and slung into the engine, and there tied fast. All this I was told; for, while the operation was performing, I lay in a profound sleep, by the force of that soporiferous medicine infused into my liquor. Fifteen hundred of the emperor's largest horses, each about four inches and a half high, were employed to draw me towards the metropolis, which, as I said, was half a mile distant.

About four hours after we began our journey, I awaked by a very ridiculous accident; for the carriage being stopped a while, to adjust something that was out of order, two or three of the young natives had the curiosity to see how I looked when I was asleep; they climbed up into the engine, and advancing very softly to my face, one of them, an officer in the guards, put the sharp end of his half-pike a good way up into my left nostril, which tickled my nose like a straw, and made me sneeze violently; whereupon they stole off unperceived, and it was three weeks before I knew the cause of my waking so suddenly. We made a long march the remaining part of the day, and, rested at night with five hundred guards on each side of me, half with torches, and half with bows and arrows, ready to shoot me if I should offer to stir. The next morning at sunrise we continued our march, and arrived within two hundred yards of the city gates about noon. The emperor, and all his court, came out to meet us; but his great officers would by no means suffer his majesty to endanger his person by mounting on my body.

At the place where the carriage stopped there stood an ancient temple, esteemed to be the largest in the whole kingdom; which, having been polluted some years before by an unnatural murder, was, according to the zeal of those people, looked upon as profane, and therefore had been applied to common use, and all the ornaments and furniture carried away. In this edifice it was determined I should lodge. The great gate fronting to the north was about four feet high, and almost two feet wide, through which I could easily creep. On each side of the gate was a small window, not above six inches from the ground: into that on the left side, the king's smith conveyed fourscore and eleven chains, like those that hang to a lady's watch in Europe, and almost as large, which were locked to my left leg with six-and-thirty padlocks. Over against this temple, on the other side of the great highway, at twenty feet distance, there was a turret at least five feet high. Here the emperor ascended, with many principal lords of his court, to have an opportunity of viewing me, as I was told, for I could not see them. It was reckoned that above a hundred thousand inhabitants came out of the town upon the same errand; and, in spite of my guards, I believe there could not be fewer than ten thousand at several times, who mounted my body by the help of ladders. But a proclamation was soon issued, to forbid it upon pain of death. When the workmen found it was impossible for me to break loose, they cut all the strings that bound me; whereupon I rose up, with as melancholy a disposition as ever I had in my life. But the noise and astonishment of the people, at seeing me rise and walk, are not to be expressed. The chains that held my left leg were about two yards long, and gave me not only the liberty of walking backwards and forwards in a semicircle, but, being fixed within four inches of the gate, allowed me to creep in, and lie at my full length in the temple.

THUMBELINA

H. C. Andersen

First published in 1835
Translated from Danish by
W. A. Craigie and J. K. Craigie, published in 1914

There was once a woman who wished for a very little child; but she did not know where she should procure one. So she went to an old witch, and said, "I do so very much wish for a little child! can you not tell me where I can get one?"

"Oh! that could easily be managed," said the witch. "There you have a barleycorn: that is not of the kind which grows in the countryman's field, and which the chickens get to eat. Put it into a flower-pot, and you shall see what you shall see."

"Thank you," said the woman; and she gave the witch a groat.

Then she went home and planted the barleycorn, and immediately there grew up a great handsome flower, which looked like a tulip; but the leaves were tightly closed, as though it were still a bud.

"It is a beautiful flower," said the woman; and she kissed its beautiful yellow and red leaves. But just as she kissed it the flower opened with a loud crack. It was a real tulip, as one could now see; but in the middle of the flower there sat upon the green stamens a little maiden, delicate and graceful to behold. She was scarcely half a thumb's length in height, and therefore she was called Thumbelina.

A neat polished walnut-shell served Thumbelina for a cradle, blue violet-leaves were her mattresses, with a rose-leaf for a coverlet. There she slept at night; but in the daytime she played upon the table, where the woman had put a plate with a wreath of flowers around it, whose stalks stood in water; on the water swam a great tulip-leaf, and on this the little maiden could sit, and row from one side of the plate to the other, with two white horse-hairs for oars. That looked pretty indeed! She could also sing, and, indeed, so delicately and sweetly, that the like had never been heard.

One night as she lay in her pretty bed, there came a horrid old Toad hopping in at the window, in which one pane was broken. The Toad was very ugly, big, and damp: it hopped straight down upon the table, where Thumbelina lay sleeping under the red rose-leaf.

"That would be a handsome wife for my son," said the Toad; and she took the walnut-shell in which Thumbelina lay asleep, and hopped with it through the window down into the garden.

There ran a great broad brook; but the margin was swampy and soft, and here the Toad dwelt with her son. Ugh! he was ugly, and looked just like his mother. "Croak! croak! brek kek-kex!" that was all he could say when he saw the graceful little maiden in the walnut-shell.

"Don't speak so loud, or she will awake," said the old Toad. "She might run away from us yet, for she is as light as a bit of swan's-down. We will put her out in the brook upon one of the broad water-lily leaves. That will be just like an island for her, she is so small and light. Then she can't get away, while we put the state-room under the mud in order, where you are to live and keep house together."

Out in the brook there grew many water-lilies with broad green leaves, which looked as if they were floating on the water. The leaf which lay farthest out was also the greatest of all, and to that the old Toad swam out and laid the walnut-shell upon it with Thumbelina. The poor little thing woke early in the morning, and when she saw where she was, she began to cry very bitterly; for there was water on every side of the great green leaf, and she could not get to land at all. The old Toad sat down in the mud, decking out her room with sedges and yellow water-lilies—it was to be made very pretty for the new daughter-in-law; then she swam out, with her ugly son, to the leaf on which Thumbelina was. They wanted to take her pretty bed, which was to be put in the bridal chamber before she went in there herself. The old Toad bowed low before her in the water, and said,

"Here is my son; he will be your husband, and you will live splendidly together in the mud."

"Croak! croak! brek-kek-kex!" was all the son could say.

Then they took the elegant little bed, and swam away with it; but Thumbelina sat all alone upon the green leaf and wept, for she did not like to live at the nasty Toad's, and have her ugly son for a husband. The little fishes swimming in the water below had both seen the Toad, and had also heard what she said; therefore they stretched forth their heads, for they wanted to see the little girl. So soon as they saw her they considered her so pretty that they felt very sorry she should have to go down to the ugly Toad. No, that must never be! They assembled together in the water around the green stalk which held the leaf on which the little maiden stood, and with their teeth they gnawed away the stalk, and so the leaf swam down the stream; and away went Thumbelina far away, where the Toad could not get at her.

Thumbelina sailed by many places, and the little birds which sat in the bushes saw her, and said, "What a lovely little girl!" The leaf swam away with her, farther and farther; so Thumbelina travelled out of the country.

A graceful little white butterfly continued to flutter round her, and at last alighted on the leaf. Thumbelina pleased him, and she was so delighted, for now the Toad could not reach her; and it was so beautiful where she was floating along—the sun shone upon the water, it was just like shining gold. She took her girdle and bound one end of it round the butterfly, fastening the other end of the ribbon to the leaf. The leaf now glided onward much faster, and Thumbelina too, for she stood upon the leaf.

There came a big Cockchafer flying up; and he saw her, and immediately clasped his claws round her slender waist, and flew with her up into a tree. The green leaf went swimming down the brook, and the butterfly with it; for he was fastened to the leaf, and could not get away from it.

Mercy! how frightened poor little Thumbelina was when the Cockchafer flew with her up into the tree! But especially she was sorry for the fine white butterfly whom she had bound fast to the leaf, for, if he could not free himself from it, he would be forced to starve to death. The Cockchafer, however, did not trouble himself at all about this. He seated himself with her upon the biggest green leaf of the tree, gave her the sweet part of the flowers to eat, and declared that she was very pretty, though she did not in the least resemble a cockchafer. Afterwards came all the other cockchafers who lived in the tree to pay a visit: they looked at Thumbelina, and the lady cockchafers shrugged their feelers and said,

"Why, she has not even more than two legs!—that has a wretched appearance."

"She has not any feelers!" cried another.

"Her waist is quite slender—fie! she looks like a human creature—how ugly she is!" said all the lady cockchafers.

And yet Thumbelina was very pretty. Even the Cockchafer who had carried her off thought so; but when all the others declared she was ugly, he believed it at last, and would not have her at all—she might go whither she liked. Then they flew down with her from the tree, and set her upon a daisy, and she wept, because she was so ugly that the cockchafers would not have her; and yet she was the loveliest little being one could imagine, and as tender and delicate as a rose-leaf.

The whole summer through poor Thumbelina lived quite alone in the great wood. She wove herself a bed out of blades of grass, and hung it up under a large burdock leaf, so that she was protected from the rain; she plucked the honey out of the flowers for food, and drank of the dew which stood every morning upon the leaves. Thus summer and autumn passed away; but now came winter, the cold long winter. All the birds who had sung so sweetly to her flew away; trees and flowers shed their leaves; the great burdock leaf under which she had lived shrivelled up, and there remained nothing of it but a yellow withered stalk; and she was dreadfully cold, for her clothes were torn, and she herself was so frail and delicate—poor little Thumbelina! she was nearly frozen. It began to snow, and every snow-flake that fell upon her was like a whole shovel-full thrown upon one of us, for we are tall, and she was only an inch long. Then she wrapped herself in a dry leaf, but that would not warm her—she shivered with cold.

Close to the wood into which she had now come lay a great corn-field, but the corn was gone long ago; only the naked dry stubble stood up out of the frozen ground. These were just like a great forest for her to wander through; and, oh! how she trembled with cold. Then she arrived at the door of the Field Mouse. This mouse had a little hole under the stubble. There the Field Mouse lived, warm and comfortable, and had a whole room-full of corn—a glorious kitchen and larder. Poor Thumbelina stood at the door just like a poor beggar girl, and begged for a little bit of a barleycorn, for she had not had the smallest morsel to eat for the last two days.

"You poor little creature," said the Field Mouse—for after all she was a good old Field Mouse—"come into my warm room and dine with me."

As she was pleased with Thumbelina, she said, "If you like you may stay with me through the winter, but you must keep my room clean and neat, and tell me stories, for I am very fond of them."

And Thumbelina did as the kind old Field Mouse bade her, and had a very good time of it.

"Now we shall soon have a visitor," said the Field Mouse. "My neighbour is in the habit of visiting me once a week. He is even better off than I am, has great rooms, and a beautiful black velvety fur. If you could only get him for your husband you would be well provided for; but he cannot see at all. You must tell him the very prettiest stories you know."

But Thumbelina did not care about this; she would not have the neighbour at all, for he was a Mole. He came and paid his visits in his black velvet coat. The Field Mouse told how rich and how learned he was, and how his house was more than twenty times larger than hers; that he had learning, but that he did not like the sun and beautiful flowers, and said nasty things about them, for he had never seen them.

Thumbelina had to sing, and she sang "Cockchafer, fly away," and "When the parson goes afield." Then the Mole fell in love with her, because of her delicious voice; but he said nothing, for he was a sedate man.

A short time before, he had dug a long passage through the earth from his own house to theirs; and Thumbelina and the Field Mouse obtained leave to walk in this passage as much as they wished. But he begged them not to be afraid of the dead bird which was lying in the passage. It was an entire bird, with wings and a beak. It certainly must have died only a short time before, when the winter began, and was now buried just where the Mole had made his passage.

The Mole took a bit of decayed wood in his mouth, for that glimmers like fire in the dark; and then he went first and lighted them through the long dark passage. When they came where the dead bird lay, the Mole thrust up his broad nose against the ceiling and pushed the earth, so that a great hole was made, through which the daylight could shine down. In the middle of the floor lay a dead Swallow, his beautiful wings pressed close against his sides, and his head and feet drawn in under his feathers: the poor bird had certainly died of cold. Thumbelina was very sorry for this; she was very fond of all the little birds, who had sung and twittered so prettily for her through the summer; but the Mole gave him a push with his short legs, and said, "Now he doesn't pipe any more. It must be miserable to be born a little bird. I'm thankful that none of my children can be that: such a bird has nothing but his 'tweet-tweet', and has to starve in the winter!"

"Yes, you may well say that, like a sensible man," observed the Field Mouse. "Of what use is all this 'tweet-tweet' to a bird when the winter comes? He must starve and freeze. But they say that's very aristocratic."

Thumbelina said nothing; but when the two others turned their backs on the bird, she bent down, put the feathers aside which covered his head, and kissed him upon his closed eyes.

"Perhaps it was he who sang so prettily to me in the summer," she thought. "How much pleasure he gave me, the dear beautiful bird!"

The Mole now closed up the hole through which the daylight shone in, and accompanied the ladies home. But at night Thumbelina could not sleep at all; so she got up out of her bed, and wove a large beautiful carpet of hay, and carried it and spread it over the dead bird, and laid soft cotton, which she had found in the Field Mouse's room, at the bird's sides, so that he might lie warm in the cold ground.

"Farewell, you pretty little bird!" said she. "Farewell! and thanks to you for your beautiful song in the summer, when all the trees were green, and the sun shone down warmly upon us." And then she laid her head on the bird's breast, but at once was greatly startled, for it felt as if something were beating inside there. That was the bird's heart. The bird was not dead; he was only lying there torpid with cold; and now he had been warmed, and came to life again.

In autumn all the swallows fly away to warm countries, but if one happens to be belated, it becomes so cold that it falls down as if dead, and lies where it falls, and then the cold snow covers it.

Thumbelina fairly trembled, she was so startled; for the bird was large, very large, compared with her, who was only an inch in height. But she took courage, laid the cotton closer round the poor bird, and brought a leaf of mint that she had used as her own coverlet, and laid it over the bird's head.

The next night she crept out to him again—and now he was alive, but quite weak; he could only open his eyes for a moment, and look at Thumbelina, who stood before him with a bit of decayed wood in her hand, for she had no other lantern.

"I thank you, you pretty little child," said the sick Swallow; "I have been famously warmed. Soon I shall get my strength back again, and I shall be able to fly about in the warm sunshine."

"Oh," she said, "it is so cold without. It snows and freezes. Stay in your warm bed, and I will nurse you."

Then she brought the Swallow water in the petal of a flower; and the Swallow drank, and told her how he had torn one of his wings in a thorn bush, and thus had not been able to fly as fast as the other swallows, which had sped away, far away, to the warm countries. So at last he had fallen to the ground, but he could remember nothing more, and did not know at all how he had come where she had found him.

The whole winter the Swallow remained there, and Thumbelina nursed and tended him heartily. Neither the Field Mouse nor the Mole heard anything about it, for they did not like the poor Swallow. So soon as the spring came, and the sun warmed the earth, the Swallow bade Thumbelina farewell, and she opened the hole which the Mole had made in the ceiling. The sun shone in upon them gloriously, and the Swallow asked if Thumbelina would go with him; she could sit upon his back, and they would fly away far into the green wood. But Thumbelina knew that the old Field Mouse would be grieved if she left her.

"No, I cannot!" said Thumbelina.

"Farewell, farewell, you good, pretty girl!" said the Swallow; and he flew out into the sunshine. Thumbelina looked after him, and the tears came into her eyes, for she was so fond of the poor Swallow.

"Tweet-weet! tweet-weet!" sang the bird, and flew intp the green forest. Thumbelina felt very sad. She did not get permission to go out into the warm sunshine. The corn which was sown in the field over the house of the Field Mouse grew up high into the air; it was quite a thick wood for the poor girl, who was only an inch in height.

"Now you must work at your outfit this summer," said the Field Mouse to her; for her neighbour, the tiresome Mole with the velvet coat, had proposed to her. "You shall have woollen and linen clothes both; you will lack nothing when you have become the Mole's wife."

Thumbelina had to turn the spindle, and the Mole hired four spiders to spin and weave for her day and night. Every evening the Mole paid her a visit; and he was always saying that when the summer should draw to a close, the sun would not shine nearly so hot, for that now it burned the earth almost as hard as a stone. Yes, when the summer should have gone, then he would keep his wedding day with Thumbelina. But she was not glad at all, for she did not like the tiresome Mole. Every morning when the sun rose, and every evening when it went down, she crept out at the door; and when the wind blew the corn ears apart, so that she could see the blue sky, she thought how bright and beautiful it was out here, and wished so much to see her dear Swallow again. But the Swallow did not come back;

he had doubtless flown far away, in the fair green forest. When autumn came on, Thumbelina had all her outfit ready.

"In four weeks you shall celebrate your wedding," said the Field Mouse to her.

But Thumbelina wept, and declared she would not have the tiresome Mole.

"Nonsense," said the Field Mouse; "don't be obstinate, or I will bite you with my white teeth. He is a very fine man whom you will marry. The queen herself has not such a black velvet fur; and his kitchen and cellar are full. Be thankful for your good fortune."

Now the wedding was to be held. The Mole had already come to fetch Thumbelina; she was to live with him, deep under the earth, and never to come out into the warm sunshine, for that he did not like. The poor little thing was very sorrowful; she was now to say farewell to the glorious sun, which, after all, she had been allowed by the Field Mouse to see from the threshold of the door.

"Farewell, thou bright sun!" she said, and stretched out her arms towards it, and walked a little way forth from the house of the Field Mouse, for now the corn had been reaped, and only the dry stubble stood in the fields. "Farewell!" she repeated, and threw her little arms round a little red flower which still bloomed there. "Greet the dear Swallow from me, if you see her again."

"Tweet-weet! tweet-weet!" a voice suddenly sounded over her head. She looked up; it was the Swallow, who was just flying by. When he saw Thumbelina he was very glad; and Thumbelina told him how loth she was to have the ugly Mole for her husband, and that she was to live deep under the earth, where the sun never shone. And she could not refrain from weeping.

"The cold winter is coming now," said the Swallow; "I am going to fly far away into the warm countries. Will you come with me? You can sit upon my back, only tie yourself fast with your sash, then we shall fly from the ugly Mole and his dark room—away, far away, over the mountains, to the warm countries, where the sun shines more beautifully than here, where it is always summer, and there are lovely flowers. Only fly with me, you dear little Thumbelina, you who saved my life when I lay frozen in the dark earthy passage."

"Yes, I will go with you!" said Thumbelina, and she seated herself on the bird's back, with her feet on his outspread wings, and bound her girdle fast to one of his strongest feathers; then the Swallow flew up into the air over forest and over sea, high up over the great mountains, where the snow always lies; and Thumbelina felt cold in the bleak air, but then she crept under the bird's warm feathers, and only put out her little head to admire all the beauties beneath her.

At last they came to the warm countries. There the sun shone far brighter than here; the sky seemed twice as high; in ditches and on the hedges grew the most beautiful blue and green grapes; lemons and oranges hung in the woods; the air was fragrant with myrtles and balsams, and on the roads the loveliest children ran about, playing with the gay butterflies. But the Swallow flew still farther, and it became more and more beautiful. Under the most glorious green trees by the blue lake stood a palace of dazzling white marble, from the olden time. Vines clustered around the lofty pillars; at the top were many swallows' nests, and in one of these the Swallow lived who carried Thumbelina.

"Here is my house," said the Swallow. "But if you will select for yourself one of the splendid flowers which grow down yonder, then I will put you into it, and you shall have everything as nice as you can wish."

"That is capital," cried she, and clapped her little hands.

A great marble pillar lay there, which had fallen to the ground and had been broken into three pieces; but between these pieces grew the most beautiful great white flowers. The Swallow flew down with Thumbelina, and set her upon one of the broad leaves. But how great was the little maid's surprise! There sat a little man in the midst of the flower, as white and transparent as if he had been made of glass; he wore the daintiest of gold crowns on his head, and the brightest wings on his shoulders; he himself was not bigger than Thumbelina. He was the angel of the flower. In each of the flowers dwelt such a little man or woman, but this one was king over them all.

"Heavens! how beautiful he is!" whispered Thumbelina to the Swallow.

The little prince was very much frightened at the Swallow; for it was quite a gigantic bird to him, who was so small. But when he saw Thumbelina, he became very glad; she was the prettiest maiden he had ever seen. Therefore he took off his golden crown, and put it upon her, asked her name, and if she would be his wife, and then she should be queen of all the flowers. Now this was truly a different kind of man to the son of the Toad, and the Mole with the black velvet fur. She therefore said "Yes" to the charming prince. And out of every flower came a lady or a lord, so pretty to behold that it was a delight: each one brought Thumbelina a present; but the best gift was a pair of beautiful wings which had belonged to a great white fly; these were fastened to Thumbelina's back, and now she could fly from flower to flower. Then there was much rejoicing; and the Swallow sat above them in her nest, and sung for them as well as she could; but yet in her heart she was sad, for she was so fond of Thumbelina, and would have liked never to part from her.

"You shall not be called Thumbelina!" said the Flower Angel to her; "that is an ugly name, and you are too fair for it—we will call you Maia."

"Farewell, farewell!" said the Swallow, and she flew away again from the warm countries, far away back to Denmark. There she had a little nest over the window of the man who can tell fairy tales. To him she sang "Tweet-weet! tweet-weet!" and from him we have the whole story.

THE LITTLE MERMAID

Hans Christian Andersen

First published in 1837
Translated from Danish by
H. P. Paull, published in 1888

Far out in the ocean, where the water is as blue as the prettiest cornflower, and as clear as crystal, it is very, very deep; so deep, indeed, that no cable could fathom it: many church steeples, piled one upon another, would not reach from the ground beneath to the surface of the water above. There dwell the Sea King and his subjects. We must not imagine that there is nothing at the bottom of the sea but bare yellow sand. No, indeed; the most singular flowers and plants grow there; the leaves and stems of which are so pliant, that the slightest agitation of the water causes them to stir as if they had life. Fishes, both large and small, glide between the branches, as birds fly among the trees here upon land. In the deepest spot of all, stands the castle of the Sea King. Its walls are built of coral, and the long, gothic windows are of the clearest amber. The roof is formed of shells, that open and close as the water flows over them. Their appearance is very beautiful, for in each lies a glittering pearl, which would be fit for the diadem of a queen.

The Sea King had been a widower for many years, and his aged mother kept house for him. She was a very wise woman, and exceedingly proud of her high birth; on that account she wore twelve oysters on her tail; while others, also of high rank, were only allowed to wear six. She was, however, deserving of very great praise, especially for her care of the little sea-princesses, her grand-daughters. They were six beautiful children; but the youngest was the prettiest of them all; her skin was as clear and delicate as a rose-leaf, and her eyes as blue as the deepest sea; but, like all the others, she had no feet, and her body ended in a fish's tail. All day long they played in the great halls of the castle, or among the living flowers that grew out of the walls. The large amber windows were open, and the fish swam in, just as the swallows fly into our houses when we open the windows, excepting that the fishes swam up to the princesses, ate out of their hands, and allowed themselves to be stroked. Outside the castle there was a beautiful garden, in which grew bright red and dark blue flowers, and blossoms like flames of fire; the fruit glittered like gold, and the leaves and stems waved to and fro continually. The earth itself was the finest sand, but blue as the flame of burning sulphur. Over everything lay a peculiar blue radiance, as if it were surrounded by the air from above, through which the blue sky shone, instead of the dark depths of the sea. In calm weather the sun could be seen, looking like a purple flower, with the light streaming from the calyx. Each of the young princesses had a little plot of ground in the garden, where she might dig and plant as she pleased. One arranged her flower-bed into the form of a whale; another thought it better to make hers like the figure of a little mermaid; but that of the youngest was round like the sun, and contained flowers as red as his rays at sunset. She was a strange child, quiet and thoughtful; and while her sisters would be delighted with the wonderful things which they obtained from the wrecks of vessels, she cared for nothing but her pretty red flowers, like the sun, excepting a beautiful marble statue. It was the representation of a handsome boy, carved out of pure white stone, which had fallen to the bottom of the sea from a wreck. She planted by the statue a rose-coloured weeping willow. It grew splendidly, and very soon hung its fresh branches over the statue, almost down to the blue sands. The shadow had a violet tint, and waved to and fro like the branches; it seemed as if the crown of the tree and the root were at play, and trying to kiss each other. Nothing gave her so much pleasure as to hear about the world above the sea. She made her old grandmother tell her all she knew of the ships and of the towns, the people and the animals. To her it seemed most wonderful and beautiful to hear that the flowers of the land should have fragrance, and not those below the sea; that the trees of the forest should be green; and that the fishes among the trees could sing so sweetly, that it was quite a pleasure to hear them. Her grandmother called the little birds fishes, or she would not have understood her; for she had never seen birds.

"When you have reached your fifteenth year," said the grand-mother, "you will have permission to rise up out of the sea, to sit on the rocks in the moonlight, while the great ships are sailing by; and then you will see both forests and towns."

In the following year, one of the sisters would be fifteen: but as each was a year younger than the other, the youngest would have to wait five years before her turn came to rise up from the bottom of the ocean, and see the earth as we do. However, each promised to tell the others what she saw on her first visit, and what she thought the most beautiful; for their grandmother could not tell them enough; there were so many things on which they wanted information. None of them longed so much for her turn to come as the youngest, she who had the longest time to wait, and who was so quiet and thoughtful. Many nights she stood by the open window, looking up through the dark blue water, and watching the fish as they splashed about with their fins and tails. She could see the moon and stars shining faintly; but through the water they looked larger than they do to our eyes. When something like a black cloud passed between her and them, she knew that it was either a whale swimming over her head, or a ship full of human beings, who never imagined that a pretty little mermaid was standing beneath them, holding out her white hands towards the keel of their ship.

As soon as the eldest was fifteen, she was allowed to rise to the surface of the ocean. When she came back, she had hundreds of things to talk about; but the most beautiful, she said, was to lie in the moonlight, on a sandbank, in the quiet sea, near the coast, and to gaze on a large town nearby, where the lights were twinkling like hundreds of stars; to listen to the sounds of the music, the noise of carriages, and the voices of human beings, and then to hear the merry bells peal out from the church steeples; and because she could not go near to all those wonderful things, she longed for them more than ever. Oh, did not the youngest sister listen eagerly to all these descriptions? and afterwards, when she stood at the open window looking up through the dark blue water, she thought of the great city, with all its bustle and noise, and even fancied she could hear the sound of the church bells, down in the depths of the sea.

In another year the second sister received permission to rise to the surface of the water, and to swim about where she pleased. She rose just as the sun was setting, and this, she said, was the most beautiful sight of all. The whole sky looked like gold, while violet and rose-coloured clouds, which she could not describe, floated over her; and, still more rapidly than the clouds, flew a large flock of wild swans towards the setting sun, looking like a long white veil across the sea. She also swam towards the sun; but it sunk into the waves, and the rosy tints faded from the clouds and from the sea.

The third sister's turn followed; she was the boldest of them all, and she swam up a broad river that emptied itself into the sea. On the banks she saw green hills covered with beautiful vines; palaces and castles peeped out from amid the proud trees of the forest; she heard the birds singing, and the rays of the sun were so powerful that she was obliged often to dive down under the water to cool her burning face. In a narrow creek she found a whole troop of little human children, quite naked, and sporting about in the water; she wanted to play with them, but they fled in a great fright; and then a little black animal came to the water; it was a dog, but she did not know that, for she had never before seen one. This animal barked at her so terribly that she became frightened, and rushed back to the open sea. But she said she should never forget the beautiful forest, the green hills, and the pretty little children who could swim in the water, although they had not fish's tails.

The fourth sister was more timid; she remained in the midst of the sea, but she said it was quite as beautiful there as nearer the land. She could see for so many miles around her, and the sky above looked like a bell of glass. She had seen the ships, but at such a great distance that they looked like sea-gulls. The dolphins sported in the waves, and the great whales spouted water from their nostrils till it seemed as if a hundred fountains were playing in every direction.

The fifth sister's birthday occurred in the winter; so when her turn came, she saw what the others had not seen the first time they went up. The sea looked quite green, and large icebergs were floating about, each like a pearl, she said, but larger and loftier than the churches built by men. They were of the most singular shapes, and glittered like diamonds. She had seated herself upon one of the largest, and let the wind play with her long hair, and she remarked that all the ships sailed by rapidly, and steered as far away as they could from the iceberg, as if they were afraid of it. Towards evening, as the sun went down, dark clouds covered the sky, the thunder rolled and the lightning flashed, and the red light glowed on the icebergs as they rocked and tossed on the heaving sea. On all the ships the sails were reefed with fear and trembling, while she sat calmly on the floating iceberg, watching the blue lightning, as it darted its forked flashes into the sea.

When first the sisters had permission to rise to the surface, they were each delighted with the new and beautiful sights they saw; but now, as grown-up girls, they could go when they pleased, and they had become indifferent about it. They wished themselves back again in the water, and after a month had passed they said it was much more beautiful down below, and pleasanter to be at home. Yet often, in the evening hours, the five sisters would twine their arms round each other, and rise to the surface, in a row. They had more beautiful voices than any human being could have; and before the approach of a storm, and when they expected a ship would be lost, they swam before the vessel, and sang sweetly of the delights to be found in the depths of the sea, and begging the sailors not to fear if they sank to the bottom. But the sailors could not understand the song, they took it for the howling of the storm. And these things were never to be beautiful for them; for if the ship sank, the men were drowned, and their dead bodies alone reached the palace of the Sea King.

When the sisters rose, arm-in-arm, through the water in this way, their youngest sister would stand quite alone, looking after them, ready to cry, only that the mermaids have no tears, and therefore they suffer more. "Oh, were I but fifteen years old," said she: "I know that I shall love the world up there, and all the people who live in it."

At last she reached her fifteenth year. "Well, now, you are grown up," said the old dowager, her grandmother; "so you must let me adorn you like your other sisters;" and she placed a wreath of white lilies in her hair, and every flower leaf was half a pearl. Then the old lady ordered eight great oysters to attach themselves to the tail of the princess to show her high rank.

"But they hurt me so," said the little mermaid.

"Pride must suffer pain," replied the old lady. Oh, how gladly she would have shaken off all this grandeur, and laid aside the heavy wreath! The red flowers in her own garden would have suited her much better, but she could not help herself: so she said, "Farewell," and rose as lightly as a bubble to the surface of the water. The sun had just set as she raised her head above the waves; but the clouds were tinted with crimson and gold, and through the glimmering twilight beamed the evening star in all its beauty. The sea was calm, and the air mild and fresh. A large ship, with three masts, lay becalmed on the water, with only one sail set; for not a breeze stiffed, and the sailors sat idle on deck or amongst the rigging. There was music and song on board; and, as darkness came on, a hundred coloured lanterns were lighted, as if the flags of all nations waved in the air. The little mermaid swam close to the cabin windows; and now and then, as the waves lifted her up, she could look in through clear glass window-panes, and see a number of well-dressed people within. Among them was a young prince, the most beautiful of all, with large black eyes; he was sixteen years of age, and his birthday was being kept with much rejoicing. The sailors were dancing on deck, but when the prince came out of the cabin, more than a hundred rockets rose in the air, making it as bright as day. The little mermaid was so startled that she dived under water; and when she again stretched out her head, it appeared as if all the stars of heaven were falling around her, she had never seen such fireworks before. Great suns spurted fire about, splendid fireflies flew into the blue air, and everything was reflected in the clear, calm sea beneath. The ship itself was so brightly illuminated that all the people, and even the smallest rope, could be distinctly and plainly seen. And how handsome the young prince looked, as he pressed the hands of all present and smiled at them, while the music resounded through the clear night air.

It was very late; yet the little mermaid could not take her eyes from the ship, or from the beautiful prince. The coloured lanterns had been extinguished, no more rockets rose in the air, and the cannon had ceased firing; but the sea became restless, and a moaning, grumbling sound could be heard beneath the waves: still the little mermaid remained by the cabin window, rocking up and down on the water, which enabled her to look in. After a while, the sails were quickly unfurled, and the noble ship continued her passage; but soon the waves rose higher, heavy clouds darkened the sky, and lightning appeared in the distance. A dreadful storm was approaching; once more the sails were reefed, and the great ship pursued her flying course over the raging sea. The waves rose mountains high, as if they would have overtopped the mast; but the ship dived like a swan between them, and then rose again on their lofty, foaming crests. To the little mermaid this appeared pleasant sport; not so to the sailors. At length the ship groaned and creaked; the thick planks gave way under the lashing of the sea as it broke over the deck; the mainmast snapped asunder like a reed; the ship lay over on her side; and the water rushed in. The little mermaid now perceived that the crew were in danger; even she herself was obliged to be careful to avoid the beams and planks of the wreck which lay scattered on the water. At one moment it was so pitch dark that she could not see a single object, but a flash of lightning revealed the whole scene; she could see every one who had been on board excepting the prince; when the ship parted, she had seen him sink into the deep waves, and she was glad, for she thought he would now be with her; and then she remembered that human beings could not live in the water, so that when he got down to her father's palace he would be quite dead. But he must not die. So she swam about among the beams and planks which strewed the surface of the sea, forgetting that they could crush her to pieces. Then she dived deeply under the dark waters, rising and falling with the waves, till at length she managed to reach the young prince, who was fast losing the power of swimming in that stormy sea. His limbs were failing him, his beautiful eyes were closed, and he would have died had not the little mermaid come to his assistance. She held his head above the water, and let the waves drift them where they would.

In the morning the storm had ceased; but of the ship not a single fragment could be seen. The sun rose up red and glowing from the water, and its beams brought back the hue of health to the prince's cheeks; but his eyes remained closed. The mermaid kissed his high, smooth forehead, and stroked back his wet hair; he seemed to her like the marble statue in her little garden, and she kissed him again, and wished that he might live. Presently they came in sight of land; she saw lofty blue mountains, on which the white snow rested as if a flock of swans were lying upon them. Near the coast were beautiful green forests, and close by stood a large building, whether a church or a convent she could not tell. Orange and citron trees grew in the garden, and before the door stood lofty palms. The sea here formed a little bay, in which the water was quite still, but very deep; so she swam with the handsome prince to the beach, which was covered with fine, white sand, and there she laid him in the warm sunshine, taking care to raise his head higher than his body. Then bells sounded in the large white building, and a number of young girls came into the garden. The little mermaid swam out farther from the shore and placed herself between some high rocks that rose out of the water; then she covered her head and neck with the foam of the sea so that her little face might not be seen, and watched to see what would become of the poor prince. She did not wait long before she saw a young girl approach the spot where he lay.

She seemed frightened at first, but only for a moment; then she fetched a number of people, and the mermaid saw that the prince came to life again, and smiled upon those who stood round him. But to her he sent no smile; he knew not that she had saved him. This made her very unhappy, and when he was led away into the great building, she dived down sorrowfully into the water, and returned to her father's castle. She had always been silent and thoughtful, and now she was more so than ever. Her sisters asked her what she had seen during her first visit to the surface of the water; but she would tell them nothing. Many an evening and morning did she rise to the place where she had left the prince. She saw the fruits in the garden ripen till they were gathered, the snow on the tops of the mountains melt away; but she never saw the prince, and therefore she returned home, always more sorrowful than before. It was her only comfort to sit in her own little garden, and fling her arm round the beautiful marble statue which was like the prince; but she gave up tending her flowers, and they grew in wild confusion over the paths, twining their long leaves and stems round the branches of the trees, so that the whole place became dark and gloomy. At length she could bear it no longer, and told one of her sisters all about it. Then the others heard the secret, and very soon it became known to two mermaids whose intimate friend happened to know who the prince was. She had also seen the festival on board ship, and she told them where the prince came from, and where his palace stood.

"Come, little sister," said the other princesses; then they entwined their arms and rose up in a long row to the surface of the water, close by the spot where they knew the prince's palace stood. It was built of bright yellow shining stone, with long flights of marble steps, one of which reached quite down to the sea. Splendid gilded cupolas rose over the roof, and between the pillars that surrounded the whole building stood life-like statues of marble. Through the clear crystal of the lofty windows could be seen noble rooms, with costly silk curtains and hangings of tapestry; while the walls were covered with beautiful paintings which were a pleasure to look at. In the centre of the largest saloon a fountain threw its sparkling jets high up into the glass cupola of the ceiling, through which the sun shone down upon the water and upon the beautiful plants growing round the basin of the fountain. Now that she knew where he lived, she spent many an evening and many a night on the water near the palace. She would swim much nearer the shore than any of the others ventured to do; indeed once she went quite up the narrow channel under the marble balcony, which threw a broad shadow on the water. Here she would sit and watch the young prince, who thought himself quite alone in the bright moonlight.

She saw him many times of an evening sailing in a pleasant boat, with music playing and flags waving. She peeped out from among the green rushes, and if the wind caught her long silvery-white veil, those who saw it believed it to be a swan, spreading out its wings. On many a night, too, when the fishermen, with their torches, were out at sea, she heard them relate so many good things about the doings of the young prince, that she was glad she had saved his life when he had been tossed about half-dead on the waves. And she remembered that his head had rested on her bosom, and how heartily she had kissed him; but he knew nothing of all this, and could not even dream of her. She grew more and more fond of human beings, and wished more and more to be able to wander about with those whose world seemed to be so much larger than her own. They could fly over the sea in ships, and mount the high hills which were far above the clouds; and the lands they possessed, their woods and their fields, stretched far away beyond the reach of her sight. There was so much that she wished to know, and her sisters were unable to answer all her questions. Then she applied to her old grandmother, who knew all about the upper world, which she very rightly called the lands above the sea.

"If human beings are not drowned," asked the little mermaid, "can they live forever? Do they never die as we do here in the sea?"

"Yes," replied the old lady, "they must also die, and their term of life is even shorter than ours. We sometimes live to three hundred years, but when we cease to exist here we only become the foam on the surface of the water, and we have not even a grave down here of those we love. We have not immortal souls, we shall never live again; but, like the green sea-weed, when once it has been cut off, we can never flourish more. Human beings, on the contrary, have a soul which lives forever, lives after the body has been turned to dust. It rises up through the clear, pure air beyond the glittering stars. As we rise out of the water, and behold all the land of the earth, so do they rise to unknown and glorious regions which we shall never see."

"Why have not we an immortal soul?" asked the little mermaid mournfully; "I would give gladly all the hundreds of years that I have to live, to be a human being only for one day, and to have the hope of knowing the happiness of that glorious world above the stars."

"You must not think of that," said the old woman; "we feel ourselves to be much happier and much better off than human beings."

"So I shall die," said the little mermaid, "and as the foam of the sea I shall be driven about never again to hear the music of the waves, or to see the pretty flowers nor the red sun. Is there anything I can do to win an immortal soul?"

"No," said the old woman, "unless a man were to love you so much that you were more to him than his father or mother; and if all his thoughts and all his love were fixed upon you, and the priest placed his right hand in yours, and he promised to be true to you here and hereafter, then his soul would glide into your body and you would obtain a share in the future happiness of mankind. He would give a soul to you and retain his own as well; but this can never happen. Your fish's tail, which amongst us is considered so beautiful, is thought on earth to be quite ugly; they do not know any better, and they think it necessary to have two stout props, which they call legs, in order to be handsome."

Then the little mermaid sighed, and looked sorrowfully at her fish's tail.

"Let us be happy," said the old lady, "and dart and spring about during the three hundred years that we have to live, which is really quite long enough; after that we can rest ourselves all the better. This evening we are going to have a court ball."

It is one of those splendid sights which we can never see on earth. The walls and the ceiling of the large ballroom were of thick, but transparent crystal. May hundreds of colossal shells, some of a deep red, others of a grass green, stood on each side in rows, with blue fire in them, which lighted up the whole saloon, and shone through the walls, so that the sea was also illuminated. Innumerable fishes, great and small, swam past the crystal walls; on some of them the scales glowed with a purple brilliancy, and on others they shone like silver and gold. Through the halls flowed a broad stream, and in it danced the mermen and the mermaids to the music of their own sweet singing. No one on earth has such a lovely voice as theirs. The little mermaid sang more sweetly than them all. The whole court applauded her with hands and tails; and for a moment her heart felt quite gay, for she knew she had the loveliest voice of any on earth or in the sea. But she soon thought again of the world above her, for she could not forget the charming prince, nor her sorrow that she had not an immortal soul like his; therefore she crept away silently out of her father's palace, and while everything within was gladness and song, she sat in her own little garden sorrowful and alone. Then she heard the bugle sounding through the water, and thought—"He is certainly sailing above, he on whom my wishes depend, and in whose hands I should like to place the happiness of my life. I will venture all for him, and to win an immortal soul, while my sisters are dancing in my father's palace, I will go to the sea witch, of whom I have always been so much afraid, but she can give me counsel and help."

And then the little mermaid went out from her garden, and took the road to the foaming whirlpools, behind which the sorceress lived. She had never been that way before: neither flowers nor grass grew there; nothing but bare, gray, sandy ground stretched out to the whirlpool, where the water, like foaming mill-wheels, whirled round everything that it seized, and cast it into the fathomless deep. Through the midst of these crushing whirlpools the little mermaid was obliged to pass, to reach the dominions of the sea witch; and also for a long distance the only road lay right across a quantity of warm, bubbling mire, called by the witch her turfmoor. Beyond this stood her house, in the centre of a strange forest, in which all the trees and flowers were polypi, half animals and half plants; they looked like serpents with a hundred heads growing out of the ground. The branches were long slimy arms, with fingers like flexible worms, moving limb after limb from the root to the top. All that could be reached in the sea they seized upon, and held fast, so that it never escaped from their clutches. The little mermaid was so alarmed at what she saw, that she stood still, and her heart beat with fear, and she was very nearly turning back; but she thought of the prince, and of the human soul for which she longed, and her courage returned. She fastened her long flowing hair round her head, so that the polypi might not seize hold of it. She laid her hands together across her bosom, and then she darted forward as a fish shoots through the water, between the supple arms and fingers of the ugly polypi, which were stretched out on each side of her. She saw that each held in its grasp something it had seized with its numerous little arms, as if they were iron bands. The white skeletons of human beings who had perished at sea, and had sunk down into the deep waters, skeletons of land animals, oars, rudders, and chests of ships were lying tightly grasped by their clinging arms; even a little mermaid, whom they had caught and strangled; and this seemed the most shocking of all to the little princess.

She now came to a space of marshy ground in the wood, where large, fat water-snakes were rolling in the mire, and showing their ugly, drab-coloured bodies. In the midst of this spot stood a house, built with the bones of shipwrecked human beings. There sat the sea witch, allowing a toad to eat from her mouth, just as people sometimes feed a canary with a piece of sugar. She called the ugly water-snakes her little chickens, and allowed them to crawl all over her bosom.

"I know what you want," said the sea witch; "it is very stupid of you, but you shall have your way, and it will bring you to sorrow, my pretty princess. You want to get rid of your fish's tail, and to have two supports instead of it, like human beings on earth, so that the young prince may fall in love with you, and that you may have an immortal soul." And then the witch laughed so loud and disgustingly, that the toad and the snakes fell to the ground, and lay there wriggling about. "You are but just in time," said the witch; "for after sunrise tomorrow I should not be able to help you till the end of another year. I will prepare a draught for you, with which you must swim to land tomorrow before sunrise, and sit down on the shore and drink it. Your tail will then disappear, and shrink up into what mankind calls legs, and you will feel great pain, as if a sword were passing through you. But all who see you will say that you are the prettiest little human being they ever saw. You will still have the same floating gracefulness of movement, and no dancer will ever tread so lightly; but at every step you take it will feel as if you were treading upon sharp knives, and that the blood must flow. If you will bear all this, I will help you."

"Yes, I will," said the little princess in a trembling voice, as she thought of the prince and the immortal soul.

"But think again," said the witch; "for when once your shape has become like a human being, you can no more be a mermaid. You will never return through the water to your sisters, or to your father's palace again; and if you do not win the love of the prince, so that he is willing to forget his father and mother for your sake, and to love you with his whole soul, and allow the priest to join your hands that you may be man and wife, then you will never have an immortal soul. The first morning after he marries another your heart will break, and you will become foam on the crest of the waves."

"I will do it," said the little mermaid, and she became pale as death.

"But I must be paid also," said the witch, "and it is not a trifle that I ask. You have the sweetest voice of any who dwell here in the depths of the sea, and you believe that you will be able to charm the prince with it also, but this voice you must give to me; the best thing you possess will I have for the price of my draught. My own blood must be mixed with it, that it may be as sharp as a two-edged sword."

"But if you take away my voice," said the little mermaid, "what is left for me?"

"Your beautiful form, your graceful walk, and your expressive eyes; surely with these you can enchain a man's heart. Well, have you lost your courage? Put out your little tongue that I may cut it off as my payment; then you shall have the powerful draught."

"It shall be," said the little mermaid.

Then the witch placed her cauldron on the fire, to prepare the magic draught.

"Cleanliness is a good thing," said she, scouring the vessel with snakes, which she had tied together in a large knot; then she pricked herself in the breast, and let the black blood drop into it. The steam that rose formed itself into such horrible shapes that no one could look at them without fear. Every moment the witch threw something else into the vessel, and when it began to boil, the sound was like the weeping of a crocodile. When at last the magic draught was ready, it looked like the clearest water. "There it is for you," said the witch. Then she cut off the mermaid's tongue, so that she became dumb, and would never again speak or sing. "If the polypi should seize hold of you as you return through the wood," said the witch, "throw over them a few drops of the potion, and their fingers will be torn into a thousand pieces." But the little mermaid had no occasion to do this, for the polypi sprang back in terror when they caught sight of the glittering draught, which shone in her hand like a twinkling star.

So she passed quickly through the wood and the marsh, and between the rushing whirlpools. She saw that in her father's palace the torches in the ballroom were extinguished, and all within asleep; but she did not venture to go in to them, for now she was dumb and going to leave them forever, she felt as if her heart would break. She stole into the garden, took a flower from the flower-beds of each of her sisters, kissed her hand a thousand times towards the palace, and then rose up through the dark blue waters. The sun had not risen when she came in sight of the prince's palace, and approached the beautiful marble steps, but the moon shone clear and bright. Then the little mermaid drank the magic draught, and it seemed as if a two-edged sword went through her delicate body: she fell into a swoon, and lay like one dead. When the sun arose and shone over the sea, she recovered, and felt a sharp pain; but just before her stood the handsome young prince. He fixed his coal-black eyes upon her so earnestly that she cast down her own, and then became aware that her fish's tail was gone, and that she had as pretty a pair of white legs and tiny feet as any little maiden could have; but she had no clothes, so she wrapped herself in her long, thick hair. The prince asked her who she was, and where she came from, and she looked at him mildly and sorrowfully with her deep blue eyes; but she could not speak. Every step she took was as the witch had said it would be, she felt as if treading upon the points of needles or sharp knives; but she bore it willingly, and stepped as lightly by the prince's side as a soap-bubble, so that he and all who saw her wondered at her graceful-swaying movements. She was very soon arrayed in costly robes of silk and muslin, and was the most beautiful creature in the palace; but she was dumb, and could neither speak nor sing.

Beautiful female slaves, dressed in silk and gold, stepped forward and sang before the prince and his royal parents: one sang better than all the others, and the prince clapped his hands and smiled at her. This was great sorrow to the little mermaid; she knew how much more sweetly she herself could sing once, and she thought, "Oh if he could only know that! I have given away my voice forever, to be with him."

The slaves next performed some pretty fairy-like dances, to the sound of beautiful music. Then the little mermaid raised her lovely white arms, stood on the tips of her toes, and glided over the floor, and danced as no one yet had been able to dance. At each moment her beauty became more revealed, and her expressive eyes appealed more directly to the heart than the songs of the slaves. Every one was enchanted, especially the prince, who called her his little foundling; and she danced again quite readily, to please him, though each time her foot touched the floor it seemed as if she trod on sharp knives."

The prince said she should remain with him always, and she received permission to sleep at his door, on a velvet cushion. He had a page's dress made for her, that she might accompany him on horseback. They rode together through the sweet-scented woods, where the green boughs touched their shoulders, and the little birds sang among the fresh leaves. She climbed with the prince to the tops of high mountains; and although her tender feet bled so that even her steps were marked, she only laughed, and followed him till they could see the clouds beneath them looking like a flock of birds travelling to distant lands. While at the prince's palace, and when all the household were asleep, she would go and sit on the broad marble steps; for it eased her burning feet to bathe them in the cold sea-water; and then she thought of all those below in the deep.

Once during the night her sisters came up arm-in-arm, singing sorrowfully, as they floated on the water. She beckoned to them, and then they recognized her, and told her how she had grieved them. After that, they came to the same place every night; and once she saw in the distance her old grandmother, who had not been to the surface of the sea for many years, and the old Sea King, her father, with his crown on his head. They stretched out their hands towards her, but they did not venture so near the land as her sisters did.

As the days passed, she loved the prince more fondly, and he loved her as he would love a little child, but it never came into his head to make her his wife; yet, unless he married her, she could not receive an immortal soul; and, on the morning after his marriage with another, she would dissolve into the foam of the sea.

"Do you not love me the best of them all?" the eyes of the little mermaid seemed to say, when he took her in his arms, and kissed her fair forehead.

"Yes, you are dear to me," said the prince; "for you have the best heart, and you are the most devoted to me; you are like a young maiden whom I once saw, but whom I shall never meet again. I was in a ship that was wrecked, and the waves cast me ashore near a holy temple, where several young maidens performed the service. The youngest of them found me on the shore, and saved my life. I saw her but twice, and she is the only one in the world whom I could love; but you are like her, and you have almost driven her image out of my mind. She belongs to the holy temple, and my good fortune has sent you to me instead of her; and we will never part."

"Ah, he knows not that it was I who saved his life," thought the little mermaid. "I carried him over the sea to the wood where the temple stands: I sat beneath the foam, and watched till the human beings came to help him. I saw the pretty maiden that he loves better than he loves me;" and the mermaid sighed deeply, but she could not shed tears. "He says the maiden belongs to the holy temple, therefore she will never return to the world. They will meet no more: while I am by his side, and see him every day. I will take care of him, and love him, and give up my life for his sake."

Very soon it was said that the prince must marry, and that the beautiful daughter of a neighbouring king would be his wife, for a fine ship was being fitted out. Although the prince gave out that he merely intended to pay a visit to the king, it was generally supposed that he really went to see his daughter. A great company were to go with him. The little mermaid smiled, and shook her head. She knew the prince's thoughts better than any of the others.

"I must travel," he had said to her; "I must see this beautiful princess; my parents desire it; but they will not oblige me to bring her home as my bride. I cannot love her; she is not like the beautiful maiden in the temple, whom you resemble. If I were forced to choose a bride, I would rather choose you, my dumb foundling, with those expressive eyes." And then he kissed her rosy mouth, played with her long waving hair, and laid his head on her heart, while she dreamed of human happiness and an immortal soul. "You are not afraid of the sea, my dumb child," said he, as they stood on the deck of the noble ship which was to carry them to the country of the neighbouring king. And then he told her of storm and of calm, of strange fishes in the deep beneath them, and of what the divers had seen there; and she smiled at his descriptions, for she knew better than any one what wonders were at the bottom of the sea.

In the moonlight, when all on board were asleep, excepting the man at the helm, who was steering, she sat on the deck, gazing down through the clear water. She thought she could distinguish her father's castle, and upon it her aged grandmother, with the silver crown on her head, looking through the rushing tide at the keel of the vessel. Then her sisters came up on the waves, and gazed at her mournfully, wringing their white hands. She beckoned to them, and smiled, and wanted to tell them how happy and well off she was; but the cabin-boy approached, and when her sisters dived down he thought it was only the foam of the sea which he saw.

The next morning the ship sailed into the harbor of a beautiful town belonging to the king whom the prince was going to visit. The church bells were ringing, and from the high towers sounded a flourish of trumpets; and soldiers, with flying colours and glittering bayonets, lined the rocks through which they passed. Every day was a festival; balls and entertainments followed one another.

But the princess had not yet appeared. People said that she was being brought up and educated in a religious house, where she was learning every royal virtue. At last she came. Then the little mermaid, who was very anxious to see whether she was really beautiful, was obliged to acknowledge that she had never seen a more perfect vision of beauty. Her skin was delicately fair, and beneath her long dark eyelashes her laughing blue eyes shone with truth and purity.

"It was you," said the prince, "who saved my life when I lay dead on the beach," and he folded his blushing bride in his arms. "Oh, I am too happy," said he to the little mermaid; "my fondest hopes are all fulfilled. You will rejoice at my happiness; for your devotion to me is great and sincere."

The little mermaid kissed his hand, and felt as if her heart were already broken. His wedding morning would bring death to her, and she would change into the foam of the sea. All the church bells rung, and the heralds rode about the town proclaiming the betrothal. Perfumed oil was burning in costly silver lamps on every altar. The priests waved the censers, while the bride and bridegroom joined their hands and received the blessing of the bishop. The little mermaid, dressed in silk and gold, held up the bride's train; but her ears heard nothing of the festive music, and her eyes saw not the holy ceremony; she thought of the night of death which was coming to her, and of all she had lost in the world. On the same evening the bride and bridegroom went on board ship; cannons were roaring, flags waving, and in the centre of the ship a costly tent of purple and gold had been erected. It contained elegant couches, for the reception of the bridal pair during the night. The ship, with swelling sails and a favourable wind, glided away smoothly and lightly over the calm sea. When it grew dark a number of coloured lamps were lit, and the sailors danced merrily on the deck. The little mermaid could not help thinking of her first rising out of the sea, when she had seen similar festivities and joys; and she joined in the dance, poised herself in the air as a swallow when he pursues his prey, and all present cheered her with wonder. She had never danced so elegantly before. Her tender feet felt as if cut with sharp knives, but she cared not for it; a sharper pang had pierced through her heart. She knew this was the last evening she should ever see the prince, for whom she had forsaken her kindred and her home; she had given up her beautiful voice, and suffered unheard-of pain daily for him, while he knew nothing of it.

This was the last evening that she would breathe the same air with him, or gaze on the starry sky and the deep sea; an eternal night, without a thought or a dream, awaited her: she had no soul and now she could never win one. All was joy and gayety on board ship till long after midnight; she laughed and danced with the rest, while the thoughts of death were in her heart. The prince kissed his beautiful bride, while she played with his raven hair, till they went arm-in-arm to rest in the splendid tent. Then all became still on board the ship; the helmsman, alone awake, stood at the helm. The little mermaid leaned her white arms on the edge of the vessel, and looked towards the east for the first blush of morning, for that first ray of dawn that would bring her death. She saw her sisters rising out of the flood: they were as pale as herself; but their long beautiful hair waved no more in the wind, and had been cut off.

"We have given our hair to the witch," said they, "to obtain help for you, that you may not die tonight. She has given us a knife: here it is, see it is very sharp. Before the sun rises you must plunge it into the heart of the prince; when the warm blood falls upon your feet they will grow together again, and form into a fish's tail, and you will be once more a mermaid, and return to us to live out your three hundred years before you die and change into the salt sea foam. Haste, then; he or you must die before sunrise. Our old grandmother moans so for you, that her white hair is falling off from sorrow, as ours fell under the witch's scissors. Kill the prince and come back; hasten: do you not see the first red streaks in the sky? In a few minutes the sun will rise, and you must die." And then they sighed deeply and mournfully, and sank down beneath the waves.

The little mermaid drew back the crimson curtain of the tent, and beheld the fair bride with her head resting on the prince's breast. She bent down and kissed his fair brow, then looked at the sky on which the rosy dawn grew brighter and brighter; then she glanced at the sharp knife, and again fixed her eyes on the prince, who whispered the name of his bride in his dreams. She was in his thoughts, and the knife trembled in the hand of the little mermaid: then she flung it far away from her into the waves; the water turned red where it fell, and the drops that spurted up looked like blood. She cast one more lingering, half-fainting glance at the prince, and then threw herself from the ship into the sea, and thought her body was dissolving into foam. The sun rose above the waves, and his warm rays fell on the cold foam of the little mermaid, who did not feel as if she were dying. She saw the bright sun, and all around her floated hundreds of transparent beautiful beings; she could see through them the white sails of the ship, and the red clouds in the sky; their speech was melodious, but too ethereal to be heard by mortal ears, as they were also unseen by mortal eyes. The little mermaid perceived that she had a body like theirs, and that she continued to rise higher and higher out of the foam. "Where am I?" asked she, and her voice sounded ethereal, as the voice of those who were with her; no earthly music could imitate it.

"Among the daughters of the air," answered one of them. "A mermaid has not an immortal soul, nor can she obtain one unless she wins the love of a human being. On the power of another hangs her eternal destiny. But the daughters of the air, although they do not possess an immortal soul, can, by their good deeds, procure one for themselves. We fly to warm countries, and cool the sultry air that destroys mankind with the pestilence. We carry the perfume of the flowers to spread health and restoration. After we have striven for three hundred years to all the good in our power, we receive an immortal soul and take part in the happiness of mankind. You, poor little mermaid, have tried with your whole heart to do as we are doing; you have suffered and endured and raised yourself to the spirit-world by your good deeds; and now, by striving for three hundred years in the same way, you may obtain an immortal soul."

The little mermaid lifted her glorified eyes towards the sun, and felt them, for the first time, filling with tears. On the ship, in which she had left the prince, there were life and noise; she saw him and his beautiful bride searching for her; sorrowfully they gazed at the pearly foam, as if they knew she had thrown herself into the waves. Unseen she kissed the forehead of her bride, and fanned the prince, and then mounted with the other children of the air to a rosy cloud that floated through the aether.

"After three hundred years, thus shall we float into the kingdom of heaven," said she. "And we may even get there sooner," whispered one of her companions. "Unseen we can enter the houses of men, where there are children, and for every day on which we find a good child, who is the joy of his parents and deserves their love, our time of probation is shortened. The child does not know, when we fly through the room, that we smile with joy at his good conduct, for we can count one year less of our three hundred years. But when we see a naughty or a wicked child, we shed tears of sorrow, and for every tear a day is added to our time of trial!"

OLIVER TWIST (AN EXCERPT)

Charles Dickens

Published in 1838

"Well! You have come here to be educated, and taught a useful trade," said the red-faced gentleman in the high chair.

"So you'll begin to pick oakum tomorrow morning at six o'clock," added the surly one in the white waistcoat.

For the combination of both these blessings in the one simple process of picking oakum, Oliver bowed low by the direction of the beadle, and was then hurried away to a large ward; where, on a rough, hard bed, he sobbed himself to sleep. What a novel illustration of the tender laws of England! They let the paupers go to sleep!

Poor Oliver! He little thought, as he lay sleeping in happy unconsciousness of all around him, that the board had that very day arrived at a decision which would exercise the most material influence over all his future fortunes. But they had. And this was it:

The members of this board were very sage, deep, philosophical men; and when they came to turn their attention to the workhouse, they found out at once, what ordinary folks would never have discovered—the poor people liked it! It was a regular place of public entertainment for the poorer classes; a tavern where there was nothing to pay; a public breakfast, dinner, tea, and supper all the year round; a brick and mortar elysium, where it was all play and no work. "Oho!" said the board, looking very knowing; "we are the fellows to set this to rights; we'll stop it all, in no time." So, they established the rule, that all poor people should have the alternative (for they would compel nobody, not they), of being starved by a gradual process in the house, or by a quick one out of it. With this view, they contracted with the water-works to lay on an unlimited supply of water; and with a corn-factor to supply periodically small quantities of oatmeal; and issued three meals of thin gruel a day, with an onion twice a week, and half a roll of Sundays. They made a great many other wise and humane regulations, having reference to the ladies, which it is not necessary to repeat; kindly undertook to divorce poor married people, in consequence of the great expense of a suit in Doctors' Commons; and, instead of compelling a man to support his family, as they had theretofore done, took his family away from him, and made him a bachelor! There is no saying how many applicants for relief, under these last two heads, might have started up in all classes of society, if it had not been coupled with the workhouse; but the board were long-headed men, and had provided for this difficulty. The relief was inseparable from the workhouse and the gruel; and that frightened people.

For the first six months after Oliver Twist was removed, the system was in full operation. It was rather expensive at first, in consequence of the increase in the undertaker's bill, and the necessity of taking in the clothes of all the paupers, which fluttered loosely on their wasted, shrunken forms, after a week or two's gruel. But the number of workhouse inmates got thin as well as the paupers; and the board were in ecstasies.

The room in which the boys were fed, was a large stone hall, with a copper at one end: out of which the master, dressed in an apron for the purpose, and assisted by one or two women, ladled the gruel at mealtimes. Of this festive composition each boy had one porringer, and no more—except on occasions of great public rejoicing, when he had two ounces and a quarter of bread besides.

The bowls never wanted washing. The boys polished them with their spoons till they shone again; and when they had performed this operation (which never took very long, the spoons being nearly as large as the bowls), they would sit staring at the copper, with such eager eyes, as if they could have devoured the very bricks of which it was composed; employing themselves, meanwhile, in sucking their fingers most assiduously, with the view of catching up any stray splashes of gruel that might have been cast thereon. Boys have generally excellent appetites. Oliver Twist and his companions suffered the tortures of slow starvation for three months: at last they got so voracious and wild with hunger, that one boy, who was tall for his age, and hadn't been used to that sort of thing (for his father had kept a small cook-shop), hinted darkly to his companions, that unless he had another basin of gruel per diem, he was afraid he might some night happen to eat the boy who slept next him, who happened to be a weakly youth of tender age. He had a wild, hungry eye; and they implicitly believed him. A council was held; lots were cast who should walk up to the master after supper that evening, and ask for more; and it fell to Oliver Twist.

The evening arrived; the boys took their places. The master, in his cook's uniform, stationed himself at the copper; his pauper assistants ranged themselves behind him; the gruel was served out; and a long grace was said over the short commons. The gruel disappeared; the boys whispered each other, and winked at Oliver; while his next neighbours nudged him. Child as he was, he was desperate with hunger, and reckless with misery. He rose from the table; and advancing to the master, basin and spoon in hand, said: somewhat alarmed at his own temerity:

"Please, sir, I want some more."

The master was a fat, healthy man; but he turned very pale. He gazed in stupefied astonishment on the small rebel for some seconds, and then clung for support to the copper. The assistants were paralysed with wonder; the boys with fear.

"What!" said the master at length, in a faint voice.

"Please, sir," replied Oliver, "I want some more."

The master aimed a blow at Oliver's head with the ladle; pinioned him in his arm; and shrieked aloud for the beadle.

The board were sitting in solemn conclave, when Mr. Bumble rushed into the room in great excitement, and addressing the gentleman in the high chair, said,

"Mr. Limbkins, I beg your pardon, sir! Oliver Twist has asked for more!"

There was a general start. Horror was depicted on every countenance.

"For *more*!" said Mr. Limbkins. "Compose yourself, Bumble, and answer me distinctly. Do I understand that he asked for more, after he had eaten the supper allotted by the dietary?"

"He did, sir," replied Bumble.

"That boy will be hung," said the gentleman in the white waistcoat. "I know that boy will be hung."

Nobody controverted the prophetic gentleman's opinion. An animated discussion took place. Oliver was ordered into instant confinement; and a bill was next morning pasted on the outside of the gate, offering a reward of five pounds to anybody who would take Oliver Twist off the hands of the parish. In other words, five pounds and Oliver

Twist were offered to any man or woman who wanted an apprentice to any trade, business, or calling.

"I never was more convinced of anything in my life," said the gentleman in the white waistcoat, as he knocked at the gate and read the bill next morning: "I never was more convinced of anything in my life, than I am that that boy will come to be hung."

As I purpose to show in the sequel whether the white waistcoated gentleman was right or not, I should perhaps mar the interest of this narrative (supposing it to possess any at all), if I ventured to hint just yet, whether the life of Oliver Twist had this violent termination or no.

THE UGLY DUCKLING

Hans Chris Andersen

First published in 1843
Translated from Danish by
H. P. Paull, published in 1888

It was lovely summer weather in the country, and the golden corn, the green oats, and the haystacks piled up in the meadows looked beautiful. The stork walking about on his long red legs chattered in the Egyptian language, which he had learnt from his mother. The corn-fields and meadows were surrounded by large forests, in the midst of which were deep pools. It was, indeed, delightful to walk about in the country. In a sunny spot stood a pleasant old farm-house close by a deep river, and from the house down to the water side grew great burdock leaves, so high, that under the tallest of them a little child could stand upright. The spot was as wild as the centre of a thick wood. In this snug retreat sat a duck on her nest, watching for her young brood to hatch; she was beginning to get tired of her task, for the little ones were a long time coming out of their shells, and she seldom had any visitors. The other Ducks liked much better to swim about in the river than to climb the slippery banks, and sit under a burdock leaf, to have a gossip with her.

At length one shell cracked, and then another, and from each egg came a living creature that lifted its head and cried, "Peep, peep."

"Quack, quack," said the mother, and then they all quacked as well as they could, and looked about them on every side at the large green leaves. Their mother allowed them to look as much as they liked, because green is good for the eyes.

"How large the world is," said the young Ducks, when they found how much more room they now had than while they were inside the egg-shell.

"Do you imagine this is the whole world?" asked the mother; "Wait till you have seen the garden; it stretches far beyond that to the parson's field, but I have never ventured to such a distance. Are you all out?" she continued, rising; "No, I declare, the largest egg lies there still. I wonder how long this is to last, I am quite tired of it;" and she seated herself again on the nest.

"Well, how are you getting on?" asked an old duck, who paid her a visit.

"One egg is not hatched yet," said the Duck, "it will not break. But just look at all the others, are they not the prettiest little ducklings you ever saw? They are the image of their father, who is so unkind, he never comes to see."

"Let me see the egg that will not break," said the Duck; "I have no doubt it is a turkey's egg. I was persuaded to hatch some once, and after all my care and trouble with the young ones, they were afraid of the water. I quacked and clucked, but all to no purpose. I could not get them to venture in. Let me look at the egg. Yes, that is a turkey's egg; take my advice, leave it where it is and teach the other children to swim."

"I think I will sit on it a little while longer," said the Duck; "as I have sat so long already, a few days will be nothing."

"Please yourself," said the old duck, and she went away.

At last the large egg broke, and a young one crept forth crying, "Peep, peep." It was very large and ugly. The Duck stared at it and exclaimed, "It is very large and not at all like the others. I wonder if it really is a turkey. We shall soon find it out, however when we go to the water. It must go in, if I have to push it myself."

On the next day the weather was delightful, and the sun shone brightly on the green burdock leaves, so the Mother Duck took her young brood down to the water, and jumped in with a splash. "Quack, quack," cried she, and one after another the little ducklings jumped in. The water closed over their heads, but they came up again in an instant, and swam about quite prettily with their legs paddling under them as easily as possible, and the ugly Duckling was also in the water swimming with them.

"Oh," said the mother, "that is not a turkey; how well he uses his legs, and how upright he holds himself! He is my own child, and he is not so very ugly after all if you look at him properly. Quack, quack! come with me now, I will take you into grand society, and introduce you to the farmyard, but you must keep close to me or you may be trodden upon; and, above all, beware of the cat."

When they reached the farmyard, there was a great disturbance, two families were fighting for an eel's head, which, after all, was carried off by the cat.

"See, children, that is the way of the world," said the Mother Duck, whetting her beak, for she would have liked the eel's head herself. "Come, now, use your legs, and let me see how well you can behave. You must bow your heads prettily to that old Duck yonder; she is the highest born of them all, and has Spanish blood, therefore, she is well off. Don't you see she has a red flag tied to her leg, which is something very grand, and a great honour for a duck; it shows that every one is anxious not to lose her, as she can be recognized both by man and beast. Come, now, don't turn your toes, a well-bred duckling spreads his feet wide apart, just like his father and mother, in this way; now bend your neck, and say 'Quack.'"

The Ducklings did as they were bid, but the other duck stared, and said, "Look, here comes another brood, as if there were not enough of us already! and what a queer looking object one of them is; we don't want him here," and then one flew out and bit him in the neck.

"Let him alone," said the mother; "he is not doing any harm."

"Yes, but he is so big and ugly," said the spiteful Duck "and therefore he must be turned out."

"The others are very pretty children," said the old Duck, with the rag on her leg, "all but that one; I wish his mother could improve him a little."

"That is impossible, your grace," replied the mother; "he is not pretty; but he has a very good disposition, and swims as well or even better than the others. I think he will grow up pretty, and perhaps be smaller; he has remained too long in the egg, and therefore his figure is not properly formed;" and then she stroked his neck and smoothed the feathers, saying, "It is a drake, and therefore not of so much consequence. I think he will grow up strong, and able to take care of himself."

"The other ducklings are graceful enough," said the old Duck. "Now make yourself at home, and if you can find an eel's head, you can bring it to me."

And so they made themselves comfortable.

But the poor Duckling, who had crept out of his shell last of all, and looked so ugly, was bitten and pushed and made fun of, not only by the ducks, but by all the poultry. "He is too big," they all said, and the turkey cock, who had been born into the world with spurs, and fancied himself really an emperor, puffed himself out like a vessel in full sail, and flew at the Duckling, and became quite red in the head with passion, so that the poor little thing did not know where to go, and was quite miserable because he was so ugly and laughed at by the whole farmyard.

So it went on from day to day till it got worse and worse. The poor Duckling was driven about by every one; even his brothers and sisters were unkind to him, and would say, "Ah, you ugly creature, I wish the cat would get you," and his mother said she wished he had never been born. The Ducks pecked him, the chickens beat him, and the girl who fed the poultry kicked him with her feet.

So at last he ran away, frightening the little birds in the hedge as he flew over the palings. "They are afraid of me because I am ugly," he said. So he closed his eyes, and flew still farther, until he came out on a large moor, inhabited by Wild Ducks. Here he remained the whole night, feeling very tired and sorrowful.

In the morning, when the Wild Ducks rose in the air, they stared at their new comrade. "What sort of a Duck are you?" they all said, coming round him. He bowed to them, and was as polite as he could be, but he did not reply to their question.

"You are exceedingly ugly," said the wild ducks, "but that will not matter if you do not want to marry one of our family." Poor thing! he had no thoughts of marriage; all he wanted was permission to lie among the rushes, and drink some of the water on the moor.

After he had been on the moor two days, there came two wild geese, or rather goslings, for they had not been out of the egg long, and were very saucy.

"Listen, friend," said one of them to the duckling, "you are so ugly, that we like you very well. Will you go with us, and become a bird of passage? Not far from here is another moor, in which there are some pretty wild geese, all unmarried. It is a chance for you to get a wife; you may be lucky, ugly as you are."

"Pop, pop," sounded in the air, and the two wild geese fell dead among the rushes, and the water was tinged with blood. "Pop, pop," echoed far and wide in the distance, and whole flocks of wild geese rose up from the rushes. The sound continued from every direction, for the sportsmen surrounded the moor, and some were even seated on branches of trees, overlooking the rushes. The blue smoke from the guns rose like clouds over the dark trees, and as it floated away across the water, a number of sporting dogs bounded in among the rushes, which bent beneath them wherever they went. How they terrified the poor Duckling! He turned away his head to hide it under his wing, and at the same moment a large terrible dog passed quite near him. His jaws were open, his tongue hung from his mouth, and his eyes glared fearfully. He thrust his nose close to the Duckling, showing his sharp teeth, and then, "splash, splash," he went into the water without touching him.

"Oh," sighed the Duckling, "how thankful I am for being so ugly; even a dog will not bite me."

And so he lay quite still, while the shot rattled through the rushes, and gun after gun was fired over him.

It was late in the day before all became quiet, but even then the poor young thing did not dare to move. He waited quietly for several hours, and then, after looking carefully around him, hastened away from the moor as fast as he could. He ran over field and meadow till a storm arose, and he could hardly struggle against it.

Towards evening, he reached a poor little cottage that seemed ready to fall, and only remained standing because it could not decide on which side to fall first. The storm continued so violent, that the Duckling could go no farther; he sat down by the cottage, and then he noticed that the door was not quite closed in consequence of one of the hinges having given way. There was therefore a narrow opening near the bottom large enough for him to slip through, which he did very quietly, and got a shelter for the night.

A woman, a Tom Cat, and a Hen lived in this cottage. The Tom Cat, whom the mistress called, *"My little son,"* was a great favourite; he could raise his back, and purr, and could even throw out sparks from his fur if it were stroked the wrong way. The Hen had very short legs, so she was called *"Chickie short legs."* She laid good eggs, and her mistress loved her as if she had been her own child.

In the morning, the strange visitor was discovered, and the tom cat began to purr, and the hen to cluck.

"What is that noise about?" said the old woman, looking round the room, but her sight was not very good; therefore, when she saw the Duckling she thought it must be a fat duck, that had strayed from home. "Oh what a prize!" she exclaimed, "I hope it is not a drake, for then I shall have some Duck's eggs. I must wait and see."

So the Duckling was allowed to remain on trial for three weeks, but there were no eggs. Now the Tom Cat was the master of the house, and the hen was mistress, and they always said, "We and the world," for they believed themselves to be half the world, and the better half too. The Duckling thought that others might hold a different opinion on the subject, but the hen would not listen to such doubts.

"Can you lay eggs?" she asked.

"No."

"Then have the goodness to hold your tongue."

"Can you raise your back, or purr, or throw out sparks?" said the Tom Cat.

"No."

"Then you have no right to express an opinion when sensible people are speaking."

So the Duckling sat in a corner, feeling very low spirited, till the sunshine and the fresh air came into the room through the open door, and then he began to feel such a great longing for a swim on the water, that he could not help telling the Hen.

"What an absurd idea," said the Hen. "You have nothing else to do, therefore you have foolish fancies. If you could purr or lay eggs, they would pass away."

"But it is so delightful to swim about on the water," said the Duckling, "and so refreshing to feel it close over your head, while you dive down to the bottom."

"Delightful, indeed!" said the Hen, "why you must be crazy! Ask the Cat, he is the cleverest animal I know, ask him how he would like to swim about on the water, or to dive under it, for I will not speak of my own opinion; ask our mistress, the old woman—there is no one in the world more clever than she is. Do you think she would like to swim, or to let the water close over her head?"

"You don't understand me," said the Duckling.

"We don't understand you? Who can understand you, I wonder? Do you consider yourself more clever than the Cat, or the old woman? I will say nothing of myself. Don't imagine such nonsense, child, and thank your good fortune that you have been received here. Are you not in a warm room, and in society from which you may learn something. But you are a chatterer, and your company is not very agreeable. Believe me, I speak only for your own good. I may tell you unpleasant truths, but that is a proof of my friendship. I advise you, therefore, to lay eggs, and learn to purr as quickly as possible."

"I believe I must go out into the world again," said the Duckling.

"Yes, do," said the hen.

So the Duckling left the cottage, and soon found water on which it could swim and dive, but was avoided by all other animals, because of its ugly appearance.

Autumn came, and the leaves in the forest turned to orange and gold. Then, as winter approached, the wind caught them as they fell and whirled them in the cold air. The clouds, heavy with hail and snowflakes, hung low in the sky, and the raven stood on the ferns crying, "Croak, croak." It made one shiver with cold to look at him. All this was very sad for the poor little Duckling.

One evening, just as the sun set amid radiant clouds, there came a large flock of beautiful birds out of the bushes. The Duckling had never seen any like them before. They were swans, and they curved their graceful necks, while their soft plumage shown with dazzling whiteness. They uttered a singular cry, as they spread their glorious wings and flew away from those cold regions to warmer countries across the sea. As they mounted higher and higher in the air, the ugly little Duckling felt quite a strange sensation as he watched them. He whirled himself in the water like a wheel, stretched out his neck towards them, and uttered a cry so strange that it frightened himself. Could he ever forget those beautiful, happy birds; and when at last they were out of his sight, he dived under the water, and rose again almost beside himself with excitement. He knew not the names of these birds, nor where they had flown, but he felt towards them as he had never felt for any other bird in the world. He was not envious of these beautiful creatures, but wished to be as lovely as they. Poor ugly creature, how gladly he would have lived even with the Ducks had they only given him encouragement.

The winter grew colder and colder; he was obliged to swim about on the water to keep it from freezing, but every night the space on which he swam became smaller and smaller. At length it froze so hard that the ice in the water crackled as he moved, and the Duckling had to paddle with his legs as well as he could, to keep the space from closing up. He became exhausted at last, and lay still and helpless, frozen fast in the ice.

Early in the morning, a peasant, who was passing by, saw what had happened. He broke the ice in pieces with his wooden shoe, and carried the Duckling home to his wife. The warmth revived the poor little creature.

But when the children wanted to play with him, the Duckling thought they would do him some harm; so he started up in terror, fluttered into the milk-pan, and splashed the milk about the room. Then the woman clapped her hands, which frightened him still more. He flew first into the butter-cask, then into the meal-tub, and out again. What a condition he was in! The woman screamed, and struck at him with the tongs; the children laughed and screamed, and tumbled over each other, in their efforts to catch him; but luckily he escaped. The door stood open; the poor creature could just manage to slip out among the bushes, and lie down quite exhausted in the newly fallen snow.

It would be very sad, were I to relate all the misery and privations which the poor little Duckling endured during the hard winter; but when it had passed, he found himself lying one morning in a moor, amongst the rushes. He felt the warm sun shining, and heard the lark singing, and saw that all around was beautiful spring.

Then the young bird felt that his wings were strong, as he flapped them against his sides, and rose high into the air. They bore him onwards, until he found himself in a large garden, before he well knew how it had happened. The apple-trees were in full blossom, and the fragrant elders bent their long green branches down to the stream which wound round a smooth lawn. Everything looked beautiful, in the freshness of early spring. From a thicket close by came three beautiful white swans, rustling their feathers, and swimming lightly over the smooth water. The Duckling remembered the lovely birds, and felt more strangely unhappy than ever.

"I will fly to those royal birds," he exclaimed, "and they will kill me, because I am so ugly, and dare to approach them; but it does not matter: better be killed by *them* than pecked by the ducks, beaten by the hens, pushed about by the maiden who feeds the poultry, or starved with hunger in the winter." Then he flew to the water, and swam towards the beautiful swans. The moment they espied the stranger, they rushed to meet him with outstretched wings. "Kill me," said the poor bird; and he bent his head down to the surface of the water, and awaited death. But what did he see in the clear stream below? His own image; no longer a dark, gray bird, ugly and disagreeable to look at, but a graceful and beautiful swan.

To be born in a Duck's nest, in a farmyard, is of no consequence to a bird, if it is hatched from a swan's egg.

He now felt glad at having suffered sorrow and trouble, because it enabled him to enjoy so much better all the pleasure and happiness around him; for the great swans swam round the new-comer, and stroked his neck with their beaks, as a welcome.

Into the garden presently came some little children, and threw bread and cake into the water.

"See," cried the youngest, "there is a new one;" and the rest were delighted, and ran to their father and mother, dancing and clapping their hands, and shouting joyously, "There is another swan come; a new one has arrived." Then they threw more bread and cake into the water, and said, "The new one is the most beautiful of all; he is so young and pretty." And the old swans bowed their heads before him.

Then he felt quite ashamed, and hid his head under his wing; for he did not know what to do, he was so happy, and yet not at all proud. He had been persecuted and despised for his ugliness, and now he heard them say he was the most beautiful of all the birds. Even the elder-tree bent down its bows into the water before him, and the sun shone warm and bright. Then he rustled his feathers, curved his slender neck, and cried joyfully, from the depths of his heart, "I never dreamed of such happiness as this, while I was an ugly Duckling."

THE SNOW-IMAGE

Nathaniel Hawthorne

Published in *Snow-image, and Other Twice-told Tales* in 1851

One afternoon of a cold winter's day, when the sun shone forth with chilly brightness, after a long storm, two children asked leave of their mother to run out and play in the new-fallen snow. The elder child was a little girl, whom, because she was of a tender and modest disposition, and was thought to be very beautiful, her parents, and other people who were familiar with her, used to call Violet. But her brother was known by the style and title of Peony, on account of the ruddiness of his broad and round little phiz, which made everybody think of sunshine and great scarlet flowers. The father of these two children, a certain Mr. Lindsey, it is important to say, was an excellent but exceedingly matter-of-fact sort of man, a dealer in hardware, and was sturdily accustomed to take what is called the common-sense view of all matters that came under his consideration. With a heart about as tender as other people's, he had a head as hard and impenetrable, and therefore, perhaps, as empty, as one of the iron pots which it was a part of his business to sell. The mother's character, on the other hand, had a strain of poetry in it, a trait of unworldly beauty,—a delicate and dewy flower, as it were, that had survived out of her imaginative youth, and still kept itself alive amid the dusty realities of matrimony and motherhood.

So, Violet and Peony, as I began with saying, besought their mother to let them run out and play in the new snow; for, though it had looked so dreary and dismal, drifting downward out of the gray sky, it had a very cheerful aspect, now that the sun was shining on it. The children dwelt in a city, and had no wider play-place than a little garden before the house, divided by a white fence from the street, and with a pear-tree and two or three plum-trees overshadowing it, and some rose-bushes just in front of the parlour-windows. The trees and shrubs, however, were now leafless, and their twigs were enveloped in the light snow, which thus made a kind of wintry foliage, with here and there a pendent icicle for the fruit.

"Yes, Violet,—yes, my little Peony," said their kind mother, "you may go out and play in the new snow."

Accordingly, the good lady bundled up her darlings in woollen jackets and wadded sacks, and put comforters round their necks, and a pair of striped gaiters on each little pair of legs, and worsted mittens on their hands, and gave them a kiss apiece, by way of a spell to keep away Jack Frost. Forth sallied the two children, with a hop-skip-and-jump, that carried them at once into the very heart of a huge snow-drift, whence Violet emerged like a snow-bunting, while little Peony floundered out with his round face in full bloom. Then what a merry time had they! To look at them, frolicking in the wintry garden, you would have thought that the dark and pitiless storm had been sent for no other purpose but to provide a new plaything for Violet and Peony; and that they themselves had beer created, as the snow-birds were, to take delight only in the tempest, and in the white mantle which it spread over the earth.

At last, when they had frosted one another all over with handfuls of snow, Violet, after laughing heartily at little Peony's figure, was struck with a new idea.

"You look exactly like a snow-image, Peony," said she, "if your cheeks were not so red. And that puts me in mind! Let us make an image out of snow,—an image of a little girl,—and it shall be our sister, and shall run about and play with us all winter long. Won't it be nice?"

"Oh yes!" cried Peony, as plainly as he could speak, for he was but a little boy. "That will be nice! And mamma shall see it!"

"Yes," answered Violet; "mamma shall see the new little girl. But she must not make her come into the warm parlour; for, you know, our little snow-sister will not love the warmth."

And forthwith the children began this great business of making a snow-image that should run about; while their mother, who was sitting at the window and overheard some of their talk, could not help smiling at the gravity with which they set about it. They really seemed to imagine that there would be no difficulty whatever in creating a live little girl out of the snow. And, to say the truth, if miracles are ever to be wrought, it will be by putting our hands to the work in precisely such a simple and undoubting frame of mind as that in which Violet and Peony now undertook to perform one, without so much as knowing that it was a miracle. So thought the mother; and thought, likewise, that the new snow, just fallen from heaven, would be excellent material to make new beings of, if it were not so very cold. She gazed at the children a moment longer, delighting to watch their little figures,—the girl, tall for her age, graceful and agile, and so delicately coloured that she looked like a cheerful thought more than a physical reality; while Peony expanded in breadth rather than height, and rolled along on his short and sturdy legs as substantial as an elephant, though not quite so big. Then the mother resumed her work. What it was I forget; but she was either trimming a silken bonnet for Violet, or darning a pair of stockings for little Peony's short legs. Again, however, and again, and yet other agains, she could not help turning her head to the window to see how the children got on with their snow-image.

Indeed, it was an exceedingly pleasant sight, those bright little souls at their task! Moreover, it was really wonderful to observe how knowingly and skilfully they managed the matter. Violet assumed the chief direction, and told Peony what to do, while, with her own delicate fingers, she shaped out all the nicer parts of the snow-figure. It seemed, in fact, not so much to be made by the children, as to grow up under their hands, while they were playing and prattling about it. Their mother was quite surprised at this; and the longer she looked, the more and more surprised she grew.

"What remarkable children mine are!" thought she, smiling with a mother's pride; and, smiling at herself, too, for being so proud of them. "What other children could have made anything so like a little girl's figure out of snow at the first trial? Well; but now I must finish Peony's new frock, for his grandfather is coming tomorrow, and I want the little fellow to look handsome."

So she took up the frock, and was soon as busily at work again with her needle as the two children with their snow-image. But still, as the needle travelled hither and thither through the seams of the dress, the mother made her toil light and happy by listening to the airy voices of Violet and Peony. They kept talking to one another all the time, their tongues being quite as active as their feet and hands. Except at intervals, she could not distinctly hear what was said, but had merely a sweet impression that they were in a most loving mood, and were enjoying themselves highly, and that the business of making the snow-image went prosperously on. Now and then, however, when Violet and Peony happened to raise their voices, the words were as audible as if they had been spoken in the very parlor where the mother sat. Oh how delightfully those words echoed in her heart, even though they meant nothing so very wise or wonderful, after all!

But you must know a mother listens with her heart much more than with her ears; and thus she is often delighted with the trills of celestial music, when other people can hear nothing of the kind.

"Peony, Peony!" cried Violet to her brother, who had gone to another part of the garden, "bring me some of that fresh snow, Peony, from the very farthest corner, where we have not been trampling. I want it to shape our little snow-sister's bosom with. You know that part must be quite pure, just as it came out of the sky!"

"Here it is, Violet!" answered Peony, in his bluff tone,—but a very sweet tone, too,—as he came floundering through the half-trodden drifts. "Here is the snow for her little bosom. O Violet, how beau-ti-ful she begins to look!"

"Yes," said Violet, thoughtfully and quietly; "our snow-sister does look very lovely. I did not quite know, Peony, that we could make such a sweet little girl as this."

The mother, as she listened, thought how fit and delightful an incident it would be, if fairies, or still better, if angel-children were to come from paradise, and play invisibly with her own darlings, and help them to make their snow-image, giving it the features of celestial babyhood! Violet and Peony would not be aware of their immortal playmates,—only they would see that the image grew very beautiful while they worked at it, and would think that they themselves had done it all.

"My little girl and boy deserve such playmates, if mortal children ever did!" said the mother to herself; and then she smiled again at her own motherly pride.

Nevertheless, the idea seized upon her imagination; and, ever and anon, she took a glimpse out of the window, half dreaming that she might see the golden-haired children of paradise sporting with her own golden-haired Violet and bright-cheeked Peony.

Now, for a few moments, there was a busy and earnest, but indistinct hum of the two children's voices, as Violet and Peony wrought together with one happy consent. Violet still seemed to be the guiding spirit, while Peony acted rather as a labourer, and brought her the snow from far and near. And yet the little urchin evidently had a proper understanding of the matter, too!

"Peony, Peony!" cried Violet; for her brother was again at the other side of the garden. "Bring me those light wreaths of snow that have rested on the lower branches of the pear-tree. You can clamber on the snowdrift, Peony, and reach them easily. I must have them to make some ringlets for our snow-sister's head!"

"Here they are, Violet!" answered the little boy. "Take care you do not break them. Well done! Well done! How pretty!"

"Does she not look sweetly?" said Violet, with a very satisfied tone; "and now we must have some little shining bits of ice, to make the brightness of her eyes. She is not finished yet. Mamma will see how very beautiful she is; but papa will say, 'Tush! nonsense!—come in out of the cold!'"

"Let us call mamma to look out," said Peony; and then he shouted lustily, "Mamma! mamma!! mamma!!! Look out, and see what a nice 'ittle girl we are making!"

The mother put down her work for an instant, and looked out of the window. But it so happened that the sun—for this was one of the shortest days of the whole year—had sunken so nearly to the edge of the world that his setting shine came obliquely into the lady's eyes. So she was dazzled, you must understand, and could not very distinctly observe what was in the garden. Still, however, through all that bright, blinding dazzle of the sun and the new snow, she beheld a small white figure in the garden, that seemed to have a wonderful deal of human likeness about it. And she saw Violet and Peony,—indeed, she looked more at them than at the image,—she saw the two children still at work; Peony bringing fresh snow, and Violet applying it to the figure as scientifically as a sculptor adds clay to his model. Indistinctly as she discerned the snow-child, the mother thought to herself that never before was there a snow-figure so cunningly made, nor ever such a dear little girl and boy to make it.

"They do everything better than other children," said she, very complacently. "No wonder they make better snow-images!"

She sat down again to her work, and made as much haste with it as possible; because twilight would soon come, and Peony's frock was not yet finished, and grandfather was expected, by railroad, pretty early in the morning. Faster and faster, therefore, went her flying fingers. The children, likewise, kept busily at work in the garden, and still the mother listened, whenever she could catch a word. She was amused to observe how their little imaginations had got mixed up with what they were doing, and carried away by it. They seemed positively to think that the snow-child would run about and play with them.

"What a nice playmate she will be for us, all winter long!" said Violet. "I hope papa will not be afraid of her giving us a cold! Shan't you love her dearly, Peony?"

"Oh yes!" cried Peony. "And I will hug her, and she shall sit down close by me and drink some of my warm milk!"

"Oh no, Peony!" answered Violet, with grave wisdom. "That will not do at all. Warm milk will not be wholesome for our little snow-sister. Little snow people, like her, eat nothing but icicles. No, no, Peony; we must not give her anything warm to drink!"

There was a minute or two of silence; for Peony, whose short legs were never weary, had gone on a pilgrimage again to the other side of the garden. All of a sudden, Violet cried out, loudly and joyfully,—"Look here, Peony! Come quickly! A light has been shining on her cheek out of that rose-colored cloud! and the colour does not go away! Is not that beautiful!"

"Yes; it is beau-ti-ful," answered Peony, pronouncing the three syllables with deliberate accuracy. "O Violet, only look at her hair! It is all like gold!"

"Oh certainly," said Violet, with tranquillity, as if it were very much a matter of course. "That color, you know, comes from the golden clouds, that we see up there in the sky. She is almost finished now. But her lips must be made very red,—redder than her cheeks. Perhaps, Peony, it will make them red if we both kiss them!"

Accordingly, the mother heard two smart little smacks, as if both her children were kissing the snow-image on its frozen mouth. But, as this did not seem to make the lips quite red enough, Violet next proposed that the snow-child should be invited to kiss Peony's scarlet cheek.

"Come, 'ittle snow-sister, kiss me!" cried Peony.

"There! she has kissed you," added Violet, "and now her lips are very red. And she blushed a little, too!"

"Oh, what a cold kiss!" cried Peony.

Just then, there came a breeze of the pure west-wind, sweeping through the garden and rattling the parlour-windows. It sounded so wintry cold, that the mother was about to tap on the window-pane with her thimbled finger, to summon the two children in, when they both cried out to her with one voice. The tone was not a tone of surprise, although they were evidently a good deal excited; it appeared rather as if they were very much rejoiced at some event that had now happened, but which they had been looking for, and had reckoned upon all along.

"Mamma! mamma! We have finished our little snow-sister, and she is running about the garden with us!"

"What imaginative little beings my children are!" thought the mother, putting the last few stitches into Peony's frock. "And it is strange, too that they make me almost as much a child as they themselves are! I can hardly help believing, now, that the snow-image has really come to life!"

"Dear mamma!" cried Violet, "pray look out and see what a sweet playmate we have!"

The mother, being thus entreated, could no longer delay to look forth from the window. The sun was now gone out of the sky, leaving, however, a rich inheritance of his brightness among those purple and golden clouds which make the sunsets of winter so magnificent. But there was not the slightest gleam or dazzle, either on the window or on the snow; so that the good lady could look all over the garden, and see everything and everybody in it. And what do you think she saw there? Violet and Peony, of course, her own two darling children. Ah, but whom or what did she see besides? Why, if you will believe me, there was a small figure of a girl, dressed all in white, with rose-tinged cheeks and ringlets of golden hue, playing about the garden with the two children! A stranger though she was, the child seemed to be on as familiar terms with Violet and Peony, and they with her, as if all the three had been playmates during the whole of their little lives. The mother thought to herself that it must certainly be the daughter of one of the neighbours, and that, seeing Violet and Peony in the garden, the child had run across the street to play with them. So this kind lady went to the door, intending to invite the little runaway into her comfortable parlour; for, now that the sunshine was withdrawn, the atmosphere, out of doors, was already growing very cold.

But, after opening the house-door, she stood an instant on the threshold, hesitating whether she ought to ask the child to come in, or whether she should even speak to her. Indeed, she almost doubted whether it were a real child after all, or only a light wreath of the new-fallen snow, blown hither and thither about the garden by the intensely cold west-wind.

There was certainly something very singular in the aspect of the little stranger. Among all the children of the neighbourhood, the lady could remember no such face, with its pure white, and delicate rose-colour, and the golden ringlets tossing about the forehead and cheeks. And as for her dress, which was entirely of white, and fluttering in the breeze, it was such as no reasonable woman would put upon a little girl, when sending her out to play, in the depth of winter. It made this kind and careful mother shiver only to look at those small feet, with nothing in the world on them, except a very thin pair of white slippers. Nevertheless, airily as she was clad, the child seemed to feel not the slightest inconvenience from the cold, but danced so lightly over the snow that the tips of her toes left hardly a print in its surface; while Violet could but just keep pace with her, and Peony's short legs compelled him to lag behind.

Once, in the course of their play, the strange child placed herself between Violet and Peony, and taking a hand of each, skipped merrily forward, and they along with her. Almost immediately, however, Peony pulled away his little fist, and began to rub it as if the fingers were tingling with cold; while Violet also released herself, though with less abruptness, gravely remarking that it was better not to take hold of hands. The white-robed damsel said not a word, but danced about, just as merrily as before. If Violet and Peony did not choose to play with her, she could make just as good a playmate of the brisk and cold west-wind, which kept blowing her all about the garden, and took such liberties with her, that they seemed to have been friends for a long time. All this while, the mother stood on the threshold, wondering how a little girl could look so much like a flying snow-drift, or how a snow-drift could look so very like a little girl.

She called Violet, and whispered to her.

"Violet my darling, what is this child's name?" asked she. "Does she live near us?"

"Why, dearest mamma," answered Violet, laughing to think that her mother did not comprehend so very plain an affair, "this is our little snow-sister whom we have just been making!"

"Yes, dear mamma," cried Peony, running to his mother, and looking up simply into her face. "This is our snow-image! Is it not a nice 'ittle child?"

At this instant a flock of snow-birds came flitting through the air. As was very natural, they avoided Violet and Peony. But—and this looked strange—they flew at once to the white-robed child, fluttered eagerly about her head, alighted on her shoulders, and seemed to claim her as an old acquaintance. She, on her part, was evidently as glad to see these little birds, old Winter's grandchildren, as they were to see her, and welcomed them by holding out both her hands. Hereupon, they each and all tried to alight on her two palms and ten small fingers and thumbs, crowding one another off, with an immense fluttering of their tiny wings. One dear little bird nestled tenderly in her bosom; another put its bill to her lips. They were as joyous, all the while, and seemed as much in their element, as you may have seen them when sporting with a snow-storm.

Violet and Peony stood laughing at this pretty sight; for they enjoyed the merry time which their new playmate was having with these small-winged visitants, almost as much as if they themselves took part in it.

"Violet," said her mother, greatly perplexed, "tell me the truth, without any jest. Who is this little girl?"

"My darling mamma," answered Violet, looking seriously into her mother's face, and apparently surprised that she should need any further explanation, "I have told you truly who she is. It is our little snow-image, which Peony and I have been making. Peony will tell you so, as well as I."

"Yes, mamma," asseverated Peony, with much gravity in his crimson little phiz; "this is 'ittle snow-child. Is not she a nice one? But, mamma, her hand is, oh, so very cold!"

While mamma still hesitated what to think and what to do, the street-gate was thrown open, and the father of Violet and Peony appeared, wrapped in a pilot-cloth sack, with a fur cap drawn down over his ears, and the thickest of gloves upon his hands. Mr. Lindsey was a middle-aged man, with a weary and yet a happy look in his wind-flushed and frost-pinched face, as if he had been busy all the day long, and was glad to get back to his quiet home. His eyes brightened at the sight of his wife and children, although he could not help uttering a word or two of surprise, at finding the whole family in the open air, on so bleak a day, and after sunset too. He soon perceived the little white stranger sporting to and fro in the garden, like a dancing snow-wreath, and the flock of snow-birds fluttering about her head.

"Pray, what little girl may that be?" inquired this very sensible man. "Surely her mother must be crazy to let her go out in such bitter weather as it has been today, with only that flimsy white gown and those thin slippers!"

"My dear husband," said his wife, "I know no more about the little thing than you do. Some neighbour's child, I suppose. Our Violet and Peony," she added, laughing at herself for repeating so absurd a story, "insist that she is nothing but a snow-image, which they have been busy about in the garden, almost all the afternoon."

As she said this, the mother glanced her eyes toward the spot where the children's snow-image had been made. What was her surprise, on perceiving that there was not the slightest trace of so much labour!—no image at all!—no piled up heap of snow!—nothing whatever, save the prints of little footsteps around a vacant space!

"This is very strange!" said she.

"What is strange, dear mother?" asked Violet. "Dear father, do not you see how it is? This is our snow-image, which Peony and I have made, because we wanted another playmate. Did not we, Peony?"

"Yes, papa," said crimson Peony. "This be our 'ittle snow-sister. Is she not beau-ti-ful? But she gave me such a cold kiss!"

"Poh, nonsense, children!" cried their good, honest father, who, as we have already intimated, had an exceedingly common-sensible way of looking at matters. "Do not tell me of making live figures out of snow. Come, wife; this little stranger must not stay out in the bleak air a moment longer. We will bring her into the parlor; and you shall give her a supper of warm bread and milk, and make her as comfortable as you can. Meanwhile, I will inquire among the neighbours; or, if necessary, send the city-crier about the streets, to give notice of a lost child."

So saying, this honest and very kind-hearted man was going toward the little white damsel, with the best intentions in the world. But Violet and Peony, each seizing their father by the hand, earnestly besought him not to make her come in.

"Dear father," cried Violet, putting herself before him, "it is true what I have been telling you! This is our little snow-girl, and she cannot live any longer than while she breathes the cold west-wind. Do not make her come into the hot room!"

"Yes, father," shouted Peony, stamping his little foot, so mightily was he in earnest, "this be nothing but our 'ittle snow-child! She will not love the hot fire!"

"Nonsense, children, nonsense, nonsense!" cried the father, half vexed, half laughing at what he considered their foolish obstinacy. "Run into the house, this moment! It is too late to play any longer, now. I must take care of this little girl immediately, or she will catch her death-a-cold!"

"Husband! dear husband!" said his wife, in a low voice,—for she had been looking narrowly at the snow-child, and was more perplexed than ever,—"there is something very singular in all this. You will think me foolish,—but—but—may it not be that some invisible angel has been attracted by the simplicity and good faith with which our children set about their undertaking? May he not have spent an hour of his immortality in playing with those dear little souls? and so the result is what we call a miracle. No, no! Do not laugh at me; I see what a foolish thought it is!"

"My dear wife," replied the husband, laughing heartily, "you are as much a child as Violet and Peony."

And in one sense so she was, for all through life she had kept her heart full of childlike simplicity and faith, which was as pure and clear as crystal; and, looking at all matters through this transparent medium, she sometimes saw truths so profound that other people laughed at them as nonsense and absurdity.

But now kind Mr. Lindsey had entered the garden, breaking away from his two children, who still sent their shrill voices after him, beseeching him to let the snow-child stay and enjoy herself in the cold west-wind. As he approached, the snow-birds took to flight. The little white damsel, also, fled backward, shaking her head, as if to say, "Pray, do not touch me!" and roguishly, as it appeared, leading him through the deepest of the snow. Once, the good man stumbled, and floundered down upon his face, so that, gathering himself up again, with the snow sticking to his rough pilot-cloth sack, he looked as white and wintry as a snow-image of the largest size. Some of the neighbours, meanwhile, seeing him from their windows, wondered what could possess poor Mr. Lindsey to be running about his garden in pursuit of a snow-drift, which the west-wind was driving hither and thither! At length, after a vast deal of trouble, he chased the little stranger into a corner, where she could not possibly escape him. His wife had been looking on, and, it being nearly twilight, was wonder-struck to observe how the snow-child gleamed and sparkled, and how she seemed to shed a glow all round about her; and when driven into the corner, she positively glistened like a star! It was a frosty kind of brightness, too, like that of an icicle in the moonlight. The wife thought it strange that good Mr. Lindsey should see nothing remarkable in the snow-child's appearance.

"Come, you odd little thing!" cried the honest man, seizing her by the hand, "I have caught you at last, and will make you comfortable in spite of yourself. We will put a nice warm pair of worsted stockings on your frozen little feet, and you shall have a good thick shawl to wrap yourself in. Your poor white nose, I am afraid, is actually frost-bitten. But we will make it all right. Come along in."

And so, with a most benevolent smile on his sagacious visage, all purple as it was with the cold, this very well-meaning gentleman took the snow-child by the hand and led her towards the house. She followed him, droopingly and reluctant; for all the glow and sparkle was gone out of her figure; and whereas just before she had resembled a bright, frosty, star-gemmed evening, with a crimson gleam on the cold horizon, she now looked as dull and languid as a thaw. As kind Mr. Lindsey led her up the steps of the door, Violet and Peony looked into his face,—their eyes full of tears, which froze before they could run down their cheeks,—and again entreated him not to bring their snow-image into the house.

"Not bring her in!" exclaimed the kind-hearted man. "Why, you are crazy, my little Violet!—quite crazy, my small Peony! She is so cold, already, that her hand has almost frozen mine, in spite of my thick gloves. Would you have her freeze to death?"

His wife, as he came up the steps, had been taking another long, earnest, almost awe-stricken gaze at the little white stranger. She hardly knew whether it was a dream or no; but she could not help fancying that she saw the delicate print of Violet's fingers on the child's neck. It looked just as if, while Violet was shaping out the image, she had given it a gentle pat with her hand, and had neglected to smooth the impression quite away.

"After all, husband," said the mother, recurring to her idea that the angels would be as much delighted to play with Violet and Peony as she herself was,—"after all, she does look strangely like a snow-image! I do believe she is made of snow!"

A puff of the west-wind blew against the snow-child, and again she sparkled like a star.

"Snow!" repeated good Mr. Lindsey, drawing the reluctant guest over his hospitable threshold. "No wonder she looks like snow. She is half frozen, poor little thing! But a good fire will put everything to rights!"

Without further talk, and always with the same best intentions, this highly benevolent and common-sensible individual led the little white damsel—drooping, drooping, drooping, more and more out of the frosty air, and into his comfortable parlour. A Heidenberg stove, filled to the brim with intensely burning anthracite, was sending a bright gleam through the isinglass of its iron door, and causing the vase of water on its top to fume and bubble with excitement. A warm, sultry smell was diffused throughout the room. A thermometer on the wall farthest from the stove stood at eighty degrees. The parlour was hung with red curtains, and covered with a red carpet, and looked just as warm as it felt. The difference betwixt the atmosphere here and the cold, wintry twilight out of doors, was like stepping at once from Nova Zembla to the hottest part of India, or from the North Pole into an oven. Oh, this was a fine place for the little white stranger!

The common-sensible man placed the snow-child on the hearth-rug, right in front of the hissing and fuming stove.

"Now she will be comfortable!" cried Mr. Lindsey, rubbing his hands and looking about him, with the pleasantest smile you ever saw. "Make yourself at home, my child."

Sad, sad and drooping, looked the little white maiden, as she stood on the hearth-rug, with the hot blast of the stove striking through her like a pestilence. Once, she threw a glance wistfully toward the windows, and caught a glimpse, through its red curtains, of the snow-covered roofs, and the stars glimmering frostily, and all the delicious intensity of the cold night. The bleak wind rattled the window-panes, as if it were summoning her to come forth. But there stood the snow-child, drooping, before the hot stove!

But the common-sensible man saw nothing amiss.

"Come wife," said he, "let her have a pair of thick stockings and a woollen shawl or blanket directly; and tell Dora to give her some warm supper as soon as the milk boils. You, Violet and Peony, amuse your little friend. She is out of spirits, you see, at finding herself in a strange place. For my part, I will go around among the neighbours, and find out where she belongs."

The mother, meanwhile, had gone in search of the shawl and stockings; for her own view of the matter, however subtle and delicate, had given way, as it always did, to the stubborn materialism of her husband.

Without heeding the remonstrances of his two children, who still kept murmuring that their little snow-sister did not love the warmth, good Mr. Lindsey took his departure, shutting the parlour-door carefully behind him. Turning up the collar of his sack over his ears, he emerged from the house, and had barely reached the street-gate, when he was recalled by the screams of Violet and Peony, and the rapping of a thimbled finger against the parlour window.

"Husband! husband!" cried his wife, showing her horror-stricken face through the window-panes. "There is no need of going for the child's parents!"

"We told you so, father!" screamed Violet and Peony, as he re-entered the parlour. "You would bring her in; and now our poor-dear-beau-ti-ful little snow-sister is thawed!

And their own sweet little faces were already dissolved in tears; so that their father, seeing what strange things occasionally happen in this every-day world, felt not a little anxious lest his children might be going to thaw too! In the utmost perplexity, he demanded an explanation of his wife. She could only reply, that, being summoned to the parlour by the cries of Violet and Peony, she found no trace of the little white maiden, unless it were the remains of a heap of snow, which, while she was gazing at it, melted quite away upon the hearth-rug.

"And there you see all that is left of it!" added she, pointing to a pool of water in front of the stove.

"Yes, father," said Violet looking reproachfully at him, through her tears, "there is all that is left of our dear little snow-sister!"

"Naughty father!" cried Peony, stamping his foot, and—I shudder to say—shaking his little fist at the common-sensible man. "We told you how it would be! What for did you bring her in?"

And the Heidenberg stove, through the isinglass of its door, seemed to glare at good Mr. Lindsey, like a red-eyed demon, triumphing in the mischief which it had done!

This, you will observe, was one of those rare cases, which yet will occasionally happen, where common-sense finds itself at fault. The remarkable story of the snow-image, though to that sagacious class of people to whom good Mr. Lindsey belongs it may seem but a childish affair, is, nevertheless, capable of being moralized in various methods, greatly for their edification. One of its lessons, for instance, might be, that it behooves men, and especially men of benevolence, to consider well what they are about, and, before acting on their philanthropic purposes, to be quite sure that they comprehend the nature and all the relations of the business in hand. What has been established as an element of good to one being may prove absolute mischief to another; even as the warmth of the parlour was proper enough for children of flesh and blood, like Violet and Peony,—though by no means very wholesome, even for them,—but involved nothing short of annihilation to the unfortunate snow-image.

But, after all, there is no teaching anything to wise men of good Mr. Lindsey's stamp. They know everything,—oh, to be sure!—everything that has been, and everything that is, and everything that, by any future possibility, can be. And, should some phenomenon of nature or providence transcend their system, they will not recognize it, even if it come to pass under their very noses.

"Wife," said Mr. Lindsey, after a fit of silence, "see what a quantity of snow the children have brought in on their feet! It has made quite a puddle here before the stove. Pray tell Dora to bring some towels and mop it up!"

THE LADY OR THE TIGER

Frank R. Stockton

Published in *The Century* in 1882

In the very olden time, there lived a semi-barbaric king, whose ideas, though somewhat polished and sharpened by the progressiveness of distant Latin neighbours, were still large, florid, and untrammelled, as became the half of him which was barbaric. He was a man of exuberant fancy, and, withal, of an authority so irresistible that, at his will, he turned his varied fancies into facts. He was greatly given to self-communing; and, when he and himself agreed upon any thing, the thing was done. When every member of his domestic and political systems moved smoothly in its appointed course, his nature was bland and genial; but whenever there was a little hitch, and some of his orbs got out of their orbits, he was blander and more genial still, for nothing pleased him so much as to make the crooked straight, and crush down uneven places.

Among the borrowed notions by which his barbarism had become semified was that of the public arena, in which, by exhibitions of manly and beastly valour, the minds of his subjects were refined and cultured.

But even here the exuberant and barbaric fancy asserted itself. The arena of the king was built, not to give the people an opportunity of hearing the rhapsodies of dying gladiators, nor to enable them to view the inevitable conclusion of a conflict between religious opinions and hungry jaws, but for purposes far better adapted to widen and develop the mental energies of the people. This vast amphitheatre, with its encircling galleries, its mysterious vaults, and its unseen passages, was an agent of poetic justice, in which crime was punished, or virtue rewarded, by the decrees of an impartial and incorruptible chance.

When a subject was accused of a crime of sufficient importance to interest the king, public notice was given that on an appointed day the fate of the accused person would be decided in the king's arena,—a structure which well deserved its name; for, although its form and plan were borrowed from afar, its purpose emanated solely from the brain of this man, who, every barleycorn a king, knew no tradition to which he owed more allegiance than pleased his fancy, and who ingrafted on every adopted form of human thought and action the rich growth of his barbaric idealism.

When all the people had assembled in the galleries, and the king, surrounded by his court, sat high up on his throne of royal state on one side of the arena, he gave a signal, a door beneath him opened, and the accused subject stepped out into the amphitheatre. Directly opposite him, on the other side of the enclosed space, were two doors, exactly alike and side by side. It was the duty and the privilege of the person on trial, to walk directly to these doors and open one of them. He could open either door he pleased: he was subject to no guidance or influence but that of the aforementioned impartial and incorruptible chance. If he opened the one, there came out of it a hungry tiger, the fiercest and most cruel that could be procured, which immediately sprang upon him, and tore him to pieces, as a punishment for his guilt. The moment that the case of the criminal was thus decided, doleful iron bells were clanged, great wails went up from the hired mourners posted on the outer rim of the arena, and the vast audience, with bowed heads and downcast hearts, wended slowly their homeward way, mourning greatly that one so young and fair, or so old and respected, should have merited so dire a fate.

But, if the accused person opened the other door, there came forth from it a lady, the most suitable to his years and station that his majesty could select among his fair subjects; and to this lady he was immediately married, as a reward of his innocence. It mattered not that he might already possess a wife and family, or that his affections might be engaged upon an object of his own selection: the king allowed no such subordinate arrangements to interfere with his great scheme of retribution and reward. The exercises, as in the other instance, took place immediately, and in the arena. Another door opened beneath the king, and a priest, followed by a band of choristers, and dancing maidens blowing joyous airs on golden horns and treading an epithalamic measure, advanced to where the pair stood, side by side; and the wedding was promptly and cheerily solemnized. Then the gay brass bells rang forth their merry peals, the people shouted glad hurrahs, and the innocent man, preceded by children strewing flowers on his path, led his bride to his home.

This was the king's semi-barbaric method of administering justice. Its perfect fairness is obvious. The criminal could not know out of which door would come the lady: he opened either he pleased, without having the slightest idea whether, in the next instant, he was to be devoured or married. On some occasions the tiger came out of one door, and on some out of the other. The decisions of this tribunal were not only fair, they were positively determinate: the accused person was instantly punished if he found himself guilty; and, if innocent, he was rewarded on the spot, whether he liked it or not. There was no escape from the judgments of the king's arena.

The institution was a very popular one. When the people gathered together on one of the great trial days, they never knew whether they were to witness a bloody slaughter or a hilarious wedding. This element of uncertainty lent an interest to the occasion which it could not otherwise have attained. Thus, the masses were entertained and pleased, and the thinking part of the community could bring no charge of unfairness against this plan; for did not the accused person have the whole matter in his own hands?

This semi-barbaric king had a daughter as blooming as his most florid fancies, and with a soul as fervent and imperious as his own. As is usual in such cases, she was the apple of his eye, and was loved by him above all humanity. Among his courtiers was a young man of that fineness of blood and lowness of station common to the conventional heroes of romance who love royal maidens. This royal maiden was well satisfied with her lover, for he was handsome and brave to a degree unsurpassed in all this kingdom; and she loved him with an ardor that had enough of barbarism in it to make it exceedingly warm and strong. This love affair moved on happily for many months, until one day the king happened to discover its existence. He did not hesitate nor waver in regard to his duty in the premises. The youth was immediately cast into prison, and a day was appointed for his trial in the king's arena. This, of course, was an especially important occasion; and his majesty, as well as all the people, was greatly interested in the workings and development of this trial. Never before had such a case occurred; never before had a subject dared to love the daughter of a king. In after-years such things became commonplace enough; but then they were, in no slight degree, novel and startling.

The tiger-cages of the kingdom were searched for the most savage and relentless beasts, from which the fiercest monster might be selected for the arena; and the ranks of maiden youth and beauty throughout the land were carefully surveyed by competent judges, in order that the young man might have a fitting bride in case fate did not determine for him a different destiny. Of course, everybody knew that the deed with which the accused was charged had been done. He had loved the princess, and neither he, she, nor any one else thought of denying the fact; but the king would not think of allowing any fact of this kind to interfere with the workings of the tribunal, in which he took such great delight and satisfaction. No matter how the affair turned out, the youth would be disposed of; and the king would take an æsthetic pleasure in watching the course of events, which would determine whether or not the young man had done wrong in allowing himself to love the princess.

The appointed day arrived. From far and near the people gathered, and thronged the great galleries of the arena; and crowds, unable to gain admittance, massed themselves against its outside walls. The king and his court were in their places, opposite the twin doors,—those fateful portals, so terrible in their similarity.

All was ready. The signal was given. A door beneath the royal party opened, and the lover of the princess walked into the arena. Tall, beautiful, fair, his appearance was greeted with a low hum of admiration and anxiety. Half the audience had not known so grand a youth had lived among them. No wonder the princess loved him! What a terrible thing for him to be there!

As the youth advanced into the arena, he turned, as the custom was, to bow to the king: but he did not think at all of that royal personage; his eyes were fixed upon the princess, who sat to the right of her father. Had it not been for the moiety of barbarism in her nature, it is probable that lady would not have been there; but her intense and fervid soul would not allow her to be absent on an occasion in which she was so terribly interested. From the moment that the decree had gone forth, that her lover should decide his fate in the king's arena, she had thought of nothing, night or day, but this great event and the various subjects connected with it. Possessed of more power, influence, and force of character than any one who had ever before been interested in such a case, she had done what no other person had done,—she had possessed herself of the secret of the doors. She knew in which of the two rooms, that lay behind those doors, stood the cage of the tiger, with its open front, and in which waited the lady. Through these thick doors, heavily curtained with skins on the inside, it was impossible that any noise or suggestion should come from within to the person who should approach to raise the latch of one of them; but gold, and the power of a woman's will, had brought the secret to the princess.

And not only did she know in which room stood the lady ready to emerge, all blushing and radiant, should her door be opened, but she knew who the lady was. It was one of the fairest and loveliest of the damsels of the court who had been selected as the reward of the accused youth, should he be proved innocent of the crime of aspiring to one so far above him; and the princess hated her. Often had she seen, or imagined that she had seen, this fair creature throwing glances of admiration upon the person of her lover, and sometimes she thought these glances were perceived and even returned. Now and then she had seen them talking together; it was but for a moment or two, but much can be said in a brief space; it may have been on most unimportant topics, but how could she know that? The girl was lovely, but she had dared to raise her eyes to the loved one of the princess; and, with all the intensity of the savage blood transmitted to her through long lines of wholly barbaric ancestors, she hated the woman who blushed and trembled behind that silent door.

When her lover turned and looked at her, and his eye met hers as she sat there paler and whiter than any one in the vast ocean of anxious faces about her, he saw, by that power of quick perception which is given to those whose souls are one, that she knew behind which door crouched the tiger, and behind which stood the lady. He had expected her to know it. He understood her nature, and his soul was assured that she would never rest until she had made plain to herself this thing, hidden to all other lookers-on, even to the king. The only hope for the youth in which there was any element of certainty was based upon the success of the princess in discovering this mystery; and the moment he looked upon her, he saw she had succeeded, as in his soul he knew she would succeed.

Then it was that his quick and anxious glance asked the question: "Which?" It was as plain to her as if he shouted it from where he stood. There was not an instant to be lost. The question was asked in a flash; it must be answered in another.

Her right arm lay on the cushioned parapet before her. She raised her hand, and made a slight, quick movement toward the right. No one but her lover saw her. Every eye but his was fixed on the man in the arena.

He turned, and with a firm and rapid step he walked across the empty space. Every heart stopped beating, every breath was held, every eye was fixed immovably upon that man. Without the slightest hesitation, he went to the door on the right, and opened it.

Now, the point of the story is this: Did the tiger come out of that door, or did the lady?

The more we reflect upon this question, the harder it is to answer. It involves a study of the human heart which leads us through devious mazes of passion, out of which it is difficult to find our way. Think of it, fair reader, not as if the decision of the question depended upon yourself, but upon that hot-blooded, semi-barbaric princess, her soul at a white heat beneath the combined fires of despair and jealousy. She had lost him, but who should have him?

How often, in her waking hours and in her dreams, had she started in wild horror, and covered her face with her hands as she thought of her lover opening the door on the other side of which waited the cruel fangs of the tiger!

But how much oftener had she seen him at the other door! How in her grievous reveries had she gnashed her teeth, and torn her hair, when she saw his start of rapturous delight as he opened the door of the lady! How her soul had burned in agony when she had seen him rush to meet that woman, with her flushing cheek and sparkling eye of triumph; when she had seen him lead her forth, his whole frame kindled with the joy of recovered life; when she had heard the glad shouts from the multitude, and the wild ringing of the happy bells; when she had seen the priest, with his joyous followers, advance to the couple, and make them man and wife before her very eyes; and when she had seen them walk away together upon their path of flowers, followed by the tremendous shouts of the hilarious multitude, in which her one despairing shriek was lost and drowned!

Would it not be better for him to die at once, and go to wait for her in the blessed regions of semi-barbaric futurity?

And yet, that awful tiger, those shrieks, that blood!

Her decision had been indicated in an instant, but it had been made after days and nights of anguished deliberation. She had known she would be asked, she had decided what she would answer, and, without the slightest hesitation, she had moved her hand to the right.

The question of her decision is one not to be lightly considered, and it is not for me to presume to set myself up as the one person able to answer it. And so I leave it with all of you: Which came out of the opened door,—the lady, or the tiger?

THE NECKLACE

Guy De Maupassant

First published in *Le Gaulois* in 1884
Translated from French by
Jonathan Sturges, published in 1889

She was one of those pretty and charming girls who are sometimes, as if by a mistake of destiny, born in a family of clerks. She had no dowry, no expectations, no means of being known, understood, loved, wedded, by any rich and distinguished man; and she let herself be married to a little clerk at the Ministry of Public Instruction.

She dressed plainly because she could not dress well, but she was as unhappy as though she had really fallen from her proper station; since with women there is neither caste nor rank; and beauty, grace, and charm act instead of family and birth. Natural fineness, instinct for what is elegant, suppleness of wit, are the sole hierarchy, and make from women of the people the equals of the very greatest ladies.

She suffered ceaselessly, feeling herself born for all the delicacies and all the luxuries. She suffered from the poverty of her dwelling, from the wretched look of the walls, from the worn-out chairs, from the ugliness of the curtains. All those things, of which another woman of her rank would never even have been conscious, tortured her and made her angry. The sight of the little Breton peasant who did her humble housework aroused in her regrets which were despairing, and distracted dreams. She thought of the silent ante-chambers hung with Oriental tapestry, lit by tall bronze candelabra, and of the two great footmen in knee-breeches who sleep in the big arm-chairs, made drowsy by the heavy warmth of the hot-air stove. She thought of the long *salons* fitted up with ancient silk, of the delicate furniture carrying priceless curiosities, and of the coquettish perfumed boudoirs made for talks at five o'clock with intimate friends, with men famous and sought after, whom all women envy and whose attention they all desire.

When she sat down to dinner, before the round table covered with a table-cloth three days old, opposite her husband, who uncovered the soup-tureen and declared with an enchanted air, "Ah, the good *pot-au-feu!* I don't know anything better than that," she thought of dainty dinners, of shining silverware, of tapestry which peopled the walls with ancient personages and with strange birds flying in the midst of a fairy forest; and she thought of delicious dishes served on marvellous plates, and of the whispered gallantries which you listen to with a sphinx-like smile, while you are eating the pink flesh of a trout or the wings of a quail.

She had no dresses, no jewels, nothing. And she loved nothing but that; she felt made for that. She would so have liked to please, to be envied, to be charming, to be sought after.

She had a friend, a former schoolmate at the convent, who was rich, and whom she did not like to go and see any more, because she suffered so much when she came back.

But, one evening, her husband returned home with a triumphant air, and holding a large envelope in his hand.

"There," said he, "here is something for you."

She tore the paper sharply, and drew out a printed card which bore these words:

"The Minister of Public Instruction and Mme. Georges Ramponneau request the honour of M. and Mme. Loisel's company at the palace of the Ministry on Monday evening, January 18th."

Instead of being delighted, as her husband hoped, she threw the invitation on the table with disdain, murmuring:

"What do you want me to do with that?"

"But, my dear, I thought you would be glad. You never go out, and this is such a fine opportunity. I had awful trouble to get it. Every one wants to go; it is very select, and they are not giving many invitations to clerks. The whole official world will be there."

She looked at him with an irritated eye, and she said, impatiently:

"And what do you want me to put on my back?"

He had not thought of that; he stammered:

"Why, the dress you go to the theatre in. It looks very well, to me."

He stopped, distracted, seeing that his wife was crying. Two great tears descended slowly from the corners of her eyes towards the corners of her mouth. He stuttered:

"What's the matter? What's the matter?"

But, by a violent effort, she had conquered her grief, and she replied, with a calm voice, while she wiped her wet cheeks:

"Nothing. Only I have no dress, and therefore I can't go to this ball. Give your card to some colleague whose wife is better equipped than I."

He was in despair. He resumed:

"Come, let us see, Mathilde. How much would it cost, a suitable dress, which you could use on other occasions, something very simple?"

She reflected several seconds, making her calculations and wondering also what sum she could ask without drawing on herself an immediate refusal and a frightened exclamation from the economical clerk.

Finally, she replied, hesitatingly:

"I don't know exactly, but I think I could manage it with four hundred francs."

He had grown a little pale, because he was laying aside just that amount to buy a gun and treat himself to a little shooting next summer on the plain of Nanterre, with several friends who went to shoot larks down there, of a Sunday.

But he said:

"All right. I will give you four hundred francs. And try to have a pretty dress."

The day of the ball drew near, and Mme. Loisel seemed sad, uneasy, anxious. Her dress was ready, however. Her husband said to her one evening:

"What is the matter? Come, you've been so queer these last three days."

And she answered:

"It annoys me not to have a single jewel, not a single stone, nothing to put on. I shall look like distress. I should almost rather not go at all."

He resumed:

"You might wear natural flowers. It's very stylish at this time of the year. For ten francs you can get two or three magnificent roses."

She was not convinced.

"No; there's nothing more humiliating than to look poor among other women who are rich."

But her husband cried:

"How stupid you are! Go look up your friend Mme. Forestier, and ask her to lend you some jewels. You're quite thick enough with her to do that."

She uttered a cry of joy:

"It's true. I never thought of it."

The next day she went to her friend and told of her distress.

Mme. Forestier went to a wardrobe with a glass door, took out a large jewel-box, brought it back, opened it, and said to Mme. Loisel:

"Choose, my dear."

She saw first of all some bracelets, then a pearl necklace, then a Venetian cross, gold, and precious stones of admirable workmanship. She tried on the ornaments before the glass, hesitated, could not make up her mind to part with them, to give them back. She kept asking:

"Haven't you any more?"

"Why, yes. Look. I don't know what you like."

All of a sudden she discovered, in a black satin box, a superb necklace of diamonds; and her heart began to beat with an immoderate desire. Her hands trembled as she took it. She fastened it around her throat, outside her high-necked dress, and remained lost in ecstasy at the sight of herself.

Then she asked, hesitating, filled with anguish:

"Can you lend me that, only that?"

"Why, yes, certainly."

She sprang upon the neck of her friend, kissed her passionately, then fled with her treasure.

The day of the ball arrived. Mme. Loisel made a great success. She was prettier than them all, elegant, gracious, smiling, and crazy with joy. All the men looked at her, asked her name, endeavoured to be introduced. All the attaches of the Cabinet wanted to waltz with her. She was remarked by the minister himself.

She danced with intoxication, with passion, made drunk by pleasure, forgetting all, in the triumph of her beauty, in the glory of her success, in a sort of cloud of happiness composed of all this homage, of all this admiration, of all these awakened desires, and of that sense of complete victory which is so sweet to woman's heart.

She went away about four o'clock in the morning. Her husband had been sleeping since mid-night, in a little deserted ante-room, with three other gentlemen whose wives were having a very good time.

He threw over her shoulders the wraps which he had brought, modest wraps of common life, whose poverty contrasted with the elegance of the ball dress. She felt this and wanted to escape so as not to be remarked by the other women, who were enveloping themselves in costly furs.

Loisel held her back.

"Wait a bit. You will catch cold outside. I will go and call a cab."

But she did not listen to him, and rapidly descended the stairs. When they were in the street they did not find a carriage; and they began to look for one, shouting after the cabmen whom they saw passing by at a distance.

They went down towards the Seine; in despair, shivering with cold. At last they found on the quay one of those ancient noctambulant coupés which, exactly as if they were ashamed to show their misery during the day, are never seen round Paris until after nightfall.

It took them to their door in the Rue des Martyrs, and once more, sadly, they climbed up homeward. All was ended, for her. And as to him, he reflected that he must be at the Ministry at ten o'clock.

She removed the wraps, which covered her shoulders, before the glass, so as once more to see herself in all her glory. But suddenly she uttered a cry. She had no longer the necklace around her neck!

Her husband, already half-undressed, demanded:

"What is the matter with you?"

She turned madly towards him:

"I have—I have—I've lost Mme. Forestier's necklace."

He stood up, distracted.

"What!—how?—Impossible!"

And they looked in the folds of her dress, in the folds of her cloak, in her pockets, everywhere. They did not find it.

He asked:

"You 're sure you had it on when you left the ball?"

"Yes, I felt it in the vestibule of the palace."

"But if you had lost it in the street we should have heard it fall. It must be in the cab."

"Yes. Probably. Did you take his number?"

"No. And you, didn't you notice it?"

"No."

They looked, thunderstruck, at one another. At last Loisel put on his clothes.

"I shall go back on foot," said he, "over the whole route which we have taken, to see if I can't find it."

And he went out. She sat waiting on a chair in her ball dress, without strength to go to bed, overwhelmed, without fire, without a thought.

Her husband came back about seven o'clock. He had found nothing.

He went to Police Headquarters, to the newspaper offices, to offer a reward; he went to the cab companies—everywhere, in fact, whither he was urged by the least suspicion of hope.

She waited all day, in the same condition of mad fear before this terrible calamity.

Loisel returned at night with a hollow, pale face; he had discovered nothing.

"You must write to your friend," said he, "that you have broken the clasp of her necklace and that you are having it mended. That will give us time to turn round."

She wrote at his dictation.

At the end of a week they had lost all hope.

And Loisel, who had aged five years, declared:

"We must consider how to replace that ornament."

The next day they took the box which had contained it, and they went to the jeweller whose name was found within. He consulted his books.

"It was not I, madame, who sold that necklace; I must simply have furnished the case."

Then they went from jeweller to jeweller, searching for a necklace like the other, consulting their memories, sick both of them with chagrin and with anguish.

They found, in a shop at the Palais Royal, a string of diamonds which seemed to them exactly like the one they looked for. It was worth forty thousand francs. They could have it for thirty-six.

So they begged the jeweller not to sell it for three days yet. And they made a bargain that he should buy it back for thirty-four thousand francs, in case they found the other one before the end of February.

Loisel possessed eighteen thousand francs which his father had left him. He would borrow the rest.

He did borrow, asking a thousand francs of one, five hundred of another, five louis here, three louis there. He gave notes, took up ruinous obligations, dealt with usurers, and all the race of lenders. He compromised all the rest of his life, risked his signature without even knowing if he could meet it; and, frightened by the pains yet to come, by the black misery which was about to fall upon him, by the prospect of all the physical privations and of all the moral tortures which he was to suffer, he went to get the new necklace, putting down upon the merchant's counter thirty-six thousand francs.

When Mme. Loisel took back the necklace Mme. Forestier said to her, with a chilly manner:

"You should have returned it sooner, I might have needed it."

She did not open the case, as her friend had so much feared. If she had detected the substitution, what would she have thought, what would she have said? Would she not have taken Mme. Loisel for a thief?

Mme. Loisel now knew the horrible existence of the needy. She took her part, moreover, all on a sudden, with heroism. That dreadful debt must be paid. She would pay it. They dismissed their servant; they changed their lodgings; they rented a garret under the roof.

She came to know what heavy house-work meant and the odious cares of the kitchen. She washed the dishes, using her rosy nails on the greasy pots and pans. She washed the dirty linen, the shirts, and the dish-cloths, which she dried upon a line; she carried the slops down to the street every morning, and carried up the water, stopping for breath at every landing. And, dressed like a woman of the people, she went to the fruiterer, the grocer, the butcher, her basket on her arm, bargaining, insulted, defending her miserable money sou by sou.

Each month they had to meet some notes, renew others, obtain more time.

Her husband worked in the evening making a fair copy of some tradesman's accounts, and late at night he often copied manuscript for five sous a page.

And this life lasted ten years.

At the end or ten years they had paid everything, everything, with the rates of usury, and the accumulations of the compound interest.

Mme. Loisel looked old now. She had become the woman of impoverished households—strong and hard and rough. With frowsy hair, skirts askew, and red hands, she talked loud while washing the floor with great swishes of water. But sometimes, when her husband was at the office, she sat down near the window, and she thought of that gay evening of long ago, of that ball where she had been so beautiful and so feted.

What would have happened if she had not lost that necklace? Who knows? who knows? How life is strange and changeful! How little a thing is needed for us to be lost or to be saved!

But, one Sunday, having gone to take a walk in the Champs Elysées to refresh herself from the labours of the week, she suddenly perceived a woman who was leading a child. It was Mme. Forestier, still young, still beautiful, still charming.

Mme. Loisel felt moved. Was she going to speak to her? Yes, certainly. And now that she had paid, she was going to tell her all about it. Why not?

She went up.

"Good-day, Jeanne."

The other, astonished to be familiarly addressed by this plain goodwife, did not recognize her at all, and stammered:

"But—madame!—I do not know—You must have mistaken."

"No. I am Mathilde Loisel."

Her friend uttered a cry.

"Oh, my poor Mathilde! How you are changed!"

"Yes, I have had days hard enough, since I have seen you, days wretched enough—and that because of you!"

"Of me! How so?"

"Do you remember that diamond necklace which you lent me to wear at the ministerial ball?"

"Yes. Well?"

"Well, I lost it."

"What do you mean? You brought it back."

"I brought you back another just like it. And for this we have been ten years paying. You can understand that it was not easy for us, us who had nothing. At last it is ended, and I am very glad."

Mme. Forestier had stopped.

"You say that you bought a necklace of diamonds to replace mine?"

"Yes. You never noticed it, then! They were very like."

And she smiled with a joy which was proud and naive at once.

Mme. Forestier, strongly moved, took her two hands.

"Oh, my poor Mathilde! Why, my necklace was paste. It was worth at most five hundred francs!"

THE HAPPY PRINCE

Oscar Wilde

Published in *The Happy Prince and Other Tales* in 1888

High above the city, on a tall column, stood the statue of the Happy Prince. He was gilded all over with thin leaves of fine gold, for eyes he had two bright sapphires, and a large red ruby glowed on his sword-hilt.

He was very much admired indeed. "He is as beautiful as a weathercock," remarked one of the Town Councillors who wished to gain a reputation for having artistic tastes; "only not quite so useful," he added, fearing lest people should think him unpractical, which he really was not.

"Why can't you be like the Happy Prince?" asked a sensible mother of her little boy who was crying for the moon. "The Happy Prince never dreams of crying for anything."

"I am glad there is someone in the world who is quite happy," muttered a disappointed man as he gazed at the wonderful statue.

"He looks just like an angel," said the Charity Children as they came out of the cathedral in their bright scarlet cloaks and their clean white pinafores.

"How do you know?" said the Mathematical Master, "you have never seen one."

"Ah! but we have, in our dreams," answered the children; and the Mathematical Master frowned and looked very severe, for he did not approve of children dreaming.

One night there flew over the city a little Swallow. His friends had gone away to Egypt six weeks before, but he had stayed behind, for he was in love with the most beautiful Reed. He had met her early in the spring as he was flying down the river after a big yellow moth, and had been so attracted by her slender waist that he had stopped to talk to her.

"Shall I love you?" said the Swallow, who liked to come to the point at once, and the Reed made him a low bow. So he flew round and round her, touching the water with his wings, and making silver ripples. This was his courtship, and it lasted all through the summer.

"It is a ridiculous attachment," twittered the other Swallows; "she has no money, and far too many relations"; and indeed the river was quite full of Reeds. Then, when the autumn came they all flew away.

After they had gone he felt lonely, and began to tire of his lady-love. "She has no conversation," he said, "and I am afraid that she is a coquette, for she is always flirting with the wind." And certainly, whenever the wind blew, the Reed made the most graceful curtseys. "I admit that she is domestic," he continued, "but I love travelling, and my wife, consequently, should love travelling also."

"Will you come away with me?" he said finally to her; but the Reed shook her head, she was so attached to her home.

"You have been trifling with me," he cried. "I am off to the Pyramids. Goodbye!" and he flew away.

All day long he flew, and at night-time he arrived at the city. "Where shall I put up?" he said; "I hope the town has made preparations."

Then he saw the statue on the tall column.

"I will put up there," he cried; "it is a fine position, with plenty of fresh air." So he alighted just between the feet of the Happy Prince.

"I have a golden bedroom," he said softly to himself as he looked round, and he prepared to go to sleep; but just as he was putting his head under his wing a large drop of water fell on him. "What a curious thing!" he cried; "there is not a single cloud in the sky, the stars are quite clear and bright, and yet it is raining. The climate in the north of Europe is really dreadful. The Reed used to like the rain, but that was merely her selfishness."

Then another drop fell.

"What is the use of a statue if it cannot keep the rain off?" he said; "I must look for a good chimney-pot," and he determined to fly away.

But before he had opened his wings, a third drop fell, and he looked up, and saw—Ah! what did he see?

The eyes of the Happy Prince were filled with tears, and tears were running down his golden cheeks. His face was so beautiful in the moonlight that the little Swallow was filled with pity.

"Who are you?" he said.

"I am the Happy Prince."

"Why are you weeping then?" asked the Swallow; "you have quite drenched me."

"When I was alive and had a human heart," answered the statue, "I did not know what tears were, for I lived in the Palace of Sans-Souci, where sorrow is not allowed to enter. In the daytime I played with my companions in the garden, and in the evening I led the dance in the Great Hall. Round the garden ran a very lofty wall, but I never cared to ask what lay beyond it, everything about me was so beautiful. My courtiers called me the Happy Prince, and happy indeed I was, if pleasure be happiness. So I lived, and so I died. And now that I am dead they have set me up here so high that I can see all the ugliness and all the misery of my city, and though my heart is made of lead yet I cannot chose but weep."

"What! is he not solid gold?" said the Swallow to himself. He was too polite to make any personal remarks out loud.

"Far away," continued the statue in a low musical voice, "far away in a little street there is a poor house. One of the windows is open, and through it I can see a woman seated at a table. Her face is thin and worn, and she has coarse, red hands, all pricked by the needle, for she is a seamstress. She is embroidering passion-flowers on a satin gown for the loveliest of the Queen's maids-of-honour to wear at the next Court ball. In a bed in the corner of the room her little boy is lying ill. He has a fever, and is asking for oranges. His mother has nothing to give him but river water, so he is crying. Swallow, Swallow, little Swallow, will you not bring her the ruby out of my sword-hilt? My feet are fastened to this pedestal and I cannot move."

"I am waited for in Egypt," said the Swallow. "My friends are flying up and down the Nile, and talking to the large lotus-flowers. Soon they will go to sleep in the tomb of the great King. The King is there himself in his painted coffin. He is wrapped in yellow linen, and embalmed with spices. Round his neck is a chain of pale green jade, and his hands are like withered leaves."

"Swallow, Swallow, little Swallow," said the Prince, "will you not stay with me for one night, and be my messenger? The boy is so thirsty, and the mother so sad."

"I don't think I like boys," answered the Swallow. "Last summer, when I was staying on the river, there were two rude boys, the miller's sons, who were always throwing stones at me. They never hit me, of course; we swallows fly far too well for that, and besides, I come of a family famous for its agility; but still, it was a mark of disrespect."

But the Happy Prince looked so sad that the little Swallow was sorry. "It is very cold here," he said; "but I will stay with you for one night, and be your messenger."

"Thank you, little Swallow," said the Prince.

So the Swallow picked out the great ruby from the Prince's sword, and flew away with it in his beak over the roofs of the town.

He passed by the cathedral tower, where the white marble angels were sculptured. He passed by the palace and heard the sound of dancing. A beautiful girl came out on the balcony with her lover. "How wonderful the stars are," he said to her, "and how wonderful is the power of love!"

"I hope my dress will be ready in time for the State-ball," she answered; "I have ordered passion-flowers to be embroidered on it; but the seamstresses are so lazy."

He passed over the river, and saw the lanterns hanging to the masts of the ships. He passed over the Ghetto, and saw the old Jews bargaining with each other, and weighing out money in copper scales. At last he came to the poor house and looked in. The boy was tossing feverishly on his bed, and the mother had fallen asleep, she was so tired. In he hopped, and laid the great ruby on the table beside the woman's thimble. Then he flew gently round the bed, fanning the boy's forehead with his wings. "How cool I feel," said the boy, "I must be getting better"; and he sank into a delicious slumber.

Then the Swallow flew back to the Happy Prince, and told him what he had done. "It is curious," he remarked, "but I feel quite warm now, although it is so cold."

"That is because you have done a good action," said the Prince. And the little Swallow began to think, and then he fell asleep. Thinking always made him sleepy.

When day broke he flew down to the river and had a bath. "What a remarkable phenomenon," said the Professor of Ornithology as he was passing over the bridge. "A swallow in winter!" And he wrote a long letter about it to the local newspaper. Everyone quoted it, it was full of so many words that they could not understand.

"Tonight I go to Egypt," said the Swallow, and he was in high spirits at the prospect. He visited all the public monuments, and sat a long time on top of the church steeple. Wherever he went the Sparrows chirruped, and said to each other, "What a distinguished stranger!" so he enjoyed himself very much.

When the moon rose he flew back to the Happy Prince. "Have you any commissions for Egypt?" he cried; "I am just starting."

"Swallow, Swallow, little Swallow," said the Prince, "will you not stay with me one night longer?"

"I am waited for in Egypt," answered the Swallow. "Tomorrow my friends will fly up to the Second Cataract. The river-horse couches there among the bulrushes, and on a great granite throne sits the God Memnon. All night long he watches the stars, and when the morning star shines he utters one cry of joy, and then he is silent. At noon the yellow lions come down to the water's edge to drink. They have eyes like green beryls, and their roar is louder than the roar of the cataract."

"Swallow, Swallow, little Swallow," said the Prince, "far away across the city I see a young man in a garret. He is leaning over a desk covered with papers, and in a tumbler by his side there is a bunch of withered violets. His hair is brown and crisp, and his lips are red as a pomegranate, and he has large and dreamy eyes. He is trying to finish a play for the Director of the Theatre, but he is too cold to write any more. There is no fire in the grate, and hunger has made him faint."

"I will wait with you one night longer," said the Swallow, who really had a good heart. "Shall I take him another ruby?"

"Alas! I have no ruby now," said the Prince; "my eyes are all that I have left. They are made of rare sapphires, which were brought out of India a thousand years ago. Pluck out one of them and take it to him. He will sell it to the jeweller, and buy food and firewood, and finish his play."

"Dear Prince," said the Swallow, "I cannot do that"; and he began to weep.

"Swallow, Swallow, little Swallow," said the Prince, "do as I command you."

So the Swallow plucked out the Prince's eye, and flew away to the student's garret. It was easy enough to get in, as there was a hole in the roof. Through this he darted, and came into the room. The young man had his head buried in his hands, so he did not hear the flutter of the bird's wings, and when he looked up he found the beautiful sapphire lying on the withered violets.

"I am beginning to be appreciated," he cried; "this is from some great admirer. Now I can finish my play," and he looked quite happy.

The next day the Swallow flew down to the harbour. He sat on the mast of a large vessel and watched the sailors hauling big chests out of the hold with ropes. "Heave a-hoy!" they shouted as each chest came up. "I am going to Egypt!" cried the Swallow, but nobody minded, and when the moon rose he flew back to the Happy Prince.

"I am come to bid you goodbye," he cried.

"Swallow, Swallow, little Swallow," said the Prince, "will you not stay with me one night longer?"

"It is winter," answered the Swallow, "and the chill snow will soon be here. In Egypt the sun is warm on the green palm-trees, and the crocodiles lie in the mud and look lazily about them. My companions are building a nest in the Temple of Baalbec, and the pink and white doves are watching them, and cooing to each other. Dear Prince, I must leave you, but I will never forget you, and next spring I will bring you back two beautiful jewels in place of those you have given away. The ruby shall be redder than a red rose, and the sapphire shall be as blue as the great sea."

"In the square below," said the Happy Prince, "there stands a little match-girl. She has let her matches fall in the gutter, and they are all spoiled. Her father will beat her if she does not bring home some money, and she is crying. She has no shoes or stockings, and her little head is bare. Pluck out my other eye, and give it to her, and her father will not beat her."

"I will stay with you one night longer," said the Swallow, "but I cannot pluck out your eye. You would be quite blind then."

"Swallow, Swallow, little Swallow," said the Prince, "do as I command you."

So he plucked out the Prince's other eye, and darted down with it. He swooped past the match-girl, and slipped the jewel into the palm of her hand. "What a lovely bit of glass," cried the little girl; and she ran home, laughing.

Then the Swallow came back to the Prince. "You are blind now," he said, "so I will stay with you always."

"No, little Swallow," said the poor Prince, "you must go away to Egypt."

"I will stay with you always," said the Swallow, and he slept at the Prince's feet.

All the next day he sat on the Prince's shoulder, and told him stories of what he had seen in strange lands. He told him of the red ibises, who stand in long rows on the banks of the Nile, and catch goldfish in their beaks; of the Sphinx, who is as old as the world itself, and lives in the desert, and knows everything; of the merchants, who walk slowly by the side of their camels, and carry amber beads in their hands; of the King of the Mountains of the Moon, who is as black as ebony, and worships a large crystal; of the great green snake that sleeps in a palm-tree, and has twenty priests to feed it with honey-cakes; and of the pygmies who sail over a big lake on large flat leaves, and are always at war with the butterflies.

"Dear little Swallow," said the Prince, "you tell me of marvellous things, but more marvellous than anything is the suffering of men and of women. There is no Mystery so great as Misery. Fly over my city, little Swallow, and tell me what you see there."

So the Swallow flew over the great city, and saw the rich making merry in their beautiful houses, while the beggars were sitting at the gates. He flew into dark lanes, and saw the white faces of starving children looking out listlessly at the black streets. Under the archway of a bridge two little boys were lying in one another's arms to try and keep themselves warm. "How hungry we are!" they said. "You must not lie here," shouted the Watchman, and they wandered out into the rain.

Then he flew back and told the Prince what he had seen.

"I am covered with fine gold," said the Prince, "you must take it off, leaf by leaf, and give it to my poor; the living always think that gold can make them happy."

Leaf after leaf of the fine gold the Swallow picked off, till the Happy Prince looked quite dull and grey. Leaf after leaf of the fine gold he brought to the poor, and the children's faces grew rosier, and they laughed and played games in the street. "We have bread now!" they cried.

Then the snow came, and after the snow came the frost. The streets looked as if they were made of silver, they were so bright and glistening; long icicles like crystal daggers hung down from the eaves of the houses, everybody went about in furs, and the little boys wore scarlet caps and skated on the ice.

The poor little Swallow grew colder and colder, but he would not leave the Prince, he loved him too well. He picked up crumbs outside the baker's door when the baker was not looking and tried to keep himself warm by flapping his wings.

But at last he knew that he was going to die. He had just strength to fly up to the Prince's shoulder once more. "Goodbye, dear Prince!" he murmured, "will you let me kiss your hand?"

"I am glad that you are going to Egypt at last, little Swallow," said the Prince, "you have stayed too long here; but you must kiss me on the lips, for I love you."

"It is not to Egypt that I am going," said the Swallow. "I am going to the House of Death. Death is the brother of Sleep, is he not?"

And he kissed the Happy Prince on the lips, and fell down dead at his feet.

At that moment a curious crack sounded inside the statue, as if something had broken. The fact is that the leaden heart had snapped right in two. It certainly was a dreadfully hard frost.

Early the next morning the Mayor was walking in the square below in company with the Town Councillors. As they passed the column he looked up at the statue: "Dear me! how shabby the Happy Prince looks!" he said.

"How shabby indeed!" cried the Town Councillors, who always agreed with the Mayor; and they went up to look at it.

"The ruby has fallen out of his sword, his eyes are gone, and he is golden no longer," said the Mayor in fact, "he is little better than a beggar!"

"Little better than a beggar," said the Town Councillors.

"And here is actually a dead bird at his feet!" continued the Mayor. "We must really issue a proclamation that birds are not to be allowed to die here." And the Town Clerk made a note of the suggestion.

So they pulled down the statue of the Happy Prince. "As he is no longer beautiful he is no longer useful," said the Art Professor at the University.

Then they melted the statue in a furnace, and the Mayor held a meeting of the Corporation to decide what was to be done with the metal. "We must have another statue, of course," he said, "and it shall be a statue of myself."

"Of myself," said each of the Town Councillors, and they quarrelled. When I last heard of them they were quarrelling still.

"What a strange thing!" said the overseer of the workmen at the foundry. "This broken lead heart will not melt in the furnace. We must throw it away." So they threw it on a dust-heap where the dead Swallow was also lying.

"Bring me the two most precious things in the city," said God to one of His Angels; and the Angel brought Him the leaden heart and the dead bird.

"You have rightly chosen," said God, "for in my garden of Paradise this little bird shall sing for evermore, and in my city of gold the Happy Prince shall praise me."

THE NIGHTINGALE AND THE ROSE

Oscar Wilde

Published in *The Happy Prince and Other Tales* in 1888

"She said that she would dance with me if I brought her red roses," cried the young Student; "but in all my garden there is no red rose."

From her nest in the holm-oak tree the Nightingale heard him, and she looked out through the leaves, and wondered.

"No red rose in all my garden!" he cried, and his beautiful eyes filled with tears. "Ah, on what little things does happiness depend! I have read all that the wise men have written, and all the secrets of philosophy are mine, yet for want of a red rose is my life made wretched."

"Here at last is a true lover," said the Nightingale. "Night after night have I sung of him, though I knew him not: night after night have I told his story to the stars, and now I see him. His hair is dark as the hyacinth-blossom, and his lips are red as the rose of his desire; but passion has made his face like pale ivory, and sorrow has set her seal upon his brow."

"The Prince gives a ball tomorrow night," murmured the young Student, "and my love will be of the company. If I bring her a red rose she will dance with me till dawn. If I bring her a red rose, I shall hold her in my arms, and she will lean her head upon my shoulder, and her hand will be clasped in mine. But there is no red rose in my garden, so I shall sit lonely, and she will pass me by. She will have no heed of me, and my heart will break."

"Here indeed is the true lover," said the Nightingale. "What I sing of, he suffers—what is joy to me, to him is pain. Surely Love is a wonderful thing. It is more precious than emeralds, and dearer than fine opals. Pearls and pomegranates cannot buy it, nor is it set forth in the marketplace. It may not be purchased of the merchants, nor can it be weighed out in the balance for gold."

"The musicians will sit in their gallery," said the young Student, "and play upon their stringed instruments, and my love will dance to the sound of the harp and the violin. She will dance so lightly that her feet will not touch the floor, and the courtiers in their gay dresses will throng round her. But with me she will not dance, for I have no red rose to give her"; and he flung himself down on the grass, and buried his face in his hands, and wept.

"Why is he weeping?" asked a little Green Lizard, as he ran past him with his tail in the air.

"Why, indeed?" said a Butterfly, who was fluttering about after a sunbeam.

"Why, indeed?" whispered a Daisy to his neighbour, in a soft, low voice.

"He is weeping for a red rose," said the Nightingale.

"For a red rose?" they cried; "how very ridiculous!" and the little Lizard, who was something of a cynic, laughed outright.

But the Nightingale understood the secret of the Student's sorrow, and she sat silent in the oak-tree, and thought about the mystery of Love.

Suddenly she spread her brown wings for flight, and soared into the air. She passed through the grove like a shadow, and like a shadow she sailed across the garden.

In the centre of the grass-plot was standing a beautiful Rose-tree, and when she saw it she flew over to it, and lit upon a spray.

"Give me a red rose," she cried, "and I will sing you my sweetest song."

But the Tree shook its head.

"My roses are white," it answered; "as white as the foam of the sea, and whiter than the snow upon the mountain. But go to my brother who grows round the old sun-dial, and perhaps he will give you what you want."

So the Nightingale flew over to the Rose-tree that was growing round the old sun-dial.

"Give me a red rose," she cried, "and I will sing you my sweetest song."

But the Tree shook its head.

"My roses are yellow," it answered; "as yellow as the hair of the mermaiden who sits upon an amber throne, and yellower than the daffodil that blooms in the meadow before the mower comes with his scythe. But go to my brother who grows beneath the Student's window, and perhaps he will give you what you want."

So the Nightingale flew over to the Rose-tree that was growing beneath the Student's window.

"Give me a red rose," she cried, "and I will sing you my sweetest song."

But the Tree shook its head.

"My roses are red," it answered, "as red as the feet of the dove, and redder than the great fans of coral that wave and wave in the ocean-cavern. But the winter has chilled my veins, and the frost has nipped my buds, and the storm has broken my branches, and I shall have no roses at all this year."

"One red rose is all I want," cried the Nightingale, "only one red rose! Is there no way by which I can get it?"

"There is a way," answered the Tree; "but it is so terrible that I dare not tell it to you."

"Tell it to me," said the Nightingale, "I am not afraid."

"If you want a red rose," said the Tree, "you must build it out of music by moonlight, and stain it with your own heart's-blood. You must sing to me with your breast against a thorn. All night long you must sing to me, and the thorn must pierce your heart, and your life-blood must flow into my veins, and become mine."

"Death is a great price to pay for a red rose," cried the Nightingale, "and Life is very dear to all. It is pleasant to sit in the green wood, and to watch the Sun in his chariot of gold, and the Moon in her chariot of pearl. Sweet is the scent of the hawthorn, and sweet are the bluebells that hide in the valley, and the heather that blows on the hill. Yet Love is better than Life, and what is the heart of a bird compared to the heart of a man?"

So she spread her brown wings for flight, and soared into the air. She swept over the garden like a shadow, and like a shadow she sailed through the grove.

The young Student was still lying on the grass, where she had left him, and the tears were not yet dry in his beautiful eyes.

"Be happy," cried the Nightingale, "be happy; you shall have your red rose. I will build it out of music by moonlight, and stain it with my own heart's-blood. All that I ask of you in return is that you will be a true lover, for Love is wiser than Philosophy, though she is wise, and mightier than Power, though he is mighty. Flame-coloured are his wings, and coloured like flame is his body. His lips are sweet as honey, and his breath is like frankincense."

The Student looked up from the grass, and listened, but he could not understand what the Nightingale was saying to him, for he only knew the things that are written down in books.

But the Oak-tree understood, and felt sad, for he was very fond of the little Nightingale who had built her nest in his branches.

"Sing me one last song," he whispered; "I shall feel very lonely when you are gone."

So the Nightingale sang to the Oak-tree, and her voice was like water bubbling from a silver jar.

When she had finished her song the Student got up, and pulled a note-book and a lead-pencil out of his pocket.

"She has form," he said to himself, as he walked away through the grove—"that cannot be denied to her; but has she got feeling? I am afraid not. In fact, she is like most artists; she is all style, without any sincerity. She would not sacrifice herself for others. She thinks merely of music, and everybody knows that the arts are selfish. Still, it must be admitted that she has some beautiful notes in her voice. What a pity it is that they do not mean anything, or do any practical good." And he went into his room, and lay down on his little pallet-bed, and began to think of his love; and, after a time, he fell asleep.

And when the Moon shone in the heavens the Nightingale flew to the Rose-tree, and set her breast against the thorn. All night long she sang with her breast against the thorn, and the cold crystal Moon leaned down and listened. All night long she sang, and the thorn went deeper and deeper into her breast, and her life-blood ebbed away from her.

She sang first of the birth of love in the heart of a boy and a girl. And on the top-most spray of the Rose-tree there blossomed a marvellous rose, petal following petal, as song followed song. Pale was it, at first, as the mist that hangs over the river—pale as the feet of the morning, and silver as the wings of the dawn. As the shadow of a rose in a mirror of silver, as the shadow of a rose in a water-pool, so was the rose that blossomed on the topmost spray of the Tree.

But the Tree cried to the Nightingale to press closer against the thorn. "Press closer, little Nightingale," cried the Tree, "or the Day will come before the rose is finished."

So the Nightingale pressed closer against the thorn, and louder and louder grew her song, for she sang of the birth of passion in the soul of a man and a maid.

And a delicate flush of pink came into the leaves of the rose, like the flush in the face of the bridegroom when he kisses the lips of the bride. But the thorn had not yet reached her heart, so the rose's heart remained white, for only a Nightingale's heart's-blood can crimson the heart of a rose.

And the Tree cried to the Nightingale to press closer against the thorn. "Press closer, little Nightingale," cried the Tree, "or the Day will come before the rose is finished."

So the Nightingale pressed closer against the thorn, and the thorn touched her heart, and a fierce pang of pain shot through her. Bitter, bitter was the pain, and wilder and wilder grew her song, for she sang of the Love that is perfected by Death, of the Love that dies not in the tomb.

And the marvellous rose became crimson, like the rose of the eastern sky. Crimson was the girdle of petals, and crimson as a ruby was the heart.

But the Nightingale's voice grew fainter, and her little wings began to beat, and a film came over her eyes. Fainter and fainter grew her song, and she felt something choking her in her throat.

Then she gave one last burst of music. The white Moon heard it, and she forgot the dawn, and lingered on in the sky. The red rose heard it, and it trembled all over with ecstasy, and opened its petals to the cold morning air. Echo bore it to her purple cavern in the hills, and woke the sleeping shepherds from their dreams. It floated through the reeds of the river, and they carried its message to the sea.

"Look, look!" cried the Tree, "the rose is finished now"; but the Nightingale made no answer, for she was lying dead in the long grass, with the thorn in her heart.

And at noon the Student opened his window and looked out.

"Why, what a wonderful piece of luck!" he cried; "here is a red rose! I have never seen any rose like it in all my life. It is so beautiful that I am sure it has a long Latin name"; and he leaned down and plucked it.

Then he put on his hat, and ran up to the Professor's house with the rose in his hand.

The daughter of the Professor was sitting in the doorway winding blue silk on a reel, and her little dog was lying at her feet.

"You said that you would dance with me if I brought you a red rose," cried the Student. "Here is the reddest rose in all the world. You will wear it tonight next your heart, and as we dance together it will tell you how I love you."

But the girl frowned.

"I am afraid it will not go with my dress," she answered; "and, besides, the Chamberlain's nephew has sent me some real jewels, and everybody knows that jewels cost far more than flowers."

"Well, upon my word, you are very ungrateful," said the Student angrily; and he threw the rose into the street, where it fell into the gutter, and a cart-wheel went over it.

"Ungrateful!" said the girl. "I tell you what, you are very rude; and, after all, who are you? Only a Student. Why, I don't believe you have even got silver buckles to your shoes as the Chamberlain's nephew has"; and she got up from her chair and went into the house.

"What a silly thing Love is," said the Student as he walked away. "It is not half as useful as Logic, for it does not prove anything, and it is always telling one of things that are not going to happen, and making one believe things that are not true. In fact, it is quite unpractical, and, as in this age to be practical is everything, I shall go back to Philosophy and study Metaphysics."

So he returned to his room and pulled out a great dusty book, and began to read.

BEAUTY AND THE BEAST

Andrew Lang

Published in *The Blue Fairy Book* in 1889

Once upon a time, in a very far-off country, there lived a merchant who had been so fortunate in all his undertakings that he was enormously rich. As he had, however, six sons and six daughters, he found that his money was not too much to let them all have everything they fancied, as they were accustomed to do.

But one day a most unexpected misfortune befell them. Their house caught fire and was speedily burnt to the ground, with all the splendid furniture, the books, pictures, gold, silver, and precious goods it contained; and this was only the beginning of their troubles. Their father, who had until this moment prospered in all ways, suddenly lost every ship he had upon the sea, either by dint of pirates, shipwreck, or fire. Then he heard that his clerks in distant countries, whom he trusted entirely, had proved unfaithful; and at last from great wealth he fell into the direst poverty.

All that he had left was a little house in a desolate place at least a hundred leagues from the town in which he had lived, and to this he was forced to retreat with his children, who were in despair at the idea of leading such a different life. Indeed, the daughters at first hoped that their friends, who had been so numerous while they were rich, would insist on their staying in their houses now they no longer possessed one. But they soon found that they were left alone, and that their former friends even attributed their misfortunes to their own extravagance, and showed no intention of offering them any help. So nothing was left for them but to take their departure to the cottage, which stood in the midst of a dark forest, and seemed to be the most dismal place upon the face of the earth. As they were too poor to have any servants, the girls had to work hard, like peasants, and the sons, for their part, cultivated the fields to earn their living. Roughly clothed, and living in the simplest way, the girls regretted unceasingly the luxuries and amusements of their former life; only the youngest tried to be brave and cheerful. She had been as sad as anyone when misfortune overtook her father, but, soon recovering her natural gaiety, she set to work to make the best of things, to amuse her father and brothers as well as she could, and to try to persuade her sisters to join her in dancing and singing. But they would do nothing of the sort, and, because she was not as doleful as themselves, they declared that this miserable life was all she was fit for. But she was really far prettier and cleverer than they were; indeed, she was so lovely that she was always called Beauty. After two years, when they were all beginning to get used to their new life, something happened to disturb their tranquillity. Their father received the news that one of his ships, which he had believed to be lost, had come safely into port with a rich cargo. All the sons and daughters at once thought that their poverty was at an end, and wanted to set out directly for the town; but their father, who was more prudent, begged them to wait a little, and, though it was harvest time, and he could ill be spared, determined to go himself first, to make inquiries. Only the youngest daughter had any doubt but that they would soon again be as rich as they were before, or at least rich enough to live comfortably in some town where they would find amusement and gay companions once more. So they all loaded their father with commissions for jewels and dresses which it would have taken a fortune to buy; only Beauty, feeling sure that it was of no use, did not ask for anything. Her father, noticing her silence, said: "And what shall I bring for you, Beauty?"

"The only thing I wish for is to see you come home safely," she answered.

But this only vexed her sisters, who fancied she was blaming them for having asked for such costly things. Her father, however, was pleased, but as he thought that at her age she certainly ought to like pretty presents, he told her to choose something.

"Well, dear father," she said, "as you insist upon it, I beg that you will bring me a rose. I have not seen one since we came here, and I love them so much."

So the merchant set out and reached the town as quickly as possible, but only to find that his former companions, believing him to be dead, had divided between them the goods which the ship had brought; and after six months of trouble and expense he found himself as poor as when he started, having been able to recover only just enough to pay the cost of his journey. To make matters worse, he was obliged to leave the town in the most terrible weather, so that by the time he was within a few leagues of his home he was almost exhausted with cold and fatigue. Though he knew it would take some hours to get through the forest, he was so anxious to be at his journey's end that he resolved to go on; but night overtook him, and the deep snow and bitter frost made it impossible for his horse to carry him any further. Not a house was to be seen; the only shelter he could get was the hollow trunk of a great tree, and there he crouched all the night which seemed to him the longest he had ever known. In spite of his weariness the howling of the wolves kept him awake, and even when at last the day broke he was not much better off, for the falling snow had covered up every path, and he did not know which way to turn.

At length he made out some sort of track, and though at the beginning it was so rough and slippery that he fell down more than once, it presently became easier, and led him into an avenue of trees which ended in a splendid castle. It seemed to the merchant very strange that no snow had fallen in the avenue, which was entirely composed of orange trees, covered with flowers and fruit. When he reached the first court of the castle he saw before him a flight of agate steps, and went up them, and passed through several splendidly furnished rooms. The pleasant warmth of the air revived him, and he felt very hungry; but there seemed to be nobody in all this vast and splendid palace whom he could ask to give him something to eat. Deep silence reigned everywhere, and at last, tired of roaming through empty rooms and galleries, he stopped in a room smaller than the rest, where a clear fire was burning and a couch was drawn up closely to it. Thinking that this must be prepared for someone who was expected, he sat down to wait till he should come, and very soon fell into a sweet sleep.

When his extreme hunger wakened him after several hours, he was still alone; but a little table, upon which was a good dinner, had been drawn up close to him, and, as he had eaten nothing for twenty-four hours, he lost no time in beginning his meal, hoping that he might soon have an opportunity of thanking his considerate entertainer, whoever it might be. But no one appeared, and even after another long sleep, from which he awoke completely refreshed, there was no sign of anybody, though a fresh meal of dainty cakes and fruit was prepared upon the little table at his elbow. Being naturally timid, the silence began to terrify him, and he resolved to search once more through all the rooms; but it was of no use. Not even a servant was to be seen; there was no sign of life in the palace! He began to wonder what he should do, and to amuse himself by pretending that all the treasures he saw were his own, and considering how he would divide them among his children. Then he went down into the garden, and though it was winter everywhere else, here the sun shone, and the birds sang, and the flowers bloomed, and the air was soft and sweet. The merchant, in ecstasies with all he saw and heard, said to himself:

"All this must be meant for me. I will go this minute and bring my children to share all these delights."

In spite of being so cold and weary when he reached the castle, he had taken his horse to the stable and fed it. Now he thought he would saddle it for his homeward journey, and he turned down the path which led to the stable. This path had a hedge of roses on each side of it, and the merchant thought he had never seen or smelt such exquisite flowers. They reminded him of his promise to Beauty, and he stopped and had just gathered one to take to her when he was startled by a strange noise behind him. Turning round, he saw a frightful Beast, which seemed to be very angry and said, in a terrible voice:

"Who told you that you might gather my roses? Was it not enough that I allowed you to be in my palace and was kind to you? This is the way you show your gratitude, by stealing my flowers! But your insolence shall not go unpunished." The merchant, terrified by these furious words, dropped the fatal rose, and, throwing himself on his knees, cried: "Pardon me, noble sir. I am truly grateful to you for your hospitality, which was so magnificent that I could not imagine that you would be offended by my taking such a little thing as a rose." But the Beast's anger was not lessened by this speech.

"You are very ready with excuses and flattery," he cried; "but that will not save you from the death you deserve."

"Alas!" thought the merchant, "if my daughter could only know what danger her rose has brought me into!"

And in despair he began to tell the Beast all his misfortunes, and the reason of his journey, not forgetting to mention Beauty's request.

"A king's ransom would hardly have procured all that my other daughters asked," he said: "but I thought that I might at least take Beauty her rose. I beg you to forgive me, for you see I meant no harm."

The Beast considered for a moment, and then he said, in a less furious tone:

"I will forgive you on one condition—that is, that you will give me one of your daughters."

"Ah!" cried the merchant, "if I were cruel enough to buy my own life at the expense of one of my children's, what excuse could I invent to bring her here?"

"No excuse would be necessary," answered the Beast. "If she comes at all she must come willingly. On no other condition will I have her. See if any one of them is courageous enough, and loves you well enough to come and save your life. You seem to be an honest man, so I will trust you to go home. I give you a month to see if either of your daughters will come back with you and stay here, to let you go free. If neither of them is willing, you must come alone, after bidding them goodbye for ever, for then you will belong to me. And do not imagine that you can hide from me, for if you fail to keep your word I will come and fetch you!" added the Beast grimly.

The merchant accepted this proposal, though he did not really think any of his daughters could be persuaded to come. He promised to return at the time appointed, and then, anxious to escape from the presence of the Beast, he asked permission to set off at once. But the Beast answered that he could not go until next day.

"Then you will find a horse ready for you," he said. "Now go and eat your supper, and await my orders."

The poor merchant, more dead than alive, went back to his room, where the most delicious supper was already served on the little table which was drawn up before a blazing fire. But he was too terrified to eat, and only tasted a few of the dishes, for fear the Beast should be angry if he did not obey his orders. When he had finished he heard a great noise in the next room, which he knew meant that the Beast was coming. As he could do nothing to escape his visit, the only thing that remained was to seem as little afraid as possible; so when the Beast appeared and asked roughly if he had supped well, the merchant answered humbly that he had, thanks to his host's kindness. Then the Beast warned him to remember their agreement, and to prepare his daughter exactly for what she had to expect.

"Do not get up tomorrow," he added, "until you see the sun and hear a golden bell ring. Then you will find your breakfast waiting for you here, and the horse you are to ride will be ready in the courtyard. He will also bring you back again when you come with your daughter a month hence. Farewell. Take a rose to Beauty, and remember your promise!"

The merchant was only too glad when the Beast went away, and though he could not sleep for sadness, he lay down until the sun rose. Then, after a hasty breakfast, he went to gather Beauty's rose, and mounted his horse, which carried him off so swiftly that in an instant he had lost sight of the palace, and he was still wrapped in gloomy thoughts when it stopped before the door of the cottage.

His sons and daughters, who had been very uneasy at his long absence, rushed to meet him, eager to know the result of his journey, which, seeing him mounted upon a splendid horse and wrapped in a rich mantle, they supposed to be favorable. He hid the truth from them at first, only saying sadly to Beauty as he gave her the rose:

"Here is what you asked me to bring you; you little know what it has cost."

But this excited their curiosity so greatly that presently he told them his adventures from beginning to end, and then they were all very unhappy. The girls lamented loudly over their lost hopes, and the sons declared that their father should not return to this terrible castle, and began to make plans for killing the Beast if it should come to fetch him. But he reminded them that he had promised to go back. Then the girls were very angry with Beauty, and said it was all her fault, and that if she had asked for something sensible this would never have happened, and complained bitterly that they should have to suffer for her folly.

Poor Beauty, much distressed, said to them:

"I have, indeed, caused this misfortune, but I assure you I did it innocently. Who could have guessed that to ask for a rose in the middle of summer would cause so much misery? But as I did the mischief it is only just that I should suffer for it. I will therefore go back with my father to keep his promise."

At first nobody would hear of this arrangement, and her father and brothers, who loved her dearly, declared that nothing should make them let her go; but Beauty was firm. As the time drew near she divided all her little possessions between her sisters, and said goodbye to everything she loved, and when the fatal day came she encouraged and cheered her father as they mounted together the horse which had brought him back. It seemed to fly rather than gallop, but so smoothly that Beauty was not frightened; indeed, she would have enjoyed the journey if she had not feared what might happen to her at the end of it. Her father still tried to persuade her to go back, but in vain. While they were talking the night fell, and then, to their great surprise, wonderful coloured lights began to shine in all directions, and splendid fireworks blazed out before them; all the forest was illuminated by them, and even felt pleasantly warm, though it had been bitterly cold before. This lasted until they reached the avenue of orange trees, where were statues holding flaming torches, and when they got nearer to the palace they saw that it was illuminated from the roof to the ground, and music sounded softly from the courtyard. "The Beast must be very hungry," said Beauty, trying to laugh, "if he makes all this rejoicing over the arrival of his prey."

But, in spite of her anxiety, she could not help admiring all the wonderful things she saw.

The horse stopped at the foot of the flight of steps leading to the terrace, and when they had dismounted her father led her to the little room he had been in before, where they found a splendid fire burning, and the table daintily spread with a delicious supper.

The merchant knew that this was meant for them, and Beauty, who was rather less frightened now that she had passed through so many rooms and seen nothing of the Beast, was quite willing to begin, for her long ride had made her very hungry. But they had hardly finished their meal when the noise of the Beast's footsteps was heard approaching, and Beauty clung to her father in terror, which became all the greater when she saw how frightened he was. But when the Beast really appeared, though she trembled at the sight of him, she made a great effort to hide her terror, and saluted him respectfully.

This evidently pleased the Beast. After looking at her he said, in a tone that might have struck terror into the boldest heart, though he did not seem to be angry:

"Good-evening, old man. Good-evening, Beauty."

The merchant was too terrified to reply, but Beauty answered sweetly: "Good-evening, Beast."

"Have you come willingly?" asked the Beast. "Will you be content to stay here when your father goes away?"

Beauty answered bravely that she was quite prepared to stay.

"I am pleased with you," said the Beast. "As you have come of your own accord, you may stay. As for you, old man," he added, turning to the merchant, "at sunrise tomorrow you will take your departure. When the bell rings get up quickly and eat your breakfast, and you will find the same horse waiting to take you home; but remember that you must never expect to see my palace again."

Then turning to Beauty, he said:

"Take your father into the next room, and help him to choose everything you think your brothers and sisters would like to have. You will find two traveling-trunks there; fill them as full as you can. It is only just that you should send them something very precious as a remembrance of yourself."

Then he went away, after saying, "Goodbye, Beauty; goodbye, old man"; and though Beauty was beginning to think with great dismay of her father's departure, she was afraid to disobey the Beast's orders; and they went into the next room, which had shelves and cupboards all round it. They were greatly surprised at the riches it contained. There were splendid dresses fit for a queen, with all the ornaments that were to be worn with them; and when Beauty opened the cupboards she was quite dazzled by the gorgeous jewels that lay in heaps upon every shelf. After choosing a vast quantity, which she divided between her sisters—for she had made a heap of the wonderful dresses for each of them—she opened the last chest, which was full of gold.

"I think, father," she said, "that, as the gold will be more useful to you, we had better take out the other things again, and fill the trunks with it." So they did this; but the more they put in the more room there seemed to be, and at last they put back all the jewels and dresses they had taken out, and Beauty even added as many more of the jewels as she could carry at once; and then the trunks were not too full, but they were so heavy that an elephant could not have carried them!

"The Beast was mocking us," cried the merchant; "he must have pretended to give us all these things, knowing that I could not carry them away."

"Let us wait and see," answered Beauty. "I cannot believe that he meant to deceive us. All we can do is to fasten them up and leave them ready."

So they did this and returned to the little room, where, to their astonishment, they found breakfast ready. The merchant ate his with a good appetite, as the Beast's generosity made him believe that he might perhaps venture to come back soon and see Beauty. But she felt sure that her father was leaving her for ever, so she was very sad when the bell rang sharply for the second time, and warned them that the time had come for them to part. They went down into the courtyard, where two horses were waiting, one loaded with the two trunks, the other for him to ride. They were pawing the ground in their impatience to start, and the merchant was forced to bid Beauty a hasty farewell; and as soon as he was mounted he went off at such a pace that she lost sight of him in an instant. Then Beauty began to cry, and wandered sadly back to her own room. But she soon found that she was very sleepy, and as she had nothing better to do she lay down and instantly fell asleep. And then she dreamed that she was walking by a brook bordered with trees, and lamenting her sad fate, when a young prince, handsomer than anyone she had ever seen, and with a voice that went straight to her heart, came and said to her, "Ah, Beauty! you are not so unfortunate as you suppose. Here you will be rewarded for all you have suffered elsewhere. Your every wish shall be gratified. Only try to find me out, no matter how I may be disguised, as I love you dearly, and in making me happy you will find your own happiness. Be as true-hearted as you are beautiful, and we shall have nothing left to wish for."

"What can I do, Prince, to make you happy?" said Beauty.

"Only be grateful," he answered, "and do not trust too much to your eyes. And, above all, do not desert me until you have saved me from my cruel misery."

After this she thought she found herself in a room with a stately and beautiful lady, who said to her:

"Dear Beauty, try not to regret all you have left behind you, for you are destined to a better fate. Only do not let yourself be deceived by appearances."

Beauty found her dreams so interesting that she was in no hurry to awake, but presently the clock roused her by calling her name softly twelve times, and then she got up and found her dressing-table set out with everything she could possibly want; and when her toilet was finished she found dinner was waiting in the room next to hers. But dinner does not take very long when you are all by yourself, and very soon she sat down cosily in the corner of a sofa, and began to think about the charming Prince she had seen in her dream.

"He said I could make him happy," said Beauty to herself.

"It seems, then, that this horrible Beast keeps him a prisoner. How can I set him free? I wonder why they both told me not to trust to appearances? I don't understand it. But, after all, it was only a dream, so why should I trouble myself about it? I had better go and find something to do to amuse myself."

So she got up and began to explore some of the many rooms of the palace.

The first she entered was lined with mirrors, and Beauty saw herself reflected on every side, and thought she had never seen such a charming room. Then a bracelet which was hanging from a chandelier caught her eye, and on taking it down she was greatly surprised to find that it held a portrait of her unknown admirer, just as she had seen him in her dream. With great delight she slipped the bracelet on her arm, and went on into a gallery of pictures, where she soon found a portrait of the same handsome Prince, as large as life, and so well painted that as she studied it he seemed to smile kindly at her. Tearing herself away from the portrait at last, she passed through into a room which contained every musical instrument under the sun, and here she amused herself for a long while in trying some of them, and singing until she was tired. The next room was a library, and she saw everything she had ever wanted to read, as well as everything she had read, and it seemed to her that a whole lifetime would not be enough to even read the names of the books, there were so many. By this time it was growing dusk, and wax candles in diamond and ruby candlesticks were beginning to light themselves in every room.

Beauty found her supper served just at the time she preferred to have it, but she did not see anyone or hear a sound, and, though her father had warned her that she would be alone, she began to find it rather dull.

But presently she heard the Beast coming, and wondered tremblingly if he meant to eat her up now.

However, as he did not seem at all ferocious, and only said gruffly:

"Good evening, Beauty," she answered cheerfully and managed to conceal her terror. Then the Beast asked her how she had been amusing herself, and she told him all the rooms she had seen.

Then he asked if she thought she could be happy in his palace; and Beauty answered that everything was so beautiful that she would be very hard to please if she could not be happy. And after about an hour's talk Beauty began to think that the Beast was not nearly so terrible as she had supposed at first. Then he got up to leave her, and said in his gruff voice:

"Do you love me, Beauty? Will you marry me?"

"Oh! what shall I say?" cried Beauty, for she was afraid to make the Beast angry by refusing.

"Say 'yes' or 'no' without fear," he replied.

"Oh! no, Beast," said Beauty hastily.

"Since you will not, good night, Beauty," he said.

And she answered, "Good night, Beast," very glad to find that her refusal had not provoked him. And after he was gone she was very soon in bed and asleep, and dreaming of her unknown Prince. She thought he came and said to her:

"Ah, Beauty! why are you so unkind to me? I fear I am fated to be unhappy for many a long day still."

And then her dreams changed, but the charming Prince figured in them all; and when morning came her first thought was to look at the portrait, and see if it was really like him, and she found that it certainly was.

This morning she decided to amuse herself in the garden, for the sun shone, and all the fountains were playing; but she was astonished to find that every place was familiar to her, and presently she came to the brook where the myrtle trees were growing where she had first met the Prince in her dream, and that made her think more than ever that he must be kept a prisoner by the Beast. When she was tired she went back to the palace, and found a new room full of materials for every kind of work—ribbons to make into bows, and silks to work into flowers. Then there was an aviary full of rare birds, which were so tame that they flew to Beauty as soon as they saw her, and perched upon her shoulders and her head.

"Pretty little creatures," she said, "how I wish that your cage was nearer to my room, that I might often hear you sing!"

So saying she opened a door, and found, to her delight, that it led into her own room, though she had thought it was quite the other side of the palace.

There were more birds in a room farther on, parrots and cockatoos that could talk, and they greeted Beauty by name; indeed, she found them so entertaining that she took one or two back to her room, and they talked to her while she was at supper; after which the Beast paid her his usual visit, and asked her the same questions as before, and then with a gruff "good night" he took his departure, and Beauty went to bed to dream of her mysterious Prince. The days passed swiftly in different amusements, and after a while Beauty found out another strange thing in the palace, which often pleased her when she was tired of being alone. There was one room which she had not noticed particularly; it was empty, except that under each of the windows stood a very comfortable chair; and the first time she had looked out of the window it had seemed to her that a black curtain prevented her from seeing anything outside. But the second time she went into the room, happening to be tired, she sat down in one of the chairs, when instantly the curtain was rolled aside, and a most amusing pantomime was acted before her; there were dances, and coloured lights, and music, and pretty dresses, and it was all so gay that Beauty was in ecstasies. After that she tried the other seven windows in turn, and there was some new and surprising entertainment to be seen from each of them, so that Beauty never could feel lonely any more. Every evening after supper the Beast came to see her, and always before saying good night asked her in his terrible voice:

"Beauty, will you marry me?"

And it seemed to Beauty, now she understood him better, that when she said, "No, Beast," he went away quite sad. But her happy dreams of the handsome young Prince soon made her forget the poor Beast, and the only thing that at all disturbed her was to be constantly told to distrust appearances, to let her heart guide her, and not her eyes, and many other equally perplexing things, which, consider as she would, she could not understand.

So everything went on for a long time, until at last, happy as she was, Beauty began to long for the sight of her father and her brothers and sisters; and one night, seeing her look very sad, the Beast asked her what was the matter. Beauty had quite ceased to be afraid of him. Now she knew that he was really gentle in spite of his ferocious looks and his dreadful voice. So she answered that she was longing to see her home once more. Upon hearing this the Beast seemed sadly distressed, and cried miserably.

"Ah! Beauty, have you the heart to desert an unhappy Beast like this? What more do you want to make you happy? Is it because you hate me that you want to escape?"

"No, dear Beast," answered Beauty softly, "I do not hate you, and I should be very sorry never to see you any more, but I long to see my father again. Only let me go for two months, and I promise to come back to you and stay for the rest of my life."

The Beast, who had been sighing dolefully while she spoke, now replied:

"I cannot refuse you anything you ask, even though it should cost me my life. Take the four boxes you will find in the room next to your own, and fill them with everything you wish to take with you. But remember your promise and come back when the two months are over, or you may have cause to repent it, for if you do not come in good time you will find your faithful Beast dead. You will not need any chariot to bring you back. Only say goodbye to all your brothers and sisters the night before you come away, and when you have gone to bed turn this ring round upon your finger and say firmly: 'I wish to go back to my palace and see my Beast again.' Good night, Beauty. Fear nothing, sleep peacefully, and before long you shall see your father once more."

As soon as Beauty was alone she hastened to fill the boxes with all the rare and precious things she saw about her, and only when she was tired of heaping things into them did they seem to be full.

Then she went to bed, but could hardly sleep for joy. And when at last she did begin to dream of her beloved Prince she was grieved to see him stretched upon a grassy bank, sad and weary, and hardly like himself.

"What is the matter?" she cried.

He looked at her reproachfully, and said:

"How can you ask me, cruel one? Are you not leaving me to my death perhaps?"

"Ah! don't be so sorrowful," cried Beauty; "I am only going to assure my father that I am safe and happy. I have promised the Beast faithfully that I will come back, and he would die of grief if I did not keep my word!"

"What would that matter to you?" said the Prince "Surely you would not care?"

"Indeed, I should be ungrateful if I did not care for such a kind Beast," cried Beauty indignantly. "I would die to save him from pain. I assure you it is not his fault that he is so ugly."

Just then a strange sound woke her—someone was speaking not very far away; and opening her eyes she found herself in a room she had never seen before, which was certainly not nearly so splendid as those she was used to in the Beast's palace. Where could she be? She got up and dressed hastily, and then saw that the boxes she had packed the night before were all in the room. While she was wondering by what magic the Beast had transported them and herself to this strange place she suddenly heard her father's voice, and rushed out and greeted him joyfully. Her brothers and sisters were all astonished at her appearance, as they had never expected to see her again, and there was no end to the questions they asked her. She had also much to hear about what had happened to them while she was away, and of her father's journey home. But when they heard that she had only come to be with them for a short time, and then must go back to the Beast's palace for ever, they lamented loudly. Then Beauty asked her father what he thought could be the meaning of her strange dreams, and why the Prince constantly begged her not to trust to appearances. After much consideration, he answered: "You tell me yourself that the Beast, frightful as he is, loves you dearly, and deserves your love and gratitude for his gentleness and kindness; I think the Prince must mean you to understand that you ought to reward him by doing as he wishes you to, in spite of his ugliness."

Beauty could not help seeing that this seemed very probable; still, when she thought of her dear Prince who was so handsome, she did not feel at all inclined to marry the Beast. At any rate, for two months she need not decide, but could enjoy herself with her sisters. But though they were rich now, and lived in town again, and had plenty of acquaintances, Beauty found that nothing amused her very much; and she often thought of the palace, where she was so happy, especially as at home she never once dreamed of her dear Prince, and she felt quite sad without him.

Then her sisters seemed to have got quite used to being without her, and even found her rather in the way, so she would not have been sorry when the two months were over but for her father and brothers, who begged her to stay, and seemed so grieved at the thought of her departure that she had not the courage to say goodbye to them. Every day when she got up she meant to say it at night, and when night came she put it off again, until at last she had a dismal dream which helped her to make up her mind. She thought she was wandering in a lonely path in the palace gardens, when she heard groans which seemed to come from some bushes hiding the entrance of a cave, and running quickly to see what could be the matter, she found the Beast stretched out upon his side, apparently dying. He reproached her faintly with being the cause of his distress, and at the same moment a stately lady appeared, and said very gravely:

"Ah! Beauty, you are only just in time to save his life. See what happens when people do not keep their promises! If you had delayed one day more, you would have found him dead."

Beauty was so terrified by this dream that the next morning she announced her intention of going back at once, and that very night she said goodbye to her father and all her brothers and sisters, and as soon as she was in bed she turned her ring round upon her finger, and said firmly, "I wish to go back to my palace and see my Beast again," as she had been told to do.

Then she fell asleep instantly, and only woke up to hear the clock saying "Beauty, Beauty" twelve times in its musical voice, which told her at once that she was really in the palace once more. Everything was just as before, and her birds were so glad to see her! But Beauty thought she had never known such a long day, for she was so anxious to see the Beast again that she felt as if suppertime would never come.

But when it did come and no Beast appeared she was really frightened; so, after listening and waiting for a long time, she ran down into the garden to search for him. Up and down the paths and avenues ran poor Beauty, calling him in vain, for no one answered, and not a trace of him could she find; until at last, quite tired, she stopped for a minute's rest, and saw that she was standing opposite the shady path she had seen in her dream. She rushed down it, and, sure enough, there was the cave, and in it lay the Beast—asleep, as Beauty thought. Quite glad to have found him, she ran up and stroked his head, but, to her horror, he did not move or open his eyes.

"Oh! he is dead; and it is all my fault," said Beauty, crying bitterly.

But then, looking at him again, she fancied he still breathed, and, hastily fetching some water from the nearest fountain, she sprinkled it over his face, and, to her great delight, he began to revive.

"Oh! Beast, how you frightened me!" she cried. "I never knew how much I loved you until just now, when I feared I was too late to save your life."

"Can you really love such an ugly creature as I am?" said the Beast faintly. "Ah! Beauty, you only came just in time. I was dying because I thought you had forgotten your promise. But go back now and rest, I shall see you again by and by."

Beauty, who had half expected that he would be angry with her, was reassured by his gentle voice, and went back to the palace, where supper was awaiting her; and afterward the Beast came in as usual, and talked about the time she had spent with her father, asking if she had enjoyed herself, and if they had all been very glad to see her.

Beauty answered politely, and quite enjoyed telling him all that had happened to her. And when at last the time came for him to go, and he asked, as he had so often asked before, "Beauty, will you marry me?"

She answered softly, "Yes, dear Beast."

As she spoke a blaze of light sprang up before the windows of the palace; fireworks crackled and guns banged, and across the avenue of orange trees, in letters all made of fire-flies, was written: "Long live the Prince and his Bride."

Turning to ask the Beast what it could all mean, Beauty found that he had disappeared, and in his place stood her long-loved Prince! At the same moment the wheels of a chariot were heard upon the terrace, and two ladies entered the room. One of them Beauty recognized as the stately lady she had seen in her dreams; the other was also so grand and queenly that Beauty hardly knew which to greet first.

But the one she already knew said to her companion:

"Well, Queen, this is Beauty, who has had the courage to rescue your son from the terrible enchantment. They love one another, and only your consent to their marriage is wanting to make them perfectly happy."

"I consent with all my heart," cried the Queen. "How can I ever thank you enough, charming girl, for having restored my dear son to his natural form?"

And then she tenderly embraced Beauty and the Prince, who had meanwhile been greeting the Fairy and receiving her congratulations.

"Now," said the Fairy to Beauty, "I suppose you would like me to send for all your brothers and sisters to dance at your wedding?"

And so she did, and the marriage was celebrated the very next day with the utmost splendour, and Beauty and the Prince lived happily ever after.

ALADDIN AND THE WONDERFUL LAMP

Andrew Lang

Published in *The Blue Fairy Book* in 1889

There once lived a poor tailor, who had a son called Aladdin, a careless, idle boy who would do nothing but play ball all day long in the streets with little idle boys like himself. This so grieved the father that he died; yet, in spite of his mother's tears and prayers, Aladdin did not mend his ways. One day, when he was playing in the streets as usual, a stranger asked him his age, and if he was not the son of Mustapha the tailor. "I am, sir," replied Aladdin; "but he died a long while ago." On this the stranger, who was a famous African magician, fell on his neck and kissed him, saying, "I am your uncle, and knew you from your likeness to my brother. Go to your mother and tell her I am coming." Aladdin ran home and told his mother of his newly found uncle. "Indeed, child," she said, "your father had a brother, but I always thought he was dead." However, she prepared supper, and bade Aladdin seek his uncle, who came laden with wine and fruit. He presently fell down and kissed the place where Mustapha used to sit, bidding Aladdin's mother not to be surprised at not having seen him before, as he had been forty years out of the country. He then turned to Aladdin, and asked him his trade, at which the boy hung his head, while his mother burst into tears. On learning that Aladdin was idle and would learn no trade, he offered to take a shop for him and stock it with merchandise. Next day he bought Aladdin a fine suit of clothes and took him all over the city, showing him the sights, and brought him home at nightfall to his mother, who was overjoyed to see her son so fine.

The next day the magician led Aladdin into some beautiful gardens a long way outside the city gates. They sat down by a fountain and the magician pulled a cake from his girdle, which he divided between them. They then journeyed onward till they almost reached the mountains. Aladdin was so tired that he begged to go back, but the magician beguiled him with pleasant stories, and led him on in spite of himself. At last they came to two mountains divided by a narrow valley. "We will go no farther," said the false uncle. "I will show you something wonderful; only do you gather up sticks while I kindle a fire." When it was lit the magician threw on it a powder he had about him, at the same time saying some magical words. The earth trembled a little and opened in front of them, disclosing a square flat stone with a brass ring in the middle to raise it by. Aladdin tried to run away, but the magician caught him and gave him a blow that knocked him down. "What have I done, uncle?" he said piteously; whereupon the magician said more kindly: "Fear nothing, but obey me. Beneath this stone lies a treasure which is to be yours, and no one else may touch it, so you must do exactly as I tell you." At the word treasure Aladdin forgot his fears, and grasped the ring as he was told, saying the names of his father and grandfather. The stone came up quite easily, and some steps appeared. "Go down," said the magician; "at the foot of those steps you will find an open door leading into three large halls. Tuck up your gown and go through them without touching anything, or you will die instantly. These halls lead into a garden of fine fruit trees. Walk on until you come to a niche in a terrace where stands a lighted lamp. Pour out the oil it contains, and bring it to me." He drew a ring from his finger and gave it to Aladdin, bidding him prosper.

Aladdin found everything as the magician had said, gathered some fruit off the trees, and, having got the lamp, arrived at the mouth of the cave. The magician cried out in a great hurry: "Make haste and give me the lamp." This Aladdin refused to do until he was out of the cave. The magician flew into a terrible passion, and throwing some more powder on to the fire, he said something, and the stone rolled back into its place.

The magician left Persia for ever, which plainly showed that he was no uncle of Aladdin's, but a cunning magician, who had read in his magic books of a wonderful lamp, which would make him the most powerful man in the world. Though he alone knew where to find it, he could only receive it from the hand of another. He had picked out the foolish Aladdin for this purpose, intending to get the lamp and kill him afterward.

For two days Aladdin remained in the dark, crying and lamenting. At last he clasped his hands in prayer, and in so doing rubbed the ring, which the magician had forgotten to take from him. Immediately an enormous and frightful genie rose out of the earth, saying: "What wouldst thou with me? I am the Slave of the Ring, and will obey thee in all things." Aladdin fearlessly replied: "Deliver me from this place!" whereupon the earth opened, and he found himself outside. As soon as his eyes could bear the light he went home, but fainted on the threshold. When he came to himself he told his mother what had passed, and showed her the lamp and the fruits he had gathered in the garden, which were, in reality, precious stones. He then asked for some food. "Alas! child," she said, "I have nothing in the house, but I have spun a little cotton and will go and sell it." Aladdin bade her keep her cotton, for he would sell the lamp instead. As it was very dirty she began to rub it, that it might fetch a higher price. Instantly a hideous genie appeared, and asked what she would have. She fainted away, but Aladdin, snatching the lamp, said boldly: "Fetch me something to eat!" The genie returned with a silver bowl, twelve silver plates containing rich meats, two silver cups, and two bottles of wine. Aladdin's mother, when she came to herself, said: "Whence comes this splendid feast?" "Ask not, but eat," replied Aladdin. So they sat at breakfast till it was dinner-time, and Aladdin told his mother about the lamp. She begged him to sell it, and have nothing to do with devils. "No," said Aladdin, "since chance hath made us aware of its virtues, we will use it, and the ring likewise, which I shall always wear on my finger." When they had eaten all the genie had brought, Aladdin sold one of the silver plates, and so on until none were left. He then had recourse to the genie, who gave him another set of plates, and thus they lived for many years.

One day Aladdin heard an order from the Sultan proclaimed that everyone was to stay at home and close his shutters while the Princess, his daughter, went to and from the bath. Aladdin was seized by a desire to see her face, which was very difficult, as she always went veiled. He hid himself behind the door of the bath, and peeped through a chink. The Princess lifted her veil as she went in, and looked so beautiful that Aladdin fell in love with her at first sight. He went home so changed that his mother was frightened. He told her he loved the Princess so deeply that he could not live without her, and meant to ask her in marriage of her father. His mother, on hearing this, burst out laughing, but Aladdin at last prevailed upon her to go before the Sultan and carry his request. She fetched a napkin and laid in it the magic fruits from the enchanted garden, which sparkled and shone like the most beautiful jewels. She took these with her to please the Sultan, and set out, trusting in the lamp. The Grand Vizier and the lords of council had just gone in as she entered the hall and placed herself in front of the Sultan. He, however, took no notice of her. She went every day for a week, and stood in the same place. When the council broke up on the sixth day the Sultan said to his Vizier: "I see a certain woman in the audience-chamber every day carrying something in a napkin. Call her next time, that I may find out what she wants." Next day, at a sign from the Vizier, she went up to the foot of the throne and remained kneeling till the Sultan said to her: "Rise, good woman, and tell me what you want." She hesitated, so the Sultan sent away all but the Vizier, and bade her speak frankly, promising to forgive her beforehand for anything she might say. She then told him of her son's violent love for the Princess. "I prayed him to forget her," she said, "but in vain; he threatened to do some desperate deed if I refused to go and ask your Majesty for the hand of the Princess. Now I pray you to forgive not me alone, but my son Aladdin." The Sultan asked her kindly what she had in the napkin, whereupon she unfolded the jewels and presented them. He was thunderstruck, and turning to the Vizier said: "What sayest thou? Ought I not to bestow the Princess on one who values her at such a price?" The Vizier, who wanted her for his own son, begged the Sultan to withhold her for three months, in the course of which he hoped his son would contrive to make him a richer present. The Sultan granted this, and told Aladdin's mother that, though he consented to the marriage, she must not appear before him again for three months.

Aladdin waited patiently for nearly three months, but after two had elapsed his mother, going into the city to buy oil, found every one rejoicing, and asked what was going on. "Do you not know," was the answer, "that the son of the Grand Vizier is to marry the Sultan's daughter tonight?" Breathless, she ran and told Aladdin, who was overwhelmed at first, but presently bethought him of the lamp. He rubbed it, and the genie appeared, saying, "What is thy will?" Aladdin replied: "The Sultan, as thou knowest, has broken his promise to me, and the Vizier's son is to have the Princess. My command is that tonight you bring hither the bride and bridegroom." "Master, I obey," said the genie. Aladdin then went to his chamber, where, sure enough, at midnight the genie transported the bed containing the Vizier's son and the Princess. "Take this new-married man," he said, "and put him outside in the cold, and return at daybreak." Whereupon the genie took the Vizier's son out of bed, leaving Aladdin with the Princess. "Fear nothing," Aladdin said to her; "you are my wife, promised to me by your unjust father, and no harm shall come to you." The Princess was too frightened to speak, and passed the most miserable night of her life, while Aladdin lay down beside her and slept soundly. At the appointed hour, the genie fetched in the shivering bridegroom, laid him in his place, and transported the bed back to the palace.

Presently the Sultan came to wish his daughter good-morning. The unhappy Vizier's son jumped up and hid himself, while the Princess would not say a word, and was very sorrowful. The Sultan sent her mother to her, who said: "How comes it, child, that you will not speak to your father? What has happened?" The Princess sighed deeply, and at last told her mother how, during the night, the bed had been carried into some strange house, and what had passed there. Her mother did not believe her in the least, but bade her rise and consider it an idle dream.

The following night exactly the same thing happened, and next morning, on the Princess's refusal to speak, the Sultan threatened to cut off her head. She then confessed all, bidding him to ask the Vizier's son if it were not so. The Sultan told the Vizier to ask his son, who owned the truth, adding that, dearly as he loved the Princess, he had rather die than go through another such fearful night, and wished to be separated from her. His wish was granted, and there was an end to feasting and rejoicing.

When the three months were over, Aladdin sent his mother to remind the Sultan of his promise. She stood in the same place as before, and the Sultan, who had forgotten Aladdin, at once remembered him, and sent for her. On seeing her poverty the Sultan felt less inclined than ever to keep his word, and asked his Vizier's advice, who counselled him to set so high a value on the Princess that no man living could come up to it. The Sultan then turned to Aladdin's mother, saying: "Good woman, a Sultan must remember his promises, and I will remember mine, but your son must first send me forty basins of gold brimful of jewels, carried by forty black slaves, led by as many white ones, splendidly dressed. Tell him that I await his answer." The mother of Aladdin bowed low and went home, thinking all was lost. She gave Aladdin the message, adding: "He may wait long enough for your answer!" "Not so long, mother, as you think," her son replied. "I would do a great deal more than that for the Princess." He summoned the genie, and in a few moments the eighty slaves arrived, and filled up the small house and garden. Aladdin made them set out to the palace, two and two, followed by his mother. They were so richly dressed, with such splendid jewels in their girdles, that everyone crowded to see them and the basins of gold they carried on their heads. They entered the palace, and, after kneeling before the Sultan, stood in a half-circle round the throne with their arms crossed, while Aladdin's mother presented them to the Sultan. He hesitated no longer, but said: "Good woman, return and tell your son that I wait for him with open arms." She lost no time in telling Aladdin, bidding him make haste. But Aladdin first called the genie. "I want a scented bath," he said, "a richly embroidered habit, a horse surpassing the Sultan's, and twenty slaves to attend me. Besides this, six slaves, beautifully dressed, to wait on my mother; and lastly, ten thousand pieces of gold in ten purses." No sooner said than done. Aladdin mounted his horse and passed through the streets, the slaves strewing gold as they went. Those who had played with him in his childhood knew him not, he had grown so handsome. When the Sultan saw him he came down from his throne, embraced him, and led him into a hall where a feast was spread, intending to marry him to the Princess that very day. But Aladdin refused, saying, "I must build a palace fit for her," and took his leave. Once home, he said to the genie: "Build me a palace of the finest marble, set with jasper, agate, and other precious stones. In the middle you shall build me a large hall with a dome, its four walls of massy gold and silver, each having six windows, whose lattices, all except one which is to be left unfinished, must be set with diamonds and rubies. There must be stables and horses and grooms and slaves; go and see about it!"

The palace was finished by the next day, and the genie carried him there and showed him all his orders faithfully carried out, even to the laying of a velvet carpet from Aladdin's palace to the Sultan's. Aladdin's mother then dressed herself carefully, and walked to the palace with her slaves, while he followed her on horseback. The Sultan sent musicians with trumpets and cymbals to meet them, so that the air resounded with music and cheers. She was taken to the Princess, who saluted her and treated her with great honour. At night the Princess said goodbye to her father, and set out on the carpet for Aladdin's palace, with his mother at her side, and followed by the hundred slaves. She was charmed at the sight of Aladdin, who ran to receive her. "Princess," he said, "blame your beauty for my boldness if I have displeased you." She told him that, having seen him, she willingly obeyed her father in this matter. After the wedding had taken place Aladdin led her into the hall, where a feast was spread, and she supped with him, after which they danced till midnight. Next day Aladdin invited the Sultan to see the palace. On entering the hall with the four-

and-twenty windows, with their rubies, diamonds, and emeralds, he cried: "It is a world's wonder! There is only one thing that surprises me. Was it by accident that one window was left unfinished?" "No, sir, by design," returned Aladdin. "I wished your Majesty to have the glory of finishing this palace." The Sultan was pleased, and sent for the best jewellers in the city. He showed them the unfinished window, and bade them fit it up like the others. "Sir," replied their spokesman, "we cannot find jewels enough." The Sultan had his own fetched, which they soon used, but to no purpose, for in a month's time the work was not half done. Aladdin, knowing that their task was vain, bade them undo their work and carry the jewels back, and the genie finished the window at his command. The Sultan was surprised to receive his jewels again, and visited Aladdin, who showed him the window finished. The Sultan embraced him, the envious Vizier meanwhile hinting that it was the work of enchantment.

Aladdin had won the hearts of the people by his gentle bearing. He was made captain of the Sultan's armies, and won several battles for him, but remained modest and courteous as before, and lived thus in peace and content for several years.

But far away in Africa the magician remembered Aladdin, and by his magic arts discovered that Aladdin, instead of perishing miserably in the cave, had escaped, and had married a princess, with whom he was living in great honour and wealth. He knew that the poor tailor's son could only have accomplished this by means of the lamp, and travelled night and day until he reached the capital of China, bent on Aladdin's ruin. As he passed through the town he heard people talking everywhere about a marvellous palace. "Forgive my ignorance," he asked, "what is this palace you speak of?" "Have you not heard of Prince Aladdin's palace," was the reply, "the greatest wonder of the world? I will direct you if you have a mind to see it." The magician thanked him who spoke, and having seen the palace, knew that it had been raised by the Genie of the Lamp, and became half mad with rage. He determined to get hold of the lamp, and again plunge Aladdin into the deepest poverty.

Unluckily, Aladdin had gone a-hunting for eight days, which gave the magician plenty of time. He bought a dozen copper lamps, put them into a basket, and went to the palace, crying: "New lamps for old!" followed by a jeering crowd. The Princess, sitting in the hall of four-and-twenty windows, sent a slave to find out what the noise was about, who came back laughing, so that the Princess scolded her. "Madam," replied the slave, "who can help laughing to see an old fool offering to exchange fine new lamps for old ones?" Another slave, hearing this, said: "There is an old one on the cornice there which he can have." Now this was the magic lamp, which Aladdin had left there, as he could not take it out hunting with him. The Princess, not knowing its value, laughingly bade the slave take it and make the exchange. She went and said to the magician: "Give me a new lamp for this." He snatched it and bade the slave take her choice, amid the jeers of the crowd. Little he cared, but left off crying his lamps, and went out of the city gates to a lonely place, where he remained till nightfall, when he pulled out the lamp and rubbed it. The genie appeared, and at the magician's command carried him, together with the palace and the Princess in it, to a lonely place in Africa.

Next morning the Sultan looked out of the window toward Aladdin's palace and rubbed his eyes, for it was gone. He sent for the Vizier and asked what had become of the palace. The Vizier looked out too, and was lost in astonishment. He again put it down to enchantment, and this time the Sultan believed him, and sent thirty men on horseback to fetch Aladdin in chains. They met him riding home, bound him, and forced him to go with them on foot. The people, however, who loved him, followed, armed, to see that he came to no harm. He was carried before the Sultan, who ordered the executioner to cut off his head. The executioner made Aladdin kneel down, bandaged his eyes, and raised his scimitar to strike. At that instant the Vizier, who saw that the crowd had forced their way into the courtyard and were scaling the walls to rescue Aladdin, called to the executioner to stay his hand. The people, indeed, looked so threatening that the Sultan gave way and ordered Aladdin to be unbound, and pardoned him in the sight of the crowd. Aladdin now begged to know what he had done. "False wretch!" said the Sultan, "come thither," and showed him from the window the place where his palace had stood. Aladdin was so amazed that he could not say a word. "Where is my palace and my daughter?" demanded the Sultan. "For the first I am not so deeply concerned, but my daughter I must have, and you must find her or lose your head." Aladdin begged for forty days in which to find her, promising, if he failed, to return and suffer death at the Sultan's pleasure. His prayer was granted, and he went forth sadly from the Sultan's presence. For three days he wandered about like a madman, asking everyone what had become of his palace, but they only laughed and pitied him. He came to the banks of a river, and knelt down to say his prayers before throwing himself in. In so doing he rubbed the magic ring he still wore. The genie he had seen in the cave appeared, and asked his will. "Save my life, genie," said Aladdin, "bring my palace back." "That is not in my power," said the genie; "I am only the Slave of the Ring; you must ask him of the lamp." "Even so," said Aladdin, "but thou canst take me to the palace, and set me down under my dear wife's window." He at once found himself in Africa, under the window of the Princess, and fell asleep out of sheer weariness.

He was awakened by the singing of the birds, and his heart was lighter. He saw plainly that all his misfortunes were owing to the loss of the lamp, and vainly wondered who had robbed him of it.

That morning the Princess rose earlier than she had done since she had been carried into Africa by the magician, whose company she was forced to endure once a day. She, however, treated him so harshly that he dared not live there altogether. As she was dressing, one of her women looked out and saw Aladdin. The Princess ran and opened the window, and at the noise she made Aladdin looked up. She called to him to come to her, and great was the joy of these lovers at seeing each other again. After he had kissed her Aladdin said: "I beg of you, Princess, in God's name, before we speak of anything else, for your own sake and mine, tell me that has become of an old lamp I left on the cornice in the hall of four-and-twenty windows, when I went a-hunting." "Alas!" she said, "I am the innocent cause of our sorrows," and told him of the exchange of the lamp. "Now I know," cried Aladdin, "that we have to thank the African magician for this! Where is the lamp?" "He carries it about with him," said the Princess. "I know, for he pulled it out of his breast to show me. He wishes me to break my faith with you and marry him, saying that you were beheaded by my father's command. He is for ever speaking ill of you but I only reply by my tears. If I persist, I doubt not but he will use violence." Aladdin comforted her, and left her for a while. He changed clothes with the first person he met in the town, and having bought a certain powder, returned to the Princess, who let him in by a little side door. "Put on your most beautiful dress," he said to her "and receive the magician with smiles, leading him to believe that you have forgotten me. Invite him to sup with you, and say you wish to taste the wine of his country. He will go for some and while he is gone I will tell you what to do." She listened carefully to

Aladdin and when he left she arrayed herself gaily for the first time since she left China. She put on a girdle and head-dress of diamonds, and, seeing in a glass that she was more beautiful than ever, received the magician, saying, to his great amazement: "I have made up my mind that Aladdin is dead, and that all my tears will not bring him back to me, so I am resolved to mourn no more, and have therefore invited you to sup with me; but I am tired of the wines of China, and would fain taste those of Africa." The magician flew to his cellar, and the Princess put the powder Aladdin had given her in her cup. When he returned she asked him to drink her health in the wine of Africa, handing him her cup in exchange for his, as a sign she was reconciled to him. Before drinking the magician made her a speech in praise of her beauty, but the Princess cut him short, saying: "Let us drink first, and you shall say what you will afterward." She set her cup to her lips and kept it there, while the magician drained his to the dregs and fell back lifeless. The Princess then opened the door to Aladdin, and flung her arms round his neck; but Aladdin put her away, bidding her leave him, as he had more to do. He then went to the dead magician, took the lamp out of his vest, and bade the genie carry the palace and all in it back to China. This was done, and the Princess in her chamber only felt two little shocks, and little thought she was at home again.

The Sultan, who was sitting in his closet, mourning for his lost daughter, happened to look up, and rubbed his eyes, for there stood the palace as before! He hastened thither, and Aladdin received him in the hall of the four-and-twenty windows, with the Princess at his side. Aladdin told him what had happened, and showed him the dead body of the magician, that he might believe. A ten days' feast was proclaimed, and it seemed as if Aladdin might now live the rest of his life in peace; but it was not to be.

The African magician had a younger brother, who was, if possible, more wicked and more cunning than himself. He travelled to China to avenge his brother's death, and went to visit a pious woman called Fatima, thinking she might be of use to him. He entered her cell and clapped a dagger to her breast, telling her to rise and do his bidding on pain of death. He changed clothes with her, colored his face like hers, put on her veil, and murdered her, that she might tell no tales. Then he went toward the palace of Aladdin, and all the people, thinking he was the holy woman, gathered round him, kissing his hands and begging his blessing. When he got to the palace there was such a noise going on round him that the Princess bade her slave look out of the window and ask what was the matter. The slave said it was the holy woman, curing people by her touch of their ailments, whereupon the Princess, who had long desired to see Fatima, sent for her. On coming to the Princess the magician offered up a prayer for her health and prosperity. When he had done the Princess made him sit by her, and begged him to stay with her always. The false Fatima, who wished for nothing better, consented, but kept his veil down for fear of discovery. The Princess showed him the hall, and asked him what he thought of it. "It is truly beautiful," said the false Fatima. "In my mind it wants but one thing." "And what is that?" said the Princess. "If only a roc's egg," replied he, "were hung up from the middle of this dome, it would be the wonder of the world."

After this the Princess could think of nothing but the roc's egg, and when Aladdin returned from hunting he found her in a very ill humour. He begged to know what was amiss, and she told him that all her pleasure in the hall was spoiled for the want of a roc's egg hanging from the dome. "If that is all," replied Aladdin, "you shall soon be happy." He left her and rubbed the lamp, and when the genie appeared commanded him to bring a roc's egg. The genie gave such a loud and terrible shriek that the hall shook. "Wretch!" he cried, "is it not enough that I have done everything for you, but you must command me to bring my master and hang him up in the midst of this dome? You and your wife and your palace deserve to be burnt to ashes, but that this request does not come from you, but from the brother of the African magician, whom you destroyed. He is now in your palace disguised as the holy woman—whom he murdered. He it was who put that wish into your wife's head. Take care of yourself, for he means to kill you." So saying, the genie disappeared.

Aladdin went back to the Princess, saying his head ached, and requesting that the holy Fatima should be fetched to lay her hands on it. But when the magician came near, Aladdin, seizing his dagger, pierced him to the heart. "What have you done?" cried the Princess. "You have killed the holy woman!" "Not so," replied Aladdin, "but a wicked magician," and told her of how she had been deceived.

After this Aladdin and his wife lived in peace. He succeeded the Sultan when he died, and reigned for many years, leaving behind him a long line of kings.

THE CABULIWALLAH

Rabindranath Tagore

First published in *Sadhana* in 1892
Translated from Bengali by
Sister Nivedita, published in
The Hungry Stones and Other Stories in 1916

My five years' old daughter Mini cannot live without chattering. I really believe that in all her life she has not wasted a minute in silence. Her mother is often vexed at this, and would stop her prattle, but I would not. To see Mini quiet is unnatural, and I cannot bear it long. And so my own talk with her is always lively.

One morning, for instance, when I was in the midst of the seventeenth chapter of my new novel, my little Mini stole into the room, and putting her hand into mine, said: "Father! Ramdayal the door-keeper calls a crow a krow! He doesn't know anything, does he?"

Before I could explain to her the differences of language in this world, she was embarked on the full tide of another subject. "What do you think, Father? Bhola says there is an elephant in the clouds, blowing water out of his trunk, and that is why it rains!"

And then, darting off anew, while I sat still making ready some reply to this last saying, "Father! what relation is Mother to you?"

"My dear little sister in the law!" I murmured involuntarily to myself, but with a grave face contrived to answer: "Go and play with Bhola, Mini! I am busy!"

The window of my room overlooks the road. The child had seated herself at my feet near my table, and was playing softly, drumming on her knees. I was hard at work on my seventeenth chapter, where Protrap Singh, the hero, had just caught Kanchanlata, the heroine, in his arms, and was about to escape with her by the third story window of the castle, when all of a sudden Mini left her play, and ran to the window, crying, "A Cabuliwallah! a Cabuliwallah!" Sure enough in the street below was a Cabuliwallah, passing slowly along. He wore the loose soiled clothing of his people, with a tall turban; there was a bag on his back, and he carried boxes of grapes in his hand.

I cannot tell what were my daughter's feelings at the sight of this man, but she began to call him loudly. "Ah!" I thought, "he will come in, and my seventeenth chapter will never be finished!" At which exact moment the Cabuliwallah turned, and looked up at the child. When she saw this, overcome by terror, she fled to her mother's protection, and disappeared. She had a blind belief that inside the bag, which the big man carried, there were perhaps two or three other children like herself. The pedlar meanwhile entered my doorway, and greeted me with a smiling face.

So precarious was the position of my hero and my heroine, that my first impulse was to stop and buy something, since the man had been called. I made some small purchases, and a conversation began about Abdurrahman, the Russians, she English, and the Frontier Policy.

As he was about to leave, he asked: "And where is the little girl, sir?"

And I, thinking that Mini must get rid of her false fear, had her brought out.

She stood by my chair, and looked at the Cabuliwallah and his bag. He offered her nuts and raisins, but she would not be tempted, and only clung the closer to me, with all her doubts increased.

This was their first meeting.

One morning, however, not many days later, as I was leaving the house, I was startled to find Mini, seated on a bench near the door, laughing and talking, with the great Cabuliwallah at her feet. In all her life, it appeared; my small daughter had never found so patient a listener, save her father. And already the corner of her little sari was stuffed with almonds and raisins, the gift of her visitor, "Why did you give her those?" I said, and taking out an eight-anna bit, I handed it to him. The man accepted the money without demur, and slipped it into his pocket.

Alas, on my return an hour later, I found the unfortunate coin had made twice its own worth of trouble! For the Cabuliwallah had given it to Mini, and her mother catching sight of the bright round object, had pounced on the child with: "Where did you get that eight-anna bit?"

"The Cabuliwallah gave it me," said Mini cheerfully.

"The Cabuliwallah gave it you!" cried her mother much shocked. "Oh, Mini! how could you take it from him?"

I, entering at the moment, saved her from impending disaster, and proceeded to make my own inquiries.

It was not the first or second time, I found, that the two had met. The Cabuliwallah had overcome the child's first terror by a judicious bribery of nuts and almonds, and the two were now great friends.

They had many quaint jokes, which afforded them much amusement. Seated in front of him, looking down on his gigantic frame in all her tiny dignity, Mini would ripple her face with laughter, and begin: "O Cabuliwallah, Cabuliwallah, what have you got in your bag?"

And he would reply, in the nasal accents of the mountaineer: "An elephant!" Not much cause for merriment, perhaps; but how they both enjoyed the witticism! And for me, this child's talk with a grown-up man had always in it something strangely fascinating.

Then the Cabuliwallah, not to be behindhand, would take his turn: "Well, little one, and when are you going to the father-in-law's house?"

Now most small Bengali maidens have heard long ago about the father-in-law's house; but we, being a little new-fangled, had kept these things from our child, and Mini at this question must have been a trifle bewildered. But she would not show it, and with ready tact replied: "Are you going there?"

Amongst men of the Cabuliwallah's class, however, it is well known that the words father-in-law's house have a double meaning. It is a euphemism for jail, the place where we are well cared for, at no expense to ourselves. In this sense would the sturdy pedlar take my daughter's question. "Ah," he would say, shaking his fist at an invisible policeman, "I will thrash my father-in-law!" Hearing this, and picturing the poor discomfited relative, Mini would go off into peals of laughter, in which her formidable friend would join.

These were autumn mornings, the very time of year when kings of old went forth to conquest; and I, never stirring from my little corner in Calcutta, would let my mind wander over the whole world. At the very name of another country, my heart would go out to it, and at the sight of a foreigner in the streets, I would fall to weaving a network of dreams,—the mountains, the glens, and the forests of his distant home, with his cottage in its setting, and the free and independent life of far-away wilds. Perhaps the scenes of travel conjure themselves up before me, and pass and repass in my imagination all the more vividly, because I lead such a vegetable existence, that a call to travel would fall upon me like a thunderbolt. In the presence of this Cabuliwallah, I was immediately transported to the foot of arid mountain peaks, with narrow little defiles twisting in and out amongst their towering heights. I could see the string of camels bearing the merchandise, and the company of turbaned merchants, carrying some of their queer old firearms, and some of their spears, journeying downward towards the plains. I could see—but at some such point Mini's mother would intervene, imploring me to "beware of that man."

Mini's mother is unfortunately a very timid lady. Whenever she hears a noise in the street, or sees people coming towards the house, she always jumps to the conclusion that they are either thieves, or drunkards, or snakes, or tigers, or malaria or cockroaches, or caterpillars, or an English sailor. Even after all these years of experience, she is not able to overcome her terror. So she was full of doubts about the Cabuliwallah, and used to beg me to keep a watchful eye on him.

I tried to laugh her fear gently away, but then she would turn round on me seriously, and ask me solemn questions.

Were children never kidnapped?

Was it, then, not true that there was slavery in Cabul?

Was it so very absurd that this big man should be able to carry off a tiny child?

I urged that, though not impossible, it was highly improbable. But this was not enough, and her dread persisted. As it was indefinite, however, it did not seem right to forbid the man the house, and the intimacy went on unchecked.

Once a year in the middle of January Rahmun, the Cabuliwallah, was in the habit of returning to his country, and as the time approached he would be very busy, going from house to house collecting his debts. This year, however, he could always find time to come and see Mini. It would have seemed to an outsider that there was some conspiracy between the two, for when he could not come in the morning, he would appear in the evening.

Even to me it was a little startling now and then, in the corner of a dark room, suddenly to surprise this tall, loose-garmented, much bebagged man; but when Mini would run in smiling, with her, "O! Cabuliwallah! Cabuliwallah!" and the two friends, so far apart in age, would subside into their old laughter and their old jokes, I felt reassured.

One morning, a few days before he had made up his mind to go, I was correcting my proof sheets in my study. It was chilly weather. Through the window the rays of the sun touched my feet, and the slight warmth was very welcome. It was almost eight o'clock, and the early pedestrians were returning home, with their heads covered. All at once, I heard an uproar in the street, and, looking out, saw Rahmun being led away bound between two policemen, and behind them a crowd of curious boys. There were blood-stains on the clothes of the Cabuliwallah, and one of the policemen carried a knife. Hurrying out, I stopped them, and enquired what it all meant. Partly from one, partly from another, I gathered that a certain neighbour had owed the pedlar something for a Rampuri shawl, but had falsely denied having bought it, and that in the course of the quarrel, Rahmun had struck him. Now in the heat of his excitement, the prisoner began calling his enemy all sorts of names, when suddenly in a verandah of my house appeared my little Mini, with her usual exclamation: "O Cabuliwallah! Cabuliwallah!" Rahmun's face lighted up as he turned to her. He had no bag under his arm today, so she could not discuss the elephant with him. She at once therefore proceeded to the next question: "Are you going to the father-in-law's house?" Rahmun laughed and said: "Just where I am going, little one!" Then seeing that the reply did not amuse the child, he held up his fettered hands. "Ali," he said, "I would have thrashed that old father-in-law, but my hands are bound!"

On a charge of murderous assault, Rahmun was sentenced to some years' imprisonment.

Time passed away, and he was not remembered. The accustomed work in the accustomed place was ours, and the thought of the once-free mountaineer spending his years in prison seldom or never occurred to us. Even my light-hearted Mini, I am ashamed to say, forgot her old friend. New companions filled her life. As she grew older, she spent more of her time with girls. So much time indeed did she spend with them that she came no more, as she used to do, to her father's room. I was scarcely on speaking terms with her.

Years had passed away. It was once more autumn and we had made arrangements for our Mini's marriage. It was to take place during the Puja Holidays. With Durga returning to Kailas, the light of our home also was to depart to her husband's house, and leave her father's in the shadow.

The morning was bright. After the rains, there was a sense of ablution in the air, and the sun-rays looked like pure gold. So bright were they that they gave a beautiful radiance even to the sordid brick walls of our Calcutta lanes. Since early dawn today the wedding-pipes had been sounding, and at each beat my own heart throbbed. The wail of the tune, Bhairavi, seemed to intensify my pain at the approaching separation. My Mini was to be married tonight.

From early morning noise and bustle had pervaded the house. In the courtyard the canopy had to be slung on its bamboo poles; the chandeliers with their tinkling sound must be hung in each room and verandah. There was no end of hurry and excitement. I was sitting in my study, looking through the accounts, when some one entered, saluting respectfully, and stood before me. It was Rahmun the Cabuliwallah. At first I did not recognise him. He had no bag, nor the long hair, nor the same vigour that he used to have. But he smiled, and I knew him again.

"When did you come, Rahmun?" I asked him.

"Last evening," he said, "I was released from jail."

The words struck harsh upon my ears. I had never before talked with one who had wounded his fellow, and my heart shrank within itself, when I realised this, for I felt that the day would have been better-omened had he not turned up.

"There are ceremonies going on," I said, "and I am busy. Could you perhaps come another day?"

At once he turned to go; but as he reached the door he hesitated, and said: "May I not see the little one, sir, for a moment?" It was his belief that Mini was still the same. He had pictured her running to him as she used, calling "O Cabuliwallah! Cabuliwallah!" He had imagined too that they would laugh and talk together, just as of old. In fact, in memory of former days he had brought, carefully wrapped up in paper, a few almonds and raisins and grapes, obtained somehow from a countryman, for his own little fund was dispersed.

I said again: "There is a ceremony in the house, and you will not be able to see any one today."

The man's face fell. He looked wistfully at me for a moment, said "Good morning," and went out. I felt a little sorry, and would have called him back, but I found he was returning of his own accord. He came close up to me holding out his offerings and said: "I brought these few things, sir, for the little one. Will you give them to her?"

I took them and was going to pay him, but he caught my hand and said: "You are very kind, sir! Keep me in your recollection. Do not offer me money!—You have a little girl, I too have one like her in my own home. I think of her, and bring fruits to your child, not to make a profit for myself."

Saying this, he put his hand inside his big loose robe, and brought out a small and dirty piece of paper. With great care he unfolded this, and smoothed it out with both hands on my table. It bore the impression of a little band. Not a photograph. Not a drawing. The impression of an ink-smeared hand laid flat on the paper. This touch of his own little daughter had been always on his heart, as he had come year after year to Calcutta, to sell his wares in the streets.

Tears came to my eyes. I forgot that he was a poor Cabuli fruit-seller, while I was—but no, what was I more than he? He also was a father. That impression of the hand of his little Parbati in her distant mountain home reminded me of my own little Mini.

I sent for Mini immediately from the inner apartment. Many difficulties were raised, but I would not listen. Clad in the red silk of her wedding-day, with the sandal paste on her forehead, and adorned as a young bride, Mini came, and stood bashfully before me.

The Cabuliwallah looked a little staggered at the apparition. He could not revive their old friendship. At last he smiled and said: "Little one, are you going to your father-in-law's house?"

But Mini now understood the meaning of the word "father-in-law," and she could not reply to him as of old. She flushed up at the question, and stood before him with her bride-like face turned down.

I remembered the day when the Cabuliwallah and my Mini had first met, and I felt sad. When she had gone, Rahmun heaved a deep sigh, and sat down on the floor. The idea had suddenly come to him that his daughter too must have grown in this long time, and that he would have to make friends with her anew. Assuredly he would not find her, as he used to know her. And besides, what might not have happened to her in these eight years?

The marriage-pipes sounded, and the mild autumn sun streamed round us. But Rahmun sat in the little Calcutta lane, and saw before him the barren mountains of Afghanistan.

I took out a bank-note, and gave it to him, saying: "Go back to your own daughter, Rahmun, in your own country, and may the happiness of your meeting bring good fortune to my child!"

Having made this present, I had to curtail some of the festivities. I could not have the electric lights I had intended, nor the military band, and the ladies of the house were despondent at it. But to me the wedding feast was all the brighter for the thought that in a distant land a long-lost father met again with his only child.

THE FIRST VOYAGE OF SINDBAD THE SAILOR

Andrew Lang

Published in *The Arabian Nights' Entertainments* in 1898

I had inherited considerable wealth from my parents, and being young and foolish I at first squandered it recklessly upon every kind of pleasure, but presently, finding that riches speedily take to themselves wings if managed as badly as I was managing mine, and remembering also that to be old and poor is misery indeed, I began to bethink me of how I could make the best of what still remained to me. I sold all my household goods by public auction, and joined a company of merchants who traded by sea, embarking with them at Balsora in a ship which we had fitted out between us.

We set sail and took our course towards the East Indies by the Persian Gulf, having the coast of Persia upon our left hand and upon our right the shores of Arabia Felix. I was at first much troubled by the uneasy motion of the vessel, but speedily recovered my health, and since that hour have been no more plagued by sea-sickness.

From time to time we landed at various islands, where we sold or exchanged our merchandise, and one day, when the wind dropped suddenly, we found ourselves becalmed close to a small island like a green meadow, which only rose slightly above the surface of the water. Our sails were furled, and the captain gave permission to all who wished to land for a while and amuse themselves. I was among the number, but when after strolling about for some time we lighted a fire and sat down to enjoy the repast which we had brought with us, we were startled by a sudden and violent trembling of the island, while at the same moment those left upon the ship set up an outcry bidding us come on board for our lives, since what we had taken for an island was nothing but the back of a sleeping whale. Those who were nearest to the boat threw themselves into it, others sprang into the sea, but before I could save myself the whale plunged suddenly into the depths of the ocean, leaving me clinging to a piece of the wood which we had brought to make our fire. Meanwhile a breeze had sprung up, and in the confusion that ensued on board our vessel in hoisting the sails and taking up those who were in the boat and clinging to its sides, no one missed me and I was left at the mercy of the waves. All that day I floated up and down, now beaten this way, now that, and when night fell I despaired for my life; but, weary and spent as I was, I clung to my frail support, and great was my joy when the morning light showed me that I had drifted against an island.

The cliffs were high and steep, but luckily for me some tree-roots protruded in places, and by their aid I climbed up at last, and stretched myself upon the turf at the top, where I lay, more dead than alive, till the sun was high in the heavens. By that time I was very hungry, but after some searching I came upon some eatable herbs, and a spring of clear water, and much refreshed I set out to explore the island. Presently I reached a great plain where a grazing horse was tethered, and as I stood looking at it I heard voices talking apparently underground, and in a moment a man appeared who asked me how I came upon the island. I told him my adventures, and heard in return that he was one of the grooms of Mihrage, the king of the island, and that each year they came to feed their master's horses in this plain. He took me to a cave where his companions were assembled, and when I had eaten of the food they set before me, they bade me think myself fortunate to have come upon them when I did, since they were going back to their master on the morrow, and without their aid I could certainly never have found my way to the inhabited part of the island.

Early the next morning we accordingly set out, and when we reached the capital I was graciously received by the king, to whom I related my adventures, upon which he ordered that I should be well cared for and provided with such things as I needed. Being a merchant I sought out men of my own profession, and particularly those who came from foreign countries, as I hoped in this way to hear news from Bagdad, and find out some means of returning thither, for the capital was situated upon the sea-shore, and visited by vessels from all parts of the world. In the meantime I heard many curious things, and answered many questions concerning my own country, for I talked willingly with all who came to me. Also to while away the time of waiting I explored a little island named Cassel, which belonged to King Mihrage, and which was supposed to be inhabited by a spirit named Deggial. Indeed, the sailors assured me that often at night the playing of timbals could be heard upon it. However, I saw nothing strange upon my voyage, saving some fish that were full two hundred cubits long, but were fortunately more in dread of us than even we were of them, and fled from us if we did but strike upon a board to frighten them. Other fishes there were only a cubit long which had heads like owls.

One day after my return, as I went down to the quay, I saw a ship which had just cast anchor, and was discharging her cargo, while the merchants to whom it belonged were busily directing the removal of it to their warehouses. Drawing nearer I presently noticed that my own name was marked upon some of the packages, and after having carefully examined them, I felt sure that they were indeed those which I had put on board our ship at Balsora. I then recognised the captain of the vessel, but as I was certain that he believed me to be dead, I went up to him and asked who owned the packages that I was looking at.

"There was on board my ship," he replied, "a merchant of Bagdad named Sindbad. One day he and several of my other passengers landed upon what we supposed to be an island, but which was really an enormous whale floating asleep upon the waves. No sooner did it feel upon its back the heat of the fire which had been kindled, than it plunged into the depths of the sea. Several of the people who were upon it perished in the waters, and among others this unlucky Sindbad. This merchandise is his, but I have resolved to dispose of it for the benefit of his family if I should ever chance to meet with them."

"Captain," said I, "I am that Sindbad whom you believe to be dead, and these are my possessions!"

When the captain heard these words he cried out in amazement, "Lackaday! and what is the world coming to? In these days there is not an honest man to be met with. Did I not with my own eyes see Sindbad drown, and now you have the audacity to tell me that you are he! I should have taken you to be a just man, and yet for the sake of obtaining that which does not belong to you, you are ready to invent this horrible falsehood."

"Have patience, and do me the favour to hear my story," said I.

"Speak then," replied the captain, "I'm all attention."

So I told him of my escape and of my fortunate meeting with the king's grooms, and how kindly I had been received at the palace. Very soon I began to see that I had made some impression upon him, and after the arrival of some of the other merchants, who showed great joy at once more seeing me alive, he declared that he also recognised me.

Throwing himself upon my neck he exclaimed, "Heaven be praised that you have escaped from so great a danger. As to your goods, I pray you take them, and dispose of them as you please." I thanked him, and praised his honesty, begging him to accept several bales of merchandise in token of my gratitude, but he would take nothing. Of the choicest of my goods I prepared a present for King Mihrage, who was at first amazed, having known that I had lost my all. However, when I had explained to him how my bales had been miraculously restored to me, he graciously accepted my gifts, and in return gave me many valuable things. I then took leave of him, and exchanging my merchandise for sandal and aloes wood, camphor, nutmegs, cloves, pepper, and ginger, I embarked upon the same vessel and traded so successfully upon our homeward voyage that I arrived in Balsora with about one hundred thousand sequins. My family received me with as much joy as I felt upon seeing them once more. I bought land and slaves, and built a great house in which I resolved to live happily, and in the enjoyment of all the pleasures of life to forget my past sufferings.

Here Sindbad paused, and commanded the musicians to play again, while the feasting continued until evening. When the time came for the porter to depart, Sindbad gave him a purse containing one hundred sequins, saying, "Take this, Hindbad, and go home, but tomorrow come again and you shall hear more of my adventures."

The porter retired quite overcome by so much generosity, and you may imagine that he was well received at home, where his wife and children thanked their lucky stars that he had found such a benefactor.

The next day Hindbad, dressed in his best, returned to the voyager's house, and was received with open arms. As soon as all the guests had arrived the banquet began as before, and when they had feasted long and merrily, Sindbad addressed them thus:

"My friends, I beg that you will give me your attention while I relate the adventures of my second voyage, which you will find even more astonishing than the first."

THE CAT THAT WALKED BY HIMSELF

Rudyard Kipling

Published in *Just So Stories* in 1902

Hear and attend and listen; for this befell and behappened and became and was, O my Best Beloved, when the Tame animals were wild. The Dog was wild, and the Horse was wild, and the Cow was wild, and the Sheep was wild, and the Pig was wild—as wild as wild could be—and they walked in the Wet Wild Woods by their wild lones. But the wildest of all the wild animals was the Cat. He walked by himself, and all places were alike to him.

Of course the Man was wild too. He was dreadfully wild. He didn't even begin to be tame till he met the Woman, and she told him that she did not like living in his wild ways. She picked out a nice dry Cave, instead of a heap of wet leaves, to lie down in; and she strewed clean sand on the floor; and she lit a nice fire of wood at the back of the Cave; and she hung a dried wild-horse skin, tail-down, across the opening of the Cave; and she said, "Wipe your feet, dear, when you come in, and now we'll keep house."

That night, Best Beloved, they ate wild sheep roasted on the hot stones, and flavoured with wild garlic and wild pepper; and wild duck stuffed with wild rice and wild fenugreek and wild coriander; and marrow-bones of wild oxen; and wild cherries, and wild grenadillas. Then the Man went to sleep in front of the fire ever so happy; but the Woman sat up, combing her hair. She took the bone of the shoulder of mutton—the big fat blade-bone—and she looked at the wonderful marks on it, and she threw more wood on the fire, and she made a Magic. She made the First Singing Magic in the world.

Out in the Wet Wild Woods all the wild animals gathered together where they could see the light of the fire a long way off, and they wondered what it meant.

Then Wild Horse stamped with his wild foot and said, "O my Friends and O my Enemies, why have the Man and the Woman made that great light in that great Cave, and what harm will it do us?"

Wild Dog lifted up his wild nose and smelled the smell of roast mutton, and said, "I will go up and see and look, and say; for I think it is good. Cat, come with me."

"Nenni!" said the Cat. "I am the Cat who walks by himself, and all places are alike to me. I will not come."

"Then we can never be friends again," said Wild Dog, and he trotted off to the Cave. But when he had gone a little way the Cat said to himself, "All places are alike to me. Why should I not go too and see and look and come away at my own liking." So he slipped after Wild Dog softly, very softly, and hid himself where he could hear everything.

When Wild Dog reached the mouth of the Cave he lifted up the dried horse-skin with his nose and sniffed the beautiful smell of the roast mutton, and the Woman, looking at the blade-bone, heard him, and laughed, and said, "Here comes the first. Wild Thing out of the Wild Woods, what do you want?"

Wild Dog said, "O my Enemy and Wife of my Enemy, what is this that smells so good in the Wild Woods?"

Then the Woman picked up a roasted mutton-bone and threw it to Wild Dog, and said, "Wild Thing out of the Wild Woods, taste and try." Wild Dog gnawed the bone, and it was more delicious than anything he had ever tasted, and he said, "O my Enemy and Wife of my Enemy, give me another."

The Woman said, "Wild Thing out of the Wild Woods, help my Man to hunt through the day and guard this Cave at night, and I will give you as many roast bones as you need."

"Ah!" said the Cat, listening. "This is a very wise Woman, but she is not so wise as I am."

Wild Dog crawled into the Cave and laid his head on the Woman's lap, and said, "O my Friend and Wife of my Friend, I will help Your Man to hunt through the day, and at night I will guard your Cave."

"Ah!" said the Cat, listening. "That is a very foolish Dog." And he went back through the Wet Wild Woods waving his wild tail, and walking by his wild lone. But he never told anybody.

When the Man waked up he said, "What is Wild Dog doing here?" And the Woman said, "His name is not Wild Dog any more, but the First Friend, because he will be our friend for always and always and always. Take him with you when you go hunting."

Next night the Woman cut great green armfuls of fresh grass from the water-meadows, and dried it before the fire, so that it smelt like new-mown hay, and she sat at the mouth of the Cave and plaited a halter out of horse-hide, and she looked at the shoulder of mutton-bone—at the big broad blade-bone—and she made a Magic. She made the Second Singing Magic in the world.

Out in the Wild Woods all the wild animals wondered what had happened to Wild Dog, and at last Wild Horse stamped with his foot and said, "I will go and see and say why Wild Dog has not returned. Cat, come with me."

"Nenni!" said the Cat. "I am the Cat who walks by himself, and all places are alike to me. I will not come." But all the same he followed Wild Horse softly, very softly, and hid himself where he could hear everything.

When the Woman heard Wild Horse tripping and stumbling on his long mane, she laughed and said, "Here comes the second. Wild Thing out of the Wild Woods what do you want?"

Wild Horse said, "O my Enemy and Wife of my Enemy, where is Wild Dog?"

The Woman laughed, and picked up the blade-bone and looked at it, and said, "Wild Thing out of the Wild Woods, you did not come here for Wild Dog, but for the sake of this good grass."

And Wild Horse, tripping and stumbling on his long mane, said, "That is true; give it me to eat."

The Woman said, "Wild Thing out of the Wild Woods, bend your wild head and wear what I give you, and you shall eat the wonderful grass three times a day."

"Ah," said the Cat, listening, "this is a clever Woman, but she is not so clever as I am." Wild Horse bent his wild head, and the Woman slipped the plaited hide halter over it, and Wild Horse breathed on the Woman's feet and said, "O my Mistress, and Wife of my Master, I will be your servant for the sake of the wonderful grass."

"Ah," said the Cat, listening, "that is a very foolish Horse." And he went back through the Wet Wild Woods, waving his wild tail and walking by his wild lone. But he never told anybody.

When the Man and the Dog came back from hunting, the Man said, "What is Wild Horse doing here?" And the Woman said, 'His name is not Wild Horse any more, but the First Servant, because he will carry us from place to place for always and always and always. Ride on his back when you go hunting.

Next day, holding her wild head high that her wild horns should not catch in the wild trees, Wild Cow came up to the Cave, and the Cat followed, and hid himself just the same as before; and everything happened just the same as before; and the Cat said the same things as before, and when Wild Cow had promised to give her milk to the Woman every day in exchange for the wonderful grass, the Cat went back through the Wet Wild Woods waving his wild tail and walking by his wild lone, just the same as before. But he never told anybody. And when the Man and the Horse and the Dog came home from hunting and asked the same questions same as before, the Woman said, 'Her name is not Wild Cow any more, but the Giver of Good Food. She will give us the warm white milk for always and always and always, and I will take care of her while you and the First Friend and the First Servant go hunting.

Next day the Cat waited to see if any other Wild thing would go up to the Cave, but no one moved in the Wet Wild Woods, so the Cat walked there by himself; and he saw the Woman milking the Cow, and he saw the light of the fire in the Cave, and he smelt the smell of the warm white milk.

Cat said, "O my Enemy and Wife of my Enemy, where did Wild Cow go?"

The Woman laughed and said, "Wild Thing out of the Wild Woods, go back to the Woods again, for I have braided up my hair, and I have put away the magic blade-bone, and we have no more need of either friends or servants in our Cave."

Cat said, "I am not a friend, and I am not a servant. I am the Cat who walks by himself, and I wish to come into your cave."

Woman said, "Then why did you not come with First Friend on the first night?"

Cat grew very angry and said, "Has Wild Dog told tales of me?"

Then the Woman laughed and said, "You are the Cat who walks by himself, and all places are alike to you. You are neither a friend nor a servant. You have said it yourself. Go away and walk by yourself in all places alike."

Then Cat pretended to be sorry and said, "Must I never come into the Cave? Must I never sit by the warm fire? Must I never drink the warm white milk? You are very wise and very beautiful. You should not be cruel even to a Cat."

Woman said, 'I knew I was wise, but I did not know I was beautiful. So I will make a bargain with you. If ever I say one word in your praise you may come into the Cave."

"And if you say two words in my praise?" said the Cat.

"I never shall," said the Woman, "but if I say two words in your praise, you may sit by the fire in the Cave."

"And if you say three words?" said the Cat.

"I never shall," said the Woman, "but if I say three words in your praise, you may drink the warm white milk three times a day for always and always and always."

Then the Cat arched his back and said, "Now let the Curtain at the mouth of the Cave, and the Fire at the back of the Cave, and the Milk-pots that stand beside the Fire, remember what my Enemy and the Wife of my Enemy has said." And he went away through the Wet Wild Woods waving his wild tail and walking by his wild lone.

That night when the Man and the Horse and the Dog came home from hunting, the Woman did not tell them of the bargain that she had made with the Cat, because she was afraid that they might not like it.

Cat went far and far away and hid himself in the Wet Wild Woods by his wild lone for a long time till the Woman forgot all about him. Only the Bat—the little upside-down Bat—that hung inside the Cave, knew where Cat hid; and every evening Bat would fly to Cat with news of what was happening.

One evening Bat said, "There is a Baby in the Cave. He is new and pink and fat and small, and the Woman is very fond of him."

"Ah," said the Cat, listening, "but what is the Baby fond of?"

"He is fond of things that are soft and tickle," said the Bat. "He is fond of warm things to hold in his arms when he goes to sleep. He is fond of being played with. He is fond of all those things."

"Ah," said the Cat, listening, "then my time has come."

Next night Cat walked through the Wet Wild Woods and hid very near the Cave till morning-time, and Man and Dog and Horse went hunting. The Woman was busy cooking that morning, and the Baby cried and interrupted. So she carried him outside the Cave and gave him a handful of pebbles to play with. But still the Baby cried.

Then the Cat put out his paddy paw and patted the Baby on the cheek, and it cooed; and the Cat rubbed against its fat knees and tickled it under its fat chin with his tail. And the Baby laughed; and the Woman heard him and smiled.

Then the Bat—the little upside-down bat—that hung in the mouth of the Cave said, "O my Hostess and Wife of my Host and Mother of my Host's Son, a Wild Thing from the Wild Woods is most beautifully playing with your Baby."

"A blessing on that Wild Thing whoever he may be," said the Woman, straightening her back, "for I was a busy woman this morning and he has done me a service."

That very minute and second, Best Beloved, the dried horse-skin Curtain that was stretched tail-down at the mouth of the Cave fell down—whoosh!—because it remembered the bargain she had made with the Cat, and when the Woman went to pick it up—lo and behold!—the Cat was sitting quite comfy inside the Cave.

"O my Enemy and Wife of my Enemy and Mother of my Enemy," said the Cat, "it is I: for you have spoken a word in my praise, and now I can sit within the Cave for always and always and always. But still I am the Cat who walks by himself, and all places are alike to me."

The Woman was very angry, and shut her lips tight and took up her spinning-wheel and began to spin. But the Baby cried because the Cat had gone away, and the Woman could not hush it, for it struggled and kicked and grew black in the face.

"O my Enemy and Wife of my Enemy and Mother of my Enemy," said the Cat, "take a strand of the wire that you are spinning and tie it to your spinning-whorl and drag it along the floor, and I will show you a magic that shall make your Baby laugh as loudly as he is now crying."

"I will do so," said the Woman, "because I am at my wits' end; but I will not thank you for it."

She tied the thread to the little clay spindle whorl and drew it across the floor, and the Cat ran after it and patted it with his paws and rolled head over heels, and tossed it backward over his shoulder and chased it between his hind-legs and pretended to lose it, and pounced down upon it again, till the Baby laughed as loudly as it had been crying, and scrambled after the Cat and frolicked all over the Cave till it grew tired and settled down to sleep with the Cat in its arms.

"Now," said the Cat, "I will sing the Baby a song that shall keep him asleep for an hour. And he began to purr, loud and low, low and loud, till the Baby fell fast asleep. The Woman smiled as she looked down upon the two of them and said, 'That was wonderfully done. No question but you are very clever, O Cat."

That very minute and second, Best Beloved, the smoke of the fire at the back of the Cave came down in clouds from the roof—puff!—because it remembered the bargain she had made with the Cat, and when it had cleared away—lo and behold!—the Cat was sitting quite comfy close to the fire.

"O my Enemy and Wife of my Enemy and Mother of My Enemy," said the Cat, "it is I, for you have spoken a second word in my praise, and now I can sit by the warm fire at the back of the Cave for always and always and always. But still I am the Cat who walks by himself, and all places are alike to me."

Then the Woman was very, very angry, and let down her hair and put more wood on the fire and brought out the broad blade-bone of the shoulder of mutton and began to make a Magic that should prevent her from saying a third word in praise of the Cat. It was not a Singing Magic, Best Beloved, it was a Still Magic; and by and by the Cave grew so still that a little wee-wee mouse crept out of a corner and ran across the floor.

"O my Enemy and Wife of my Enemy and Mother of my Enemy," said the Cat, "is that little mouse part of your magic?"

"Ouh! Chee! No indeed!" said the Woman, and she dropped the blade-bone and jumped upon the footstool in front of the fire and braided up her hair very quick for fear that the mouse should run up it.

"Ah," said the Cat, watching, "then the mouse will do me no harm if I eat it?"

"No," said the Woman, braiding up her hair, "eat it quickly and I will ever be grateful to you."

Cat made one jump and caught the little mouse, and the Woman said, "A hundred thanks. Even the First Friend is not quick enough to catch little mice as you have done. You must be very wise."

That very moment and second, O Best Beloved, the Milk-pot that stood by the fire cracked in two pieces—ffft—because it remembered the bargain she had made with the Cat, and when the Woman jumped down from the footstool—lo and behold!—the Cat was lapping up the warm white milk that lay in one of the broken pieces.

"O my Enemy and Wife of my Enemy and Mother of my Enemy, said the Cat, "it is I; for you have spoken three words in my praise, and now I can drink the warm white milk three times a day for always and always and always. But still I am the Cat who walks by himself, and all places are alike to me."

Then the Woman laughed and set the Cat a bowl of the warm white milk and said, "O Cat, you are as clever as a man, but remember that your bargain was not made with the Man or the Dog, and I do not know what they will do when they come home."

"What is that to me?" said the Cat. "If I have my place in the Cave by the fire and my warm white milk three times a day I do not care what the Man or the Dog can do."

That evening when the Man and the Dog came into the Cave, the Woman told them all the story of the bargain while the Cat sat by the fire and smiled. Then the Man said, "Yes, but he has not made a bargain with me or with all proper Men after me." Then he took off his two leather boots and he took up his little stone axe (that makes three) and he fetched a piece of wood and a hatchet (that is five altogether), and he set them out in a row and he said, "Now we will make our bargain. If you do not catch mice when you are in the Cave for always and always and always, I will throw these five things at you whenever I see you, and so shall all proper Men do after me."

"Ah," said the Woman, listening, "this is a very clever Cat, but he is not so clever as my Man."

The Cat counted the five things (and they looked very knobby) and he said, "I will catch mice when I am in the Cave for always and always and always; but still I am the Cat who walks by himself, and all places are alike to me."

"Not when I am near," said the Man. "If you had not said that last I would have put all these things away for always and always and always; but I am now going to throw my two boots and my little stone axe (that makes three) at you whenever I meet you. And so shall all proper Men do after me!"

Then the Dog said, "Wait a minute. He has not made a bargain with me or with all proper Dogs after me." And he showed his teeth and said, "If you are not kind to the Baby while I am in the Cave for always and always and always, I will hunt you till I catch you, and when I catch you I will bite you. And so shall all proper Dogs do after me."

"Ah," said the Woman, listening, "this is a very clever Cat, but he is not so clever as the Dog."

Cat counted the Dog's teeth (and they looked very pointed) and he said, "I will be kind to the Baby while I am in the Cave, as long as he does not pull my tail too hard, for always and always and always. But still I am the Cat that walks by himself, and all places are alike to me."

"Not when I am near," said the Dog. "If you had not said that last I would have shut my mouth for always and always and always; but now I am going to hunt you up a tree whenever I meet you. And so shall all proper Dogs do after me."

Then the Man threw his two boots and his little stone axe (that makes three) at the Cat, and the Cat ran out of the Cave and the Dog chased him up a tree; and from that day to this, Best Beloved, three proper Men out of five will always throw things at a Cat whenever they meet him, and all proper Dogs will chase him up a tree. But the Cat keeps his side of the bargain too. He will kill mice and he will be kind to Babies when he is in the house, just as long as they do not pull his tail too hard. But when he has done that, and between times, and when the moon gets up and night comes, he is the Cat that walks by himself, and all places are alike to him. Then he goes out to the Wet Wild Woods or up the Wet Wild Trees or on the Wet Wild Roofs, waving his wild tail and walking by his wild lone.

Pussy can sit by the fire and sing,
Pussy can climb a tree,
Or play with a silly old cork and string
To 'muse herself, not me.
But I like Binkie my dog, because
He knows how to behave;
So, Binkie's the same as the First Friend was,
And I am the Man in the Cave.

Pussy will play man-Friday till
It's time to wet her paw
And make her walk on the window-sill
(For the footprint Crusoe saw);
Then she fluffles her tail and mews,
And scratches and won't attend.

But Binkie will play whatever I choose,
And he is my true First Friend.

Pussy will rub my knees with her head
Pretending she loves me hard;
But the very minute I go to my bed
Pussy runs out in the yard,
And there she stays till the morning-light;
So I know it is only pretend;
But Binkie, he snores at my feet all night,
And he is my Firstest Friend!

HOW THE FIRST LETTER WAS WRITTEN

Rudyard Kipling

Published in *Just So Stories* in 1902

Once upon a most early time was a Neolithic man. He was not a Jute or an Angle, or even a Dravidian, which he might well have been, Best Beloved, but never mind why. He was a Primitive, and he lived cavily in a Cave, and he wore very few clothes, and he couldn't read and he couldn't write and he didn't want to, and except when he was hungry he was quite happy. His name was Tegumai Bopsulai, and that means, "Man-who-does-not-put-his-foot-forward-in-a-hurry"; but we, O Best Beloved, will call him Tegumai, for short. And his wife's name was Teshumai Tewindrow, and that means, "Lady-who-asks-a-very-many-questions"; but we, O Best Beloved, will call her Teshumai, for short. And his little girl-daughter's name was Taffimai Metallumai, and that means, "Small-person-without-any-manners-who-ought-to-be-spanked"; but I'm going to call her Taffy. And she was Tegumai Bopsulai's Best Beloved and her own Mummy's Best Beloved, and she was not spanked half as much as was good for her; and they were all three very happy. As soon as Taffy could run about she went everywhere with her Daddy Tegumai, and sometimes they would not come home to the Cave till they were hungry, and then Teshumai Tewindrow would say, "Where in the world have you two been to, to get so shocking dirty? Really, my Tegumai, you're no better than my Taffy."

Now attend and listen!

One day Tegumai Bopsulai went down through the beaver-swamp to the Wagai river to spear carp-fish for dinner, and Taffy went too. Tegumai's spear was made of wood with shark's teeth at the end, and before he had caught any fish at all he accidentally broke it clean across by jabbing it down too hard on the bottom of the river. They were miles and miles from home (of course they had their lunch with them in a little bag), and Tegumai had forgotten to bring any extra spears.

"Here's a pretty kettle of fish!" said Tegumai. "It will take me half the day to mend this."

"There's your big black spear at home," said Taffy. "Let me run back to the Cave and ask Mummy to give it me."

"It's too far for your little fat legs," said Tegumai. "Besides, you might fall into the beaver-swamp and be drowned. We must make the best of a bad job." He sat down and took out a little leather mendy-bag, full of reindeer-sinews and strips of leather, and lumps of beeswax and resin, and began to mend the spear.

Taffy sat down too, with her toes in the water and her chin in her hand, and thought very hard. Then she said—"I say, Daddy, it's an awful nuisance that you and I don't know how to write, isn't it? If we did we could send a message for the new spear."

"Taffy," said Tegumai, "how often have I told you not to use slang? 'Awful' isn't a pretty word, but it could be a convenience, now you mention it, if we could write home."

Just then a Stranger-man came along the river, but he belonged to a far tribe, the Tewaras, and he did not understand one word of Tegumai's language. He stood on the bank and smiled at Taffy, because he had a little girl-daughter of his own at home. Tegumai drew a hank of deer-sinews from his mendy-bag and began to mend his spear.

"Come here," said Taffy. "Do you know where my Mummy lives?" And the Stranger-man said, "Um!" being, as you know, a Tewara.

"Silly!" said Taffy, and she stamped her foot, because she saw a shoal of very big carp going up the river just when her Daddy couldn't use his spear.

"Don't bother grown-ups," said Tegumai, so busy with his spear-mending that he did not turn round.

"I aren't," said Taffy. "I only want him to do what I want him to do, and he won't understand."

"Then don't bother me," said Tegumai, and he went on pulling and straining at the deer-sinews with his mouth full of loose ends. The Stranger-man—a genuine Tewara he was—sat down on the grass, and Taffy showed him what her Daddy was doing. The Stranger-man thought, this is a very wonderful child. She stamps her foot at me and she makes faces. She must be the daughter of that noble Chief who is so great that he won't take any notice of me. So he smiled more politely than ever.

"Now," said Taffy, "I want you to go to my Mummy, because your legs are longer than mine, and you won't fall into the beaver-swamp, and ask for Daddy's other spear—the one with the black handle that hangs over our fireplace."

The Stranger-man (and he was a Tewara) thought, "This is a very, very wonderful child. She waves her arms and she shouts at me, but I don't understand a word of what she says. But if I don't do what she wants, I greatly fear that that haughty Chief, Man-who-turns-his-back-on-callers, will be angry." He got up and twisted a big flat piece of bark off a birch-tree and gave it to Taffy. He did this, Best Beloved, to show that his heart was as white as the birch-bark and that he meant no harm; but Taffy didn't quite understand.

"Oh!" said she. "Now I see! You want my Mummy's living-address? Of course I can't write, but I can draw pictures if I've anything sharp to scratch with. Please lend me the shark's tooth off your necklace."

The Stranger-man (and he was a Tewara) didn't say anything, So Taffy put up her little hand and pulled at the beautiful bead and seed and shark-tooth necklace round his neck.

The Stranger-man (and he was a Tewara) thought, "This is a very, very, very wonderful child. The shark's tooth on my necklace is a magic shark's tooth, and I was always told that if anybody touched it without my leave they would immediately swell up or burst, but this child doesn't swell up or burst, and that important Chief, Man-who-attends-strictly-to-his-business, who has not yet taken any notice of me at all, doesn't seem to be afraid that she will swell up or burst. I had better be more polite."

So he gave Taffy the shark's tooth, and she lay down flat on her tummy with her legs in the air, like some people on the drawing-room floor when they want to draw pictures, and she said, "Now I'll draw you some beautiful pictures! You can look over my shoulder, but you mustn't joggle. First I'll draw Daddy fishing. It isn't very like him; but Mummy will know, because I've drawn his spear all broken. Well, now I'll draw the other spear that he wants, the black-handled spear. It looks as if it was sticking in Daddy's back, but that's because the shark's tooth slipped and this piece of bark isn't big enough. That's the spear I want you to fetch; so I'll draw a picture of me myself 'splaining to you. My hair doesn't stand up like I've drawn, but it's easier to draw that way. Now I'll draw you. I think you're very nice really, but I can't make you pretty in the picture, so you mustn't be 'fended. Are you 'fended?"

The Stranger-man (and he was a Tewara) smiled. He thought, "There must be a big battle going to be fought somewhere, and this extraordinary child, who takes my magic shark's tooth but who does not swell up or burst, is telling me to call all the great Chief's tribe to help him. He is a great Chief, or he would have noticed me."

"Look," said Taffy, drawing very hard and rather scratchily, "now I've drawn you, and I've put the spear that Daddy wants into your hand, just to remind you that you're to bring it. Now I'll show you how to find my Mummy's living-address. You go along till you come to two trees (those are trees), and then you go over a hill (that's a hill), and then you come into a beaver-swamp all full of beavers. I haven't put in all the beavers, because I can't draw beavers, but I've drawn their heads, and that's all you'll see of them when you cross the swamp. Mind you don't fall in! Then our Cave is just beyond the beaver-swamp. It isn't as high as the hills really, but I can't draw things very small. That's my Mummy outside. She is beautiful. She is the most beautifullest Mummy there ever was, but she won't be 'fended when she sees I've drawn her so plain. She'll be pleased of me because I can draw. Now, in case you forget, I've drawn the spear that Daddy wants outside our Cave. It's inside really, but you show the picture to my Mummy and she'll give it you. I've made her holding up her hands, because I know she'll be so pleased to see you. Isn't it a beautiful picture? And do you quite understand, or shall I 'splain again?"

The Stranger-man (and he was a Tewara) looked at the picture and nodded very hard. He said to himself, "If I do not fetch this great Chief's tribe to help him, he will be slain by his enemies who are coming up on all sides with spears. Now I see why the great Chief pretended not to notice me! He feared that his enemies were hiding in the bushes and would see him. Therefore he turned to me his back, and let the wise and wonderful child draw the terrible picture showing me his difficulties. I will away and get help for him from his tribe." He did not even ask Taffy the road, but raced off into the bushes like the wind, with the birch-bark in his hand, and Taffy sat down most pleased.

Now this is the picture that Taffy had drawn for him!

"What have you been doing, Taffy?" said Tegumai. He had mended his spear and was carefully waving it to and fro.

"It's a little berangement of my own, Daddy dear," said Taffy. "If you won't ask me questions, you'll know all about it in a little time, and you'll be surprised. You don't know how surprised you'll be, Daddy! Promise you'll be surprised."

"Very well," said Tegumai, and went on fishing.

The Stranger-man—did you know he was a Tewara?—hurried away with the picture and ran for some miles, till quite by accident he found Teshumai Tewindrow at the door of her Cave, talking to some other Neolithic ladies who had come in to a Primitive lunch. Taffy was very like Teshumai, especially about the upper part of the face and the eyes, so the Stranger-man—always a pure Tewara—smiled politely and handed Teshumai the birch-bark. He had run hard, so that he panted, and his legs were scratched with brambles, but he still tried to be polite.

As soon as Teshumai saw the picture she screamed like anything and flew at the Stranger-man. The other Neolithic ladies at once knocked him down and sat on him in a long line of six, while Teshumai pulled his hair.

"It's as plain as the nose on this Stranger-man's face," she said. "He has stuck my Tegumai all full of spears, and frightened poor Taffy so that her hair stands all on end; and not content with that, he brings me a horrid picture of how it was done. Look!" She showed the picture to all the Neolithic ladies sitting patiently on the Stranger-man. "Here is my Tegumai with his arm broken; here is a spear sticking into his back; here is a man with a spear ready to throw; here is another man throwing a spear from a Cave, and here are a whole pack of people" (they were Taffy's beavers really, but they did look rather like people) "coming up behind Tegumai. Isn't it shocking!"

"Most shocking!" said the Neolithic ladies, and they filled the Stranger-man's hair with mud (at which he was surprised), and they beat upon the Reverberating Tribal Drums, and called together all the chiefs of the Tribe of Tegumai, with their Hetmans and Dolmans, all Neguses, Woons, and Akhoonds of the organisation, in addition to the Warlocks, Angekoks, Juju-men, Bonzes, and the rest, who decided that before they chopped the Stranger-man's head off he should instantly lead them down to the river and show them where he had hidden poor Taffy.

By this time the Stranger-man (in spite of being a Tewara) was really annoyed. They had filled his hair quite solid with mud; they had rolled him up and down on knobby pebbles; they had sat upon him in a long line of six; they had thumped him and bumped him till he could hardly breathe; and though he did not understand their language, he was almost sure that the names the Neolithic ladies called him were not ladylike. However, he said nothing till all the Tribe of Tegumai were assembled, and then he led them back to the bank of the Wagai river, and there they found Taffy making daisy-chains, and Tegumai carefully spearing small carp with his mended spear.

"Well, you have been quick!" said Taffy. "But why did you bring so many people? Daddy dear, this is my surprise. Are you surprised, Daddy?"

"Very," said Tegumai; "but it has ruined all my fishing for the day. Why, the whole dear, kind, nice, clean, quiet Tribe is here, Taffy."

And so they were. First of all walked Teshumai Tewindrow and the Neolithic ladies, tightly holding on to the Stranger-man, whose hair was full of mud (although he was a Tewara). Behind them came the Head Chief, the Vice-Chief, the Deputy and Assistant Chiefs (all armed to the upper teeth), the Hetmans and Heads of Hundreds, Platoffs with their Platoons, and Dolmans with their Detachments; Woons, Neguses, and Akhoonds ranking in the rear (still armed to the teeth). Behind them was the Tribe in hierarchical order, from owners of four caves (one for each season), a private reindeer-run, and two salmon-leaps, to feudal and prognathous Villeins, semi-entitled to half a bearskin of winter nights, seven yards from the fire, and adscript serfs, holding the reversion of a scraped marrow-bone under heriot (Aren't those beautiful words, Best Beloved?). They were all there, prancing and shouting, and they frightened every fish for twenty miles, and Tegumai thanked them in a fluid Neolithic oration.

Then Teshumai Tewindrow ran down and kissed and hugged Taffy very much indeed; but the Head Chief of the Tribe of Tegumai took Tegumai by the top-knot feathers and shook him severely.

"Explain! Explain! Explain!" cried all the Tribe of Tegumai.

"Goodness' sakes alive!" said Tegumai. "Let go of my top-knot. Can't a man break his carp-spear without the whole countryside descending on him? You're a very interfering people."

"I don't believe you've brought my Daddy's black-handled spear after all," said Taffy. "And what are you doing to my nice Stranger-man?"

They were thumping him by twos and threes and tens till his eyes turned round and round. He could only gasp and point at Taffy.

"Where are the bad people who speared you, my darling?" said Teshumai Tewindrow.

"There weren't any," said Tegumai. "My only visitor this morning was the poor fellow that you are trying to choke. Aren't you well, or are you ill, O Tribe of Tegumai?"

"He came with a horrible picture," said the Head Chief, "a picture that showed you were full of spears."

"Er-um-P'raps I'd better 'splain that I gave him that picture," said Taffy, but she did not feel quite comfy.

"You!" said the Tribe of Tegumai all together. "Small-person-with-no-manners-who-ought-to-be-spanked! You?"

"Taffy dear, I'm afraid we're in for a little trouble," said her Daddy, and put his arm round her, so she didn't care.

"Explain! Explain! Explain!" said the Head Chief of the Tribe of Tegumai, and he hopped on one foot.

"I wanted the Stranger-man to fetch Daddy's spear, so I drawded it," said Taffy. "There wasn't lots of spears. There was only one spear. I drawded it three times to make sure. I couldn't help it looking as if it stuck into Daddy's head—there wasn't room on the birch-bark; and those things that Mummy called bad people are my beavers. I drawded them to show him the way through the swamp; and I drawded Mummy at the mouth of the Cave looking pleased because he is a nice Stranger-man, and I think you are just the stupidest people in the world," said Taffy. "He is a very nice man. Why have you filled his hair with mud? Wash him!"

Nobody said anything at all for a long time, till the Head Chief laughed; then the Stranger-man (who was at least a Tewara) laughed; then Tegumai laughed till he fell down flat on the bank; then all the Tribe laughed more and worse and louder. The only people who did not laugh were Teshumai Tewindrow and all the Neolithic ladies. They were very polite to all their husbands, and said "Idiot!" ever so often.

Then the Head Chief of the Tribe of Tegumai cried and said and sang, "O Small-person-with-out-any-manners-who-ought-to-be-spanked, you've hit upon a great invention!"

"I didn't intend to; I only wanted Daddy's black-handled spear," said Taffy.

"Never mind. It is a great invention, and some day men will call it writing. At present it is only pictures, and, as we have seen today, pictures are not always properly understood. But a time will come, O Babe of Tegumai, when we shall make letters—all twenty-six of 'em,—and when we shall be able to read as well as to write, and then we shall always say exactly what we mean without any mistakes. Let the Neolithic ladies wash the mud out of the stranger's hair."

"I shall be glad of that," said Taffy, "because, after all, though you've brought every single other spear in the Tribe of Tegumai, you've forgotten my Daddy's black-handled spear."

Then the Head Chief cried and said and sang, "Taffy dear, the next time you write a picture-letter, you'd better send a man who can talk our language with it, to explain what it means. I don't mind it myself, because I am a Head Chief, but it's very bad for the rest of the Tribe of Tegumai, and, as you can see, it surprises the stranger."

Then they adopted the Stranger-man (a genuine Tewara of Tewar) into the Tribe of Tegumai, because he was a gentleman and did not make a fuss about the mud that the Neolithic ladies had put into his hair. But from that day to this (and I suppose it is all Taffy's fault), very few little girls have ever liked learning to read or write. Most of them prefer to draw pictures and play about with their Daddies—just like Taffy.

There runs a road by Merrow Down—
A grassy track today it is
An hour out of Guildford town,
Above the river Wey it is.

Here, when they heard the horse-bells ring,
The ancient Britons dressed and rode
To watch the dark Phoenicians bring
Their goods along the Western Road.

And here, or hereabouts, they met
To hold their racial talks and such—
To barter beads for Whitby jet,
And tin for gay shell torques and such.

But long and long before that time
(When bison used to roam on it)
Did Taffy and her Daddy climb
That down, and had their home on it.

Then beavers built in Broadstone brook
And made a swamp where Bramley stands:

And bears from Shere would come and look
For Taffimai where Shamley stands.

The Wey, that Taffy called Wagai,
Was more than six times bigger then;
And all the Tribe of Tegumai
They cut a noble figure then!

HOW THE CAMEL GOT HIS HUMP

Rudyard Kipling

Published in *Just So Stories* in 1902

In the beginning of years, when the world was so new and all, and the Animals were just beginning to work for Man, there was a Camel, and he lived in the middle of a Howling Desert because he did not want to work; and besides, he was a Howler himself. So he ate sticks and thorns and tamarisks and milkweed and prickles, most 'scruciating idle; and when anybody spoke to him he said "Humph!" Just "Humph!" and no more.

Presently the Horse came to him on Monday morning, with a saddle on his back and a bit in his mouth, and said, "Camel, O Camel, come out and trot like the rest of us."

"Humph!" said the Camel; and the Horse went away and told the Man.

Presently the Dog came to him, with a stick in his mouth, and said, "Camel, O Camel, come and fetch and carry like the rest of us."

"Humph!" said the Camel; and the Dog went away and told the Man.

Presently the Ox came to him, with the yoke on his neck and said, "Camel, O Camel, come and plough like the rest of us."

"Humph!" said the Camel; and the Ox went away and told the Man.

At the end of the day the Man called the Horse and the Dog and the Ox together, and said, "Three, O Three, I'm very sorry for you (with the world so new-and-all); but that Humph-thing in the Desert can't work, or he would have been here by now, so I am going to leave him alone, and you must work double-time to make up for it."

That made the Three very angry (with the world so new-and-all), and they held a palaver, and an *indaba*, and a *punchayet*, and a pow-wow on the edge of the Desert; and the Camel came chewing on milkweed *most* 'scruciating idle, and laughed at them. Then he said "Humph!" and went away again.

Presently there came along the Djinn in charge of All Deserts, rolling in a cloud of dust (Djinns always travel that way because it is Magic), and he stopped to palaver and pow-pow with the Three.

"Djinn of All Deserts," said the Horse, "is it right for anyone to be idle, with the world so new-and-all?"

"Certainly not," said the Djinn.

"Well," said the Horse, "there's a thing in the middle of your Howling Desert (and he's a Howler himself) with a long neck and long legs, and he hasn't done a stroke of work since Monday morning. He won't trot."

"Whew!" said the Djinn, whistling, "that's my Camel, for all the gold in Arabia! What does he say about it?"

"He says 'Humph!'" said the Dog; "and he won't fetch and carry."

"Does he say anything else?"

"Only 'Humph!' and he won't plough," said the Ox.

"Very good," said the Djinn. "I'll humph him if you will kindly wait a minute."

The Djinn rolled himself up in his dust-cloak, and took a bearing across the desert, and found the Camel most 'scruciatingly idle, looking at his own reflection in a pool of water.

"My long and bubbling friend," said the Djinn, "what's this I hear of your doing no work, with the world so new-and-all?"

"Humph!" said the Camel.

The Djinn sat down, with his chin in his hand, and began to think a Great Magic, while the Camel looked at his own reflection in the pool of water.

"You've given the Three extra work ever since Monday morning, all on account of your 'scruciating idleness," said the Djinn; and he went on thinking Magics, with his chin in his hand.

"Humph!" said the Camel.

"I shouldn't say that again if I were you," said the Djinn; "you might say it once too often. Bubbles, I want you to work."

And the Camel said "Humph!" again; but no sooner had he said it than he saw his back, that he was so proud of, puffing up and puffing up into a great big lolloping humph.

"Do you see that?" said the Djinn. "That's your very own humph that you've brought upon your very own self by not working. Today is Thursday, and you've done no work since Monday, when the work began. Now you are going to work."

"How can I," said the Camel, "with this humph on my back?"

"That's made a-purpose," said the Djinn, "all because you missed those three days. You will be able to work now for three days without eating, because you can live on your humph; and don't you ever say I never did anything for you. Come out of the Desert and go to the Three, and behave. Humph yourself!"

And the Camel humphed himself, humph and all, and went away to join the Three. And from that day to this the Camel always wears a humph (we call it "hump" now, not to hurt his feelings); but he has never yet caught up with the three days that he missed at the beginning of the world, and he has never yet learned how to behave.

The Camel's hump is an ugly lump
Which well you may see at the Zoo;
But uglier yet is the hump we get
From having too little to do.

Kiddies and grown-ups too-oo-oo,
If we haven't enough to do-oo-oo,
We get the hump—
Cameelious hump—
The hump that is black and blue!

We climb out of bed with a frouzly head
And a snarly-yarly voice.
We shiver and scowl and we grunt and we growl
At our bath and our boots and our toys;

And there ought to be a corner for me
(And I know there is one for you)
When we get the hump—
Cameelious hump—
The hump that is black and blue!

The cure for this ill is not to sit still,
Or frowst with a book by the fire;
But to take a large hoe and a shovel also,
And dig till you gently perspire;

And then you will find that the sun and the wind.
And the Djinn of the Garden too,
Have lifted the hump—
The horrible hump—
The hump that is black and blue!

I get it as well as you-oo-oo—
If I haven't enough to do-oo-oo—
We all get hump—
Cameelious hump—
Kiddies and grown-ups too!

A KIDNAPPED SANTA CLAUS

L. Frank Baum

Published in *The Delineator* in 1904

Santa Claus lives in the Laughing Valley, where stands the big, rambling castle in which his toys are manufactured. His workmen, selected from the ryls, knooks, pixies and fairies, live with him, and every one is as busy as can be from one year's end to another.

It is called the Laughing Valley because everything there is happy and gay. The brook chuckles to itself as it leaps rollicking between its green banks; the wind whistles merrily in the trees; the sunbeams dance lightly over the soft grass, and the violets and wild flowers look smilingly up from their green nests. To laugh one needs to be happy; to be happy one needs to be content. And throughout the Laughing Valley of Santa Claus contentment reigns supreme.

On one side is the mighty Forest of Burzee. At the other side stands the huge mountain that contains the Caves of the Daemons. And between them the Valley lies smiling and peaceful.

One would thing that our good old Santa Claus, who devotes his days to making children happy, would have no enemies on all the earth; and, as a matter of fact, for a long period of time he encountered nothing but love wherever he might go.

But the Daemons who live in the mountain caves grew to hate Santa Claus very much, and all for the simple reason that he made children happy.

The Caves of the Daemons are five in number. A broad pathway leads up to the first cave, which is a finely arched cavern at the foot of the mountain, the entrance being beautifully carved and decorated. In it resides the Daemon of Selfishness. Back of this is another cavern inhabited by the Daemon of Envy. The cave of the Daemon of Hatred is next in order, and through this one passes to the home of the Daemon of Malice—situated in a dark and fearful cave in the very heart of the mountain. I do not know what lies beyond this. Some say there are terrible pitfalls leading to death and destruction, and this may very well be true. However, from each one of the four caves mentioned there is a small, narrow tunnel leading to the fifth cave—a cozy little room occupied by the Daemon of Repentance. And as the rocky floors of these passages are well worn by the track of passing feet, I judge that many wanderers in the Caves of the Daemons have escaped through the tunnels to the abode of the Daemon of Repentance, who is said to be a pleasant sort of fellow who gladly opens for one a little door admitting you into fresh air and sunshine again.

Well, these Daemons of the Caves, thinking they had great cause to dislike old Santa Claus, held a meeting one day to discuss the matter.

"I'm really getting lonesome," said the Daemon of Selfishness. "For Santa Claus distributes so many pretty Christmas gifts to all the children that they become happy and generous, through his example, and keep away from my cave."

"I'm having the same trouble," rejoined the Daemon of Envy. "The little ones seem quite content with Santa Claus, and there are few, indeed, that I can coax to become envious."

"And that makes it bad for me!" declared the Daemon of Hatred. "For if no children pass through the Caves of Selfishness and Envy, none can get to MY cavern."

"Or to mine," added the Daemon of Malice.

"For my part," said the Daemon of Repentance, "it is easily seen that if children do not visit your caves they have no need to visit mine; so that I am quite as neglected as you are."

"And all because of this person they call Santa Claus!" exclaimed the Daemon of Envy. "He is simply ruining our business, and something must be done at once."

To this they readily agreed; but what to do was another and more difficult matter to settle. They knew that Santa Claus worked all through the year at his castle in the Laughing Valley, preparing the gifts he was to distribute on Christmas Eve; and at first they resolved to try to tempt him into their caves, that they might lead him on to the terrible pitfalls that ended in destruction.

So the very next day, while Santa Claus was busily at work, surrounded by his little band of assistants, the Daemon of Selfishness came to him and said:

"These toys are wonderfully bright and pretty. Why do you not keep them for yourself? It's a pity to give them to those noisy boys and fretful girls, who break and destroy them so quickly."

"Nonsense!" cried the old graybeard, his bright eyes twinkling merrily as he turned toward the tempting Daemon. "The boys and girls are never so noisy and fretful after receiving my presents, and if I can make them happy for one day in the year I am quite content."

So the Daemon went back to the others, who awaited him in their caves, and said:

"I have failed, for Santa Claus is not at all selfish."

The following day the Daemon of Envy visited Santa Claus. Said he: "The toy shops are full of playthings quite as pretty as those you are making. What a shame it is that they should interfere with your business! They make toys by machinery much quicker than you can make them by hand; and they sell them for money, while you get nothing at all for your work."

But Santa Claus refused to be envious of the toy shops.

"I can supply the little ones but once a year—on Christmas Eve," he answered; "for the children are many, and I am but one. And as my work is one of love and kindness I would be ashamed to receive money for my little gifts. But throughout all the year the children must be amused in some way, and so the toy shops are able to bring much happiness to my little friends. I like the toy shops, and am glad to see them prosper."

In spite of the second rebuff, the Daemon of Hatred thought he would try to influence Santa Claus. So the next day he entered the busy workshop and said:

"Good morning, Santa! I have bad news for you."

"Then run away, like a good fellow," answered Santa Claus. "Bad news is something that should be kept secret and never told."

"You cannot escape this, however," declared the Daemon; "for in the world are a good many who do not believe in Santa Claus, and these you are bound to hate bitterly, since they have so wronged you."

"Stuff and rubbish!" cried Santa.

"And there are others who resent your making children happy and who sneer at you and call you a foolish old rattlepate! You are quite right to hate such base slanderers, and you ought to be revenged upon them for their evil words."

"But I don't hate 'em!" exclaimed Santa Claus positively. "Such people do me no real harm, but merely render themselves and their children unhappy. Poor things! I'd much rather help them any day than injure them."

Indeed, the Daemons could not tempt old Santa Claus in any way. On the contrary, he was shrewd enough to see that their object in visiting him was to make mischief and trouble, and his cheery laughter disconcerted the evil ones and showed to them the folly of such an undertaking. So they abandoned honeyed words and determined to use force.

It was well known that no harm can come to Santa Claus while he is in the Laughing Valley, for the fairies, and ryls, and knooks all protect him. But on Christmas Eve he drives his reindeer out into the big world, carrying a sleighload of toys and pretty gifts to the children; and this was the time and the occasion when his enemies had the best chance to injure him. So the Daemons laid their plans and awaited the arrival of Christmas Eve.

The moon shone big and white in the sky, and the snow lay crisp and sparkling on the ground as Santa Claus cracked his whip and sped away out of the Valley into the great world beyond. The roomy sleigh was packed full with huge sacks of toys, and as the reindeer dashed onward our jolly old Santa laughed and whistled and sang for very joy. For in all his merry life this was the one day in the year when he was happiest—the day he lovingly bestowed the treasures of his workshop upon the little children.

It would be a busy night for him, he well knew. As he whistled and shouted and cracked his whip again, he reviewed in mind all the towns and cities and farmhouses where he was expected, and figured that he had just enough presents to go around and make every child happy. The reindeer knew exactly what was expected of them, and dashed along so swiftly that their feet scarcely seemed to touch the snow-covered ground.

Suddenly a strange thing happened: a rope shot through the moonlight and a big noose that was in the end of it settled over the arms and body of Santa Claus and drew tight. Before he could resist or even cry out he was jerked from the seat of the sleigh and tumbled head foremost into a snowbank, while the reindeer rushed onward with the load of toys and carried it quickly out of sight and sound.

Such a surprising experience confused old Santa for a moment, and when he had collected his senses he found that the wicked Daemons had pulled him from the snowdrift and bound him tightly with many coils of the stout rope. And then they carried the kidnapped Santa Claus away to their mountain, where they thrust the prisoner into a secret cave and chained him to the rocky wall so that he could not escape.

"Ha, ha!" laughed the Daemons, rubbing their hands together with cruel glee. "What will the children do now? How they will cry and scold and storm when they find there are no toys in their stockings and no gifts on their Christmas trees! And what a lot of punishment they will receive from their parents, and how they will flock to our Caves of Selfishness, and Envy, and Hatred, and Malice! We have done a mighty clever thing, we Daemons of the Caves!"

Now it so chanced that on this Christmas Eve the good Santa Claus had taken with him in his sleigh Nuter the Ryl, Peter the Knook, Kilter the Pixie, and a small fairy named Wisk—his four favourite assistants. These little people he had often found very useful in helping him to distribute his gifts to the children, and when their master was so suddenly dragged from the sleigh they were all snugly tucked underneath the seat, where the sharp wind could not reach them.

The tiny immortals knew nothing of the capture of Santa Claus until some time after he had disappeared. But finally they missed his cheery voice, and as their master always sang or whistled on his journeys, the silence warned them that something was wrong.

Little Wisk stuck out his head from underneath the seat and found Santa Claus gone and no one to direct the flight of the reindeer.

"Whoa!" he called out, and the deer obediently slackened speed and came to a halt.

Peter and Nuter and Kilter all jumped upon the seat and looked back over the track made by the sleigh. But Santa Claus had been left miles and miles behind.

"What shall we do?" asked Wisk anxiously, all the mirth and mischief banished from his wee face by this great calamity.

"We must go back at once and find our master," said Nuter the Ryl, who thought and spoke with much deliberation.

"No, no!" exclaimed Peter the Knook, who, cross and crabbed though he was, might always be depended upon in an emergency. "If we delay, or go back, there will not be time to get the toys to the children before morning; and that would grieve Santa Claus more than anything else."

"It is certain that some wicked creatures have captured him," added Kilter thoughtfully, "and their object must be to make the children unhappy. So our first duty is to get the toys distributed as carefully as if Santa Claus were himself present. Afterward we can search for our master and easily secure his freedom."

This seemed such good and sensible advice that the others at once resolved to adopt it. So Peter the Knook called to the reindeer, and the faithful animals again sprang forward and dashed over hill and valley, through forest and plain, until they came to the houses wherein children lay sleeping and dreaming of the pretty gifts they would find on Christmas morning.

The little immortals had set themselves a difficult task; for although they had assisted Santa Claus on many of his journeys, their master had always directed and guided them and told them exactly what he wished them to do. But now they had to distribute the toys according to their own judgment, and they did not understand children as well as did old Santa. So it is no wonder they made some laughable errors.

Mamie Brown, who wanted a doll, got a drum instead; and a drum is of no use to a girl who loves dolls. And Charlie Smith, who delights to romp and play out of doors, and who wanted some new rubber boots to keep his feet dry, received a sewing box filled with coloured worsteds and threads and needles, which made him so provoked that he thoughtlessly called our dear Santa Claus a fraud.

Had there been many such mistakes the Daemons would have accomplished their evil purpose and made the children unhappy. But the little friends of the absent Santa Claus laboured faithfully and intelligently to carry out their master's ideas, and they made fewer errors than might be expected under such unusual circumstances.

And, although they worked as swiftly as possible, day had begun to break before the toys and other presents were all distributed; so for the first time in many years the reindeer trotted into the Laughing Valley, on their return, in broad daylight, with the brilliant sun peeping over the edge of the forest to prove they were far behind their accustomed hours.

Having put the deer in the stable, the little folk began to wonder how they might rescue their master; and they realized they must discover, first of all, what had happened to him and where he was.

So Wisk the Fairy transported himself to the bower of the Fairy Queen, which was located deep in the heart of the Forest of Burzee; and once there, it did not take him long to find out all about the naughty Daemons and how they had kidnapped the good Santa Claus to prevent his making children happy. The Fairy Queen also promised her assistance, and then, fortified by this powerful support, Wisk flew back to where Nuter and Peter and Kilter awaited him, and the four counselled together and laid plans to rescue their master from his enemies.

It is possible that Santa Claus was not as merry as usual during the night that succeeded his capture. For although he had faith in the judgment of his little friends he could not avoid a certain amount of worry, and an anxious look would creep at times into his kind old eyes as he thought of the disappointment that might await his dear little children. And the Daemons, who guarded him by turns, one after another, did not neglect to taunt him with contemptuous words in his helpless condition.

When Christmas Day dawned the Daemon of Malice was guarding the prisoner, and his tongue was sharper than that of any of the others.

"The children are waking up, Santa!" he cried. "They are waking up to find their stockings empty! Ho, ho! How they will quarrel, and wail, and stamp their feet in anger! Our caves will be full today, old Santa! Our caves are sure to be full!"

But to this, as to other like taunts, Santa Claus answered nothing. He was much grieved by his capture, it is true; but his courage did not forsake him. And, finding that the prisoner would not reply to his jeers, the Daemon of Malice presently went away, and sent the Daemon of Repentance to take his place.

This last personage was not so disagreeable as the others. He had gentle and refined features, and his voice was soft and pleasant in tone.

"My brother Daemons do not trust me overmuch," said he, as he entered the cavern; "but it is morning, now, and the mischief is done. You cannot visit the children again for another year."

"That is true," answered Santa Claus, almost cheerfully; "Christmas Eve is past, and for the first time in centuries I have not visited my children."

"The little ones will be greatly disappointed," murmured the Daemon of Repentance, almost regretfully; "but that cannot be helped now. Their grief is likely to make the children selfish and envious and hateful, and if they come to the Caves of the Daemons today I shall get a chance to lead some of them to my Cave of Repentance."

"Do you never repent, yourself?" asked Santa Claus, curiously.

"Oh, yes, indeed," answered the Daemon. "I am even now repenting that I assisted in your capture. Of course it is too late to remedy the evil that has been done; but repentance, you know, can come only after an evil thought or deed, for in the beginning there is nothing to repent of."

"So I understand," said Santa Claus. "Those who avoid evil need never visit your cave."

"As a rule, that is true," replied the Daemon; "yet you, who have done no evil, are about to visit my cave at once; for to prove that I sincerely regret my share in your capture I am going to permit you to escape."

This speech greatly surprised the prisoner, until he reflected that it was just what might be expected of the Daemon of Repentance. The fellow at once busied himself untying the knots that bound Santa Claus and unlocking the chains that fastened him to the wall. Then he led the way through a long tunnel until they both emerged in the Cave of Repentance.

"I hope you will forgive me," said the Daemon pleadingly. "I am not really a bad person, you know; and I believe I accomplish a great deal of good in the world."

With this he opened a back door that let in a flood of sunshine, and Santa Claus sniffed the fresh air gratefully.

"I bear no malice," said he to the Daemon, in a gentle voice; "and I am sure the world would be a dreary place without you. So, good morning, and a Merry Christmas to you!"

With these words he stepped out to greet the bright morning, and a moment later he was trudging along, whistling softly to himself, on his way to his home in the Laughing Valley.

Marching over the snow toward the mountain was a vast army, made up of the most curious creatures imaginable. There were numberless knooks from the forest, as rough and crooked in appearance as the gnarled branches of the trees they ministered to. And there were dainty ryls from the fields, each one bearing the emblem of the flower or plant it guarded. Behind these were many ranks of pixies, gnomes and nymphs, and in the rear a thousand beautiful fairies floated along in gorgeous array.

This wonderful army was led by Wisk, Peter, Nuter, and Kilter, who had assembled it to rescue Santa Claus from captivity and to punish the Daemons who had dared to take him away from his beloved children.

And, although they looked so bright and peaceful, the little immortals were armed with powers that would be very terrible to those who had incurred their anger. Woe to the Daemons of the Caves if this mighty army of vengeance ever met them!

But lo! coming to meet his loyal friends appeared the imposing form of Santa Claus, his white beard floating in the breeze and his bright eyes sparkling with pleasure at this proof of the love and veneration he had inspired in the hearts of the most powerful creatures in existence.

And while they clustered around him and danced with glee at his safe return, he gave them earnest thanks for their support. But Wisk, and Nuter, and Peter, and Kilter, he embraced affectionately.

"It is useless to pursue the Daemons," said Santa Claus to the army. "They have their place in the world, and can never be destroyed. But that is a great pity, nevertheless," he continued musingly.

So the fairies, and knooks, and pixies, and ryls all escorted the good man to his castle, and there left him to talk over the events of the night with his little assistants.

Wisk had already rendered himself invisible and flown through the big world to see how the children were getting along on this bright Christmas morning; and by the time he returned, Peter had finished telling Santa Claus of how they had distributed the toys.

"We really did very well," cried the fairy, in a pleased voice; "for I found little unhappiness among the children this morning. Still, you must not get captured again, my dear master; for we might not be so fortunate another time in carrying out your ideas."

He then related the mistakes that had been made, and which he had not discovered until his tour of inspection. And Santa Claus at once sent him with rubber boots for Charlie Smith, and a doll for Mamie Brown; so that even those two disappointed ones became happy.

As for the wicked Daemons of the Caves, they were filled with anger and chagrin when they found that their clever capture of Santa Claus had come to naught. Indeed, no one on that Christmas Day appeared to be at all selfish, or envious, or hateful. And, realizing that while the children's saint had so many powerful friends it was folly to oppose him, the Daemons never again attempted to interfere with his journeys on Christmas Eve.

THREE QUESTIONS

Leo Tolstoy

First published in *What Men Live by and Other Tales* in 1906
Translated from Russian by
Louise and Aylmer Maude

It once occurred to a certain king, that if he always knew the right time to begin everything; if he knew who were the right people to listen to, and whom to avoid; and, above all, if he always knew what was the most important thing to do, he would never fail in anything he might undertake.

And this thought having occurred to him, he had it proclaimed throughout his kingdom that he would give a great reward to anyone who would teach him what was the right time for every action, and who were the most necessary people, and how he might know what was the most important thing to do.

And learned men came to the King, but they all answered his questions differently.

In reply to the first question, some said that to know the right time for every action, one must draw up in advance, a table of days, months and years, and must live strictly according to it. Only thus, said they, could everything be done at its proper time. Others declared that it was impossible to decide beforehand the right time for every action; but that, not letting oneself be absorbed in idle pastimes, one should always attend to all that was going on, and then do what was most needful. Others, again, said that however attentive the King might be to what was going on, it was impossible for one man to decide correctly the right time for every action, but that he should have a Council of wise men, who would help him to fix the proper time for everything.

But then again others said there were some things which could not wait to be laid before a Council, but about which one had at once to decide whether to undertake them or not. But in order to decide that, one must know beforehand what was going to happen. It is only magicians who know that; and, therefore, in order to know the right time for every action, one must consult magicians.

Equally various were the answers to the second question. Some said, the people the King most needed were his councilors;

others, the priests; others, the doctors; while some said the warriors were the most necessary.

To the third question, as to what was the most important occupation: some replied that the most important thing in the world was science. Others said it was skill in warfare; and others, again, that it was religious worship.

All the answers being different, the King agreed with none of them, and gave the reward to none. But still wishing to find the right answers to his questions, he decided to consult a hermit, widely renowned for his wisdom.

The hermit lived in a wood which he never quitted, and he received none but common folk. So the King put on simple clothes, and before reaching the hermit's cell dismounted from his horse, and, leaving his bodyguard behind, went on alone.

When the King approached, the hermit was digging the ground in front of his hut. Seeing the King, he greeted him and went on digging. The hermit was frail and weak, and each time he stuck his spade into the ground and turned a little earth, he breathed heavily.

The King went up to him and said: "I have come to you, wise hermit, to ask you to answer three questions: How can I learn to do the right thing at the right time? Who are the people I most need, and to whom should I, therefore, pay more attention than to the rest? And, what affairs are the most important, and need my first attention?"

The hermit listened to the King, but answered nothing. He just spat on his hand and recommenced digging.

"You are tired," said the King, "let me take the spade and work awhile for you."

"Thanks!" said the hermit, and, giving the spade to the King, he sat down on the ground.

When he had dug two beds, the King stopped and repeated his questions. The hermit again gave no answer, but rose, stretched out his hand for the spade, and said:

"Now rest awhile—and let me work a bit."

But the King did not give him the spade, and continued to dig. One hour passed, and another. The sun began to sink behind the trees, and the King at last stuck the spade into the ground, and said:

"I came to you, wise man, for an answer to my questions. If you can give me none, tell me so, and I will return home."

"Here comes someone running," said the hermit, "let us see who it is."

The King turned round, and saw a bearded man come running out of the wood. The man held his hands pressed against his stomach, and blood was flowing from under them. When he reached the King, he fell fainting on the ground moaning feebly. The King and the hermit unfastened the man's clothing. There was a large wound in his stomach. The King washed it as best he could, and bandaged it with his handkerchief and with a towel the hermit had. But the blood would not stop flowing, and the King again and again removed the bandage soaked with warm blood, and washed and rebandaged the wound. When at last the blood ceased flowing, the man revived and asked for something to drink. The King brought fresh water and gave it to him. Meanwhile the sun had set, and it had become cool. So the King, with the hermit's help, carried the wounded man into the hut and laid him on the bed. Lying on the bed the man closed his eyes and was quiet; but the King was so tired with his walk and with the work he had done, that he crouched down on the threshold, and also fell asleep—so soundly that he slept all through the short summer night. When he awoke in the morning, it was long before he could remember where he was, or who was the strange bearded man lying on the bed and gazing intently at him with shining eyes.

"Forgive me!" said the bearded man in a weak voice, when he saw that the King was awake and was looking at him.

"I do not know you, and have nothing to forgive you for," said the King.

"You do not know me, but I know you. I am that enemy of yours who swore to revenge himself on you, because you executed his brother and seized his property. I knew you had gone alone to see the hermit, and I resolved to kill you on your way back. But the day passed and you did not return. So I came out from my ambush to find you, and I came upon your bodyguard, and they recognized me, and wounded me. I escaped from them, but should have bled to death had you not dressed my wound. I wished to kill you, and you have saved my life. Now, if I live, and if you wish it, I will serve you as your most faithful slave, and will bid my sons do the same. Forgive me!"

The King was very glad to have made peace with his enemy so easily, and to have gained him for a friend, and he not only forgave him, but said he would send his servants and his own physician to attend him, and promised to restore his property.

Having taken leave of the wounded man, the King went out into the porch and looked around for the hermit. Before going away he wished once more to beg an answer to the questions he had put. The hermit was outside, on his knees, sowing seeds in the beds that had been dug the day before.

The King approached him, and said:

"For the last time, I pray you to answer my questions, wise man."

"You have already been answered!" said the hermit still crouching on his thin legs, and looking up at the King, who stood before him.

"How answered? What do you mean?" asked the King.

"Do you not see," replied the hermit. "If you had not pitied my weakness yesterday, and had not dug those beds for me, but had gone your way, that man would have attacked you, and you would have repented of not having stayed with me. So the most important time was when you were digging the beds; and I was the most important man; and to do me good was your most important business. Afterwards when that man ran to us, the most important time was when you were attending to him, for if you had not bound up his wounds he would have died without having made peace with you. So he was the most important man, and what you did for him was your most important business. Remember then: there is only one time that is important—Now! It is the most important time because it is the only time when we have any power. The most necessary man is he with whom you are, for no man knows whether he will ever have dealings with anyone else: and the most important affair is, to do him good, because for that purpose alone was man sent into this life!"

AFTER TWENTY YEARS

O. Henry

Published in *The Four Million* in 1906

The policeman on the beat moved up the avenue impressively. The impressiveness was habitual and not for show, for spectators were few. The time was barely 10 o'clock at night, but chilly gusts of wind with a taste of rain in them had well nigh de-peopled the streets.

Trying doors as he went, twirling his club with many intricate and artful movements, turning now and then to cast his watchful eye adown the pacific thoroughfare, the officer, with his stalwart form and slight swagger, made a fine picture of a guardian of the peace. The vicinity was one that kept early hours. Now and then you might see the lights of a cigar store or of an all-night lunch counter; but the majority of the doors belonged to business places that had long since been closed.

When about midway of a certain block the policeman suddenly slowed his walk. In the doorway of a darkened hardware store a man leaned, with an unlighted cigar in his mouth. As the policeman walked up to him the man spoke up quickly.

"It's all right, officer," he said, reassuringly. "I'm just waiting for a friend. It's an appointment made twenty years ago. Sounds a little funny to you, doesn't it? Well, I'll explain if you'd like to make certain it's all straight. About that long ago there used to be a restaurant where this store stands—'Big Joe' Brady's restaurant."

"Until five years ago," said the policeman. "It was torn down then."

The man in the doorway struck a match and lit his cigar. The light showed a pale, square-jawed face with keen eyes, and a little white scar near his right eyebrow. His scarfpin was a large diamond, oddly set.

"Twenty years ago tonight," said the man, "I dined here at 'Big Joe' Brady's with Jimmy Wells, my best chum, and the finest chap in the world. He and I were raised here in New York, just like two brothers, together. I was eighteen and Jimmy was twenty. The next morning I was to start for the

West to make my fortune. You couldn't have dragged Jimmy out of New York; he thought it was the only place on earth. Well, we agreed that night that we would meet here again exactly twenty years from that date and time, no matter what our conditions might be or from what distance we might have to come. We figured that in twenty years each of us ought to have our destiny worked out and our fortunes made, whatever they were going to be."

"It sounds pretty interesting," said the policeman. "Rather a long time between meets, though, it seems to me. Haven't you heard from your friend since you left?"

"Well, yes, for a time we corresponded," said the other. "But after a year or two we lost track of each other. You see, the West is a pretty big proposition, and I kept hustling around over it pretty lively. But I know Jimmy will meet me here if he's alive, for he always was the truest, stanchest old chap in the world. He'll never forget. I came a thousand miles to stand in this door tonight, and it's worth it if my old partner turns up."

The waiting man pulled out a handsome watch, the lids of it set with small diamonds.

"Three minutes to ten," he announced. "It was exactly ten o'clock when we parted here at the restaurant door."

"Did pretty well out West, didn't you?" asked the policeman.

"You bet! I hope Jimmy has done half as well. He was a kind of plodder, though, good fellow as he was. I've had to compete with some of the sharpest wits going to get my pile. A man gets in a groove in New York. It takes the West to put a razor-edge on him."

The policeman twirled his club and took a step or two.

"I'll be on my way. Hope your friend comes around all right. Going to call time on him sharp?"

"I should say not!" said the other. "I'll give him half an hour at least. If Jimmy is alive on earth he'll be here by that time. So long, officer."

"Good night, sir," said the policeman, passing on along his beat, trying doors as he went.

There was now a fine, cold drizzle falling, and the wind had risen from its uncertain puffs into a steady blow. The few foot passengers astir in that quarter hurried dismally and silently along with coat collars turned high and pocketed hands. And in the door of the hardware store the man who had come a thousand miles to fill an appointment, uncertain almost to absurdity, with the friend of his youth, smoked his cigar and waited.

About twenty minutes he waited, and then a tall man in a long overcoat, with collar turned up to his ears, hurried across from the opposite side of the street. He went directly to the waiting man.

"Is that you, Bob?" he asked, doubtfully.

"Is that you, Jimmy Wells?" cried the man in the door.

"Bless my heart!" exclaimed the new arrival, grasping both the other's hands with his own. "It's Bob, sure as fate. I was certain I'd find you here if you were still in existence. Well, well, well!—twenty years is a long time. The old restaurant's gone, Bob; I wish it had lasted, so we could have had another dinner there. How has the West treated you, old man?"

"Bully; it has given me everything I asked it for. You've changed lots, Jimmy. I never thought you were so tall by two or three inches."

"Oh, I grew a bit after I was twenty."

"Doing well in New York, Jimmy?"

"Moderately. I have a position in one of the city departments. Come on, Bob; we'll go around to a place I know of, and have a good long talk about old times."

The two men started up the street, arm in arm. The man from the West, his egotism enlarged by success, was beginning to outline the history of his career. The other, submerged in his overcoat, listened with interest.

At the corner stood a drug store, brilliant with electric lights. When they came into this glare each of them turned simultaneously to gaze upon the other's face.

The man from the West stopped suddenly and released his arm.

"You're not Jimmy Wells," he snapped. "Twenty years is a long time, but not long enough to change a man's nose from a Roman to a pug."

"It sometimes changes a good man into a bad one," said the tall man. "You've been under arrest for ten minutes, 'Silky' Bob. Chicago thinks you may have dropped over our way and wires us she wants to have a chat with you. Going quietly, are you? That's sensible. Now, before we go on to the station here's a note I was asked to hand you. You may read it here at the window. It's from Patrolman Wells."

The man from the West unfolded the little piece of paper handed him. His hand was steady when he began to read, but it trembled a little by the time he had finished. The note was rather short.

Bob: I was at the appointed place on time. When you struck the match to light your cigar I saw it was the face of the man wanted in Chicago. Somehow I couldn't do it myself, so I went around and got a plain clothes man to do the job.

Jimmy

A MIDSUMMER NIGHT'S DREAM

E. Nesbit

Published in *Beautiful Stories from Shakespeare* in 1907

Hermia and Lysander were lovers; but Hermia's father wished her to marry another man, named Demetrius. Now, in Athens, where they lived, there was a wicked law, by which any girl who refused to marry according to her father's wishes, might be put to death. Hermia's father was so angry with her for refusing to do as he wished, that he actually brought her before the Duke of Athens to ask that she might be killed, if she still refused to obey him. The Duke gave her four days to think about it, and, at the end of that time, if she still refused to marry Demetrius, she would have to die.

Lysander of course was nearly mad with grief, and the best thing to do seemed to him for Hermia to run away to his aunt's house at a place beyond the reach of that cruel law; and there he would come to her and marry her. But before she started, she told her friend, Helena, what she was going to do.

Helena had been Demetrius' sweetheart long before his marriage with Hermia had been thought of, and being very silly, like all jealous people, she could not see that it was not poor Hermia's fault that Demetrius wished to marry her instead of his own lady, Helena. She knew that if she told Demetrius that Hermia was going, as she was, to the wood outside Athens, he would follow her, "and I can follow him, and at least I shall see him," she said to herself. So she went to him, and betrayed her friend's secret.

Now this wood where Lysander was to meet Hermia, and where the other two had decided to follow them, was full of fairies, as most woods are, if one only had the eyes to see them, and in this wood on this night were the King and Queen of the fairies, Oberon and Titania. Now fairies are very wise people, but now and then they can be quite as foolish as mortal folk. Oberon and Titania, who might have been as happy as the days were long, had thrown away all their joy in a foolish quarrel. They never met without saying disagreeable things to each other, and scolded each other so dreadfully that all their little fairy followers, for fear, would creep into acorn cups and hide them there.

So, instead of keeping one happy Court and dancing all night through in the moonlight as is fairies' use, the King with his attendants wandered through one part of the wood, while the Queen with hers kept state in another. And the cause of all this trouble was a little Indian boy whom Titania had taken to be one of her followers. Oberon wanted the child to follow him and be one of his fairy knights; but the Queen would not give him up.

On this night, in a mossy moonlit glade, the King and Queen of the fairies met.

"Ill met by moonlight, proud Titania," said the King.

"What! jealous, Oberon?" answered the Queen. "You spoil everything with your quarrelling. Come, fairies, let us leave him. I am not friends with him now."

"It rests with you to make up the quarrel," said the King.

"Give me that little Indian boy, and I will again be your humble servant and suitor."

"Set your mind at rest," said the Queen. "Your whole fairy kingdom buys not that boy from me. Come, fairies."

And she and her train rode off down the moonbeams.

"Well, go your ways," said Oberon. "But I'll be even with you before you leave this wood."

Then Oberon called his favourite fairy, Puck. Puck was the spirit of mischief. He used to slip into the dairies and take the cream away, and get into the churn so that the butter would not come, and turn the beer sour, and lead people out of their way on dark nights and then laugh at them, and tumble people's stools from under them when they were going to sit down, and upset their hot ale over their chins when they were going to drink.

"Now," said Oberon to this little sprite, "fetch me the flower called Love-in-idleness. The juice of that little purple flower laid on the eyes of those who sleep will make them, when they wake, to love the first thing they see. I will put some of the juice of that flower on my Titania's eyes, and when she wakes she will love the first thing she sees, were it lion, bear, or wolf, or bull, or meddling monkey, or a busy ape."

While Puck was gone, Demetrius passed through the glade followed by poor Helena, and still she told him how she loved him and reminded him of all his promises, and still he told her that he did not and could not love her, and that his promises were nothing. Oberon was sorry for poor Helena, and when Puck returned with the flower, he bade him follow Demetrius and put some of the juice on his eyes, so that he might love Helena when he woke and looked on her, as much as she loved him. So Puck set off, and wandering through the wood found, not Demetrius, but Lysander, on whose eyes he put the juice; but when Lysander woke, he saw not his own Hermia, but Helena, who was walking through the wood looking for the cruel Demetrius; and directly he saw her he loved her and left his own lady, under the spell of the purple flower.

When Hermia woke she found Lysander gone, and wandered about the wood trying to find him. Puck went back and told Oberon what he had done, and Oberon soon found that he had made a mistake, and set about looking for Demetrius, and having found him, put some of the juice on his eyes. And the first thing Demetrius saw when he woke was also Helena. So now Demetrius and Lysander were both following her through the wood, and it was Hermia's turn to follow her lover as Helena had done before. The end of it was that Helena and Hermia began to quarrel, and Demetrius and Lysander went off to fight. Oberon was very sorry to see his kind scheme to help these lovers turn out so badly. So he said to Puck:

"These two young men are going to fight. You must overhang the night with drooping fog, and lead them so astray, that one will never find the other. When they are tired out, they will fall asleep. Then drop this other herb on Lysander's eyes. That will give him his old sight and his old love. Then each man will have the lady who loves him, and they will all think that this has been only a Midsummer Night's Dream. Then when this is done, all will be well with them."

So Puck went and did as he was told, and when the two had fallen asleep without meeting each other, Puck poured the juice on Lysander's eyes, and said:

"When thou wakest,
Thou takest

True delight
In the sight
Of thy former lady's eye:
Jack shall have Jill;
Nought shall go ill."

Meanwhile Oberon found Titania asleep on a bank where grew wild thyme, oxlips, and violets, and woodbine, musk-roses and eglantine. There Titania always slept a part of the night, wrapped in the enamelled skin of a snake. Oberon stooped over her and laid the juice on her eyes, saying:

"What thou seest when thou wake,
Do it for thy true love take."

Now, it happened that when Titania woke the first thing she saw was a stupid clown, one of a party of players who had come out into the wood to rehearse their play. This clown had met with Puck, who had clapped an ass's head on his shoulders so that it looked as if it grew there. Directly Titania woke and saw this dreadful monster, she said, "What angel is this? Are you as wise as you are beautiful?"

"If I am wise enough to find my way out of this wood, that's enough for me," said the foolish clown.

"Do not desire to go out of the wood," said Titania. The spell of the love-juice was on her, and to her the clown seemed the most beautiful and delightful creature on all the earth. "I love you," she went on. "Come with me, and I will give you fairies to attend on you."

So she called four fairies, whose names were Peaseblossom, Cobweb, Moth, and Mustardseed.

"You must attend this gentleman," said the Queen. "Feed him with apricots and dewberries, purple grapes, green figs, and mulberries. Steal honey-bags for him from the bumble-bees, and with the wings of painted butterflies fan the moonbeams from his sleeping eyes."

"I will," said one of the fairies, and all the others said, "I will."

"Now, sit down with me," said the Queen to the clown, "and let me stroke your dear cheeks, and stick musk-roses in your smooth, sleek head, and kiss your fair large ears, my gentle joy."

"Where's Peaseblossom?" asked the clown with the ass's head. He did not care much about the Queen's affection, but he was very proud of having fairies to wait on him. "Ready," said Peaseblossom.

"Scratch my head, Peaseblossom," said the clown. "Where's Cobweb?" "Ready," said Cobweb.

"Kill me," said the clown, "the red bumble-bee on the top of the thistle yonder, and bring me the honey-bag. Where's Mustardseed?"

"Ready," said Mustardseed.

"Oh, I want nothing," said the clown. "Only just help Cobweb to scratch. I must go to the barber's, for methinks I am marvelous hairy about the face."

"Would you like anything to eat?" said the fairy Queen.

"I should like some good dry oats," said the clown—for his donkey's head made him desire donkey's food—"and some hay to follow."

"Shall some of my fairies fetch you new nuts from the squirrel's house?" asked the Queen.

"I'd rather have a handful or two of good dried peas," said the clown. "But please don't let any of your people disturb me; I am going to sleep."

Then said the Queen, "And I will wind thee in my arms."

And so when Oberon came along he found his beautiful Queen lavishing kisses and endearments on a clown with a donkey's head.

And before he released her from the enchantment, he persuaded her to give him the little Indian boy he so much desired to have. Then he took pity on her, and threw some juice of the disenchanting flower on her pretty eyes; and then in a moment she saw plainly the donkey-headed clown she had been loving, and knew how foolish she had been.

Oberon took off the ass's head from the clown, and left him to finish his sleep with his own silly head lying on the thyme and violets.

Thus all was made plain and straight again. Oberon and Titania loved each other more than ever. Demetrius thought of no one but Helena, and Helena had never had any thought of anyone but Demetrius.

As for Hermia and Lysander, they were as loving a couple as you could meet in a day's march, even through a fairy wood.

So the four mortal lovers went back to Athens and were married; and the fairy King and Queen live happily together in that very wood at this very day.

HAMLET

E. Nesbit

Published in *Beautiful Stories from Shakespeare* in 1907

Hamlet was the only son of the King of Denmark. He loved his father and mother dearly—and was happy in the love of a sweet lady named Ophelia. Her father, Polonius, was the King's Chamberlain.

While Hamlet was away studying at Wittenberg, his father died. Young Hamlet hastened home in great grief to hear that a serpent had stung the King, and that he was dead. The young Prince had loved his father so tenderly that you may judge what he felt when he found that the Queen, before yet the King had been laid in the ground a month, had determined to marry again—and to marry the dead King's brother.

Hamlet refused to put off mourning for the wedding.

"It is not only the black I wear on my body," he said, "that proves my loss. I wear mourning in my heart for my dead father. His son at least remembers him, and grieves still."

Then said Claudius the King's brother, "This grief is unreasonable. Of course you must sorrow at the loss of your father, but—"

"Ah," said Hamlet, bitterly, "I cannot in one little month forget those I love."

With that the Queen and Claudius left him, to make merry over their wedding, forgetting the poor good King who had been so kind to them both.

And Hamlet, left alone, began to wonder and to question as to what he ought to do. For he could not believe the story about the snake-bite. It seemed to him all too plain that the wicked Claudius had killed the King, so as to get the crown and marry the Queen. Yet he had no proof, and could not accuse Claudius.

And while he was thus thinking came Horatio, a fellow student of his, from Wittenberg.

"What brought you here?" asked Hamlet, when he had greeted his friend kindly.

"I came, my lord, to see your father's funeral."

"I think it was to see my mother's wedding," said Hamlet, bitterly. "My father! We shall not look upon his like again."

"My lord," answered Horatio, "I think I saw him yesternight."

Then, while Hamlet listened in surprise, Horatio told how he, with two gentlemen of the guard, had seen the King's ghost on the battlements. Hamlet went that night, and true enough, at midnight, the ghost of the King, in the armour he had been wont to wear, appeared on the battlements in the chill moonlight. Hamlet was a brave youth. Instead of running away from the ghost he spoke to it—and when it beckoned him he followed it to a quiet place, and there the ghost told him that what he had suspected was true. The wicked Claudius had indeed killed his good brother the King, by dropping poison into his ear as he slept in his orchard in the afternoon.

"And you," said the ghost, "must avenge this cruel murder—on my wicked brother. But do nothing against the Queen—for I have loved her, and she is your mother. Remember me."

Then seeing the morning approach, the ghost vanished.

"Now," said Hamlet, "there is nothing left but revenge. Remember thee—I will remember nothing else—books, pleasure, youth—let all go—and your commands alone live on my brain."

So when his friends came back he made them swear to keep the secret of the ghost, and then went in from the battlements, now gray with mingled dawn and moonlight, to think how he might best avenge his murdered father.

The shock of seeing and hearing his father's ghost made him feel almost mad, and for fear that his uncle might notice that he was not himself, he determined to hide his mad longing for revenge under a pretended madness in other matters.

And when he met Ophelia, who loved him—and to whom he had given gifts, and letters, and many loving words—he behaved so wildly to her, that she could not but think him mad. For she loved him so that she could not believe he would be as cruel as this, unless he were quite mad. So she told her father, and showed him a pretty letter from Hamlet. And in the letter was much folly, and this pretty verse—

"Doubt that the stars are fire;
Doubt that the sun doth move;

Doubt truth to be a liar;
But never doubt I love."

And from that time everyone believed that the cause of Hamlet's supposed madness was love.

Poor Hamlet was very unhappy. He longed to obey his father's ghost—and yet he was too gentle and kindly to wish to kill another man, even his father's murderer. And sometimes he wondered whether, after all, the ghost spoke truly.

Just at this time some actors came to the Court, and Hamlet ordered them to perform a certain play before the King and Queen. Now, this play was the story of a man *who had been murdered in his garden by a near relation, who afterwards married the dead man's wife.*

You may imagine the feelings of the wicked King, as he sat on his throne, with the Queen beside him and all his Court around, and saw, acted on the stage, the very wickedness that he had himself done. And when, in the play, the wicked relation poured poison into the ear of the sleeping man, the wicked Claudius suddenly rose, and staggered from the room—the Queen and others following.

Then said Hamlet to his friends—

"Now I am sure the ghost spoke true. For if Claudius had not done this murder, he could not have been so distressed to see it in a play."

Now the Queen sent for Hamlet, by the King's desire, to scold him for his conduct during the play, and for other matters; and Claudius, wishing to know exactly what happened, told old Polonius to hide himself behind the hangings in the Queen's room. And as they talked, the Queen got frightened at Hamlet's rough, strange words, and cried for help, and Polonius behind the curtain cried out too. Hamlet, thinking it was the King who was hidden there, thrust with his sword at the hangings, and killed, not the King, but poor old Polonius.

So now Hamlet had offended his uncle and his mother, and by bad hap killed his true love's father.

"Oh! what a rash and bloody deed is this," cried the Queen.

And Hamlet answered bitterly, "Almost as bad as to kill a king, and marry his brother." Then Hamlet told the Queen plainly all his thoughts and how he knew of the murder, and begged her, at least, to have no more friendship or kindness of the base Claudius, who had killed the good

King. And as they spoke the King's ghost again appeared before Hamlet, but the Queen could not see it. So when the ghost had gone, they parted.

When the Queen told Claudius what had passed, and how Polonius was dead, he said, "This shows plainly that Hamlet is mad, and since he has killed the Chancellor, it is for his own safety that we must carry out our plan, and send him away to England."

So Hamlet was sent, under charge of two courtiers who served the King, and these bore letters to the English Court, requiring that Hamlet should be put to death. But Hamlet had the good sense to get at these letters, and put in others instead, with the names of the two courtiers who were so ready to betray him. Then, as the vessel went to England, Hamlet escaped on board a pirate ship, and the two wicked courtiers left him to his fate, and went on to meet theirs.

Hamlet hurried home, but in the meantime a dreadful thing had happened. Poor pretty Ophelia, having lost her lover and her father, lost her wits too, and went in sad madness about the Court, with straws, and weeds, and flowers in her hair, singing strange scraps of songs, and talking poor, foolish, pretty talk with no heart of meaning to it. And one day, coming to a stream where willows grew, she tried to bang a flowery garland on a willow, and fell into the water with all her flowers, and so died.

And Hamlet had loved her, though his plan of seeming madness had made him hide it; and when he came back, he found the King and Queen, and the Court, weeping at the funeral of his dear love and lady.

Ophelia's brother, Laertes, had also just come to Court to ask justice for the death of his father, old Polonius; and now, wild with grief, he leaped into his sister's grave, to clasp her in his arms once more.

"I loved her more than forty thousand brothers," cried Hamlet, and leapt into the grave after him, and they fought till they were parted.

Afterwards Hamlet begged Laertes to forgive him.

"I could not bear," he said, "that any, even a brother, should seem to love her more than I."

But the wicked Claudius would not let them be friends. He told Laertes how Hamlet had killed old Polonius, and between them they made a plot to slay Hamlet by treachery.

Laertes challenged him to a fencing match, and all the Court were present. Hamlet had the blunt foil always used in fencing, but Laertes had prepared for himself a sword, sharp, and tipped with poison. And the wicked King had made ready a bowl of poisoned wine, which he meant to give poor Hamlet when he should grow warm with the sword play, and should call for drink.

So Laertes and Hamlet fought, and Laertes, after some fencing, gave Hamlet a sharp sword thrust. Hamlet, angry at this treachery—for they had been fencing, not as men fight, but as they play—closed with Laertes in a struggle; both dropped their swords, and when they picked them up again, Hamlet, without noticing it, had exchanged his own blunt sword for Laertes' sharp and poisoned one. And with one thrust of it he pierced Laertes, who fell dead by his own treachery.

At this moment the Queen cried out, "The drink, the drink! Oh, my dear Hamlet! I am poisoned!"

She had drunk of the poisoned bowl the King had prepared for Hamlet, and the King saw the Queen, whom, wicked as he was, he really loved, fall dead by his means.

Then Ophelia being dead, and Polonius, and the Queen, and Laertes, and the two courtiers who had been sent to England, Hamlet at last found courage to do the ghost's bidding and avenge his father's murder—which, if he had braced up his heart to do long before, all these lives had been spared, and none had suffered but the wicked King, who well deserved to die.

Hamlet, his heart at last being great enough to do the deed he ought, turned the poisoned sword on the false King.

"Then—venom—do thy work!" he cried, and the King died.

So Hamlet in the end kept the promise he had made his father. And all being now accomplished, he himself died. And those who stood by saw him die, with prayers and tears, for his friends and his people loved him with their whole hearts. Thus ends the tragic tale of Hamlet, Prince of Denmark.

THE COMEDY OF ERRORS

E. Nesbit

Published in *Beautiful Stories from Shakespeare* in 1907

Aegeon was a merchant of Syracuse, which is a seaport in Sicily. His wife was Aemilia, and they were very happy until Aegeon's manager died, and he was obliged to go by himself to a place called Epidamnum on the Adriatic. As soon as she could Aemilia followed him, and after they had been together some time two baby boys were born to them. The babies were exactly alike; even when they were dressed differently they looked the same.

And now you must believe a very strange thing. At the same inn where these children were born, and on the same day, two baby boys were born to a much poorer couple than Aemilia and Aegeon; so poor, indeed, were the parents of these twins that they sold them to the parents of the other twins.

Aemilia was eager to show her children to her friends in Syracuse, and in treacherous weather she and Aegeon and the four babies sailed homewards.

They were still far from Syracuse when their ship sprang a leak, and the crew left it in a body by the only boat, caring little what became of their passengers.

Aemilia fastened one of her children to a mast and tied one of the slave-children to him; Aegeon followed her example with the remaining children. Then the parents secured themselves to the same masts, and hoped for safety.

The ship, however, suddenly struck a rock and was split in two, and Aemilia, and the two children whom she had tied, floated away from Aegeon and the other children. Aemilia and her charges were picked up by some people of Epidamnum, but some fishermen of Corinth took the babies from her by force, and she returned to Epidanmum alone, and very miserable. Afterwards she settled in Ephesus, a famous town in Asia Minor.

Aegeon and his charges were also saved; and, more fortunate than Aemilia, he was able to return to Syracuse and keep them till they were eighteen. His own child he called Antipholus, and the slavechild he called Dromio; and, strangely enough, these were the names given to the children who floated away from him.

At the age of eighteen the son who was with Aegeon grew restless with a desire to find his brother. Aegeon let him depart with his servant, and the young men are henceforth known as Antipholus of Syracuse and Dromio of Syracuse.

Let alone, Aegeon found his home too dreary to dwell in, and travelled for five years. He did not, during his absence, learn all the news of Syracuse, or he would never have gone to Ephesus.

As it was, his melancholy wandering ceased in that town, where he was arrested almost as soon as he arrived. He then found that the Duke of Syracuse had been acting in so tyrannical a manner to Ephesians unlucky enough to fall into his hands, that the Government of Ephesus had angrily passed a law which punished by death or a fine of a thousand pounds any Syracusan who should come to Ephesus. Aegeon was brought before Solinus, Duke of Ephesus, who told him that he must die or pay a thousand pounds before the end of the day.

You will think there was fate in this when I tell you that the children who were kidnapped by the fishermen of Corinth were now citizens of Ephesus, whither they had been brought by Duke Menaphon, an uncle of Duke Solinus. They will henceforth be called Antipholus of Ephesus and Dromio of Ephesus.

Moreover, on the very day when Aegeon was arrested, Antipholus of Syracuse landed in Ephesus and pretended that he came from Epidamnum in order to avoid a penalty. He handed his money to his servant Dromio of Syracuse, and bade him take it to the Centaur Inn and remain there till he came.

In less than ten minutes he was met on the Mart by Dromio of Ephesus, his brother's slave, and immediately mistook him for his own Dromio. "Why are you back so soon? Where did you leave the money?" asked Antipholus of Syracuse.

This Dromio knew of no money except sixpence, which he had received on the previous Wednesday and given to the saddler; but he did know that his mistress was annoyed because his master was not in to dinner, and he asked Antipholus of Syracuse to go to a house called The Phoenix without delay. His speech angered the hearer, who would have beaten him if he had not fled. Antipholus of Syracuse them went to The Centaur, found that his gold had been deposited there, and walked out of the inn.

He was wandering about Ephesus when two beautiful ladies signalled to him with their hands. They were sisters, and their names were Adriana and Luciana. Adriana was the wife of his brother Antipholus of Ephesus, and she had made up her mind, from the strange account given her by Dromio of Ephesus, that her husband preferred another woman to his wife. "Ay, you may look as if you did not know me," she said to the man who was really her brother-in-law, "but I can remember when no words were sweet unless I said them, no meat flavoursome unless I carved it."

"Is it I you address?" said Antipholus of Syracuse stiffly. "I do not know you."

"Fie, brother," said Luciana. "You know perfectly well that she sent Dromio to you to bid you come to dinner;" and Adriana said, "Come, come; I have been made a fool of long enough. My truant husband shall dine with me and confess his silly pranks and be forgiven."

They were determined ladies, and Antipholus of Syracuse grew weary of disputing with them, and followed them obediently to The Phoenix, where a very late "mid-day" dinner awaited them.

They were at dinner when Antipholus of Ephesus and his slave Dromio demanded admittance. "Maud, Bridget, Marian, Cecily, Gillian, Ginn!" shouted Dromio of Ephesus, who knew all his fellow-servants' names by heart.

From within came the reply, "Fool, dray-horse, coxcomb, idiot!" It was Dromio of Syracuse unconsciously insulting his brother.

Master and man did their best to get in, short of using a crowbar, and finally went away; but Antipholus of Ephesus felt so annoyed with his wife that he decided to give a gold chain which he had promised her, to another woman.

Inside The Phoenix, Luciana, who believed Antipholus of Syracuse to be her sister's husband, attempted, by a discourse in rhyme, when alone with him, to make him kinder to Adriana. In reply he told her that he was not married, but that he loved her so much that, if Luciana were a mermaid, he would gladly lie on the sea if he might feel beneath him her floating golden hair.

Luciana was shocked and left him, and reported his lovemaking to Adriana, who said that her husband was old and ugly, and not fit to be seen or heard, though secretly she was very fond of him.

Antipholus of Syracuse soon received a visitor in the shape of Angelo the goldsmith, of whom Antipholus of Ephesus had ordered the chain which he had promised his wife and intended to give to another woman.

The goldsmith handed the chain to Antipholus of Syracuse, and treated his "I bespoke it not" as mere fun, so that the puzzled merchant took the chain as good-humouredly as he had partaken of Adriana's dinner. He offered payment, but Angelo foolishly said he would call again.

The consequence was that Angelo was without money when a creditor of the sort that stands no nonsense, threatened him with arrest unless he paid his debt immediately. This creditor had brought a police officer with him, and Angelo was relieved to see Antipholus of Ephesus coming out of the house where he had been dining because he had been locked out of The Phoenix. Bitter was Angelo's dismay when Antipholus denied receipt of the chain. Angelo could have sent his mother to prison if she had said that, and he gave Antipholus of Ephesus in charge.

At this moment up came Dromio of Syracuse and told the wrong Antipholus that he had shipped his goods, and that a favourable wind was blowing. To the ears of Antipholus of Ephesus this talk was simple nonsense. He would gladly have beaten the slave, but contented himself with crossly telling him to hurry to Adriana and bid her send to her arrested husband a purse of money which she would find in his desk.

Though Adriana was furious with her husband because she thought he had been making love to her sister, she did not prevent Luciana from getting the purse, and she bade Dromio of Syracuse bring home his master immediately.

Unfortunately, before Dromio could reach the police station he met his real master, who had never been arrested, and did not understand what he meant by offering him a purse. Antipholus of Syracuse was further surprised when a lady whom he did not know asked him for a chain that he had promised her. She was, of course, the lady with whom Antipholus of Ephesus had dined when his brother was occupying his place at table. "Avaunt, thou witch!" was the answer which, to her astonishment, she received.

Meanwhile Antipholus of Ephesus waited vainly for the money which was to have released him. Never a good-tempered man, he was crazy with anger when Dromio of Ephesus, who, of course, had not been instructed to fetch a purse, appeared with nothing more useful than a rope. He beat the slave in the street despite the remonstrance of the police officer; and his temper did not mend when Adriana, Luciana, and a doctor arrived under the impression that he was mad and must have his pulse felt. He raged so much that men came forward to bind him. But the kindness of Adriana spared him this shame. She promised to pay the sum demanded of him, and asked the doctor to lead him to The Phoenix.

Angelo's merchant creditor being paid, the two were friendly again, and might soon have been seen chatting before an abbey about the odd behaviour of Antipholus of Ephesus. "Softly," said the merchant at last, "that's he, I think."

It was not; it was Antipholus of Syracuse with his servant Dromio, and he wore Angelo's chain round his neck! The reconciled pair fairly pounced upon him to know what he meant by denying the receipt of the chain he had the impudence to wear. Antipholus of Syracuse lost his temper, and drew his sword, and at that moment Adriana and several others appeared. "Hold!" shouted the careful wife. "Hurt him not; he is mad. Take his sword away. Bind him—and Dromio too."

Dromio of Syracuse did not wish to be bound, and he said to his master, "Run, master! Into that abbey, quick, or we shall be robbed!"

They accordingly retreated into the abbey.

Adriana, Luciana, and a crowd remained outside, and the Abbess came out, and said, "People, why do you gather here?"

"To fetch my poor distracted husband," replied Adriana.

Angelo and the merchant remarked that they had not known that he was mad.

Adriana then told the Abbess rather too much about her wifely worries, for the Abbess received the idea that Adriana was a shrew, and that if her husband was distracted he had better not return to her for the present.

Adriana determined, therefore, to complain to Duke Solinus, and, lo and behold! a minute afterwards the great man appeared with officers and two others. The others were Aegeon and the headsman. The thousand marks had not been found, and Aegeon's fate seemed sealed.

Ere the Duke could pass the abbey Adriana knelt before him, and told a woeful tale of a mad husband rushing about stealing jewellery and drawing his sword, adding that the Abbess refused to allow her to lead him home.

The Duke bade the Abbess be summoned, and no sooner had he given the order than a servant from The Phoenix ran to Adriana with the tale that his master had singed off the doctor's beard.

"Nonsense!" said Adriana, "he's in the abbey."

"As sure as I live I speak the truth," said the servant.

Antipholus of Syracuse had not come out of the abbey, before his brother of Ephesus prostrated himself in front of the Duke, exclaiming, "Justice, most gracious Duke, against that woman." He pointed to Adriana. "She has treated another man like her husband in my own house."

Even while he was speaking Aegeon said, "Unless I am delirious, I see my son Antipholus."

No one noticed him, and Antipholus of Ephesus went on to say how the doctor, whom he called "a threadbare juggler," had been one of a gang who tied him to his slave Dromio, and thrust them into a vault whence he had escaped by gnawing through his bonds.

The Duke could not understand how the same man who spoke to him was seen to go into the abbey, and he was still wondering when Aegeon asked Antipholus of Ephesus if he was not his son. He replied, "I never saw my father in my life;" but so deceived was Aegeon by his likeness to the brother whom he had brought up, that he said, "Thou art ashamed to acknowledge me in misery."

Soon, however, the Abbess advanced with Antipholus of Syracuse and Dromio of Syracuse.

Then cried Adriana, "I see two husbands or mine eyes deceive me;" and Antipholus, espying his father, said, "Thou art Aegeon or his ghost."

It was a day of surprises, for the Abbess said, "I will free that man by paying his fine, and gain my husband whom I lost. Speak, Aegeon, for I am thy wife Aemilia."

The Duke was touched. "He is free without a fine," he said.

So Aegeon and Aemilia were reunited, and Adriana and her husband reconciled; but no one was happier than Antipholus of Syracuse, who, in the Duke's presence, went to Luciana and said, "I told you I loved you. Will you be my wife?"

Her answer was given by a look, and therefore is not written.

The two Dromios were glad to think they would receive no more beatings.

TO BUILD A FIRE

Jack London

Published in *Lost Face* in 1910

Day had broken cold and grey, exceedingly cold and grey, when the man turned aside from the main Yukon trail and climbed the high earth-bank, where a dim and little-travelled trail led eastward through the fat spruce timberland. It was a steep bank, and he paused for breath at the top, excusing the act to himself by looking at his watch. It was nine o'clock. There was no sun nor hint of sun, though there was not a cloud in the sky. It was a clear day, and yet there seemed an intangible pall over the face of things, a subtle gloom that made the day dark, and that was due to the absence of sun. This fact did not worry the man. He was used to the lack of sun. It had been days since he had seen the sun, and he knew that a few more days must pass before that cheerful orb, due south, would just peep above the sky-line and dip immediately from view.

The man flung a look back along the way he had come. The Yukon lay a mile wide and hidden under three feet of ice. On top of this ice were as many feet of snow. It was all pure white, rolling in gentle undulations where the ice-jams of the freeze-up had formed. North and south, as far as his eye could see, it was unbroken white, save for a dark hair-line that curved and twisted from around the spruce-covered island to the south, and that curved and twisted away into the north, where it disappeared behind another spruce-covered island. This dark hair-line was the trail—the main trail—that led south five hundred miles to the Chilcoot Pass, Dyea, and salt water; and that led north seventy miles to Dawson, and still on to the north a thousand miles to Nulato, and finally to St. Michael on Bering Sea, a thousand miles and half a thousand more.

But all this—the mysterious, far-reaching hairline trail, the absence of sun from the sky, the tremendous cold, and the strangeness and weirdness of it all—made no impression on the man. It was not because he was long used to it. He was a new-comer in the land, a *chechaquo*, and this was his first winter. The trouble with him was that he was without imagination. He was quick and alert in the things of life, but only in the things, and not in the significances. Fifty degrees below zero meant eighty odd degrees of frost. Such fact impressed him as being cold and uncomfortable, and that was all. It did not lead him to meditate upon his frailty as a creature of temperature, and upon man's frailty in general, able only to live within certain narrow limits of heat and cold; and from there on it did not lead him to the conjectural field of immortality and man's place in the universe. Fifty degrees below zero stood for a bite of frost that hurt and that must be guarded against by the use of mittens, ear-flaps, warm moccasins, and thick socks. Fifty degrees below zero was to him just precisely fifty degrees below zero. That there should be anything more to it than that was a thought that never entered his head.

As he turned to go on, he spat speculatively. There was a sharp, explosive crackle that startled him. He spat again. And again, in the air, before it could fall to the snow, the spittle crackled. He knew that at fifty below spittle crackled on the snow, but this spittle had crackled in the air. Undoubtedly it was colder than fifty below—how much colder he did not know. But the temperature did not matter. He was bound for the old claim on the left fork of Henderson Creek, where the boys were already. They had come over across the divide from the Indian Creek country, while he had come the roundabout way to take a look at the possibilities of getting out logs in the spring from the islands in the Yukon. He would be in to camp by six o'clock; a bit after dark, it was true, but the boys would be there, a fire would be going, and a hot supper would be ready. As for lunch, he pressed his hand against the protruding bundle under his jacket. It was also under his shirt, wrapped up in a handkerchief and lying against the naked skin. It was the only way to keep the biscuits from freezing. He smiled agreeably to himself as he thought of those biscuits, each cut open and sopped in bacon grease, and each enclosing a generous slice of fried bacon.

He plunged in among the big spruce trees. The trail was faint. A foot of snow had fallen since the last sled had passed over, and he was glad he was without a sled, travelling light. In fact, he carried nothing but the lunch wrapped in the handkerchief. He was surprised, however, at the cold. It certainly was cold, he concluded, as he rubbed his numbed nose and cheek-bones with his mittened hand. He was a warm-whiskered man, but the hair on his face did not protect the high cheek-bones and the eager nose that thrust itself aggressively into the frosty air.

At the man's heels trotted a dog, a big native husky, the proper wolf-dog, grey-coated and without any visible or temperamental difference from its brother, the wild wolf. The animal was depressed by the tremendous cold. It knew that it was no time for travelling. Its instinct told it a truer tale than was told to the man by the man's judgment. In reality, it was not merely colder than fifty below zero; it was colder than sixty below, than seventy below. It was seventy-five below zero. Since the freezing-point is thirty-two above zero, it meant that one hundred and seven degrees of frost obtained. The dog did not know anything about thermometers. Possibly in its brain there was no sharp consciousness of a condition of very cold such as was in the man's brain. But the brute had its instinct. It experienced a vague but menacing apprehension that subdued it and made it slink along at the man's heels, and that made it question eagerly every unwonted movement of the man as if expecting him to go into camp or to seek shelter somewhere and build a fire. The dog had learned fire, and it wanted fire, or else to burrow under the snow and cuddle its warmth away from the air.

The frozen moisture of its breathing had settled on its fur in a fine powder of frost, and especially were its jowls, muzzle, and eyelashes whitened by its crystalled breath. The man's red beard and moustache were likewise frosted, but more solidly, the deposit taking the form of ice and increasing with every warm, moist breath he exhaled. Also, the man was chewing tobacco, and the muzzle of ice held his lips so rigidly that he was unable to clear his chin when he expelled the juice. The result was that a crystal beard of the colour and solidity of amber was increasing its length on his chin. If he fell down it would shatter itself, like glass, into brittle fragments. But he did not mind the appendage. It was the penalty all tobacco-chewers paid in that country, and he had been out before in two cold snaps. They had not been so cold as this, he knew, but by the spirit thermometer at Sixty Mile he knew they had been registered at fifty below and at fifty-five.

He held on through the level stretch of woods for several miles, crossed a wide flat of nigger-heads, and dropped down a bank to the frozen bed of a small stream. This was Henderson Creek, and he knew he was ten miles from the forks. He looked at his watch. It was ten o'clock. He was making four miles an hour, and he calculated that he would arrive at the forks at half-past twelve. He decided to celebrate that event by eating his lunch there.

The dog dropped in again at his heels, with a tail drooping discouragement, as the man swung along the creek-bed. The furrow of the old sled-trail was plainly visible, but a dozen inches of snow covered the marks of the last runners. In a month no man had come up or down that silent creek. The man held steadily on. He was not much given to thinking, and just then particularly he had nothing to think about save that he would eat lunch at the forks and that at six o'clock he would be in camp with the boys. There was nobody to talk to and, had there been, speech would have been impossible because of the ice-muzzle on his mouth. So he continued monotonously to chew tobacco and to increase the length of his amber beard.

Once in a while the thought reiterated itself that it was very cold and that he had never experienced such cold. As he walked along he rubbed his cheek-bones and nose with the back of his mittened hand. He did this automatically, now and again changing hands. But rub as he would, the instant he stopped his cheek-bones went numb, and the following instant the end of his nose went numb. He was sure to frost his cheeks; he knew that, and experienced a pang of regret that he had not devised a nose-strap of the sort Bud wore in cold snaps. Such a strap passed across the cheeks, as well, and saved them. But it didn't matter much, after all. What were frosted cheeks? A bit painful, that was all; they were never serious.

Empty as the man's mind was of thoughts, he was keenly observant, and he noticed the changes in the creek, the curves and bends and timber-jams, and always he sharply noted where he placed his feet. Once, coming around a bend, he shied abruptly, like a startled horse, curved away from the place where he had been walking, and retreated several paces back along the trail. The creek he knew was frozen clear to the bottom—no creek could contain water in that arctic winter—but he knew also that there were springs that bubbled out from the hillsides and ran along under the snow and on top the ice of the creek. He knew that the coldest snaps never froze these springs, and he knew likewise their danger. They were traps. They hid pools of water under the snow that might be three inches deep, or three feet. Sometimes a skin of ice half an inch thick covered them, and in turn was covered by the snow. Sometimes there were alternate layers of water and ice-skin, so that when one broke through he kept on breaking through for a while, sometimes wetting himself to the waist.

That was why he had shied in such panic. He had felt the give under his feet and heard the crackle of a snow-hidden ice-skin. And to get his feet wet in such a temperature meant trouble and danger. At the very least it meant delay, for he would be forced to stop and build a fire, and under its protection to bare his feet while he dried his socks and moccasins. He stood and studied the creek-bed and its banks, and decided that the flow of water came from the right. He reflected awhile, rubbing his nose and cheeks, then skirted to the left, stepping gingerly and testing the footing for each step. Once clear of the danger, he took a fresh chew of tobacco and swung along at his four-mile gait.

In the course of the next two hours he came upon several similar traps. Usually the snow above the hidden pools had a sunken, candied appearance that advertised the danger. Once again, however, he had a close call; and once, suspecting danger, he compelled the dog to go on in front. The dog did not want to go. It hung back until the man shoved it forward, and then it went quickly across the white, unbroken surface. Suddenly it broke through, floundered to one side, and got away to firmer footing. It had wet its forefeet and legs, and almost immediately the water that clung to it turned to ice. It made quick efforts to lick the ice off its legs, then dropped down in the snow and began to bite out the ice that had formed between the toes. This was a matter of instinct. To permit the ice to remain would mean sore feet. It did not know this. It merely obeyed the mysterious prompting that arose from the deep crypts of its being. But the man knew, having achieved a judgment on the subject, and he removed the mitten from his right hand and helped tear out the ice-particles. He did not expose his fingers more than a minute, and was astonished at the swift numbness that smote them. It certainly was cold. He pulled on the mitten hastily, and beat the hand savagely across his chest.

At twelve o'clock the day was at its brightest. Yet the sun was too far south on its winter journey to clear the horizon. The bulge of the earth intervened between it and Henderson Creek, where the man walked under a clear sky at noon and cast no shadow. At half-past twelve, to the minute, he arrived at the forks of the creek. He was pleased at the speed he had made. If he kept it up, he would certainly be with the boys by six. He unbuttoned his jacket and shirt and drew forth his lunch. The action consumed no more than a quarter of a minute, yet in that brief moment the numbness laid hold of the exposed fingers. He did not put the mitten on, but, instead, struck the fingers a dozen sharp smashes against his leg. Then he sat down on a snow-covered log to eat. The sting that followed upon the striking of his fingers against his leg ceased so quickly that he was startled, he had had no chance to take a bite of biscuit. He struck the fingers repeatedly and returned them to the mitten, baring the other hand for the purpose of eating. He tried to take a mouthful, but the ice-muzzle prevented. He had forgotten to build a fire and thaw out. He chuckled at his foolishness, and as he chuckled he noted the numbness creeping into the exposed fingers. Also, he noted that the stinging which had first come to his toes when he sat down was already passing away. He wondered whether the toes were warm or numbed. He moved them inside the moccasins and decided that they were numbed.

He pulled the mitten on hurriedly and stood up. He was a bit frightened. He stamped up and down until the stinging returned into the feet. It certainly was cold, was his thought. That man from Sulphur Creek had spoken the truth when telling how cold it sometimes got in the country. And he had laughed at him at the time! That showed one must not be too sure of things. There was no mistake about it, it was cold. He strode up and down, stamping his feet and threshing his arms, until reassured by the returning warmth. Then he got out matches and proceeded to make a fire. From the undergrowth, where high water of the previous spring had lodged a supply of seasoned twigs, he got his firewood. Working carefully from a small beginning, he soon had a roaring fire, over which he thawed the ice from his face and in the protection of which he ate his biscuits. For the moment the cold of space was outwitted. The dog took satisfaction in the fire, stretching out close enough for warmth and far enough away to escape being singed.

When the man had finished, he filled his pipe and took his comfortable time over a smoke. Then he pulled on his mittens, settled the ear-flaps of his cap firmly about his ears, and took the creek trail up the left fork. The dog was disappointed and yearned back toward the fire. This man did not know cold. Possibly all the generations of his ancestry had been ignorant of cold, of real cold, of cold one hundred and seven degrees below freezing-point. But the dog knew; all its ancestry knew, and it had inherited the knowledge. And it knew that it was not good to walk abroad in such fearful cold. It was the time to lie snug in a hole in the snow and wait for a curtain of cloud to be drawn across the face of outer space whence this cold came.

On the other hand, there was keen intimacy between the dog and the man. The one was the toil-slave of the other, and the only caresses it had ever received were the caresses of the whip-lash and of harsh and menacing throat-sounds that threatened the whip-lash. So the dog made no effort to communicate its apprehension to the man. It was not concerned in the welfare of the man; it was for its own sake that it yearned back toward the fire. But the man whistled, and spoke to it with the sound of whip-lashes, and the dog swung in at the man's heels and followed after.

The man took a chew of tobacco and proceeded to start a new amber beard. Also, his moist breath quickly powdered with white his moustache, eyebrows, and lashes. There did not seem to be so many springs on the left fork of the Henderson, and for half an hour the man saw no signs of any. And then it happened. At a place where there were no signs, where the soft, unbroken snow seemed to advertise solidity beneath, the man broke through. It was not deep. He wetted himself half-way to the knees before he floundered out to the firm crust.

He was angry, and cursed his luck aloud. He had hoped to get into camp with the boys at six o'clock, and this would delay him an hour, for he would have to build a fire and dry out his foot-gear. This was imperative at that low temperature—he knew that much; and he turned aside to the bank, which he climbed. On top, tangled in the underbrush about the trunks of several small spruce trees, was a high-water deposit of dry firewood—sticks and twigs principally, but also larger portions of seasoned branches and fine, dry, last-year's grasses. He threw down several large pieces on top of the snow. This served for a foundation and prevented the young flame from drowning itself in the snow it otherwise would melt. The flame he got by touching a match to a small shred of birch-bark that he took from his pocket. This burned even more readily than paper. Placing it on the foundation, he fed the young flame with wisps of dry grass and with the tiniest dry twigs.

He worked slowly and carefully, keenly aware of his danger. Gradually, as the flame grew stronger, he increased the size of the twigs with which he fed it. He squatted in the snow, pulling the twigs out from their entanglement in the brush and feeding directly to the flame. He knew there must be no failure. When it is seventy-five below zero, a man must not fail in his first attempt to build a fire—that is, if his feet are wet. If his feet are dry, and he fails, he can run along the trail for half a mile and restore his circulation. But the circulation of wet and freezing feet cannot be restored by running when it is seventy-five below. No matter how fast he runs, the wet feet will freeze the harder.

All this the man knew. The old-timer on Sulphur Creek had told him about it the previous fall, and now he was appreciating the advice. Already all sensation had gone out of his feet. To build the fire he had been forced to remove his mittens, and the fingers had quickly gone numb. His pace of four miles an hour had kept his heart pumping blood to the surface of his body and to all the extremities. But the instant he stopped, the action of the pump eased down. The cold of space smote the unprotected tip of the planet, and he, being on that unprotected tip, received the full force of the blow. The blood of his body recoiled before it. The blood was alive, like the dog, and like the dog it wanted to hide away and cover itself up from the fearful cold. So long as he walked four miles an hour, he pumped that blood, willy-nilly, to the surface; but now it ebbed away and sank down into the recesses of his body. The extremities were the first to feel its absence. His wet feet froze the faster, and his exposed fingers numbed the faster, though they had not yet begun to freeze. Nose and cheeks were already freezing, while the skin of all his body chilled as it lost its blood.

But he was safe. Toes and nose and cheeks would be only touched by the frost, for the fire was beginning to burn with strength. He was feeding it with twigs the size of his finger. In another minute he would be able to feed it with branches the size of his wrist, and then he could remove his wet foot-gear, and, while it dried, he could keep his naked feet warm by the fire, rubbing them at first, of course, with snow. The fire was a success. He was safe. He remembered the advice of the old-timer on Sulphur Creek, and smiled. The old-timer had been very serious in laying down the law that no man must travel alone in the Klondike after fifty below. Well, here he was; he had had the accident; he was alone; and he had saved himself. Those old-timers were rather womanish, some of them, he thought. All a man had to do was to keep his head, and he was all right. Any man who was a man could travel alone. But it was surprising, the rapidity with which his cheeks and nose were freezing. And he had not thought his fingers could go lifeless in so short a time. Lifeless they were, for he could scarcely make them move together to grip a twig, and they seemed remote from his body and from him. When he touched a twig, he had to look and see whether or not he had hold of it. The wires were pretty well down between him and his finger-ends.

All of which counted for little. There was the fire, snapping and crackling and promising life with every dancing flame. He started to untie his moccasins. They were coated with ice; the thick German socks were like sheaths of iron half-way to the knees; and the mocassin strings were like rods of steel all twisted and knotted as by some conflagration. For a moment he tugged with his numbed fingers, then, realizing the folly of it, he drew his sheath-knife.

But before he could cut the strings, it happened. It was his own fault or, rather, his mistake. He should not have built the fire under the spruce tree. He should have built it in the open. But it had been easier to pull the twigs from the brush and drop them directly on the fire. Now the tree under which he had done this carried a weight of snow on its boughs. No wind had blown for weeks, and each bough was fully freighted. Each time he had pulled a twig he had communicated a slight agitation to the tree—an imperceptible agitation, so far as he was concerned, but an agitation sufficient to bring about the disaster. High up in the tree one bough capsized its load of snow. This fell on the boughs beneath, capsizing them. This process continued, spreading out and involving the whole tree. It grew like an avalanche, and it descended without warning upon the man and the fire, and the fire was blotted out! Where it had burned was a mantle of fresh and disordered snow.

The man was shocked. It was as though he had just heard his own sentence of death. For a moment he sat and stared at the spot where the fire had been. Then he grew very calm. Perhaps the old-timer on Sulphur Creek was right. If he had only had a trail-mate he would have been in no danger now. The trail-mate could have built the fire. Well, it was up to him to build the fire over again, and this second time there must be no failure. Even if he succeeded, he would most likely lose some toes. His feet must be badly frozen by now, and there would be some time before the second fire was ready.

Such were his thoughts, but he did not sit and think them. He was busy all the time they were passing through his mind, he made a new foundation for a fire, this time in the open; where no treacherous tree could blot it out. Next, he gathered dry grasses and tiny twigs from the high-water flotsam. He could not bring his fingers together to pull them out, but he was able to gather them by the handful. In this way he got many rotten twigs and bits of green moss that were undesirable, but it was the best he could do. He worked methodically, even collecting an armful of the larger branches to be used later when the fire gathered strength. And all the while the dog sat and watched him, a certain yearning wistfulness in its eyes, for it looked upon him as the fire-provider, and the fire was slow in coming.

When all was ready, the man reached in his pocket for a second piece of birch-bark. He knew the bark was there, and, though he could not feel it with his fingers, he could hear its crisp rustling as he fumbled for it. Try as he would, he could not clutch hold of it. And all the time, in his consciousness, was the knowledge that each instant his feet were freezing. This thought tended to put him in a panic, but he fought against it and kept calm. He pulled on his mittens with his teeth, and threshed his arms back and forth, beating his hands with all his might against his sides. He did this sitting down, and he stood up to do it; and all the while the dog sat in the snow, its wolf-brush of a tail curled around warmly over its forefeet, its sharp wolf-ears pricked forward intently as it watched the man. And the man as he beat and threshed with his arms and hands, felt a great surge of envy as he regarded the creature that was warm and secure in its natural covering.

After a time he was aware of the first far-away signals of sensation in his beaten fingers. The faint tingling grew stronger till it evolved into a stinging ache that was excruciating, but which the man hailed with satisfaction. He stripped the mitten from his right hand and fetched forth the birch-bark. The exposed fingers were quickly going numb again. Next he brought out his bunch of sulphur matches. But the tremendous cold had already driven the life out of his fingers. In his effort to separate one match from the others, the whole bunch fell in the snow. He tried to pick it out of the snow, but failed. The dead fingers could neither touch nor clutch. He was very careful. He drove the thought of his freezing feet; and nose, and cheeks, out of his mind, devoting his whole soul to the matches. He watched, using the sense of vision in place of that of touch, and when he saw his fingers on each side the bunch, he closed them—that is, he willed to close them, for the wires were drawn, and the fingers did not obey. He pulled the mitten on the right hand, and beat it fiercely against his knee. Then, with both mittened hands, he scooped the bunch of matches, along with much snow, into his lap. Yet he was no better off.

After some manipulation he managed to get the bunch between the heels of his mittened hands. In this fashion he carried it to his mouth. The ice crackled and snapped when by a violent effort he opened his mouth. He drew the lower jaw in, curled the upper lip out of the way, and scraped the bunch with his upper teeth in order to separate a match. He succeeded in getting one, which he dropped on his lap. He was no better off. He could not pick it up. Then he devised a way. He picked it up in his teeth and scratched it on his leg. Twenty times he scratched before he succeeded in lighting it. As it flamed he held it with his teeth to the birch-bark. But the burning brimstone went up his nostrils and into his lungs, causing him to cough spasmodically. The match fell into the snow and went out.

The old-timer on Sulphur Creek was right, he thought in the moment of controlled despair that ensued: after fifty below, a man should travel with a partner. He beat his hands, but failed in exciting any sensation. Suddenly he bared both hands, removing the mittens with his teeth. He caught the whole bunch between the heels of his hands. His arm-muscles not being frozen enabled him to press the hand-heels tightly against the matches. Then he scratched the bunch along his leg. It flared into flame, seventy sulphur matches at once! There was no wind to blow them out. He kept his head to one side to escape the strangling fumes, and held the blazing bunch to the birch-bark. As he so held it, he became aware of sensation in his hand. His flesh was burning. He could smell it. Deep down below the surface he could feel it. The sensation developed into pain that grew acute. And still he endured it, holding the flame of the matches clumsily to the bark that would not light readily because his own burning hands were in the way, absorbing most of the flame.

At last, when he could endure no more, he jerked his hands apart. The blazing matches fell sizzling into the snow, but the birch-bark was alight. He began laying dry grasses and the tiniest twigs on the flame. He could not pick and choose, for he had to lift the fuel between the heels of his hands. Small pieces of rotten wood and green moss clung to the twigs, and he bit them off as well as he could with his teeth. He cherished the flame carefully and awkwardly. It meant life, and it must not perish. The withdrawal of blood from the surface of his body now made him begin to shiver, and he grew more awkward. A large piece of green moss fell squarely on the little fire. He tried to poke it out with his fingers, but his shivering frame made him poke too far, and he disrupted the nucleus of the little fire, the burning grasses and tiny twigs separating and scattering. He tried to poke them together again, but in spite of the tenseness of the effort, his shivering got away with him, and the twigs were hopelessly scattered. Each twig gushed a puff of smoke and went out. The fire-provider had failed. As he looked apathetically about him, his eyes chanced on the dog, sitting across the ruins of the fire from him, in the snow, making restless, hunching movements, slightly lifting one forefoot and then the other, shifting its weight back and forth on them with wistful eagerness.

The sight of the dog put a wild idea into his head. He remembered the tale of the man, caught in a blizzard, who killed a steer and crawled inside the carcass, and so was saved. He would kill the dog and bury his hands in the warm body until the numbness went out of them. Then he could build another fire. He spoke to the dog, calling it to him; but in his voice was a strange note of fear that frightened the animal, who had never known the man to speak in such way before. Something was the matter, and its suspicious nature sensed danger,—it knew not what danger but somewhere, somehow, in its brain arose an apprehension of the man. It flattened its ears down at the sound of the man's voice, and its restless, hunching movements and the liftings and shiftings of its forefeet became more pronounced but it would not come to the man. He got on his hands and knees and crawled toward the dog. This unusual posture again excited suspicion, and the animal sidled mincingly away.

The man sat up in the snow for a moment and struggled for calmness. Then he pulled on his mittens, by means of his teeth, and got upon his feet. He glanced down at first in order to assure himself that he was really standing up, for the absence of sensation in his feet left him unrelated to the earth. His erect position in itself started to drive the webs of suspicion from the dog's mind; and when he spoke peremptorily, with the sound of whip-lashes in his voice, the dog rendered its customary allegiance and came to him. As it came within reaching distance, the man lost his control. His arms flashed out to the dog, and he experienced genuine surprise when he discovered that his hands could not clutch, that there was neither bend nor feeling in the lingers. He had forgotten for the moment that they were frozen and that they were freezing more and more. All this happened quickly, and before the animal could get away, he encircled its body with his arms. He sat down in the snow, and in this fashion held the dog, while it snarled and whined and struggled.

But it was all he could do, hold its body encircled in his arms and sit there. He realized that he could not kill the dog. There was no way to do it. With his helpless hands he could neither draw nor hold his sheath-knife nor throttle the animal. He released it, and it plunged wildly away, with tail between its legs, and still snarling. It halted forty feet away and surveyed him curiously, with ears sharply pricked forward. The man looked down at his hands in order to locate them, and found them hanging on the ends of his arms. It struck him as curious that one should have to use his eyes in order to find out where his hands were. He began threshing his arms back and forth, beating the mittened hands against his sides. He did this for five minutes, violently, and his heart pumped enough blood up to the surface to put a stop to his shivering. But no sensation was aroused in the hands. He had an impression that they hung like weights on the ends of his arms, but when he tried to run the impression down, he could not find it.

A certain fear of death, dull and oppressive, came to him. This fear quickly became poignant as he realized that it was no longer a mere matter of freezing his fingers and toes, or of losing his hands and feet, but that it was a matter of life and death with the chances against him. This threw him into a panic, and he turned and ran up the creek-bed along the old, dim trail. The dog joined in behind and kept up with him. He ran blindly, without intention, in fear such as he had never known in his life. Slowly, as he ploughed and floundered through the snow, he began to see things again—the banks of the creek, the old timber-jams, the leafless aspens, and the sky. The running made him feel better. He did not shiver. Maybe, if he ran on, his feet would thaw out; and, anyway, if he ran far enough, he would reach camp and the boys. Without doubt he would lose some fingers and toes and some of his face; but the boys would take care of him, and save the rest of him when he got there. And at the same time there was another thought in his mind that said he would never get to the camp and the boys; that it was too many miles away, that the freezing had too great a start on him, and that he would soon be stiff and dead. This thought he kept in the background and refused to consider. Sometimes it pushed itself forward and demanded to be heard, but he thrust it back and strove to think of other things.

It struck him as curious that he could run at all on feet so frozen that he could not feel them when they struck the earth and took the weight of his body. He seemed to himself to skim along above the surface and to have no connection with the earth. Somewhere he had once seen a winged Mercury, and he wondered if Mercury felt as he felt when skimming over the earth.

His theory of running until he reached camp and the boys had one flaw in it: he lacked the endurance. Several times he stumbled, and finally he tottered, crumpled up, and fell. When he tried to rise, he failed. He must sit and rest, he decided, and next time he would merely walk and keep on going. As he sat and regained his breath, he noted that he was feeling quite warm and comfortable. He was not shivering, and it even seemed that a warm glow had come to his chest and trunk. And yet, when he touched his nose or cheeks, there was no sensation. Running would not thaw them out. Nor would it thaw out his hands and feet. Then the thought came to him that the frozen portions of his body must be extending. He tried to keep this thought down, to forget it, to think of something else; he was aware of the panicky feeling that it caused, and he was afraid of the panic. But the thought asserted itself, and persisted, until it produced a vision of his body totally frozen. This was too much, and he made another wild run along the trail. Once he slowed down to a walk, but the thought of the freezing extending itself made him run again.

And all the time the dog ran with him, at his heels. When he fell down a second time, it curled its tail over its forefeet and sat in front of him facing him curiously eager and intent. The warmth and security of the animal angered him, and he cursed it till it flattened down its ears appeasingly. This time the shivering came more quickly upon the man. He was losing in his battle with the frost. It was creeping into his body from all sides. The thought of it drove him on, but he ran no more than a hundred feet, when he staggered and pitched headlong. It was his last panic. When he had recovered his breath and control, he sat up and entertained in his mind the conception of meeting death with dignity. However, the conception did not come to him in such terms. His idea of it was that he had been making a fool of himself, running around like a chicken with its head cut off—such was the simile that occurred to him. Well, he was bound to freeze anyway, and he might as well take it decently. With this new-found peace of mind came the first glimmerings of drowsiness. A good idea, he thought, to sleep off to death. It was like taking an anæsthetic. Freezing was not so bad as people thought. There were lots worse ways to die.

He pictured the boys finding his body next day. Suddenly he found himself with them, coming along the trail and looking for himself. And, still with them, he came around a turn in the trail and found himself lying in the snow. He did not belong with himself any more, for even then he was out of himself, standing with the boys and looking at himself in the snow. It certainly was cold, was his thought. When he got back to the States he could tell the folks what real cold was. He drifted on from this to a vision of the old-timer on Sulphur Creek. He could see him quite clearly, warm and comfortable, and smoking a pipe.

"You were right, old hoss; you were right," the man mumbled to the old-timer of Sulphur Creek.

Then the man drowsed off into what seemed to him the most comfortable and satisfying sleep he had ever known. The dog sat facing him and waiting. The brief day drew to a close in a long, slow twilight. There were no signs of a fire to be made, and, besides, never in the dog's experience had it known a man to sit like that in the snow and make no fire. As the twilight drew on, its eager yearning for the fire mastered it, and with a great lifting and shifting of forefeet, it whined softly, then flattened its ears down in anticipation of being chidden by the man. But the man remained silent. Later, the dog whined loudly. And still later it crept close to the man and caught the scent of death. This made the animal bristle and back away. A little longer it delayed, howling under the stars that leaped and danced and shone brightly in the cold sky. Then it turned and trotted up the trail in the direction of the camp it knew, where were the other food-providers and fire-providers.

THE HARE AND THE TORTOISE

Aesop

Translated by V. S. Vernon Jones, published in 1912

A Hare was one day making fun of a Tortoise for being so slow upon his feet. "Wait a bit," said the Tortoise; "I'll run a race with you, and I'll wager that I win." "Oh, well," replied the Hare, who was much amused at the idea, "let's try and see"; and it was soon agreed that the fox should set a course for them, and be the judge. When the time came both started off together, but the Hare was soon so far ahead that he thought he might as well have a rest: so down he lay and fell fast asleep. Meanwhile the Tortoise kept plodding on, and in time reached the goal. At last the Hare woke up with a start, and dashed on at his fastest, but only to find that the Tortoise had already won the race.

Slow and steady wins the race.

THE CROW AND THE PITCHER

Aesop

Translated by V. S. Vernon Jones, published in 1912

A thirsty Crow found a Pitcher with some water in it, but so little was there that, try as she might, she could not reach it with her beak, and it seemed as though she would die of thirst within sight of the remedy. At last she hit upon a clever plan. She began dropping pebbles into the Pitcher, and with each pebble the water rose a little higher until at last it reached the brim, and the knowing bird was enabled to quench her thirst.

Necessity is the mother of invention.

THE GRASSHOPPER AND THE ANTS

Aesop

Translated by V. S. Vernon Jones, published in 1912

One fine day in winter, some Ants were busy drying their store of corn, which had got rather damp during a long spell of rain. Presently, up came a Grasshopper and begged them to spare her a few grains, "For," she said, "I'm simply starving." The Ants stopped work for a moment, though this was against their principles. "May we ask," said they, "what you were doing with yourself all last summer? Why didn't you collect a store of food for the winter?" "The fact is," replied the Grasshopper, "I was so busy singing that I hadn't the time." "If you spent the summer singing," replied the Ants, "you can't do better than spend the winter dancing." And they chuckled and went on with their work.

THE OPEN WINDOW

Saki

Published in *Beasts and Super-Beasts* in 1914

"My aunt will be down presently, Mr. Nuttel," said a very self-possessed young lady of fifteen; "in the meantime you must try and put up with me."

Framton Nuttel endeavoured to say the correct something which should duly flatter the niece of the moment without unduly discounting the aunt that was to come. Privately he doubted more than ever whether these formal visits on a succession of total strangers would do much towards helping the nerve cure which he was supposed to be undergoing.

"I know how it will be," his sister had said when he was preparing to migrate to this rural retreat; "you will bury yourself down there and not speak to a living soul, and your nerves will be worse than ever from moping. I shall just give you letters of introduction to all the people I know there. Some of them, as far as I can remember, were quite nice."

Framton wondered whether Mrs. Sappleton, the lady to whom he was presenting one of the letters of introduction, came into the nice division.

"Do you know many of the people round here?" asked the niece, when she judged that they had had sufficient silent communion.

"Hardly a soul," said Framton. "My sister was staying here, at the rectory, you know, some four years ago, and she gave me letters of introduction to some of the people here."

He made the last statement in a tone of distinct regret.

"Then you know practically nothing about my aunt?" pursued the self-possessed young lady.

"Only her name and address," admitted the caller. He was wondering whether Mrs. Sappleton was in the married or widowed state. An undefinable something about the room seemed to suggest masculine habitation.

"Her great tragedy happened just three years ago," said the child; "that would be since your sister's time."

"Her tragedy?" asked Framton; somehow in this restful country spot tragedies seemed out of place.

"You may wonder why we keep that window wide open on an October afternoon," said the niece, indicating a large French window that opened on to a lawn.

"It is quite warm for the time of the year," said Framton; "but has that window got anything to do with the tragedy?"

"Out through that window, three years ago to a day, her husband and her two young brothers went off for their day's shooting. They never came back. In crossing the moor to their favourite snipe-shooting ground they were all three engulfed in a treacherous piece of bog. It had been that dreadful wet summer, you know, and places that were safe in other years gave way suddenly without warning. Their bodies were never recovered. That was the dreadful part of it." Here the child's voice lost its self-possessed note and became falteringly human. "Poor aunt always thinks that they will come back some day, they and the little brown spaniel that was lost with them, and walk in at that window just as they used to do. That is why the window is kept open every evening till it is quite dusk. Poor dear aunt, she has often told me how they went out, her husband with his white waterproof coat over his arm, and Ronnie, her youngest brother, singing 'Bertie, why do you bound?' as he always did to tease her, because she said it got on her nerves. Do you know, sometimes on still, quiet evenings like this, I almost get a creepy feeling that they will all walk in through that window—"

She broke off with a little shudder. It was a relief to Framton when the aunt bustled into the room with a whirl of apologies for being late in making her appearance.

"I hope Vera has been amusing you?" she said.

"She has been very interesting," said Framton.

"I hope you don't mind the open window," said Mrs. Sappleton briskly; "my husband and brothers will be home directly from shooting, and they always come in this way. They've been out for snipe in the marshes today, so they'll make a fine mess over my poor carpets. So like you men-folk, isn't it?"

She rattled on cheerfully about the shooting and the scarcity of birds, and the prospects for duck in the winter. To Framton it was all purely horrible. He made a desperate but only partially successful effort to turn the talk on to a less ghastly topic; he was conscious that his hostess was giving him only a fragment of her attention, and her eyes were constantly straying past him to the open window and the lawn beyond. It was certainly an unfortunate coincidence that he should have paid his visit on this tragic anniversary.

"The doctors agree in ordering me complete rest, an absence of mental excitement, and avoidance of anything in the nature of violent physical exercise," announced Framton, who laboured under the tolerably widespread delusion that total strangers and chance acquaintances are hungry for the least detail of one's ailments and infirmities, their cause and cure. "On the matter of diet they are not so much in agreement," he continued.

"No?" said Mrs. Sappleton, in a voice which only replaced a yawn at the last moment. Then she suddenly brightened into alert attention—but not to what Framton was saying.

"Here they are at last!" she cried. "Just in time for tea, and don't they look as if they were muddy up to the eyes!"

Framton shivered slightly and turned towards the niece with a look intended to convey sympathetic comprehension. The child was staring out through the open window with dazed horror in her eyes. In a chill shock of nameless fear Framton swung round in his seat and looked in the same direction.

In the deepening twilight three figures were walking across the lawn towards the window; they all carried guns under their arms, and one of them was additionally burdened with a white coat hung over his shoulders. A tired brown spaniel kept close at their heels. Noiselessly they neared the house, and then a hoarse young voice chanted out of the dusk: "I said, Bertie, why do you bound?"

Framton grabbed wildly at his stick and hat; the hall-door, the gravel-drive, and the front gate were dimly-noted stages in his headlong retreat. A cyclist coming along the road had to run into the hedge to avoid an imminent collision.

"Here we are, my dear," said the bearer of the white mackintosh, coming in through the window; "fairly muddy, but most of it's dry. Who was that who bolted out as we came up?"

"A most extraordinary man, a Mr. Nuttel," said Mrs. Sappleton; "could only talk about his illnesses, and dashed off without a word of goodbye or apology when you arrived. One would think he had seen a ghost."

"I expect it was the spaniel," said the niece calmly; "he told me he had a horror of dogs. He was once hunted into a cemetery somewhere on the banks of the Ganges by a pack of pariah dogs, and had to spend the night in a newly dug grave with the creatures snarling and grinning and foaming just above him. Enough to make anyone lose their nerve."

Romance at short notice was her speciality.

A FABLE

Mark Twain

Published in *The Mysterious Stranger and Other Stories* in 1916

Once upon a time an artist who had painted a small and very beautiful picture placed it so that he could see it in the mirror. He said, "This doubles the distance and softens it, and it is twice as lovely as it was before."

The animals out in the woods heard of this through the housecat, who was greatly admired by them because he was so learned, and so refined and civilized, and so polite and high-bred, and could tell them so much which they didn't know before, and were not certain about afterward. They were much excited about this new piece of gossip, and they asked questions, so as to get at a full understanding of it. They asked what a picture was, and the cat explained.

"It is a flat thing," he said; "wonderfully flat, marvellously flat, enchantingly flat and elegant. And, oh, so beautiful!"

That excited them almost to a frenzy, and they said they would give the world to see it. Then the bear asked:

"What is it that makes it so beautiful?"

"It is the looks of it," said the cat.

This filled them with admiration and uncertainty, and they were more excited than ever. Then the cow asked:

"What is a mirror?"

"It is a hole in the wall," said the cat. "You look in it, and there you see the picture, and it is so dainty and charming and ethereal and inspiring in its unimaginable beauty that your head turns round and round, and you almost swoon with ecstasy."

The ass had not said anything as yet; he now began to throw doubts. He said there had never been anything as beautiful as this before, and probably wasn't now. He said that when it took a whole basketful of sesquipedalian adjectives to whoop up a thing of beauty, it was time for suspicion.

It was easy to see that these doubts were having an effect upon the animals, so the cat went off offended. The subject was dropped for a couple of days, but in the meantime curiosity was taking a fresh start, and there was a revival of interest perceptible.

Then the animals assailed the ass for spoiling what could possibly have been a pleasure to them, on a mere suspicion that the picture was not beautiful, without any evidence that such was the case. The ass was not troubled; he was calm, and said there was one way to find out who was in the right, himself or the cat: he would go and look in that hole, and come back and tell what he found there. The animals felt relieved and grateful, and asked him to go at once—which he did.

But he did not know where he ought to stand; and so, through error, he stood between the picture and the mirror. The result was that the picture had no chance, and didn't show up. He returned home and said:

"The cat lied. There was nothing in that hole but an ass. There wasn't a sign of a flat thing visible. It was a handsome ass, and friendly, but just an ass, and nothing more."

The elephant asked:

"Did you see it good and clear? Were you close to it?"

"I saw it good and clear, O Hathi, King of Beasts. I was so close that I touched noses with it."

"This is very strange," said the elephant; "the cat was always truthful before—as far as we could make out. Let another witness try. Go, Baloo, look in the hole, and come and report."

So the bear went. When he came back, he said:

"Both the cat and the ass have lied; there was nothing in the hole but a bear."

Great was the surprise and puzzlement of the animals. Each was now anxious to make the test himself and get at the straight truth. The elephant sent them one at a time.

First, the cow. She found nothing in the hole but a cow.

The tiger found nothing in it but a tiger.

The lion found nothing in it but a lion.

The leopard found nothing in it but a leopard.

The camel found a camel, and nothing more.

Then Hathi was wroth, and said he would have the truth, if he had to go and fetch it himself. When he returned, he abused his whole subjectry for liars, and was in an unappeasable fury with the moral and mental blindness of the cat. He said that anybody but a near-sighted fool could see that there was nothing in the hole but an elephant.

MORAL, BY THE CAT

You can find in a text whatever you bring, if you will stand between it and the mirror of your imagination. You may not see your ears, but they will be there.

THE DOLL'S HOUSE

Katherine Mansfield

Published in *The Nation and Athenaeum* in 1922

When dear old Mrs. Hay went back to town after staying with the Burnells she sent the children a doll's house. It was so big that the carter and Pat carried it into the courtyard, and there it stayed, propped up on two wooden boxes beside the feed-room door. No harm could come to it; it was summer. And perhaps the smell of paint would have gone off by the time it had to be taken in. For, really, the smell of paint coming from that doll's house ("Sweet of old Mrs. Hay, of course; most sweet and generous!") —but the smell of paint was quite enough to make anyone seriously ill, in Aunt Beryl's opinion. Even before the sacking was taken off. And when it was . . .

There stood the Doll's house, a dark, oily, spinach green, picked out with bright yellow. Its two solid little chimneys, glued on to the roof, were painted red and white, and the door, gleaming with yellow varnish, was like a little slab of toffee. Four windows, real windows, were divided into panes by a broad streak of green. There was actually a tiny porch, too, painted yellow, with big lumps of congealed paint hanging along the edge.

But perfect, perfect little house! Who could possibly mind the smell. It was part of the joy, part of the newness.

"Open it quickly, someone!"

The hook at the side was stuck fast. Pat pried it open with his penknife, and the whole house front swung back, and—there you were, gazing at one and the same moment into the drawing-room and dining-room, the kitchen and two bedrooms. That is the way for a house to open! Why don't all houses open like that? How much more exciting than peering through the slit of a door into a mean little hall with a hat-stand and two umbrellas! That is—isn't it?—what you long to know about a house when you put your hand on the knocker. Perhaps it is the way God opens houses at the dead of night when He is taking a quiet turn with an angel . . .

"O-oh!" The Burnell children sounded as though they were in despair. It was too marvellous; it was too much for them. They had never seen anything like it in their lives. All the rooms were papered. There were pictures on the walls, painted on the paper, with gold frames complete. Red carpet covered all the floors except the kitchen; red plush chairs in the drawing-room, green in the dining-room; tables, beds with real bedclothes, a cradle, a stove, a dresser with tiny plates and one big jug. But what Kezia liked more than anything, what she liked frightfully, was the lamp. It stood in the middle of the dining-room table, an exquisite little amber lamp with a white globe. It was even filled all ready for lighting, though, of course, you couldn't light it. But there was something inside that looked like oil and moved when you shook it.

The father and mother dolls, who sprawled very stiff as though they had fainted in the drawing-room, and their two little children asleep upstairs, were really too big for the doll's house. They didn't look as though they belonged. But the lamp was perfect. It seemed to smile at Kezia, to say, "I live here." The lamp was real.

The Burnell children could hardly walk to school fast enough the next morning. They burned to tell everybody, to describe, to—well—to boast about their doll's house before the school-bell rang.

"I'm to tell," said Isabel, "because I'm the eldest. And you two can join in after. But I'm to tell first."

There was nothing to answer. Isabel was bossy, but she was always right, and Lottie and Kezia knew too well the powers that went with being eldest. They brushed through the thick buttercups at the road edge and said nothing.

"And I'm to choose who's to come and see it first. Mother said I might."

For it had been arranged that while the doll's house stood in the courtyard they might ask the girls at school, two at a time, to come and look. Not to stay to tea, of course, or to come traipsing through the house. But just to stand quietly in the courtyard while Isabel pointed out the beauties, and Lottie and Kezia looked pleased . . .

But hurry as they might, by the time they had reached the tarred palings of the boys' playground the bell had begun to jangle. They only just had time to whip off their hats and fall into line before the roll was called. Never mind. Isabel tried to make up for it by looking very important and mysterious and by whispering behind her hand to the girls near her, "Got something to tell you at playtime."

Playtime came and Isabel was surrounded. The girls of her class nearly fought to put their arms round her, to walk away with her, to beam flatteringly, to be her special friend. She held quite a court under the huge pine trees at the side of the playground. Nudging, giggling together, the little girls pressed up close. And the only two who stayed outside the ring were the two who were always outside, the little Kelveys. They knew better than to come anywhere near the Burnells.

For the fact was, the school the Burnell children went to was not at all the kind of place their parents would have chosen if there had been any choice. But there was none. It was the only school for miles. And the consequence was all the children of the neighbourhood, the Judge's little girls, the doctor's daughters, the store-keeper's children, the milkman's, were forced to mix together. Not to speak of there being an equal number of rude, rough little boys as well. But the line had to be drawn somewhere. It was drawn at the Kelveys. Many of the children, including the Burnells, were not allowed even to speak to them. They walked past the Kelveys with their heads in the air, and as they set the fashion in all matters of behaviour, the Kelveys were shunned by everybody. Even the teacher had a special voice for them, and a special smile for the other children when Lil Kelvey came up to her desk with a bunch of dreadfully common-looking flowers.

They were the daughters of a spry, hardworking little washerwoman, who went about from house to house by the day. This was awful enough. But where was Mr. Kelvey? Nobody knew for certain. But everybody said he was in prison. So they were the daughters of a washerwoman and a gaolbird. Very nice company for other people's children! And they looked it. Why Mrs. Kelvey made them so conspicuous was hard to understand. The truth was they were dressed in "bits" given to her by the people for whom she worked. Lil, for instance, who was a stout, plain child, with big freckles, came to school in a dress made from a green art-serge table-cloth of the Burnells', with red plush sleeves from the Logans' curtains. Her hat, perched on top of her high forehead, was a grown-up woman's hat, once the property of Miss Lecky, the postmistress. It was turned up at the back and trimmed with a large scarlet quill. What a little guy she looked! It was impossible not to laugh. And her little sister, our

Else, wore a long white dress, rather like a nightgown, and a pair of little boy's boots. But whatever our Else wore she would have looked strange. She was a tiny wishbone of a child, with cropped hair and enormous solemn eyes—a little white owl. Nobody had ever seen her smile; she scarcely ever spoke. She went through life holding on to Lil, with a piece of Lil's skirt screwed up in her hand. Where Lil went, our Else followed. In the playground, on the road going to and from school, there was Lil marching in front and our Else holding on behind. Only when she wanted anything, or when she was out of breath, our Else gave Lil a tug, a twitch, and Lil stopped and turned round. The Kelveys never failed to understand each other.

Now they hovered at the edge; you couldn't stop them listening. When the little girls turned round and sneered, Lil, as usual, gave her silly, shamefaced smile, but our Else only looked.

And Isabel's voice, so very proud, went on telling. The carpet made a great sensation, but so did the beds with real bedclothes, and the stove with an oven door.

When she finished Kezia broke in. "You've forgotten the lamp, Isabel."

"Oh, yes," said Isabel, "and there's a teeny little lamp, all made of yellow glass, with a white globe that stands on the dining-room table. You couldn't tell it from a real one."

"The lamp's best of all," cried Kezia. She thought Isabel wasn't making half enough of the little lamp. But nobody paid any attention. Isabel was choosing the two who were to come back with them that afternoon and see it. She chose Emmie Cole and Lena Logan. But when the others knew they were all to have a chance, they couldn't be nice enough to Isabel. One by one they put their arms round Isabel's waist and walked her off. They had something to whisper to her, a secret. "Isabel's *my* friend."

Only the little Kelveys moved away forgotten; there was nothing more for them to hear. Days passed, and as more children saw the doll's house, the fame of it spread. It became the one subject, the rage. The one question was, "Have you seen Burnells' doll's house? Oh, ain't it lovely!" "Haven't you seen it? Oh, I say!"

Even the dinner hour was given up to talking about it. The little girls sat under the pines eating their thick mutton sandwiches and big slabs of johnny cake spread with butter. While always, as near as they could get, sat the Kelveys, our Else holding on to Lil, listening too, while they chewed their jam sandwiches out of a newspaper soaked with large red blobs . . .

"Mother," said Kezia, "can't I ask the Kelveys just once?"

"Certainly not, Kezia."

"But why not?"

"Run away, Kezia; you know quite well why not."

At last everybody had seen it except them. On that day the subject rather flagged. It was the dinner hour. The children stood together under the pine trees, and suddenly, as they looked at the Kelveys eating out of their paper, always by themselves, always listening, they wanted to be horrid to them. Emmie Cole started the whisper.

"Lil Kelvey's going to be a servant when she grows up."

"O-oh, how awful!" said Isabel Burnell, and she made eyes at Emmie.

Emmie swallowed in a very meaning way and nodded to Isabel as she'd seen her mother do on those occasions.

"It's true—it's true—it's true," she said.

Then Lena Logan's little eyes snapped. "Shall I ask her?" she whispered.

"Bet you don't," said Jessie May.

"Pooh, I'm not frightened," said Lena. Suddenly she gave a little squeal and danced in front of the other girls. "Watch! Watch me! Watch me now!" said Lena. And sliding, gliding, dragging one foot, giggling behind her hand, Lena went over to the Kelveys.

Lil looked up from her dinner. She wrapped the rest quickly away. Our Else stopped chewing. What was coming now?

"Is it true you're going to be a servant when you grow up, Lil Kelvey?" shrilled Lena.

Dead silence. But instead of answering, Lil only gave her silly, shamefaced smile. She didn't seem to mind the question at all. What a sell for Lena! The girls began to titter.

Lena couldn't stand that. She put her hands on her hips; she shot forward. "Yah, yer father's in prison!" she hissed, spitefully. This was such a marvellous thing to have said that the little girls rushed away in a body, deeply, deeply excited, wild with joy. Someone found a long rope, and they began skipping. And never did they skip so high, run in and out so fast, or do such daring things as on that morning.

In the afternoon Pat called for the Burnell children with the buggy and they drove home. There were visitors. Isabel and Lottie, who liked visitors, went upstairs to change their pinafores. But Kezia thieved out at the back. Nobody was about; she began to swing on the big white gates of the courtyard. Presently, looking along the road, she saw two little dots. They grew bigger, they were coming towards her. Now she could see that one was in front and one close behind. Now she could see that they were the Kelveys. Kezia stopped swinging. She slipped off the gate as if she was going to run away. Then she hesitated. The Kelveys came nearer, and beside them walked their shadows, very long, stretching right across the road with their heads in the buttercups. Kezia clambered back on the gate; she had made up her mind; she swung out.

"Hullo," she said to the passing Kelveys.

They were so astounded that they stopped. Lil gave her silly smile. Our Else stared.

"You can come and see our doll's house if you want to," said Kezia, and she dragged one toe on the ground. But at that Lil turned red and shook her head quickly.

"Why not?" asked Kezia.

Lil gasped, then she said, "Your ma told our ma you wasn't to speak to us."

"Oh, well," said Kezia. She didn't know what to reply. "It doesn't matter. You can come and see our doll's house all the same. Come on. Nobody's looking."

But Lil shook her head still harder.

"Don't you want to?" asked Kezia.

Suddenly there was a twitch, a tug at Lil's skirt. She turned round. Our Else was looking at her with big, imploring eyes; she was frowning; she wanted to go. For a moment Lil looked at our Else very doubtfully. But then our Else twitched her skirt again. She started forward. Kezia led the way. Like two little stray cats they followed across the courtyard to where the doll's house stood.

"There it is," said Kezia.

There was a pause. Lil breathed loudly, almost snorted; our Else was still as stone.

"I'll open it for you," said Kezia kindly. She undid the hook and they looked inside.

"There's the drawing-room and the dining-room, and that's the—"

"Kezia!"

Oh, what a start they gave!

"Kezia!"

It was Aunt Beryl's voice. They turned round. At the back door stood Aunt Beryl, staring as if she couldn't believe what she saw.

"How dare you ask the little Kelveys into the courtyard?" said her cold, furious voice. "You know as well as I do, you're not allowed to talk to them. Run away, children, run away at once. And don't come back again," said Aunt Beryl. And she stepped into the yard and shooed them out as if they were chickens.

"Off you go immediately!" she called, cold and proud.

They did not need telling twice. Burning with shame, shrinking together, Lil huddling along like her mother, our Else dazed, somehow they crossed the big courtyard and squeezed through the white gate.

"Wicked, disobedient little girl!" said Aunt Beryl bitterly to Kezia, and she slammed the doll's house to.

The afternoon had been awful. A letter had come from Willie Brent, a terrifying, threatening letter, saying if she did not meet him that evening in Pulman's Bush, he'd come to the front door and ask the reason why! But now that she had frightened those little rats of Kelveys and given Kezia a good scolding, her heart felt lighter. That ghastly pressure was gone. She went back to the house humming.

When the Kelveys were well out of sight of Burnells', they sat down to rest on a big red drainpipe by the side of the road. Lil's cheeks were still burning; she took off the hat with the quill and held it on her knee. Dreamily they looked over the hay paddocks, past the creek, to the group of wattles where Logan's cows stood waiting to be milked. What were their thoughts? Presently our Else nudged up close to her sister. But now she had forgotten the cross lady. She put out a finger and stroked her sister's quill; she smiled her rare smile.

"I seen the little lamp," she said, softly.

Then both were silent once more.

CHILDREN

Anton Chekhov

Published in *The Cook's Wedding and Other Stories*
Translated by Constance Garnett, published in 1922

Papa and mamma and Aunt Nadya are not at home. They have gone to a christening party at the house of that old officer who rides on a little grey horse. While waiting for them to come home, Grisha, Anya, Alyosha, Sonya, and the cook's son, Andrey, are sitting at the table in the dining-room, playing at loto. To tell the truth, it is bedtime, but how can one go to sleep without hearing from mamma what the baby was like at the christening, and what they had for supper? The table, lighted by a hanging lamp, is dotted with numbers, nutshells, scraps of paper, and little bits of glass. Two cards lie in front of each player, and a heap of bits of glass for covering the numbers. In the middle of the table is a white saucer with five kopecks in it. Beside the saucer, a half-eaten apple, a pair of scissors, and a plate on which they have been told to put their nutshells. The children are playing for money. The stake is a kopeck. The rule is: if anyone cheats, he is turned out at once. There is no one in the dining-room but the players, and nurse, Agafya Ivanovna, is in the kitchen, showing the cook how to cut a pattern, while their elder brother, Vasya, a schoolboy in the fifth class, is lying on the sofa in the drawing-room, feeling bored.

They are playing with zest. The greatest excitement is expressed on the face of Grisha. He is a small boy of nine, with a head cropped so that the bare skin shows through, chubby cheeks, and thick lips like a negro's. He is already in the preparatory class, and so is regarded as grown up, and the cleverest. He is playing entirely for the sake of the money. If there had been no kopecks in the saucer, he would have been asleep long ago. His brown eyes stray uneasily and jealously over the other players' cards. The fear that he may not win, envy, and the financial combinations of which his cropped head is full, will not let him sit still and concentrate his mind. He fidgets as though he were sitting on thorns. When he wins, he snatches up the money greedily, and instantly puts it in his pocket. His sister, Anya, a girl of eight, with a sharp chin and clever shining eyes, is also afraid that someone else may win. She flushes and turns pale, and watches the players keenly. The kopecks do not interest her. Success in the game is for her a question of vanity. The other sister, Sonya, a child of six with a curly head, and a complexion such as is seen only in very healthy children, expensive dolls, and the faces on bonbon boxes, is playing loto for the process of the game itself. There is bliss all over her face. Whoever wins, she laughs and claps her hands. Alyosha, a chubby, spherical little figure, gasps, breathes hard through his nose, and stares open-eyed at the cards. He is moved neither by covetousness nor vanity. So long as he is not driven out of the room, or sent to bed, he is thankful. He looks phlegmatic, but at heart he is rather a little beast. He is not there so much for the sake of the loto, as for the sake of the misunderstandings which are inevitable in the game. He is greatly delighted if one hits another, or calls him names. He ought to have run off somewhere long ago, but he won't leave the table for a minute, for fear they should steal his counters or his kopecks. As he can only count the units and numbers which end in nought, Anya covers his numbers for him. The fifth player, the cook's son, Andrey, a dark-skinned and sickly looking boy in a cotton shirt, with a copper cross on his breast, stands motionless, looking dreamily at the numbers. He takes no interest in winning, or in the success of the others, because he is entirely engrossed by the arithmetic of the game, and it's far from complex theory; "How many numbers there are in the world," he is thinking, "and how is it they don't get mixed up?"

They all shout out the numbers in turn, except Sonya and Alyosha. To vary the monotony, they have invented in the course of time a number of synonyms and comic nicknames. Seven, for instance, is called the "ovenrake," eleven the "sticks," seventy-seven "Semyon Semyonitch," ninety "grandfather," and so on. The game is going merrily.

"Thirty-two," cries Grisha, drawing the little yellow cylinders out of his father's cap. "Seventeen! Ovenrake! Twenty-eight! Lay them straight . . ."

Anya sees that Andrey has let twenty-eight slip. At any other time she would have pointed it out to him, but now when her vanity lies in the saucer with the kopecks, she is triumphant.

"Twenty-three!" Grisha goes on, "Semyon Semyonitch! Nine!"

"A beetle, a beetle," cries Sonya, pointing to a beetle running across the table. "Aie!"

"Don't kill it," says Alyosha, in his deep bass, "perhaps it's got children . . ."

Sonya follows the black beetle with her eyes and wonders about its children: what tiny little beetles they must be!

"Forty-three! One!" Grisha goes on, unhappy at the thought that Anya has already made two fours. "Six!"

"Game! I have got the game!" cries Sonya, rolling her eyes coquettishly and giggling.

The players' countenances lengthen.

"Must make sure!" says Grisha, looking with hatred at Sonya.

Exercising his rights as a big boy, and the cleverest, Grisha takes upon himself to decide. What he wants, that they do. Sonya's reckoning is slowly and carefully verified, and to the great regret of her fellow players, it appears that she has not cheated. Another game is begun.

"I did see something yesterday!" says Anya, as though to herself. "Filipp Filippitch turned his eyelids inside out somehow and his eyes looked red and dreadful, like an evil spirit's."

"I saw it too," says Grisha. "Eight! And a boy at our school can move his ears. Twenty-seven!"

Andrey looks up at Grisha, meditates, and says:

"I can move my ears too . . ."

"Well then, move them."

Andrey moves his eyes, his lips, and his fingers, and fancies that his ears are moving too. Everyone laughs.

"He is a horrid man, that Filipp Filippitch," sighs Sonya. "He came into our nursery yesterday, and I had nothing on but my chemise . . . And I felt so improper!"

"Game!" Grisha cries suddenly, snatching the money from the saucer. "I've got the game! You can look and see if you like."

The cook's son looks up and turns pale.

"Then I can't go on playing any more," he whispers.

"Why not?"

"Because . . . because I have got no more money."

"You can't play without money," says Grisha.

Andrey ransacks his pockets once more to make sure. Finding nothing in them but crumbs and a bitten pencil, he drops the corners of his mouth and begins blinking miserably. He is on the point of crying . . .

"I'll put it down for you!" says Sonya, unable to endure his look of agony. "Only mind you must pay me back afterwards."

The money is brought and the game goes on.

"I believe they are ringing somewhere," says Anya, opening her eyes wide.

They all leave off playing and gaze open-mouthed at the dark window. The reflection of the lamp glimmers in the darkness.

"It was your fancy."

"At night they only ring in the cemetery," says Andrey.

"And what do they ring there for?"

"To prevent robbers from breaking into the church. They are afraid of the bells."

"And what do robbers break into the church for?" asks Sonya.

"Everyone knows what for: to kill the watchmen."

A minute passes in silence. They all look at one another, shudder, and go on playing. This time Andrey wins.

"He has cheated," Alyosha booms out, apropos of nothing.

"What a lie, I haven't cheated."

Andrey turns pale, his mouth works, and he gives Alyosha a slap on the head! Alyosha glares angrily, jumps up, and with one knee on the table, slaps Andrey on the cheek! Each gives the other a second blow, and both howl. Sonya, feeling such horrors too much for her, begins crying too, and the dining-room resounds with lamentations on various notes. But do not imagine that that is the end of the game. Before five minutes are over, the children are laughing and talking peaceably again. Their faces are tear-stained, but that does not prevent them from smiling; Alyosha is positively blissful, there has been a squabble!

Vasya, the fifth form schoolboy, walks into the dining-room. He looks sleepy and disillusioned.

"This is revolting!" he thinks, seeing Grisha feel in his pockets in which the kopecks are jingling. "How can they give children money? And how can they let them play games of chance? A nice way to bring them up, I must say! It's revolting!"

But the children's play is so tempting that he feels an inclination to join them and to try his luck.

"Wait a minute and I'll sit down to a game," he says.

"Put down a kopeck!"

"In a minute," he says, fumbling in his pockets. "I haven't a kopeck, but here is a rouble. I'll stake a rouble."

"No, no, no . . . You must put down a kopeck."

"You stupids. A rouble is worth more than a kopeck anyway," the schoolboy explains. "Whoever wins can give me change."

"No, please! Go away!"

The fifth form schoolboy shrugs his shoulders, and goes into the kitchen to get change from the servants. It appears there is not a single kopeck in the kitchen.

"In that case, you give me change," he urges Grisha, coming back from the kitchen. "I'll pay you for the change. Won't you? Come, give me ten kopecks for a rouble."

Grisha looks suspiciously at Vasya, wondering whether it isn't some trick, a swindle.

"I won't," he says, holding his pockets.

Vasya begins to get cross, and abuses them, calling them idiots and blockheads.

"I'll put down a stake for you, Vasya!" says Sonya. "Sit down." He sits down and lays two cards before him. Anya begins counting the numbers.

"I've dropped a kopeck!" Grisha announces suddenly, in an agitated voice. "Wait!"

He takes the lamp, and creeps under the table to look for the kopeck. They clutch at nutshells and all sorts of nastiness, knock their heads together, but do not find the kopeck. They begin looking again, and look till Vasya takes the lamp out of Grisha's hands and puts it in its place. Grisha goes on looking in the dark. But at last the kopeck is found. The players sit down at the table and mean to go on playing.

"Sonya is asleep!" Alyosha announces.

Sonya, with her curly head lying on her arms, is in a sweet, sound, tranquil sleep, as though she had been asleep for an hour. She has fallen asleep by accident, while the others were looking for the kopeck.

"Come along, lie on mamma's bed!" says Anya, leading her away from the table. "Come along!"

They all troop out with her, and five minutes later mamma's bed presents a curious spectacle. Sonya is asleep. Alyosha is snoring beside her. With their heads to the others' feet, sleep Grisha and Anya. The cook's son, Andrey too, has managed to snuggle in beside them. Near them lie the kopecks, that have lost their power till the next game. Good night!

MONKEY AND THE CROCODILE

First published in *Panchatantra*
Translated from Sanskrit by
Arthur William Ryder, published in 1925

On the shore of the sea was a great rose-apple tree that was never without fruit. In it lived a monkey named Red-Face.

Now one day a crocodile named Ugly-Mug crawled out of the ocean under the tree and burrowed in the soft sand. Then Red-Face said: "You are my guest, sir. Pray eat these rose-apples which I throw you. You will find them like nectar. You know the proverb:

"A fool or scholar let him be,
Pleasant or hideous to see,
A guest, when offerings are given,
Is useful as a bridge to heaven.

"Ask not his home or education,
His family or reputation,
But offer thanks and sacrifice:
For so prescribes the lawbook wise.

"And again:

"By honouring the guests who come
Wayworn from some far-distant home
To share the sacrifice, you go
The noblest way that mortals know.

"And once again:

"If guests unhonoured leave your door,
And sadly sighing come no more,
Your fathers and the gods above
Turn from you and forget their love."

Thus he spoke and offered rose-apples. And the crocodile ate them and enjoyed a long and pleasant conversation with the monkey before returning to his home. So the monkey and the crocodile rested each day in the shade of the rose-apple tree. They spent the time in cheerful conversation on various subjects, and were happy.

Now the crocodile went home and gave his wife the rose-apples which he had not eaten. And one day she asked him: "My dear husband, where do you get such fruits? They are like nectar."

"My dear," he said, "I have an awfully good friend, a monkey named Red-Face. He gives me these fruits in the most courteous manner."

Then she said: "If anyone eats such nectar fruit every day, his heart must be turned to nectar. So, if you value your wife, give me his heart, and I will eat it. Then I shall never grow old or sick, but will be a delightful companion for you."

But he objected: "In the first place, my dear, he is our adopted brother. Secondly, he gives us fruit. I cannot kill him. Please do not insist. Besides, there is a proverb:

"To give us birth, we need a mother;
For second birth we need another:
And friendship's brothers seem by far
More dear than natural brothers are."

But she said: "You have never refused me before. So I am sure it is a she-monkey. You love her and spend the whole day with her. That is why you will not give me what I want. And when you meet me at night, your sighs are hot as a flame of fire. And when you hold me and kiss me, you do not hug me tight. I know some other woman has stolen into your heart."

Then the crocodile was quite dejected, and said to his wife:

"When I am at your feet
And at your service, sweet,
Why do you look at me
With peevish jealousy?"

But her face swam in tears when she heard him, and she said:

"You love her, you deceiver;
Your wishes never leave her;
"Her pretty shamming steals upon your heart.
My rivalry is vain, sir;
And so I pray abstain, sir,
From service that is only tricky art.

"Besides, if you do not love her, why not kill her when I ask you? And if it is really a he-monkey, why should you love him? Enough! Unless I eat his heart, I shall starve myself to death in your house."

Now when he saw how determined she was, he was distracted with anxiety, and said: "Ah, the proverb is right:

"Remember that a single grab
Suffices for a fish or crab,
For fool or woman; and 'tis so
For sot, cement, or indigo.

"Oh, what shall I do? How can I kill him?" With these thoughts in mind, he visited the monkey.

Now the monkey had missed his friend, and when he saw him afflicted, he said: "My friend, why have you not been here this long time? Why don't you speak cheerfully, and repeat something witty?"

The crocodile replied: "My friend and brother, my wife scolded me today. She said: 'You ungrateful wretch! Do not show me your face. You are living daily at a friend's expense, and make him no return. You do not even show him the door of your house. You cannot possibly make amends for this. There is a saying:

"'The Brahman-murderer or thief,
Drunkard or liar, finds relief;
While for ingratitude alone
No expiation will atone.

"'I regard this monkey as my brother-in-law. So bring him home, and we will make some return for his kindness. If you refuse, I will see you later in heaven.' Now I could not come to you until she had finished her scolding. And this long time passed while I was quarreling with her about you. So please come home with me. Your brother's wife has set up an awning. She has fixed her clothes and gems and rubies and all that, to pay you a fitting welcome. She has hung holiday garlands on the doorposts. And she is waiting impatiently."

"My friend and brother," said the monkey, "your lady is very kind. It is quite according to the proverb:

"Six things are done by friends:
To take, and give again;
To listen, and to talk;
To dine, to entertain.

"But we monkeys live in trees, and your home is in the water. How can I go there? Rather bring your lady here, brother, that I may bow down and receive her blessing."

The crocodile said: "My friend, our home is on a lovely sand-bank under the water. So climb on my back and travel comfortably with nothing to fear."

When the monkey heard this, he was delighted and said: "If that is possible, my friend, then hasten. Why delay? Here I am on your back."

But as he sat there and saw the crocodile swimming in the bottomless ocean, the monkey was terribly frightened and said: "Go slow, brother. My whole body is drenched by the great waves."

And the crocodile thought when he heard this: "If he fell from my back, he could not move an inch, the water is so deep. He is in my power. So I will tell him my purpose, and then he can pray to his favorite god."

And he said: "Sir, I have deceived you and brought you to your death, because my wife bade me do it. So pray to your favorite god."

"Brother," said the monkey, "what harm have I done her or you? Why have you planned to kill me?"

"Well," replied the crocodile, "those nectar fruits tasted so sweet that she began to long to eat your heart. That is why I have done this."

Then the quick-witted monkey said: "If that is the case, sir, why didn't you tell me on shore? For then I might have brought with me another heart, very sweet indeed, which I keep in a hole in the rose-apple tree. As it is, I am forlorn in this heart, at being taken to her in vain, without my sweet heart."

When he heard this, the crocodile was delighted and said: "If you feel so, my friend, give me that other heart. And my cross wife will eat it and give up starving herself. Now I will take you back to the rose-apple tree."

So he turned back and swam toward the rose-apple tree, while the monkey murmured a hundred prayers to every kind of a god. And when at last he came to shore, he hopped and jumped farther and farther, climbed up the rose-apple tree, and thought: "Hurrah! My life is saved. Surely, the saying is a good one:

"We dare not trust a rogue; nor must
We trust in those deserving trust:
For danger follows, and we fall
Destroyed and ruined, roots and all.

"So today is my rebirthday."

The crocodile said: "My friend and brother, give me the heart, so that my wife may eat it and give up starving herself."

Then the monkey laughed, and scolded him, saying: "You fool! You traitor! How can anyone have two hearts? Go home, and never come back under the rose-apple tree. You know the proverb:

"Whoever trusts a faithless friend
And twice in him believes,
Lays hold on death as certainly
As when a mule conceives."

Now the crocodile was embarrassed when he heard this, and he thought: "Oh, why was I such a fool as to tell him my plan? If I can possibly win his confidence again, I will do it." So he said: "My friend, she has no need of a heart. What I said was just a joke to test your sentiments. Please come to our house as a guest. Your brother's wife is most eager for you."

The monkey said: "Rascal! Go away this moment. I will not come. For

"The hungry man at nothing sticks;
The poor man has his heartless tricks.
Tell Handsome, miss, that Theodore
Will see him in the well no more."

"How was that?" asked the crocodile. And the monkey told the story of 'Handsome and Theodore'.

THE CAT'S JUDGMENT

First published in *Panchatantra*
Translated from Sanskrit by
Arthur William Ryder, published in 1925

At one time I was myself living in a certain tree. And beneath the same tree dwelt another bird, a partridge. So by virtue of our near neighbourhood there sprang up between us a firm friendship. Every day after taking our meals and airings we spent the evening hours in a round of amusements, such as repeating witty sayings, telling tales from the old story-books, solving puzzles and conundrums, or exchanging presents.

One day the partridge went foraging with other birds to a spot where the rice was ripe and abundant, and he did not return at nightfall. Of course, I missed him greatly and I thought: "Alas! Why does not my friend the partridge come home tonight? I am much afraid he is caught in some trap, or has even been killed." And many days passed while I grieved in this way.

Now one evening a rabbit named Speedy made himself at home in the partridge's old nest in the hole. Nor did I say him nay, for I despaired of seeing the partridge again.

However, one fine day the partridge, who had grown extremely plump from eating rice, remembered his old home and returned. This, indeed, is not to be wondered at.

No mortal has such joy, although
In heaven's fields he roam,
As in his city, in his land,
And in his humble home.

Now when he saw the rabbit in the hole, he said reproachfully: "Come now, rabbit, you have done a shabby thing in occupying my apartment. Please begone, and lose no time about it."

"You fool!" said the rabbit, "don't you know that a dwelling is yours only while you occupy it?" "Very well, then," said the partridge, "suppose we ask the neighbors. For, to give you a legal quotation,

"For ownership of cisterns, tanks,
Wells, groves, and houses, too,
The neighbors' testimony goes—
Such is the legal view.

"And again:

"When house or field or well or grove
Or land is in dispute,
A neighbor's testimony is
Decisive of the suit."

Then the rabbit said: "You fool! Are you ignorant of the consecrated tradition which says:

"Suppose beside your neighbor you
For ten long years abide,
What weight have learnèd arguments?
Eyewitnesses decide.

"Fool! Fool! Did you never hear the dictum of the sage Narada?

"The title to possession is
A ten years' habitation
With men. But with the birds and beasts
Mere present occupation.

"Hence, even supposing this apartment to be yours, still it was unoccupied when I moved in, and now it is mine."

"Well, well!" replied the partridge, "if you appeal to consecrated tradition, come with me, and we will consult the specialists. It shall be yours or mine according to their decision." "Very well," said the other, and together they started off to have their suit decided. I, too, was at their heels, out of curiosity. "I will just see what comes of all this," I said to myself.

Now they had not traveled far when the rabbit asked the partridge: "My good fellow, who is to pass judgment on our disagreement?" And the partridge answered: "On a sand-bank by the sacred Ganges—where there is sweet music from the dancing waves that intercross and break when the water is swept by nimble breezes—there dwells a tomcat whose name is Curd-Ear. He abides unshaken in his vow of penance and self-denial, and character has begotten compassion."

But when the rabbit spied the cat, his soul staggered with terror, and he said: "No, no! He is a seedy rascal. You must have heard the proverb:

"Oh, never trust a rogue for all
His pharisaic puzzling:
At holy shrines some saints are found
Quite capable of guzzling."

Upon hearing this, Curd-Ear, whose manner of life had been assumed for the purpose of making an easy livelihood, desired to win their confidence. He therefore gazed straight at the sun, stood on his hind-legs, lifted his fore-paws, blinked his eyes, and in order to deceive them by pious sentiments, delivered the following moral discourse. "Alas! Alas! All is vanity. This fragile life passes in a moment. Union with the beloved is an empty dream. Family endearments are a conjurer's trick. But for the moral law, there would be no escape. Oh, listen to Scripture!

"Each transitory day, O man,
To moral living give;
Else, like the blacksmith's bellows, you
Suck air, but do not live.

"And furthermore:

"Non-moral learning is a curse,
A dog's tail, nothing less,
That does not save from flies and fleas,
Nor cover nakedness.

"And yet again:

"A rotten ear among the wheat,
Among the birds a bat,

Is he who spurns the moral law;
The merest living gnat.

"The flowers and fruit are better than the tree;
Better than curds is butter said to be;
Better than oil-cake, oil that trickles free;
Better than mortal man, morality.

"The praise of constant steadfastness
Some wise professors sing;
But moral earnestness is swift,
Though many fetters cling.

"Forget your prosings manifold;
The moral law is briefly told:
To help your neighbor—this is good;
To injure him is devilhood."

Having listened to this moral discourse, the rabbit said: "Friend partridge, here on the river-bank is the saint who expounds the moral law. Let us ask him."

But the partridge said: "After all, he is our natural enemy. Let us ask him from a distance." So together they began to question him: "O holy moralist, a dispute has arisen between us. Pray give judgment in accordance with the moral law. And whichever of us is found to speak falsely, him you may eat."

"Dear friends," said the cat, "I implore you not to speak thus. My soul abhors every act of cruelty, that street-sign pointing to hell. Surely, you know the Scripture:

"The holy first commandment runs—
Not harsh, but kindly be—
And therefore lavish mercy on
Mosquito, louse, and flea.

"Why speak of hurting innocence?
For he, with purpose fell

Who injures even noxious beasts,
Is plunged in ghastly hell.

"Nay, even those who slay living creatures in the act of sacrifice are befuddled, and their hermeneutic theology is at fault. And if you object to me the passage, 'One should sacrifice with goats,' in that passage the word 'goats' signifies grain that has aged seven years. 'Go, oats'—such is the true exegesis. And then, consider the passage:

"If he who cuts down trees or cattle,
Or makes a bloody slime in battle,
Should thereby win to heaven—well,
Who (let me ask you) goes to hell?

"No, no. I shall eat nobody. However, I am somewhat old and do not readily distinguish your voices from a distance. So how am I to determine winner and loser? In view of this, pray draw near and make me acquainted with the case. Then I can pronounce a judgment that discriminates the essence of the matter, and thus causes no impediment in my march to the other world. You know the stanza:

"If any man, from pride or greed,
Timidity or wrath,
Judge falsely, he has set his foot
On hell's down-sloping path.

"And again:

"Who wrongs a sheep, slays kinsmen five;
Who wrongs a cow, slays ten;
A hundred die for maidens wronged;
A thousand die for men.

"Therefore confide in me and speak clearly at the edge of my ear."

Why spin it out? That seedy rogue won their trust so fully that both drew near him. Then, of course, he seized them simultaneously, one with his paw, the other with the saw of his teeth. And when they were dead, he ate them both.

"And that is why I say:
A seedy umpire is not very . . .

and the rest of it.

"Just so, you, too, being blind at night, if you take as overlord this seedy fellow who is blind in the daytime, will go the way of the rabbit and the partridge. Reflect on this, then do what seems proper."

And all the birds, after listening to the crow's remarks, said: "He speaks well," and they flew to their homes, planning to reassemble for consultation on the question of a king. Only the owl remained with his consort, for he was blind in the daytime. There he sat in his chair of state, awaiting the anointing. And he called out: "Ho, there! Who takes my orders? Why is the ceremony delayed?"

Thereupon his consort said: "My dear sir, the crow has found means to hold up the ceremony. And the birds have gone flying away. Only that crow, for some reason or other, remains here all alone. Rise at once, and I will conduct you home."

Then the owl was deeply disappointed, and he said: "You monster! Why have you wronged me by preventing the regal anointing? From this day there is enmity between us. For the proverb says:

"When arrows pierce or axes wound
A tree, it grows together sound;
From cruel, ugly speech you feel
A wound that time will never heal."

Thereupon he went home with his consort, while the crow reflected: "Dear me! I have burdened myself with a needless enmity by speaking so. I should have remembered:

"All spoken words, if harsh and heedless
And inappropriate and needless,
Are self-condemnatory slips
That turn to poison on the lips.

"And again:

"However wise and strong you be,
Beware the needless enemy:
You would not swallow poison down
Because a doctor lives in town.

"No man of sense vituperates
Another, while the public waits;
For even truth should be concealed,
If causing sorrow when revealed.

"And finally:

"Reflect with many a chosen friend;
Reflect alone, and to the end;
Then act. You are intelligent,
And fame's and wealth's recipient."

"After these reflections, the crow also left the spot.

"For this cause, my son, we have an inherited feud with the owls."

"Father," said Cloudy, "what should we do under the circumstances?" And Live-Strong answered: "Even in these circumstances there is an effective procedure other than the six expedients. This I will adopt, and will myself lead the way to conquer the enemy. I will deceive them and put them in a fatal situation. For the saying goes:

"The strong, deft, clever rascals note,
Who robbed the Brahman of his goat."

"How was that?" asked Cloudy. And Live-Strong told the story of 'The Brahman's Goat'.

THE MICE THAT SET ELEPHANTS FREE

First published in *Panchatantra*
Translated from Sanskrit by
Arthur William Ryder, published in 1925

There was once a region where people, houses, and temples had fallen into decay. So the mice, who were old settlers there, occupied the chinks in the floors of stately dwellings with sons, grandsons (both in the male and female line), and further descendants as they were born, until their holes formed a dense tangle. They found uncommon happiness in a variety of festivals, dramatic performances (with plots of their own invention), wedding-feasts, eating-parties, drinking-bouts, and similar diversions. And so the time passed.

But into this scene burst an elephant-king, whose retinue numbered thousands. He, with his herd, had started for the lake upon information that there was water there. As he marched through the mouse community, he crushed faces, eyes, heads, and necks of such mice as he encountered.

Then the survivors held a convention. "We are being killed," they said, "by these lumbering elephants—curse them! If they come this way again, there will not be mice enough for seed. Besides:

"An elephant will kill you, if
He touch; a serpent if he sniff;
King's laughter has a deadly sting;
A rascal kills by honoring.

"Therefore let us devise a remedy effective in this crisis."

When they had done so, a certain number went to the lake, bowed before the elephant-king, and said respectfully: "O King, not far from here is our community, inherited from a long line of ancestors. There we have prospered through a long succession of sons and grandsons. Now you gentlemen, while coming here to water, have destroyed us by the thousand. Furthermore, if you travel that way again, there will not be enough of us for seed. If then you feel compassion toward us, pray travel another path.

Consider the fact that even creatures of our size will some day prove of some service."

And the elephant-king turned over in his mind what he had heard, decided that the statement of the mice was entirely logical, and granted their request.

Now in the course of time a certain king commanded his elephant-trappers to trap elephants. And they constructed a so-called water-trap, caught the king with his herd, three days later dragged him out with a great tackle made of ropes and things, and tied him to stout trees in that very bit of forest.

When the trappers had gone, the elephant-king reflected thus: "In what manner, or through whose assistance, shall I be delivered?" Then it occurred to him: "We have no means of deliverance except those mice."

So the king sent the mice an exact description of his disastrous position in the trap through one of his personal retinue, an elephant-cow who had not ventured into the trap, and who had previous information of the mouse community.

When the mice learned the matter, they gathered by the thousand, eager to return the favor shown them, and visited the elephant herd. And seeing king and herd fettered, they gnawed the guy-ropes where they stood, then swarmed up the branches, and by cutting the ropes aloft, set their friends free.

"And that is why I say:
"Make friends, make friends, however strong, . . .

and the rest of it."

When Slow had listened to this, he said: "Be it even so, my dear fellow. Have no fear. In this place you are at home. Pray dismiss anxieties and behave as in your own dwelling." So they all took food and recreation at such hours as suited each, met at the noon hour in the shade of crowding trees beside the broad lake, and spent their time in reciprocated friendship, discussing a variety of masterly works on religion, economics, and similar subjects. And this seems quite natural:

For men of sense, good poetry
And science will suffice:
The time of dunderheads is spent
In squabbling, sleep, and vice.

And again:

A thrill
Will fill
The wisest heart,
When flow
Bons mots
Composed with art,
Though fe-
Males be
Removed apart.

Now one day Spot failed to appear at the regular hour. And the others, missing him, alarmed also by an evil omen that appeared at that moment, drew the conclusion that he was in trouble, and could not keep up their spirits. Then Slow and Gold said to Swift: "Dear fellow, we two are prevented by locomotive limitations from hunting for our dear friend. We beg you, therefore, to hunt about and learn whether the poor fellow is eaten by a lion, or singed by forest fire, or fallen into the power of hunters and such creatures. There is a saying:

"One quickly fears for loved ones who
In pleasure-gardens play:
What, then, if they in forests grim
And peril-bristling stay?

"By all means go, search out precise news concerning Spot, and return quickly."

On hearing this, Swift flew a little distance to the edge of a swamp, and finding Spot caught in a stout trap braced with pegs of acacia-wood, he sorrowfully said: "My dear friend, how did you fall into this distress?"

"My friend," said Spot, "there is no time for delay. Listen to me.

"When life is near an end,
The presence of a friend
Brings happiness, allying
The living with the dying.

"Oh, pardon any expressions of friendly impatience I may have used in our discussions. Likewise, say to Gold and Slow in my name:

"If any ugly word
Was willy-nilly heard,
I pray you both, forgive—
Let only friendship live."

On hearing this, Swift replied: "Feel no fear, my dear fellow, while you have friends like us. I will return with all speed, bringing Gold to cut your bonds."

Thereupon, with his heart in a flutter, he found Slow and Gold, explained the nature of Spot's captivity, then returned to Spot, carrying Gold in his beak. Gold, for his part, on seeing the plight of his friend, sorrowfully said: "My dear fellow, you always had a wary mind and a shrewd eye. How, then, did you fall into this dreadful captivity?"

And Spot rejoined: "Why ask, my friend? Fate, you know, does what it will. As the saying goes:

"What mortal flies
(However wise)
When billows rise
To fatal size
On seas of woe?
"In dead of night,
Or broad daylight,
Grim fate may smite;
Ah, who can fight
An unseen foe?

"You, my saintly friend, are familiar with the caprices of constraining destiny. Therefore be quick. Cut my bonds before the pitiless hunter comes."

"Have no fear," said Gold, "while I am at your side. In my heart, however, is great sorrow, which I beg you to remove by telling your story. You are guided by an eye of wisdom. How did you fall into this captivity?"

"Well," said Spot, "if you insist on knowing, listen, and learn how I have been made captive a second time, having once before suffered the woes of captivity."

"Tell me," said Gold, "how once before you suffered the woes of captivity. I am eager to learn the full detail." And Spot told the story of 'Spot's Captivity'.